My Heart is Hurting

S.E. Reed

WILD INK PUBLISHING

A Wild Ink Publishing Publishing Original
Wild Ink Publishing
wild-ink-publishing.com

Copyright © 2023 S.E. Reed

Edited by Brittany McMunn
Design and Layout by Abigail Wild

ISBN: 978-1-958531-25-9

Any references to historical events, real people, or real places are used fictitiously. Names, characters, and places are products of the author's imagination.

For my husband and children—
my loves, my inspiration.

– Chapter One –
You want me to do what?

My name is Jinny Buffett.

J-I-N-N-Y… not Jimmy, and definitely not Jimmy Buffett.

Everyone in Hollywood knows who Jimmy Buffett is because of the huge, flashing neon signs and music blaring from the Margaritaville Beach Resort on Ocean Drive. That's where my Mama works every, single, stupid night for two reasons. One, she loves singing Jimmy Buffett songs and two, she uses her job as a cocktail waitress to pick up men.

It's the end of a long, hot, boring summer and I dread going back to school next week. But, maybe, if I'm lucky, no one will shout JINNY CHEESEBURGER or sing "Cheeseburger in Paradise" when I walk down the hallway, since I've grown four inches and lost fifteen pounds.
Shantel Greenburg can suck on that.

The tender white skin on my thighs prickle when I slump down to the steps outside my crappy apartment complex. Over my shoulder, the Hernandez brothers throw rocks at the green dented dumpster in the parking lot. That's when I see a familiar face walking between the cars, heading my way. Ms. Fleming, my ninth-grade English teacher from last year. She's not in her usual polo and khakis, but instead she's wearing a floral dress, like she's going to church.

"Hey, Ms. Fleming," I say slowly, raising an eyebrow. "Whatcha doin' slummin' over here? I didn't think teachers made house calls."

"Hello, Jinny. I'm glad you're home. Do you have a few minutes to chat?" She walks up the steps and stands in front of me.

"I guess… I was gonna run to the beach and look for shells," I say and point down at my unlaced knock-offs from Walmart. I know it's babyish to look for seashells at my age, but they are fascinating. My room is filled with unique shells I found mixed into the soft, wet sand during low tide.

"This won't take long. I was at school preparing my classroom and I happened to see your FSA scores from last year," Ms. Fleming explains.

Ugh, the annual Florida State Assessment test. Yawn! I swear I finished mine before most of the dummies in my class ever made it to the second page.

I shrug and lean forward to tie my laces.

"Really Jinny? Aren't you even a little interested?"

Her voice is plucky and drenched with hope. I shade my eyes to look at her and stifle a groan when I see that gleam in her eyes, the one I've seen over the years from idealistic teachers who want to save me.

"I don't care what I scored."

Mama says I'm smarter than she is, and it pisses her off to no end. I don't need a test score to prove it.

"Well, I'm going to tell you anyway. You had the highest score in the entire state of Florida!" She claps her dainty hands together with pride.

"Oh." The only sound I manage to loosen from my throat before she continues.

"Do you know how big this is? What kind of opportunities this will open for you? You are the brightest student I've ever taught. This is huge news!" She smiles and opens her arms like she expects me to embrace her in the greatest hug of all time.

"So, what."

Her smile fades, but I don't care. I don't want to be her brightest student. I don't want her to hug me. All I can do is picture what Mama's gonna say when she finds out.

Oh, you think you're so smart, Jinny? You gonna go off to college and get a fancy job with a fancy house, just so you can tell everyone you're better than me?

The rusted metal handrail rattles when I jump up and take the steps two-at-a-time to get the hell away from this conversation.

"Wait, there's more. I spoke with Principal Guthrie and he—"

"Why are you talkin' to Principal Guthrie about me?" I spin around and demand. "Am I in trouble?" I raise my voice. "You think I cheated? Is that it? You come 'round here to call me a cheater?"

"No, no, Jinny, you misunderstand— you aren't in trouble." Ms. Fleming puts her hands up, sweat rolling down her forehead. "We know the scores are accurate. You aced my class last year without much effort and I went back and looked at your file at all your grades and scores, they were off the charts... We think a girl like you needs some extra guidance, that's all." She trembles and looks around, afraid of what I might say, afraid of the neighborhood.

"A girl like me huh?" I know exactly what she means. A poor, white-trash girl like me. A girl with a Mama like mine and a dead Daddy from the swamps. A girl living in a place like this.

"Listen, all I'm trying to say, very badly I'm afraid, is that I want to work with you. I want to help you find something to get involved with on campus, an extracurricular activity to help you develop and explore your intellectual talents. I don't want to see you to end up like your—" Ms. Fleming grows flustered and stops herself. She tries to be diplomatic, but what she really wants to say is she doesn't want me to end up like my Mama.

"Just back off, Ms. Fleming," I yell and head for the parking lot. The heat rises up in little waves from the black pavement, smelling like gasoline and trash.

She has no idea what it's like to be me. Does she really think I'd let myself end up like my Mama?

"Ooooh, Jinny Cheeseburger, you rude!" laughs Sabrina Elliot.

I should have known she was sitting on the porch below my apartment listening to this entire conversation. Sabrina's a drop-out, a year older than me, who was forced to move in with her Grann Ruth last summer. She rarely leaves the porch, except to use her fake ID to buy cigarettes.

I will myself to keep walking, but my emotions choke me. I want to yell at someone, anyone!

"Shut your ugly pizza face, Sabrina! And tell Grann Ruth to quit smokin' pot in her bedroom. It floats through the floors and stinks up my clothes," I shout at her then glare at Ms. Fleming on my steps, looking embarrassed and confused.

Sabrina laughs. "Loser."

"Argh!" I scream and turn around, letting my feet guide me as my eyes fill with tears. I can feel Ms. Fleming's disappointed eyes on me, her mouth probably hanging open like an ugly rockfish. The dead kind I see washed up on shore.

Who does Ms. Fleming think she is anyway? Showing up at my apartment completely unannounced and ruining my day. Did she even consider I might not want to be labeled smart or participate in extracurricular activities? I sure as hell don't need her to remind me not to turn into my Mama.

I run for half-a-mile until I reach Hollywood Blvd, my long, dirty hair flopping across my neck and back. I'm tempted to run home for a ponytail holder, but the smooth pavement feels good under my feet. I push myself faster toward the Atlantic Ocean where the cool ocean breeze will soak up my sweat. A horn honks next to me, and without looking, I reach up to flip them off.

Men of all ages love to honk at teenage girls, especially around here.

I look over to make sure the driver caught my gesture, ready to flip another bird, but it's only Ms. Fleming waving at me. I could keep going. I want to keep going. But Ms. Fleming veers her car to the side of the road, blocking my path.

"Did you flip me off?" she asks through the open window.

"Sorry, I thought you were just another Hollywood Beach pervert."

"Wait, Jinny, can I give you a ride to the beach? I'll leave you alone the rest of the summer if you hear what I have to say."

"School starts in less than a week!" I protest. She looks desperate. I feel bad because I don't want to break her Anne-of-Green-Gables spirit or anything.

"Please?" she asks again.

"Fine."

When I open the door to her shiny Mazda and crawl in, I'm surprised by how clean it smells. Not like Mama's BMW, a gift from one of her regulars at Tootsie's Nude Cabaret in downtown Miami, where she worked when I was little. Mama loves her BMW, but I hate it. It reeks of musky cologne and her menthol cigarettes.

"I'm sorry I showed up out of the blue today. I realize I may have made you— uncomfortable," Ms. Fleming apologizes as she turns on her blinker and pulls back into traffic.

I don't respond.

"The thing is, Jinny; I want to see you succeed."

"You want to see me succeed? You already know I get straight A's." I fold my arms over my chest.

She pulls to a stop at the intersection. The crashing azure waves of the Atlantic Ocean are directly in front of us, so close I can practically touch them. I reach for the door handle, but hesitate.

She lets out a sigh. "It's not about getting straight A's Jinny. That's not what I'm trying to say. Have you ever heard of a girl named Laura Dekker? She sailed around the world by herself when she was fourteen. Or Malala Yousafzai who won the Nobel Peace Prize at seventeen? Or Jordan Romero? He climbed Mount Everest when he was thirteen? I could go on and on about smart and successful young people. I'm not saying you have to sail around the world, but I think we can find an exciting project at school for you to get involved with."

I frown. Most days I don't know if Mama's coming home at night or if there's food in the fridge. Does Ms. Fleming really think I care about some extra school project? I want to be angry and tell her to mind her own business, but it is kind of sweet that she seems genuinely interested in me. Or annoying– I'm not sure which.

"So, like, what do you want me to do? You better not say, help the school go green or something corny."

She pulls over at the entrance to the beach and puts the car in park.

"No, Jinny. But recycling is nothing to joke about. Global warming is a serious issue. We should all be working together to save our planet and–"

"Ms. Fleming!" I interrupt.

"Sorry," she says. "Okay, so what I'd really love is to see you start an after-school club. You can pick anything that interests you. I'll teach you how to write the bi-laws and you can use my classroom afterschool on Tuesdays and Thursdays. I won't even be there because I'm teaching a creative writing class at the community college those afternoons. So, it would give you the chance to be in charge and take real ownership of something. I was thinking you could plan a field trip for your club. Of course, I'll chaperone. Now… how does that sound?"

"Ugh…" I complain.

Her lengthy "I want you to be successful" speech was to get me to start an afterschool club?

Unbelievable.

"Yeah, I'll think about it."

My voice, an octave lower than it usually is, tries to mask my disappointment. I open the door and flee as fast as I can, rushing toward the boardwalk, a series of wooden planks in the sand tucked between the naupaka plants and palmetto bushes.

I'm glad that's over.

Why are teachers so annoying?

"I promise it will be fun!" she shouts, her voice a drift on the ocean breeze, barely audible over the crashing waves.

Yeah right, loads of fun… forming a school club, writing bi-laws and planning field trips.

I slip off my shoes and socks and let the velvety hot sand fill the spaces between my toes. I run toward the sparkling water, and just as I'm about to reach the frothy salt foam lapping up on the shore, I hear my name.

"JINNY BUFFETT!"

I look over my shoulder and see Ms. Fleming waving a hot pink flier in her hand. "Here's the form. Fill this out and bring it to me at school. I'll be there Monday working on lesson plans," she says out of breath.

"Thanks," I mumble.

I shove the flier in my pocket. The beach is normally the one place I find peace, but now I'm flustered. The hot pink paper burns my skin through my shorts.

Did I just agree to start a club?

– Chapter Two –
But I need new clothes!

"Why was that nosey-ass teacher here?" Mama asks the next morning after she comes in.

Her mascara is clumpy from not washing her face and her mouth looks kind of red and raw– whoever she was with last night must have had a beard. She drops a styrofoam container on the table, filled with a half-eaten western omelet.

"How'd you know Ms. Fleming was here?" I set down my worn copy of Lord of the Flies and take a bite of the cold, rubbery eggs.

"Marco said you called the restaurant lookin' for food, but I'd already agreed to go out with a friend after work. Since you been workin' on losin' weight, I knew you wouldn't mind skipping a meal. If you want to have a body like I do, baby girl, you have to take care of your assets." She smooths her hands over her hips and turns around, wagging her butt at me.

I try not to gag on the eggs.

"Come on Jinny, why was she here?" She tries to coax it out of me.

Why did Marco have to go and tell Mama about Ms. Fleming? Normally I like Marco. He was my Daddy's best friend before he died. They grew up together, deep in the Everglades, far from civilization, yet a looming presence on those of us living on the coast.

Now Marco works at Margaritaville as a cook. Sometimes he's such a gossip!

I scan Mama's face for clues. Is she pissed? No. Not exactly. She's jealous, I see the telltale flick in her left eye.

"She didn't want nothin' Mama. Just bringin' me something for school. Maybe, uh, you can teach me your squats." I change the subject to get her off my case.

She lights up like our cheap pre-lit Christmas tree.

"Jinny, I've been waiting for this day. I told you after you got your period, you'd start behaving like a real woman." She points her long, red acrylic nail at me. I nod and fight the urge to roll my eyes. "That's right. It's time you act like a queen– know the power you hold in those hips."

"The world doesn't make queens of girls who hide in houses and dreams–" I recall something from one of the books I'm reading.

"What are you goin' on about?" She snarls.

"Nothing Mama, it's from a book…"

"Just like your Daddy, spouting off things to make you sound smart." She opens a cupboard and slams it shut. Her momentary excitement to teach me the power in my hips is gone, replaced with rage.

I get up from the table to go back to my room and leave her alone. She probably hasn't slept and is going to be nasty all day, no matter what I do or say.

But then I remember what today is.

"Can we still go school shopping?"

I can tell from her face, she forgot.

"I'm gonna get some rest. I picked up an extra shift later today… Don't give me that look."

"But it's the last tax-free day," I whine. "I need school supplies and clothes. You promised! Nothin' fits me no more Mama!"

She looks me up and down, as if noticing my baggy sweat shorts and faded Madonna t-shirt for the first time. "You got a point. Here's a few bucks. Walk to Target and get what you need. You best not buy any junk food with it either!"

"Thanks Mama!" I run over and hug her, taking the money before she can change her mind. She recoils from my embrace, like touching me disgusts her. I don't care, I'm still grateful. Money in hand, I rush into my room and shut the door.

"Meow!" cries Pearl, my little gray striped kitten.

I tickle her fur and she quiets. I don't want Mama to hear her, she has a strict no pet policy. I found Pearl tangled in an iridescent nylon fishing net on the beach a few weeks ago and couldn't leave her there crying.

Mama still hasn't noticed.

I look at the money and count it. Oh my God, she gave me a hundred dollars. I open my closet and do a quick inventory of what I need for school, a few shirts and shorts, probably a new bra. The one I'm wearing doesn't fit anymore. Even though I'm taller and thinner, my chest is one place that keeps growing, which makes me feel both uncomfortable and kind of happy at the same time; a strange combination.

Pearl wrestles with my pair of cheap yellow flip-flops and knocks the lid off the shoe box I keep hidden in the back.

"Go on now," I scoot her from the closet and retrieve the box.

It's where I keep the few things I have from my Daddy. There's a picture of him when he was my age— standing on a big swamp-cabin porch, the kind built up from the ground so gators and snakes can't crawl in. It has a rusted tin roof draped with lights along the edges. The house is bordered with ratty palm trees and old cars in the driveway.

What I love is how happy he looks, leaning against the post with his Mama and six sisters surrounding him. All the faces of people I wish I knew. They look back at me, like they wish they knew me too.

If I close my eyes and listen really hard, I swear I can hear them calling my name.

There isn't much else from my Daddy in the box. The picture, an old note I found in Mama's underwear drawer asking why she kept breaking up with him, and his favorite faded Miami Dolphins t-shirt. His scent is long gone, but I still remember it. The metallic, greasy smell from working on cars mixed with sweet, citrus oranges.

Daddy always ate oranges.

After he died, Mama packed up everything he owned and took it to the dumpster behind the Dollar General.

Like he meant nothing.

Like he was just a pile of trash, instead of a person— the other half of me. Like maybe someday I wouldn't want something to remind me of him.

– Chapter Three –
Shut up, it's NOT a crush...

It's weird being at school when no one is around. Every sound echoes through the long, empty hallways. Footsteps. Doors. Voices.

"I'm gay mom, not deaf. I can hear you talking about me."

When I turn the corner by the front office I see a cute dark-haired guy and his mom arguing at the desk by Miss Charmaine, the office secretary.

"I know you can hear me, Thomas. But you're on your phone texting, so I was just asking if there are any clubs we can sign you up for. I know you want to make new friends," his mom hisses.

"Mom, stop stressing out. It's just a new school. I'll figure it out."

The guy, Thomas, looks at me as I walk by, but I avert my gaze. If I was enrolling at a new school with my Mama... I shudder. That would be the worst. I wouldn't want anyone to look at me or talk to me.

"Jinny, I'm so happy to see you!" Ms. Fleming says with a beaming, white smile as I walk into her classroom.

"Ma'am." I hold out the hot pink flier.

"Great! I can't wait to see what kind of club you've decided to form. I'm sure it's something very inspiring." She looks at what I've written on the paper and then at me. Her doe eyes dim as the light in them fades with disappointment. "Is this a joke?"

"No. Why would I walk all the way here to give you a joke?"

Although, I was expecting her to react this way.

"The Occult Club? Is this really what I think it is?"

"Did you read the description?" I ask, pointing to the paper.

She looks it over again as the brown toe of her loafer taps against the freshly waxed linoleum floor.

"Well, Jinny, I was hoping you'd come up with something a little less... outside the box. Maybe something a bit more mainstream. It says here you want your club to discuss the weird, strange, and unexplained. You've even mentioned spirit boards and performing seances to speak with the dead."

"You said anything I want," I remind her.

"Yes, I did, but within reason. I mean, how can I sponsor a club like this? Florida is part of the Bible Belt last time I checked. I'm not sure parents would appreciate our school having a club linked to the occult. Do you understand what I'm trying to say?" Her lips purse as she inhales a deep breath.

I shrug. I thought it was a good idea. I was inspired by the picture in my shoebox and something Marco said when I called to ask when Mama was coming home from work. Uh, your Mama left a while ago kiddo. But don't you worry, your Daddy's spirit always lookin out for you girl. You gotta believe that, he said over the noises in the Margaritaville kitchen.

But maybe there's some truth in it. Maybe his spirit is watching over me– and maybe I should dig deeper and find a way to talk to him.

I stare at Ms. Fleming. There's no way I can tell her I want to contact the spirit of my dead Daddy–

"How about I help you come up with an idea? What about a poetry club! We don't have one of those at school. You could explore different kinds of forms and themes."

"Iambic pentameter? Yuck."

"Well, I won't sanction this." Ms. Fleming holds firm on her decision.

"Ugh, you're no fun," I snap at her. "Why did I even come here? I could be at home playing with my kitten Pearl and watching Netflix or re-reading The Hobbit."

"Jinny, you didn't tell me you're a Tolkien fan. That's perfect! Why don't you make your club a J. R. R. Tolkien book club?" She practically jumps up and down with joy.

"God no. I don't want people to know I read The Hobbit. Shantel and her dumb cheerleader friends will lock me in a bathroom stall and steal my phone." I shake my head furiously.

"There are plenty of kids at Hollywood Hills High School who read fantasy books and are proud of it. I should know, I'm an English teacher!"

"No." I fold my arms over my chest.

"Well, what kind of compromise can we make here?"

I snatch the flier from her and quickly scribble something over my original idea and hand it back. She remains silent as she looks over it carefully.

The Mysterious Magical Book Club
We will read fantasy books and do other stuff

"This is perfect. It's a book club, with a touch of ambiguity, so if you kids want to discuss ghosts and swamp monsters, well you can. I approve your club! I'll type a description and hang it in the main hall outside the English Department with directions for signing-up."

"Okay, thanks I guess. Um, I should go." I turn around to leave before she can sucker me into anything else.

"Jinny, I'm proud of you! See you when school starts," she yells as I walk out the door.

Sometimes I wish Mama would be proud of me for school stuff. But I know she won't be.

"Is that you Cheeseburger?" A voice comes up behind me in the empty hallway.

I am so sick of that nickname.

"Asshole," I mutter. I think I know who it is but turn to look anyway.

Victor Suarez, hottest guy in tenth grade, and captain of the junior varsity football team. Also, the on-again-off-again boyfriend of my nemesis Shantel, which makes him a jerk by association.

"Whoa! Calm down Jinny, I'm just teasing," he says with a grin.

Why does he have to be so cute?

"What do you want, Victor?"

"Just saying hello. Football started today and I had to come drop off something for coach."

"Oh."

"What are you doing here? Are you on a team this year?" he asks, as if he cares.

"None of your business."

He laughs. "Well, my dad's outside waiting, so I better go. You wanna ride home?" Like he already knows Mama isn't waiting for me in her shitty BMW. Like he already knows I'm walking home in the sweltering heat of a late Florida summer afternoon.

"No. I'll walk."

"Suit yourself Chee—I mean Jinny."

He runs ahead, pushing open the double doors, and holds one open for me. Does he think being charming will change my mind about him? I don't say thanks or anything. He keeps pace with my long strides and stops before getting into his dad's shiny, black Lincoln Navigator that's parked at the end of the sidewalk.

"You look really good Jinny," he says casually as he opens the SUV door. "Maybe we'll have some classes together this year." His eyes sparkle.

Okay, so maybe he is kind of charming.

"Uh, thanks. Yeah, I started running," I manage to say while forcing my lips from curling into a smile.

I can't believe Victor Suarez went from calling me Cheeseburger to saying I look good, and he hopes we have a class together this year. Can he see the burnt hues of embarrassment rising in my cheeks? He smiles once more before jumping into the vehicle; I stand frozen, watching his face in the rearview mirror as they drive away.

Our eyes lock and no matter how hard I try; I can't look away.

- Chapter Four -
Are you listening to me?

Today is the first day of school and Mama didn't come home last night. Which means I have to walk or catch a ride on the disgusting school bus with the freshman and weirdos. Not that she would have given me a ride anyway, but at least we could have argued about it.

What a crappy way to start my first day. She's such a selfish person. She thinks because she sent me a text at midnight, that I'll forgive her.

MAMA:
Picked up a late shift sweetie
I'm sure you understand!
I'll bring home dinner tomorrow

I'm not holding my breath on dinner. Mama comes home less and less lately...

Marco sent me a text too.

MARCO:
Sophomore year!
Good luck kiddo
ur daddy is proud of you,
wherever he is...

I grab the picture of me and Daddy from the top drawer of my dresser, where I keep it hidden from Mama. The one of us when I was three, right before he died. He's stone faced with a dark neck tattoo peeking out from under the collar of his shirt. I'm on his lap and have a stupid look on my face with gapped baby teeth and pigtails. I try hard to remember that day, but it was so long ago.

I like to imagine he bought me an ice cream cone from the stand by the big playground near the beach. My heart longs to believe I felt loved that day. A feeling I don't have very often…

I look at my phone and sigh, it's time to start walking if I want to make it to school on time. One final look in the mirror. I have on a pair of jean shorts and a black shirt with a silver vampire cat on the front and black slip-on Vans. I washed my long hair and used Mama's flat iron to take the waves out of it. I slicked a bit of mascara on my lashes to frame my hazel eyes but that's all the make-up I can stand. I've got a few freckles, like Mama, but she covers hers with ten pounds of foundation while I leave mine untouched.

"Well? What do you think?" I turn and ask Pearl.

"Meow!" She lunges at me in playful approval.

"Sorry, no kittens at school." I remove her from my leg and put her on the bed. She curls up and nearly disappears in the blanket.

***

Walking into school I try to hold my head up high.

I hear Ms. Fleming's voice echoing in my mind, You had the highest score in the entire state of Florida. Maybe, just maybe, I am special.

Maybe this year will be my year.

I make it to the tenth-grade hallway and find my locker. I'm busy trying to figure out the combination when someone walks up behind me.

"Looks like someone forgot to feed Cheeseburger this summer." Shantel Greenburg laughs, her perfect french manicured nail points at me when I turn to face her.

All her cheer friends are laughing too. My cheeks bloom with heat and my heart races, as the hallway feels like it's spinning, causing my knees to wobble.

"Awe, look, Cheeseburger is embarrassed and there's no one around to save her," Shantel says and smirks, proud of how her tormenting has evoked a physical response from me.

I clench my fists and will myself to pull it together! For the love of all that's holy, don't just stand here and do nothing! I open my mouth, not sure of what might come out.

"Fuck-off Shantel!" I scream and my eyes get big. I wasn't expecting that, neither was anyone else and the cheer girls look dumbfounded, like no one has ever stood up to Shantel before.

This year I will keep my head up.

"You can't talk to me like that," Shantel gasps.

José Lopez walks by and whispers, "Nice one." Then puts out his fist.

I bump it back.

"Yeah, fuck that dumb–" Jonelle Jackson says as she strolls up next to me, but Mr. Aarons materializes out of thin air, like a ghost.

"Jonelle, you should stop whatever dribble is about to come out of your mouth."

He's serious. Shantel and the Cheers scatter.

"I didn't say nothin!" Jonelle puffs up her chest.

"Go to class girls and don't start anything else today, alright?"

Mr. Aarons disappears down the ninth-grade hallway before we can argue that we didn't start anything, it was Shantel.

"Jinny! You got all tall and skinny and shit. Girl, I'm seriously jealous!"

Jonelle is still taller than me even after my summer sprouting. She's got to be the tallest girl in school, built like a football player too.

"I started running and mostly eating vegetables and salad," I tell her. I don't tell her it's because my Mama's stopped buying food and I haven't had a real meal in weeks.

"NAH!" She laughs. "Salad and shit, that's for rabbits. I ain't no rabbit."

"What'd you do this summer?" I ask.

"Took care of my brothers. Taught the youngest one to read, cause my pops works and my mom took off last year." She looks around when she says it.

I nod. Wow. Jonelle taught her brother to read, that couldn't have been easy.

"Do you like to read?" I ask.

"Yah, my texts…"

The bell rings and we go down separate halls.

I take my seat in the back of Mr. Pearson's first period Algebra II class, and solve all the "Brain Teasers" posted on the walls within seconds. My schedule says I'm in every accelerated class again, just like last year.

Mr. Pearson describes our workload for the semester and I yawn. I'll have every assignment for the year finished in a month. I put my head down on the desk and contemplate if I should ask him for extra work to keep me busy, or if I should bring a book with me. I'm leaning towards bringing a book. I can already tell I'm not going to like Mr. Pearson; he's condescending.

The room goes quiet.

I lift my head and look around.

"Are you even listening to me, Jinny?" He singles me out.

"No," I reply. "This is boring."

He snorts.

"For a girl as 'smart' as they say you are, it's extremely disappointing to see your lack of effort on the first day," he says snidely and uses air quotes. Like my intelligence is a big fucking joke.

The other students laugh, and my blood boils.

"Rude!" I snap back, louder than I expected.

"Get out," he says and points to the door.

"Blah, blah, blah," I say as I walk out of the room and straight to the Main Office.

Usually I'm not a snitch, it doesn't get you far in my neighborhood, but I don't appreciate teachers picking on me.

"I want to see Principal Guthrie."

"He's busy dear," says Miss Charmaine.

She reminds me of Sabrina's Grann Ruth, old and cranky. But at least Miss Charmaine doesn't smell like skunk weed.

"I'll wait." I plant my feet like the thick roots of a Banyan tree, willing to stay here all day if I have to.

"Have a seat." She points to an open chair.

There's someone familiar sitting in the other chair. His black shaggy hair covers half his face, and this time he's the one avoiding eye contact, but I remember him.

Thomas.

The new kid, who is gay and not deaf. I wonder what he did on his first day to be sent to the principal's office. That's when I see red oozing from the knees of his jeans. The rips aren't intentional. They're fresh and jagged, like he hit the ground– hard. I notice the palms of his hands are scraped and bleeding, too.

"Who did that to you?" I ask him.

"Why do you care?" The carefree and confident tone he had when he was here with his mom is gone. Replaced by a scared boy.

"Jinny Buffett. I'm in tenth grade. First day?"

I use a different tactic to get him to open up, even though I already know the answer.

Thomas doesn't say anything for a second, but finally replies, "Yeah, first day. We moved here from Seattle a few weeks ago."

He lifts his head and shakes his hair from his eyes to look at me. I smile, hoping to give him a reason to trust me. Recognition flashes across his face.

"I saw you here the other day, registering for classes," I answer his silent question.

Thomas relaxes a little and laughs.

"God, did you hear my Mom? Going on and on about signing me up for clubs. She's so extra."

"At least she cares."

"Sometimes too much. Ever since my parent's divorce last spring, she's been over the top," he informs me, temporarily forgetting his injuries.

I think it's really brave of him to be so open with me. I keep everything bottled up, never letting anyone in. If I had a therapist, they'd call it, trust issues.

Miss Charmaine stares at us like we are a scene from her favorite daytime TV drama.

I want to tell her to mind her own effing business, but instead I say, "Miss Charmaine, shouldn't you get him some Band-Aids or something? He's bleeding on the floor."

Thomas smirks. "Yeah, Charmaine, it's practically a puddle."

We laugh and I feel better knowing I helped Thomas relax. He smiles, "Thanks, Jinny."

Awe, he's really cute, and I want to know more about him.

Miss Charmaine's intercom beeps and I hear Principal Guthrie ask her to send me in. I stand and walk toward the door.

"Thomas, I don't know where you live, but if you wanna walk home together after school I'll be out front, past the bus loop, for fifteen minutes. Meet me there?"

Thomas looks like he could use someone to walk home with him. And for some reason, I have a feeling that person is supposed to be me. Plus, I still want to know who pushed him. I know why they did it… he's a gay boy from Seattle. I don't know what that feels like. But I do know what it feels like to be picked on. I don't wait for him to answer. If he wants to walk home with me he'll be there after school.

Now, the real reason I came here. I march into Mr. Guthrie's office and explode!

– Chapter Five –
You put my name on it?

"Mr. Pearson is an ASSHOLE," I yell the moment I walk into the office.

"Nice to see you too, Jinny. Please, take a seat." Principal Guthrie is unphased by my cursing and points to one of the chairs in front of his desk. He comes around and sits down in the other chair, turning so he can face me. "Why don't you tell me what happened?" His brows furrow and he leans toward me like he cares. Like he's concerned about me.

"Mr. Pearson passed out the syllabus and I read it. Then he started running his mouth about expectations, but I was already bored and put my head down. I literally know how to do every stupid thing on the syllabus and when he asked if I was listening, I said no. He said for a girl as smart as me, he's very disappointed... But I don't need HIS approval!"

"I see."

"He even used air quotes when he said, smart. Everyone in class started laughing at me..."

Principal Guthrie gets up and takes a file from one of the cabinets, then sits at his desk and picks up the phone. He flips through the file quickly while he's waiting for someone to answer on the other end. Oh crap.

"Are you calling my Mama?"

He holds a finger up, the don't interrupt me move.

I gasp. "Look, Sir, I mean Principal Guthrie, I'm sorry. I won't be disrespectful. Please don't call my Mama. You don't know her!"

The thing I dread the most, someone calling Mama, and her showing up here at school. I can only imagine– she'll stroll in wearing her shortest jean skirt and her biggest push-up bra. Then she'll start screaming at anyone and everyone, causing a huge "look at me" scene. I just know it. My heart pounds like a drum and I drop my face into my hands. I should have kept my big mouth shut about Mr. Pearson.

This is what I get for snitching.

"Hello, this is Principal Guthrie over at Hollywood Hills High School. Is Director Evans from the Mathematics Department available?"

I look up–

Did he say Mathematics Department?

So, he isn't calling Mama?

"Director Evans? Yes, yes, remember that student I told you about? The one with the FSA scores? Yes, Jinny Buffett… Good. Well, she's in my office right now... As you suspected, tenth grade Algebra II is far too easy for her. Can she take the online course you suggested? Yes, the Advanced Calculus II... Perfect!" Then he writes something down on a sticky pad. "I'll give it to her. She can do the work during her first period in the library. Thanks again."

He hangs up the phone.

"Seriously?" I ask. My heart relaxes and the pumping sound in my ears subsides.

He nods and smiles. "Oh, by the way, I really thought your book club idea was clever. Ms. Fleming is extremely proud to have you as her student."

"Um... Thank you." I've never been comfortable with praise.

My skin itches.

"Alright, I think we've solved this. Why don't you head to the library. Tell Ms. Franklin, you'll be in there for first period from now on. If she has questions, she can call me. And Jinny, no more getting kicked out of class. If the work is too easy, we can come up with an alternative for you."

He peels off a yellow sticky note and hands it to me. It's the email address for Director Evans.

"Thanks Principal Guthrie."

"My pleasure. If you don't mind, can you let Thomas know it's his turn."

I head for the door but stop when I think of Thomas out there with his bloody knees on his first day of school. "Someone hurt him, because he's the new kid, or because he's gay. Hopefully he'll tell you who did it and you can suspend their intolerant ass– because that kind of shit is not okay."

Principal Guthrie nods and I walk out of his office, ready to face the rest of the school day. "Your turn Thomas. I'll see you after school, don't forget."

His smile tells me he won't.

Ms. Franklin, the librarian, gives me the stink eye when I ask for a computer.

"Call Principal Guthrie if you don't believe me."

She huffs and assigns me to one of the desktops. I open my school account and email Director Evans thanking her for the opportunity.

Now what.

I look at my schedule and my next class is art. The only class I have that's not considered accelerated. "You have to go to one of the charter schools for accelerated art," they told me. No thank you! I am not riding a bus half-way across the city for one class. Maybe Jonelle will be in art with me. I could text her and ask, but Hollywood Hills High teachers are jerk-offs. They claim if they see your phone they will take it for a whole week, like we are babies and can't manage technology without their permission.

I guess since I'm starting a book club, I could look at the books. I like the library when it's empty. The way it smells like antique paper. All the possibilities living in solitude on the shelves. But the bell rings before I have a chance to look.

The next three periods drag until lunch. The cafeteria is a zoo, but I spot Angie in line. Outside of Jonelle, she's the only other person at school I'd consider a friend, even though we don't talk much. Her dad, Mr. Bailey, is the art teacher and always smells like patchouli oil.

"You look different," she says when I stand next to her.

"I started running. How was your summer?"

"It was okay. I got a job babysitting the neighbor girl everyday at five a.m."

She has dark circles under her eyes.

"Five a.m.? Girl, you're crazy," Jonelle says as she walks up behind us.

"It's not bad. Emily has Down syndrome. We mostly watch cartoons and draw."

Something in my heart tugs. I know Angie is a goodie-two-shoes, but taking a job helping a kid with Down syndrome, now that's selfless.

We slowly snake through the lunch line and take our trays of mystery food to a table at the corner of the crowded room. But before I can put a bite in my mouth, someone unexpected sits down next to me.

"How's your first day going Jinny?"

Victor smiles, his teeth perfectly straight and bright. I subconsciously run my tongue over my teeth, praying I remembered to brush this morning.

"I got kicked out of math."

Jonelle tilts her head back and howls with laughter. It's the kind of infectious sound that makes us all laugh with her. Then Ang tells us about her day while Jonelle cuts in about who broke up over the summer, who moved away, and any other gossip she can think of. Victor tells us about football.

Is this really happening? Is Victor hanging out with me and my friends?

"VICTOR!" shouts Matt Bowland. "Bro, why are you sitting with these rejects? Come on, I've got a spot for you at our table." He grabs at Victor's arm to pull him away from us.

I want to punch Matt for ruining this moment.

"Rejects?" Jonelle stands up. "Who you callin' a reject?"

She's taller and broader than Matt and could knock his ass out in a heartbeat if she wanted to. He's such a creep. He stares at her with a sultry look on his face, like he actually wishes she would punch him. Mama has names for guys like that. Names even I'm embarrassed to repeat.

"Jonelle, don't you have Ms. Fleming's class right now? Come on, walk with me?" I say to interrupt the weird tension. I stand and put myself between the two of them.

"Nah, I'm heading to P.E. Ang, let's get out of here, I'm sick of clowns." Jonelle lifts her chin up in defiance.

Victor jumps from his seat. "I have Ms. Fleming's class. I'll walk with you Jinny."

"But, bro! Lunch isn't even over." Matt shouts after us as we walk out of the cafeteria.

"Matt's an idiot," Victor says and shakes his head.

I couldn't agree more.

In Ms. Fleming's room, Victor slides into a seat next to me, and keeps glancing over in my direction.

"What is it?" I hiss.

"I've never been in an accelerated class before," he whispers and wipes his palms on his jeans.

"It's easy. Don't stress."

He sits up straight in his chair as soon as Ms. Fleming starts talking.

"Welcome to tenth grade accelerated English. This class is going to help you transition to upper level course work and college level–"

I want to pay attention, I really do. But, I look at her syllabus and I've read every book on it, most of them two or three times. *The Great Gatsby, 1984, To Kill a Mockingbird, The Help, Catcher in the Rye...*

I find books in the trash all the time. The Classics. Garbage to people in Hollywood. Sometimes I find new ones down on the beach too. Books, left by lazy vacationers. I like to think the ghost of my Daddy leads me to them. To keep my mind entertained. I keep all the books I find under my bed and read them at night.

I guess starting a book club wasn't really that far of a stretch.

I smile for a second until–

Oh my god. There's a sign for my book club posted on the wall. Ms.

Fleming made a great big poster board with glittery letters and a sign-up sheet.

Do you ever find Magic in the words you read?
Do you ever want to talk to kids your own age about books out-side of the classroom?
If so, join Jinny Buffett's Mysterious Magical Book Club
Meets in Ms. Fleming's room @ 3pm on Tuesday and Thursday

I cannot believe she put my name on the poster. Holy shit! I'm never going to live this down. Why the hell did I agree to this? Now everyone at school will know what a nerd I am.

I put my head down on my desk and take several sudden and urgent breaths.

"Jinny, do you want to say anything?" Ms. Fleming asks.

I look up quickly. I don't know what's going on. Everyone is staring at me.

"I was just suggesting that if our class reading list doesn't grab the attention of this group, they could join your book club," she restates herself.

"Um. Yes. Book Club." My voice is dry and cracks. Someone laughs.

"Well, okay then, the sign-up is on the wall over there and I have one out in the main hallway, for other grades to sign-up. It starts next week on Tuesday."

Ms. Fleming moves on to the next thing on the syllabus and I put my head back down against the cool wood grain of the desk.

- Chapter Six -
Friends & Fish Tacos

I'm still mortified by Ms. Fleming. How could she do this to me? The final bell rings at the end of school and I go outside to wait for Thomas. I hope he lives close to me, so I don't have to back-track across town, but I would do it for him.

"Awe, Jinny Cheeseburger, you started your own nerd club. Aren't you special?" says Britney McConnal.

The spineless group of cheers all laugh along with her as they round the corner heading to practice. At least Shantel isn't with them, I can't take any more of her crap today.

"Cheeseburger? Like the Jimmy Buffett song?" Thomas says as he walks up behind me.

"Yeah."

"They're just jealous," Thomas says and smiles.

I shrug– I'd never thought of it that way. If I was them I wouldn't be jealous of me. They are the ones with the expensive clothes and live in the nice neighborhoods with perfect, loving, two-parent households.

"So, Thomas, where do you live?"

Please let it be close to me.

"The Hollywood Plaza Condos. Is that near you?" he asks.

"YES! It's like two blocks from me."

I would have walked him home no matter where he lived. It's not like I have anything else to do after school.

"So how do you like being in Florida? Have you been to the ocean yet?" I ask as we start walking home.

"It's okay. I've been dying to go to the beach, but Mom is all nervous, and won't let me go without her. But like, I don't want to go to the beach with my mom."

"I go practically every weekend. You can come with me next time if you want. What's your number?" I pull my phone from my jean shorts and type his number as he spouts it off to me. Then I text him quick.

ME:
Hey it's me

THOMAS:
Hey girl ☺

He puts his phone in his back pocket. "I'm glad we met, it's been kind of weird and painful, starting a new school," he admits, joking about his injuries. At least his hands and knees have been cleaned up.

"I can show you around and fill you in on who hangs with who."

Getting to know new people can be awkward, I know, that's why I generally avoid it. But, there's something different about Thomas. Maybe because he's not from around here. He doesn't look at me the way everyone else does, like I'm white trash.

Or like my Mama slept with their Daddy.

It doesn't take long before we are laughing and talking as if we've always been friends.

"I signed up for your book club," he says as we round the corner a few blocks from school. "There was this cute guy signing up for something, and when I went to check it out I was like, hey, that's the girl Jinny I met. You don't mind right? Like it's a book club for anyone?"

"What? You signed up for my book club? And so did someone else? I thought, uh, I thought everyone would think it's a joke…"

I can't believe it.

"Why would starting a club be a joke? I think it's awesome."

"You do?"

"Yeah! I'm glad it was a book club and not something like math," Thomas says.

I laugh. If he only knew all the drama I had with math today.

"Do you like to read?"

"I just got done with the Lemony Snickets series. Don't judge… I know they are for elementary kids."

"Oh my gosh, I've read them a thousand times, it can be our secret." I wink.

"Yaaassss!" He gives me an unexpected hug.

We both laugh.

"Well, there's your place." I point toward Thomas's condo complex. "Wanna meet me here tomorrow morning so we can walk together?"

"Of course!"

Then Thomas hugs me again.

I watch him run off and enter the gate code. He waves goodbye and I smile the rest of the two blocks home, ignoring the sweat running down my back.

***

I turn Spotify on my phone and connect it to Mama's fake Bose speaker in the kitchen when I walk in the door. Mama's not home to bitch and moan about me using her things so I turn it up all the way.

I'm starving. I check the fridge. Not much, but better than empty. There's a zucchini and a head of lettuce. I'm so hungry I would have pulled out and eaten all of my hair if the fridge had been bare again. Instead I flip my head over and I pull my long hair into a messy bun and make a salad. I use stale oyster crackers for croutons. I really wish we had real food. Ever since I got my period last spring, Mama literally stopped grocery shopping. I'm pretty sure she has actually said that since I'm a woman now, I have to stop eating if I want a body like hers. Gross!

Body shaming at its worst.

I hate her sometimes, okay all the time.

"Come here Pearl, you want to explore?" I open my bedroom door. "Just don't claw up Mama's couch." The first thing she does is claw the couch. Little asshole.

My phone beeps. A text from Thomas.

THOMAS:
Hey new bestie!
What u doing?

ME:
Playin w/my kitten Pearl.
What u up2?

THOMAS:
Thinkin about that cute boy
who signed up for book club
his name was Josè Lopez

ME:
OMG he is cute!
I'll intro u 2morrow
he's prfct 4 u
I swear   <3

THOMAS:
YAASSSSS!!!!
bbl mom needs me

I take Pearl back to my room in case Mama actually comes home with dinner. I look at the books I have under my bed and try to figure out what one we should use for Mysterious Magical Book Club, but when I look at all my books, I start getting anxious. Maybe no one will want to read my kind of books. Maybe I should let Josè or Thomas pick the first book. That sounds good, taking turns reading our favorite books. Is that what adults do at book clubs? Or is it just about drinking wine and gossiping?

I spend a few hours reading and drawing pictures of seashells and start wondering if Mama's ever coming home tonight, but then I hear the front door.

"JINNY!" Mama's voice rings out. I rush from my room and find her in the kitchen. "How was your first day sweetheart?"

I'm immediately suspicious. Asking about my first day? Calling me sweetheart? But, she has food with her and I'm starving, my stomach flips, twice.

"I'm so hungry."

"And?" She's wearing her six-inch black heels and tight blue dress. I wonder where she's been all day, it's not one of her normal outfits for cocktail waitressing. She taps her toe impatiently.

"Thank you for bringing home dinner, Ma'am," I mumble the words I think she wants to hear.

"Jinny, don't be stupid. I mean, are you going to tell me? How was it? Did you make any friends? I thought you might call me after school." She pouts. "Why dontchu you call your Mama anymore." She uses that creepy scrunched up baby voice, the one she uses to manipulate men. 'Oh pwetty pwease, put gas in my car so I don't break a nail'

Puke.

I look at her and shrug.

Then, completely out of character, she takes the two real plates we own and dishes up the food. Normally, she plops the take-out containers on the table and I take what I want to my room.

She's up to something… But I take a seat at the table anyway.

"Sorry I didn't call," I say and take a bite of the crispy fish tacos. The food is so good I can hardly stand it, and almost forgive her. "And yes, I made some friends. There's this boy from Seattle. We are going to walk to school together."

"I knew once you lost some weight the boys would be all over you. Is that what you wore today? You really should try a little harder. You're getting old enough, you could show more skin." She flashes a smile.

My heart sinks. Typical Mama.

"Yeah, maybe."

"I'm serious Jinny, I was about your age when I started working tables at the cocktail bar in Miami. I always say, if you want the tips you gotta show a little–"

"Stop, Mama," I cut her off before things get vulgar. I wish she'd shut up. I just want to eat without gagging.

"Hrmph, your loss," she answers me coldly. Then she takes out a cigarette and lights it instead of eating her food.

Her mood changes are instant.

I silently eat my food, ignoring the smoke rings she blows at me. For some reason I think about the picture she has of me hanging in her bedroom from the Hollywood Little Darling Beauty Pageant. It was right after Daddy died. She sold his mechanics toolbox and used the money to buy me a custom dress and pay the entry fee. She told everyone at her work I was going to win her the five thousand dollar grand prize.

I didn't win.

And she was furious.

The judges said the dress was too scandalous for a four-year old. Mama screamed something at the judges, knocked over their table, and forced them to take my picture before the cops came to remove us.

"So, Jinny, how would you feel if I took a trip with one of my friends? Now that you're back in school, you'll hardly notice I'm gone." She gets up and makes me a glass of ice water and even puts a lemon wedge in it, like I'm just some customer she's schmoozing to get tips from.

I knew she was up to something! I let out a sigh, knowing she's not really asking for my permission. Mama always does whatever she wants. She'll go and leave me home alone whether I want her to or not.

"Can you leave me some money for food?" I whisper.

"Of course! I knew you wouldn't mind. It's one of the regulars at work, he's taking a business trip to Islamorada in the Keys, and he wants my company. I put in so many hours last month, they owe me a week off." She beams and starts bouncing around. "I have so much to pack!"

She's never left me alone for a week before... a few days yes, but never a week. She's so selfish. Selfish and stupid. A week with a regular? She'll dump him before they get half-way through the trip. I push my plate away, the sight of the food mixed with the smell of her smoke is sickening.

"Can I go to my room now?"

She flits around like a songbird in spring. I go to my room and try not to slam the door, even though I want to slam it so hard it knocks the pictures off the wall. I want to punch the mirror over my dresser and give myself seven years of bad luck.

Instead, I lie on my bed and cry myself to sleep.

***

"Jinny," a voice says my name.

I sit up and rub the sleep from my eyes. I don't see anyone, but it's dark, the apartment quiet, no music or TV coming from Mama's room, and no humming of the air conditioner. Just silence.

"Hello?" I ask. "Is that you, Marco?"

He does have a key for emergencies. I don't know who else would be in the apartment at this hour.

"Jinny."

Shivers go up my spine. My heart races and my breathing quickens. I reach around in the covers for my phone to turn on the flashlight, just as I clasp the screen, I see a wispy shadow figure standing in the corner of the room.

"Is Mama okay? Why are you in my room?"

That's definitely not Marco! My lips tremble, ready to release a scream, but then I smell something citrus and sweet...

"Daddy? Is that you?"

"I'll keep watch while she's gone," the spirit figure says to me. "You got folks out there who love you, girl."

"Who's out there Daddy?" I ask.

But as suddenly as he appeared, he's gone, without an answer. I jump and rush to where he stood. A fine mist still lingers, smelling like greasy motor oil. I look down and discover a fresh orange peel left on the floor.

I crawl back into my bed and pull Pearl closer to me.

"Am I crazy?"

She licks my nose and I nuzzle her soft gray fur. I toss and turn for hours, until finally sleep drags me into its clutches. I dream about being lost, and I call out for my Mama, but it's Daddy and his six sisters who appear.

"Tag, you're it!" One of them taps me on the shoulder and we spend hours running around, playing freeze tag in the swamp.

– Chapter Seven –
You're such a little FREAK!

Beep, beep, beep!

My alarm goes off and I moan. I'm slow to open my heavy eyelids as the sun shines brightly through the slits of the cheap, white plastic blinds. I'm tired from waking up in the middle of the night and playing tag in my dreams, my legs even ache, as if I was actually running. I sit up and look around. I don't see the orange peels and I wonder if Daddy's spirit really did visit me, or if it was all just part of my dream. An emptiness settles in my heart.

I drag myself from my room. Mama's bedroom door is open and her bed is empty. I rush to the kitchen, hoping to find her sitting at the table drinking coffee, but it's empty too. There's forty dollars sitting on the table with a note in her oversized swirly script.

Jinny,
Text me every day. Call Marco if you need anything!

XOXO
Crystal Diamond Buffett

Mama always signs her full name on everything, even her notes to me. Like I might forget who she is. As if she'd let me.

I get ready for school. Another pair of jean shorts and a gray shirt that says Snooze on the front, fits my mood. I yawn. Mama's lucky— if I was any other teenager, I'd crawl back into bed and skip school. But, she knows I won't miss school and risk the truancy officer getting involved. My phone rings.

It's Marco.

I don't answer. I have to go to school. So I text him while I walk to meet Thomas.

ME:
I'm fine I'll call u if i
need anything

MARCO:
Sounds good kiddo. Work hard
in school today!

ME:
K, bye

"Jinny!" Thomas sits on the painted, cinder block wall that surrounds his condo complex. He jumps down and rushes toward me with a smile on his face. He's wearing black skinny jeans and a plain white t-shirt.

"You look like James Franco," I say as we hug hello.

"Have you seen him as James Dean? I'm in love!" He fans his face and surprises me by singing while we walk on the cracked sidewalk toward school. It's humid and loud from morning traffic and cicadas buzzing. But, his voice, it's magical, cutting through the background noises. I stop dead in my tracks.

"Thomas, oh my god, your voice! Have you even heard yourself?"

"Nah, it's no big deal." He shades his eyes with his black hair and laughs nervously.

Just then, a familiar black Lincoln Navigator crawls by and honks. The window rolls down and Victor sticks his head out.

"HEY JINNY!" he shouts and waves before his dad speeds up and drives off. My heart beats faster and I try not to blush, but I feel the warmth flood my freckled face.

Thomas grabs me by the shoulders, "Girl, who was that?" He bats his eye lashes at me.

"Just Victor Suarez. He's nobody."

"Nobody? Yeah right. He loooooves you. Did you see those eyes?" Thomas teases.

I squeak.

"Here, listen to this." He hands me one of his Airpods and I put it in my left ear. "It's like she's singing to my soul," he says and sings along.

I can't get over how such a big voice like that can come out of a skinny gay boy like him. I love him even more now. We walk and listen to music the rest of the way to school. I know my voice sounds like shit but Thomas doesn't say so.

When we get to school, Matt Bowland stands on the stairs waiting for something, or someone. Thomas tenses and slows down. He grabs my arm to stop me from walking any further.

"Slow down. Let's just wait before we go inside." He turns to walk back the other direction.

"Thomas, is that the asshole who pushed you around yesterday?" I ask. I swear to God I'll kill Matt.

"JINNY, wait up!" It's Jonelle hollering from the other direction. Thomas and I wait for her to run over to us. "Who are you?" She says to Thomas when she gets closer. She looks him up and down.

She's suspicious and I smile, knowing that feeling. Girls like us, we have a lot of trust issues. But I know how to ease the tension.

"Jonelle, this is Thomas. He just moved here from Seattle and lives by me. He's cool," I provide the necessary introduction for Thomas.

"Sup." Jonelle nods her head at him. She looks over and sees Matt with his shoulders pushed back and his chest up. "Who's that dick waiting for?"

"Me... he hates me," Thomas says. "He lives next door to my Mom's cousin, so when we moved here, I said hey to him. I mean, he's cute. But, I should have known better. Guys like him are no good for guys like me."

"Fuck him! You're hanging with me and Jinny now. Ain't no one gonna mess with us, not if they know what's good for them." Jonelle cracks her knuckles. "Oh... Jinny, I signed up for your mysterious magical shit. So, what's the deal? We get to hang out after school and play Bloody Mary? If we conjure up any nasty spirits, I'm sending them to Matt Bowland's house to haunt the shit out of him. Little prick." Jonelle bumps her shoulder into me and winks. Then she shakes with laughter.

Thomas smirks. "I like you Jonelle," he says.

"JINNY!" It's Ang. She just got off the handicapped bus and runs towards us.

"Hey Ang." I give her a hug.

"I'm going to sign up for your club," she says and smiles. "I like to read books too! What a good idea for a new club."

"Really?"

I can't believe it. People actually want to read books with me in my stupid club. The bell rings and everyone piles into the building. We linger, letting the place clear out.

"See you at lunch," Jonelle says and her and Ang head in.

Thomas still stands next to me. I wonder if he's nervous to go inside alone. "I have to go to the Library. I'll walk with you to your class, Thomas."

I link arms with him and walk into the building. He holds his head up as we march through the ninth grade hallway. Not a lot of tenth graders down here, but it is the fastest way for me to go to the Library.

"Thanks girl." He hugs me before entering his classroom.

When I get to the library I sign on to the computer and check my email. Director Evans sent directions for logging on to Advanced Calculus II. I finish the work in fifteen minutes. It's better than Mr. Pearson's class, but still easy. I put my head down, maybe I'll take a nap. I'm still tired after not sleeping well last night.

"Who does that little skank think she is?"

"Yeah, what a bitch!"

I hear a group of girls coming into the library laughing and making noise. I peek and see Shantel standing with Britney and a couple of the other cheerleaders. Of course.

"Starting her own club? Talking to Victor? Having attitude with me! I will crush her," Shantel shrieks.

"She's a nobody," Britney replies.

"Yeah, forget her," Faith adds.

I get out of my seat. Britney and Faith gasp when they see me. I march right up to Shantel. My fists are balled at my side and I'm trembling. I don't know what I am going to do, but I want to knock out her teeth. Then I remember, Mama isn't home. If I get into a fight and the school calls her, she will make my life a living hell.

My breathing is labored as I wrestle with my emotions.

"What do you think you're doing?" Shantel asks me.

Just then, the door to the library opens behind her and the perfect person walks in. My hands loosen and I plaster a smile across my face.

"Shantel, um, there is still room if you want to join my book club. The first meeting is next week on Tuesday. I hope you'll think about it," I say as loud and sweet as I can, my heart pounds in my ears. This better work.

"Gross! Get away from me! Why would I join your pathetic club, you little FREAK!" she screams and puts her hands up like she's going to push me away from her.

"MISS GREENBURG, my office NOW!"

Shantel jumps a foot in the air.

Ha, ha! Dumb asses didn't see Principal Guthrie walk in behind them. I quickly make a sad face, so he can see how damaged I am from girls like Shantel bullying me. I mean, it's true, but right now it's on my terms.

Shantel spins around and heads for the door. The rest of the cheers are frozen statues. "Go to class, now!" Principal Guthrie snaps at them. They yip and run out of the library like scolded puppies.

"Jinny, are you alright?" He looks distraught, like he didn't know this kind of shit happens all the time. Not just to me, but to a lot of kids. Just look at what happened to Thomas.

"I'm fine. I better go, too," I say and grab my bag.

"I stopped in to see how you're doing. I'm sorry about Shantel. That was unfortunate and I will not tolerate that kind of behavior."

"It's okay, I'm used to girls like her... And my new math class was easy. I finished in fifteen minutes. Don't get me wrong, it's a lot more interesting than Algebra II. Seriously, thank you again," I tell him.

He shakes his head. "Jinny, how did we get this far in your education and not challenge you more?"

What a loaded question.

I wonder for a split second if he wants me to answer. Well Principal Guthrie, we got this far because my name is Jinny Buffett and every teacher in south Florida thinks that's the funniest thing they ever heard and they actually laugh at me when they see my name on their class roster. Strike one. Then there's that little detail about me being poor white trash. Strike two. Let's see, how about the fact that my Daddy was from the Everglades and died selling drugs. Strike three.

Oh, the worst part, the real clincher is that my Mama is a cocktail waitress who moonlights as a prostitute in every hotel in Hollywood.

"I don't know." I shrug and walk out.

– Chapter Eight –
Wait? How many people signed up?

I can't wait to see Jonelle and Ang and tell them about what happened with Shantel in the library. I'm still laughing at the look of shock and disgust on her face when she got caught tormenting me. The bell rings for lunch and I practically run through the halls to get to the cafeteria, weaving and ducking between the sea of students.

"Jonelle, hey girl," I'm out of breath when I see her in the lunch line. "You'll never guess what I did in first period." I tell her all about my run-in with Shantel and Principal Guthrie, not leaving out any of the juicy details.

"You're ruthless! This is why we're gonna hang out more. Not just for your magic club," she says and puts her arm around me.

"Yeah, we should hang more." I nod.

"Grab yo shit, let's go find Ang." Jonelle pushes me forward in line and I take a salad and apple from the case and check out. She takes a cheeseburger. I try not to flinch.

Ang is already waiting for us at the same table as yesterday. We sit down with her and she smiles. "I did it! I signed-up for your club. I texted Miguel and Sarah to let them know I won't be able to help Emily on the bus home on Tuesday and Thursday. It's cool– they knew I'd have stuff once school started again." She takes her pb&j sandwich out of her packed cold lunch.

I'm going crazy!

Another person signed-up for the Mysterious Magical Book Club. That's five of us. I wonder if there will be any more names when I get to Ms. Fleming's class.

"Thanks, Ang. I hope it's worth it."

I'm kind of getting nervous now– there's going to be this expectation from everyone. They are giving up their normal afterschool plans to be in my club. I've never had to be responsible for the way others feel and spend their time. I look at my shiny green apple. I'm not very hungry, but I take a big bite anyway. The tang makes my mouth pucker.

"Maybe Victor will sign-up," Jonelle announces and raises her eyebrows up and down. "I seen the way he lookin' at you Jinny. He wants to get into your pants."

I choke and sour apple chunks shoot out the side of my mouth.

"Don't be a pig," I say to her. "He's been in Shantel's pants. I don't want nothin' to do with him."

"You sure 'bout that?" She leans forward and motions me closer to whisper, "Maybe it's his pickle you want to tickle." Jonelle throws her head back and laughs as loud as she can and smacks her hands on the lunch table. She's an animal.

Now I remember why I never hung out with her that much last year. But, I'm trying. I really do want friends this year. Even if they are disgusting.

"Jonelle don't say shit like that." I'm embarrassed.

She wipes her tears away from all the laughing. Ang is chuckling too, with a mouth full of sandwich. I frown at them. Bitches... But, this is what friends do right? Talk crap, tease, act silly during lunch. I look around the crowded lunchroom to confirm.

After lunch I decide to check on the sign-up sheet in the hallway. The one Thomas said he put his name on.

The Mysterious Magical Book Club
Please print your name & grade
Jose Lopez 9th
Thomas Grady 9th
Ashley Jaleek 9th
Hector Mann 10th

Oh my God. That makes seven of us! I don't know Hector or Ashley, but I'll ask Jonelle and Ang if they do. I walk to Ms. Fleming's class and check the other sign-up sheet in her room.

The Mysterious Magical Book Club
Please print your name & grade
Jonelle Jackson 10th
Angie Bailey 10th
Kaei Summer 9th
Victor Suarez 10th (when football ends)
Kristin Amick 11th

I don't know why, but I take my phone out and snap a picture of the list before Ms. Fleming sees me with it. I'm in shock. People actually want to read books with me. That's ten of us. And Victor! What game is he playing? Is Jonelle right? I make a face. I'm not ready for any of that shit. I've never kissed anyone, let alone thought about what was in their pants. God, my head is spinning right now.

"Jinny, can you have a seat?" Ms. Fleming says.

Someone laughs. I'm the only one still standing. I take my seat as fast as I can and feel their eyes on me. More laughter. I want to blurt out SHUT UP and STOP LOOKING AT ME! But instead I get out my notebook and start taking notes and try to ignore them. After a minute the room is quiet, except little pencil scratches on paper as we all try to keep up with Ms. Fleming's lecture on deciphering universal themes in literature.

"You want to identify the subtle clues within the plot. Look for how the main character has personal growth. It's not always going to be obvious," she keeps going.

But, I get bored and put down my pencil. Understanding charactive motive is easy. What's not easy is knowing real people's motives. Like, why did ten people sign up for my book club? What do they expect? My chest feels tight. Did the air stop working? Why is it suddenly so hot in this class?

Finally, after what seems like an eternity in hell, the bell rings.

"Ms. Fleming?" I walk up to her at the end of class. "Did you see—"

"Jinny! I'm thrilled." She cuts me off, knowing what I'm going to say. "You have ten people in your club. I knew this would happen. You are going to surprise yourself when you see how good it feels to lead this club. Aren't you proud?" She picks up some papers and shuffles them at her desk. Then she looks me square in the eye.

If we were standing in my neighborhood, I'd think she was getting ready to say some shit and my shoulders tense up, confused. But then she softens and smiles.

"Do you know what book you will read first in your club? Do you need any ideas?"

I let out the breath in my lungs. Actually, I do have an idea, and I'd been waiting for the right time to tell her. "I was thinking about As I Lay Dying by William Faulkner. Have you read that one? I know it's not very magical, but it explores the theme of death, and I uh– " I fumble on the words. I had this big thing prepared, about how my Daddy is dead, how I've been thinking about him a lot lately, and his ghost. I thought maybe if we read it, I could segway it into a conversation about the real meaning of life and–

She coughs.

"Uh, yes, Jinny. Of course that's a good option. Great idea!" She is scrambling and I'm perplexed. Does she really think it's a great idea or is she just trying to appease me? "I have another idea, though. Have you read The Raven Boys by Maggie Stiefvater? I think it might be the perfect first book, considering your audience." She pulls a book from her desk and hands it to me. I take it, quickly reading the back cover while she talks.

"That's my copy. Read it this weekend and text me if you like it. I'll order enough copies on Amazon with my class budget to get them here by Tuesday for your first club meeting. You'll have to do some fundraising after that to buy other books, but you can decide as a group how many books you'll read. I think it would be wonderful for you each to keep all the books you read, like trophies, from being in the club together. Then you can write in the margins, make notes..." She pauses to see if I want to add anything.

I can see she's thought about this and I don't hate her idea.

"Okay." I put the book in my bag. "What's your number?" I pull out my phone and put her number in.

"Now, how are your other classes? I understand you're taking online calculus through the college. Do you need to bump up a grade level in your other classes?" She looks at me and blinks hard.

"Um... Most of 'em are easy... and... I already read all the books you have on your list for this class." Damn. I didn't want to do that, but I think she'd rather me be honest.

"I'm glad to hear it. I'll assign you more advanced topics for the writing portions, the kinds of things you'll see later in college and grad school. I use the classics in this class, because you'll see them again and again in the academic world."

"Okay, more advanced writing, I'd like that."

"I want to start meeting with you once a week to discuss what you plan on doing for college. I really think we need to start preparing your applications early—"

"College? I'm not going to college." I cut her off. "My Mama hates school. She won't let me go." I turn to leave.

"Jinny, wait. I'm serious. Plan on every Wednesday. We can meet for thirty minutes after school. Please."

I let out a long sigh. If I tell Ms. Fleming no, I'll have to stare at her disappointed face every day in class. But, if I tell Mama I'm starting college prep and working on applications, she will absolutely lose her mind. I'm stuck between a rock and a hard place.

"FINE!" I run out and slam her door.

I look up and down the hallway and hope no one saw me do that. I don't want to start some rumors about me fighting with the teachers. The bell is already ringing and everyone rushes into their next class. Saved by the bell. I walk toward my next period, and since I'm all alone in the hallway, I text Ms. Fleming.

ME:
I didn't mean 2 slam the door
sorry

MS. FLEMING:
It's okay Jinny

ME:
K, bye

MS. FLEMING:
Put your phone away

ME:
I have 2 ask u
somthn important

MS. FLEMING:
??

ME:
Can we play bloody mary in
Mysterious Magical Book Club?

MS. FLEMING:
GO to class!
And absolutely NO evoking
demons in my classroom!
:)

ME:
K, bye

I put my phone away quick and stroll into my last class with a smile painted on my face. I should be pissed at Ms. Fleming, sticking her nose in my life, asking about college, and making me do her dumb weekly check-ins. But, instead, I feel relieved and hopeful that my life is finally turning in a direction I might actually be proud of.

This is the best year at school I've ever had.

And it's only the second day.

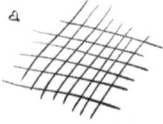

– Chapter Nine –
Hey y'all, it's dance time!

After school Thomas waits for me outside by the steps. "Girl you have a lot of names on your sheet for Mysterious Magical Book Club." He looks happy. Maybe he is having a good second day too.

"Right?! There are ten people! I'm shocked."

"I'm not surprised at all, Jinny. You're like the sun. People gravitate to you." Thomas spins a perfect pirouette and stops with a stomp. I laugh.

"Shut up. You're the one who's a star. Look at that spin," I say before I grab his hand and lace my fingers through his.

He squeezes hard and we walk proudly away from school.

"Do you want to come over and look at my yearbook from last year? I can point out all the people who joined the Mysterious Magical Book Club. School pictures are always so funny. No filters in a yearbook." I make a goofy face at him and he laughs.

"YASSSS! I'd love to hang with you girl," he exclaims.

"Should we stop by and ask your mom first if you can come over? I know you said she's kind of overprotective."

"Yeah, we can. She's dying to meet you. Does your mom care if I come over?"

I shake my head no. "She's at work all night." It's not exactly a lie. She is on a job and she will be gone all night...

"Perfect! We can be loud," he says it like he already knows we will be. "Ooooh, I have a song for us." He pulls out his Airpods and puts one in my ear. Taylor Swift. We sing at the top of our lungs as we walk home.

His voice is like an angel.

Mine is like a cat being ran over.

***

I don't know what to expect when we go through the gate and into Thomas's condo complex. I've passed here a million times, but never been inside the fenced property. The buildings are clean, new and modern. Expensive foreign cars are dotted throughout the covered parking spots. Manicured bushes, lush pink bougainvillea vines, and bright yellow hibiscus flowers complete the landscape.

This block used to be filled with old rent-controlled apartments like mine, but they tore them down after a hurricane a few years ago and put the condos up in their place.

It's the kind of place I wish me and Mama lived.

Thomas uses the key to let us inside. It smells new and fresh inside and the furniture is fancy, not like the cheap wicker crap we have in our apartment.

"Oh, you really think your lawyers can get your child support reduced? Go ahead and try it! You're such a piece of SHIT!" His mom yells from the far room.

Thomas looks at me and shrugs.

We walk down the hall and into the kitchen. He opens the fridge and grabs two Diet Cokes and hands one to me. "I can go home if you want. We can hang out this weekend," I offer just in case he's embarrassed by his Mom, but doesn't want to tell me.

"MOM!" he screams.

His mom comes rushing into the room. "Thomas! You're home!" She's a tiny woman with dark hair and Botox features. He hugs her and she actually hugs him back.

Mama acts like I'm the plague anytime I try that move. I'd be jealous, but it's adorable seeing Thomas hug his mom… I smile.

"THIS is Jinny. The girl I told you about. I'm going to her house to look at her old yearbooks," he says.

"Hi Mrs—"

"Jinny Buffett!" His mom practically shouts and rushes to hug me, cutting me off before I can finish saying hi. Her fake boobs feel like rocks against my stomach. She's really short and I was not prepared for her to hug me like that. I steady myself so we don't fall over backward. She steps back and looks me up and down. "You're right Thomas, she's fabulous."

I blush.

"Where are my manners?" She says each word punchy. "I'm Thomas's mom, Silvia Arnold. I went back to my maiden name in case you were wondering. But, you can just call me Sil." She's dramatic. I kind of like it. It must be where Thomas gets it from.

"Nice to meet you, Ma'am." It comes out twangy, like when Mama slips back into her thick panhandle accent.

Thomas and Sil look back and forth at one another. Then they both start to giggle. Oh God! I'm such a dork.

"See mom, I told you. They have southern accents in Florida. Jinny's is perfect! Watch, let me try– Nice to meet you, Ma'am." He copies me and laughs.

I pretend pout.

"Ma'am," he says again at his mom. He's so extra around her, not like at school where he seems less vibrant.

It inspires me, so I put a hand on my hip to play up my fake southern charm, channeling how Mama acts when she's waitressing at Margaritaville.

"Howdy y'all! Welcome to the Sunshine State." I flip my hair and smile big.

"Well you're as cute as a button Jinny! You can come over and say "Howdy y'all" anytime you like," Sil teases me back.

No one's ever called me cute as a button. I'm not sure if I should say thank you.

My heart beats faster, maybe letting myself out of my shell might have been a bad idea. Maybe Thomas is going to get mad at me. Maybe I shouldn't have come over to his house at all. Then Sil's phone rings and she gets distracted and waves bye to us.

"Okay come on girl… Let's go back to your place to look at yearbooks and watch TikTok. You can teach me more of that southern twang." Thomas tugs at me.

The tension on my heart relaxes when I see how happy and excited he is to hang out with me. I don't know why I get so worked up and scared when I'm having a good time. I've got to get it through my head that it's okay to be myself.

"I'll walk Thomas home when we're done," I say to Sil as we are walking out the door.

She's still on the phone but smiles and waves.

We are past the end of the sidewalk, ready to leave through the gate of his condo complex, when Sil comes running up behind us. "Thomas! Jinny! Wait, what's your phone number?" She's out of breath from running.

I look at her funny.

"Just in case of an emergency, you know."

"God Mom, I could have texted it to you!" Thomas says.

"Well maybe I wanted to hear Jinny say it in her cute little accent," Sil retorts.

I give her my number and she enters it into her phone. "Home by seven for dinner," she yells as we walk out of the gate.

"God, sorry about that," Thomas says.

"I think it's nice that she cares." I don't tell him how lucky he is to have a mom who worries about his safety and wants to make sure he's home on time for dinner.

As soon as I unlock my apartment, I can tell Grann Ruth had a hard day. The entire place reeks of her medical grade pot. I grab the Febreze as fast as I can and go from room to room spritzing everything. "Sorry, the neighbor downstairs has cancer and smokes pot all day," I explain, but he doesn't seem to mind.

He goes right to my room, flops on my bed, and turns on some music on his phone. He's busy admiring the seashells and drawings I've done of buildings and other things I have scattered about my room.

I find my yearbook from last year in one of the many stacks of books in my closet and we look at the pictures of everyone who signed up for Mysterious Magical Book Club. We compare the school pictures to their social profiles and laugh.

"Don't look at mine." I slam it closed before he can see, but he takes it from me anyway and finds my picture from last school year.

I shove a pillow over my face.

"Awe, Jinny, you're soooooo cute! Look at you," Thomas croons.

I peek out from behind the pillow and narrow my eyes on him.

"What? Aren't you gonna say how FAT I was?"

Thomas turns his head sideways, like a puppy. "You know I'd never say that."

I let out a deep breath. "Sorry. I mean. I shouldn't be salty about it. I was like that for a reason. Food was basically my babysitter when I was younger. My Mama would load up the place and go out at night," I try, badly, to explain myself, each word sounds worse than the last and I stop.

"You don't have to defend yourself to me girl, I get it," he says.

But does he?

How could he ever get who I am?

Then he finds another picture and puts his hand over it before he shows me.

"Have you ever had a boyfriend?" He changes the subject.

"No, why?" I try to peek at the picture he has covered. But he slaps my hand away. I pretend to be offended and he smirks.

"Have you ever had a boyfriend, Thomas?" I ask, flipping the question back on him.

"No. But, I used to kiss this hot guy named Jared last year. He was on the hockey team," he says and finds a picture on his phone and shows me. It's a selfie of a pretty cute guy. He swipes through a bunch of pictures and stops on one of them kissing. It's awkward and hot at the same time. I can see angst in the guy's eyes. Which are wide open by the way.

"He's kind of hot. What happened?"

"He was sweet at first, as long as we were alone. When I tried to hold hands with him out in public he turned into a total asshole," he admits. "Like a serious closeted jerk-off." He puts his phone down.

"Thomas, do you think Victor is cute?"

"YAASSSS! I knew it. I knew you liked him Jinny! You should text him," he says and flips back to the yearbook. The page he was hiding before was the page with Victor's picture. That perfect smile. Those beautiful brown eyes. My heart pumps faster.

I'm lost in his gaze for a split second and Thomas grabs my phone.

"Do you have his number?" He's scrolling.

"No! You don't know what that would do. He used to go out with Shantel Greenburg and she hates me. I am NOT dealing with all that," I practically scream. I think I scare Thomas. His eyes get big.

But instead, he says, "Dish it. Tell me everything."

So I curl up next to him and tell him all about me. About Jinny Buffett and Jimmy Buffett and Jinny Cheeseburger and my dead drug dealing Daddy from the Everglades and my Mama who is in the Keys with some man and all of her Uncles.

"Wait? Her uncles?"

"Thomas, you're so innocent!" I laugh.

"What? No I'm not!"

"Uncle is code for men who pay for sex."

He gasps.

And the words keep pouring out of my mouth like a pitcher of sweet tea on a covered porch and I can't seem to shut the hell up. The more I talk, the more I realize I don't want to shut up, I want to get everything out.

"Jinny, I love you," he says when I finally close my big-fat-mouth.

"I love you too Thomas. I'm so happy we met." I really am. I didn't know I needed a BFF so badly.

"Can I spend the night tomorrow?" he asks. "Since your mom is gone, I don't want you to be all alone. Plus, my mom doesn't care if I stay at a girls house since I'm gay." He jumps up and stands on my bed and does a dance. Then he looks over at the mirror on my dresser and blows himself a kiss.

"YASSSS!" I shout it like he does and laugh.

"Perfect! Oh, and if my mom asks, I'll just tell her your mom works the Margaritaville night shift. She'll understand." He jumps off the bed with a twirl, and for the first time I notice Pearl, curled up on the edge of the bed, looking mad about being bounced around.

Later I walk Thomas home, the sun starting to drift away, and our shadows dancing around mimicking our happiness. We are so excited for our sleepover tomorrow we can't stop gushing and twirling around! We agree to meet for school at 7:15 before we hug goodbye.

I practically skip all the way home.

When I reach the parking lot of my apartment, I hear tires squeal from around the corner. It's Sabrina in her Grann's van. She almost hits me so I flip her off.

"Learn how to drive asshole," I shout when she gets out.

"Shut up, Cheeseburger," she snaps and slams the door.

She carries a six-pack, a carton of cigarettes, and heads for the porch.

"Wait, Sabrina. Can you take me to the grocery store later? I'll give you five bucks."

I have to get snacks if I'm having a sleepover, and it's too late to walk alone.

"We can go now. If I go back inside, Grann will want me to hand over the keys. Pay up now, so I can use the money when we get there. Ten minutes. That's it Jinny." She's in a foul mood but she takes me anyway after I run up and grab my money.

Sabrina honks the entire way there and screams at everyone we pass. I don't ask her what's wrong. I don't care.

She parks in the handicapped spot in the front and I run inside as fast as I can. Sabrina will literally leave me and drive off if I don't get back to the van before she does and I really don't want to walk home alone this time of night.

Thomas is skinny, so he probably doesn't eat much, I think to myself. But, even so, for a sleepover we have to have snacks. At least that's what sleepovers in books and movies are like– friends laughing and staying up all night talking and eating. I've never actually had a real sleepover with a friend before.

"Why you eatin' that shit Jinny? Tryin' to get fat again?" Sabrina asks when she sees I have a can of Pringles, two Twix Bars, a box of Velveeta mac and cheese, and a 2-liter bottle of Diet Coke.

"No. Shut up."

Part of me wants to throw the food out the window. I have such a love hate with food. I'm so uncomfortable in my own skin.

Sabrina drives like a maniac all the way home and hits the handicapped sign when she parks. I don't say thank you. I paid her dumb-ass to take me, that was thank you enough. I walk up to my apartment and see a note taped to the front door.

Oh shit. What is this?

My heart pounds. If it's an eviction notice, so help me god, I'm going to lose my mind. I've paid all of Mama's bills this month. She has no idea how to pay anything online, so I do it all for her. But rent, that's a paper check or cash. She promised me she walked the check down to the front office two weeks ago. I will literally kill her if she stole the rent money for something stupid, like new clothes, again.

My hands are shaky as I open it.

Jinny,
Just stopped by to say hi after football practice.
Victor

What the actual fuck.

Maybe it's a joke. Maybe Shantel and her cheerleading idiots did this to get me to act stupid and text Victor. Jokes on them! I don't have Victor's number. I contemplate texting Thomas about the note. He'll probably say it's a fake too.

But, what if– what if it is real.

What if Victor actually wrote this note? Sweat forms around my hairline and there's a tingly feeling in my toes. Could the hottest guy at school like me?

But then I remember him laughing at me last year, along with everyone else, when Shantel sang Cheeseburger in Paradise at the top of her lungs.

If this note was from him, he's got to be up to something, so I crumple it up, throw the note in the trash bin, and try to pretend it was never here in the first place. I text Marco and tell him I'm fine then I text Mama too.

No response from either of them.

What a surprise.

I go to bed and think about how much fun I had with Thomas tonight and try NOT to think about Victor.

"Jinny."

This time I know it's Daddy, the smell of oranges is strong. I sit up and Pearl scoots herself right into my spot, snuggling against my pillow. "Pillow thief," I hiss at her before addressing the spirit. "Daddy, why do you keep visiting me?" Might as well just ask him.

"A storm is brewing," he says.

"Like a hurricane?" It is storm season. For a split second I think of Mama in the Keys. Maybe Daddy is warning me that Mama is in trouble. But, I didn't see anything on the news about a hurricane, they usually talk about loading up on bottled water and putting out the storm shutters.

"She is the storm," Daddy's spirit says, then he's gone again, the faint mist in the moonlight, the only thing that remains.

I exhale loudly before falling back onto my pillow. Pearl yowls and I jump.

"Sorry kitty." I grab her and hold her close to my chest, listening to her purr and try to go back to sleep. But, my head is jumbled with thoughts of my Mama and Daddy and hurricanes and the fact that I am all alone.

– Chapter Ten –
Two weeks, more like FOREVER!

I wake up before my alarm. Pearl licks my nose with her scratchy pink tongue and bites at me like I'm a tasty piece of meat.

"Ugh, go to sleep." I swat her away, harder than I mean to. "I was having horrible dreams!" I pull the thin, holey blanket I've had for as long as I can remember, back over my head and try to get ten more minutes of sleep. But, I can't shake the feeling that something is wrong with Mama.

After Daddy's spirit visited me again last night, warning me of a storm, I tossed and turned until I had one of those dreams that was so real it hurt. I dreamed about Mama's favorite movie, Cocktails, with Tom Cruise. A hurricane blew and the palm trees leaned sideways and all the string lights flickered and blinked, and whipped like an electric snake.
That's when I saw her legs dangle over the side of a dumpster outside the bar. A crowd had formed and everyone pointed and laughed while I screamed and cried.

I get up and reach for my phone. I'm going to call her and make sure she's still alive. But, she texted while I was sleeping.

MAMA:
I'm coming home late tonight to
Grab a few things...
I picked up a different job last night,
Lasts two weeks, better pay
Love you! 🖤

No wonder I had such a bad dream. Daddy's ghost must have known this was going to happen. I get out of bed and check the bills in the kitchen, the ones I need to pay in the next two weeks. I log on to Mama's bank account online and see if there is any money to pay them. She's such an ASSHOLE!

What's gonna happen to her job at Margaritaville if she's gone for two more weeks? This better be worth it. I'm not moving again. I kind of like it here. I kind of don't mind Sabrina. I kind of don't mind the rusted metal railing. I kind of don't mind living close to Thomas. Even the skunk smell from Grann Ruth's pot has become, well, predictable. It's better than some of the shit I've seen and smelled in places we lived before moving here. We bounced around a lot after Daddy died. The Hollywood Apartment Complex has been my home for four years.

I don't even know what to say to Mama. How could she do this to me? Two weeks is like an eternity. I want to tell her how selfish she is. How trashy it makes me feel to know she'd rather be out there with some guy she just met, then here with me. But, I don't have it in me to argue with her this morning.

ME:
I need 2 pay the bills
Make sure u don't spend the $
for rent. And I need some
more $ for food

MAMA:
Morning sunshine!
I'll leave some cash for food.
Will you be home tonight
When I pick up my stuff?

ME:
Where else would I be?

MAMA:
It's Friday night!
Don't you have any
friends to go out with?

ME:
Whatevs! Actually, that
new guy friend I told u
bout, he's spending the nite
He's gay so don't
freak out!!!

MAMA:

Don't let him steal my
clothes...

ME:

DUH. k bye

I get ready for school quickly, throw my hair up in a sloppy bun, and put on my sunglasses. I'm so pissed off at Mama. I swear, I don't have time for her drama anymore. How can she live with herself? Acting like she does.

I'm embarrassed for both of us.

"I will NEVER be like YOU!" I scream at a picture of her hanging on the wall.

If I don't do something to change things around here, then I'm destined to be just like her. The thought of it gives me the creepy crawlies. I have to get out of here!

I grab my bag and head for the door. Ms. Fleming says I have to start planning my future and college. Maybe she's right. How else am I going to get away from Mama? Maybe I could become a scientist or an architect or I don't know... Anything but this.

I'm lost in thought when I reach Thomas. He's waiting for me, as planned, outside his condo complex.

"JINNY! Girl your hair is so cute up and messy. Love the sunglasses. Soooo Audrey Hepburn, in Breakfast at Tiffany's," Thomas gushes when I approach. My mood lifts drastically.

"Thank God today is Friday. This has been the longest week of my life... I could not handle another day!" I complain to him.

He pulls out his Airpods and puts one in my ear for me, turning on Demi Lovato.

"This can be our Friday song," he says and sings along for a while. "Oh hey, can we stop back at my place and get my stuff after school?" he asks.

"Totally."

"I thought we could go to the beach tomorrow, to look for shells. Do you think your Mom would be comfortable with that?"

"OMG Yasssss! If I'm with you, I'm sure it will be fine."

We walk to school, talking about the beach, and I forget all about Mama and her shit. I also forget to tell Thomas about the note from Victor until we get to school and I see him on the steps talking to his football crew and throwing the ball up in the air in a perfect spiral. He's wearing his jersey and looks amazing. Tonight is the first home football game. When he spots us, he leaves his boys and comes strutting over.

"Hey, Jinny, sorry I missed you last night. Did you get my note?" He asks with a grin.

I can see Thomas's eyes fall out of his head. I guess it's good to know the note was actually from Victor and not a joke from the cheerleaders.

But then, for some reason, instead of being flattered or excited, I get pissed off.

"What the hell gives you the nerve to show up at my house?" I snap at him.

He blinks twice and looks at Thomas who shrugs.
"Uh, sorry Jinny, I just wanted to ask about the Mysterious Magical Book Club. I want to join, but we have Football every day after school. I thought I could read the books at home, and maybe once the season ends in November, I can start coming to the club."

"Oh really?" I ask.

He laughs and wipes his palms on his pants. "My mom wants me to get involved in other activities in case football doesn't pan out. There's a lot of good QB's in our district..." A drop of sweat rolls down the side of his face.

Oh my god, he's nervous.

Why did I yell at him?

Because Jinny, he used to make fun of you! My brain screams.

Then, my heart decides it's going to answer my brain. PEOPLE CAN CHANGE! You've changed! LOOK AT YOU! Be his friend!

I take a deep breath to calm my stupid arguing insides.

"Sorry, I had some difficult family news last night... Guess I'm not feeling myself... Yes, of course you can be in my club." I force a half-smile. "I'll get you a copy of our first book so you can keep up," I tell him.

He relaxes and smiles with those perfect teeth. I run my tongue over mine. They feel gross, I think I forgot to brush them. How embarrassing.

"Awesome! Thanks Jinny. And sorry for whatever happened to your family." He leans in with both arms and hugs me!

Are you kidding? Victor just hugged me in front of people at school.

"HA! I told you so," Jonelle comes up behind me and pulls me backward by my backpack after Victor turns and runs back to the football players. I stumble, but she catches me. "Tickle, tickle," she whispers in my ear.

"Jonelle, you're nasty, you know that?" I glare at her.

Her and Thomas bust up laughing.

We wait for Ang to arrive before walking inside, four across, all of us laughing and smiling and happy.

"See you at lunch," I wave as we head in different directions.

Thomas walks with me toward the library. "Jinny, girl, you gotta dish. What was all that about with Victor and the note? And difficult family news? What's wrong? Are you okay?" I can tell he's concerned, and maybe annoyed I didn't say anything on our walk to school.

"After I got home last night, there was a note on my door from Victor, saying he stopped by to see me. I thought it was a joke, but apparently not. And Mama is gonna be gone another two weeks! I was going to tell you about it all tonight at our sleepover, but now you know," I explain as fast as I can. I should have texted him before school.

"Geeeeze Jinny!" The bell rings and we hug and run our separate ways.

***

At lunch Jonelle won't stop talking about Victor and I'm paranoid he's going to come over and try to sit with us again and hear her teasing me.

"Can we just talk about this later?" I hiss.

"But it's Friday girl and I won't see you till Monday," she pouts and folds her arms over her chest.

"Well, why don't you and Ang meet me and Thomas at the beach tomorrow," I suggest.

"I dunno, maybe. I'll ask my pops," Jonelle says, but I can tell she's not real sure he will say yes. Maybe she's watching her brothers again.

"The beach will be fun. I'll ask," Ang says. Then she starts telling a story about the last time she went to the beach and Jonelle finally stops talking about Victor.

My shoulders relax and I take a few bites of my food.

"Don't look now Jinny, but lover boy is right behind you," Jonelle says, straight faced. I spin around and knock my tray on the floor.

"Made you look!" Jonelle starts howling with laughter.

"Real funny."

But we all start laughing, because it is kind of funny.

"You should have seen your face!" She teases as we leave the lunch room and head for our next classes.

"Okay guys, I want you to break into pairs. We are starting our fall project on F. Scott Fitzgerald's classic American novel, The Great Gatsby. You're going to start a writing journal as a team and you can use the prompts on the board or create your own. Once you get into the story and have honest discussions with your partner, I'm hoping the words start flowing from a deep place inside of you. I want you to think of Nick, Daisy, and Gatsby as real people and compare them to your own lives and future selves." Ms. Fleming writes things on the board as she talks and I look around the room.

I catch eyes with Jessie Lesters. I usually pair up with her for projects. She's quiet and gets her shit done, we work well together.

"Now, to make this a little interesting, and to get different points of view, I want you to choose a partner of the opposite sex, or orientation, from yourself. This way we can see how we view things with the preconceived notions we approach in our lives based on modern day gender-roles." Ms. Fleming turns to look at the class.

I glare at her. She did this on purpose. Now I have to pick someone other than Jessie. I look around again.

"Jinny, will you be my partner?" Victor asks, loudly, even though he's sitting right next to me. It's like he wants everyone to hear.

"Fine." Why fight it?

"Looks like we have our first team. Jinny and Victor." Ms. Fleming writes our names on the board. Everyone else starts talking and picking partners.

I get up and take a green notebook from the pile Ms. Fleming sets out for the project.

"Have you read Great Gatsby yet?" Victor asks when I sit back down.

"Three times."

"Impressive. I'll work on it this weekend. Do you have any ideas for the journal?" he asks. "If not, we can just use one of the prompts Ms. Fleming put on the board."

I cock my head and look at him. Is he really into this or just putting on a show?

"Yeah, I have an idea. To start, we can talk about Daisy and how she represents femininity and what that says about society and gender and relationships in the past versus present day... or some shit like that. I don't care." I put my head down.

"Jinny, are you okay?" Victor asks.

I lift my head up and look at him. "I'm fine. Sorry."

"Oh okay, well that sounded perfect. Can you say it one more time, so I can write it in our journal?" He's got his pencil ready.

So, I say it again slower and he writes down my words. He's left handed and he pushes his bottom lip out a tiny bit when he concentrates. I never noticed it before. I wonder what else I've never noticed about Victor. He's bouncing his knee just a little, like there's a song playing in his head. And his bicep looks bigger than I remember last year. My chest aches in a way that's new and exciting.

Oh my god.

I'm crushing on Victor.

The bell rings and I leave without saying goodbye.

***

After school I go outside and Thomas is already waiting for me. He's with Jonelle. I don't see Ang. She's probably on the bus heading to the elementary school to get Emily.

"Jonelle said she's going to the beach tomorrow! YAAASSSS!!" Thomas does a dance and Jonelle starts dancing with him.

"So you can go?" I ask her.

"I texted Pops. He said yes. He don't have to work."

She looks happy. I wonder how often she goes out with friends. I realize I don't see her with anyone else at lunch or after school. Are me and Ang and Thomas her only friends too? She used to hang out with some of the kids on my block, but they are pretty sketchy. Probably not a place her Pops lets her hang now. I wonder if he'd ever let her come to my house?

"Wanna meet us at the 7-11 by North Beach at 1 p.m.?" I ask.

"Yeah girl, I'll make Ang's parents pick me up. You fools walking?"

"My mom will probably drive us. She's super nosy," Thomas says.

Then Jonelle sees her ride and runs off waving like a big goofball and Thomas and I wave back just as silly and over exaggerated.

Thomas puts his Airpod in my ear. Our new ritual. We sing and dance while we walk home.

"Thomas, have you thought about joining choir or dance team?" I ask. "You're like better than anyone I ever met." I mean it. He's good. Like he should be on Broadway or American Idol.

"You think?" he asks.

"Don't play me like that. You know you're good," I elbow him then twirl and slow step, trying to imitate one of the moves he makes. He laughs, then does the move himself, proving just how good he is.

"Can I confess something?" he says.

"Of course!"

"My parents got divorced because of me. My dad couldn't handle me being gay, and into dance and singing. He wanted me to play sports and be some man's man. My mom told him she wouldn't stay married to a homophobe and moved us here."

"Thomas, you can't blame yourself. People are dirtbags," I say to comfort him. "Sounds like your dad is a world class prick and I'm sure your mom and him had other problems, but your mom just got a lot cooler in my book."

I hug him and he holds me for a few extra seconds.

I think we both needed a hug. We walk the rest of the way to his place singing. I watch him dance and it makes my heart want to explode. He's amazing and I can't believe he wants to be my friend. Me, some stupid white trash girl, and he's like this future superstar.

When we get to his condo to grab his stuff it seems quiet– probably because his mom isn't on the phone screaming at his dad.

"Be right back. Just go in and make yourself at home. MOM get Jinny a diet coke!" He screams down the hall before running upstairs.

I walk into the kitchen and find Sil painting her nails.

"Howdy Ma'am." I smile.

"Oh Jinny!" She lights up when she sees me. "Thomas is so excited for tonight." She puts her polish down and gets up. "Grab a coke and come tell me about school today." She heads over to the couch. I obey, grabbing a can from the fridge, and follow her to the couch. She pats the spot next to her, so I plunk down.

"School was okay. My favorite part was walking home watching Thomas sing and dance. He's, like, incredible." I take a drink.

She waves her hands up and down to dry the wet, pink polish. I can see she's proud of her son. It's something that I don't know much about. Having a parent look all glowing for something good their kid has done.

Mama never looks like that over me.

"He's a special guy," she gushes.

"Yeah, you should take him to audition for the Miami Fine Arts Academy. A lot of the students there end up in movies or get a record deal." I pull out my phone and open up TikTok. "I follow them. Their videos always go viral." I scroll through and find the one I want her to watch. "Thomas is a helluva lot better than that, and it got three-million hits," I say as she watches. "Thomas is a star," I tell her with such passion.

After learning about his parents divorce, I want to see Thomas do something amazing, just to prove to his bigot father what a creep he is. I have this new, overwhelming feeling blooming inside of me. I need to protect the people I love, because I've had a hard time protecting myself.

"He's going to be goddamn famous," I say.

Her eyes get big.

And she looks at me funny.

"Oops, sorry, Ma'am." I put my head down cause I forgot not to swear in front of a parent. I really need to learn to watch my mouth and use some manners. I'm such trash sometimes. Uhhhgggg...

"Oh please." She laughs. "What's that place called again?" Sil grabs her phone and I tell her Miami Fine Arts Academy. She plugs it in her phone and starts looking. She dials the number and walks into the other room.

"I'm ready!" Thomas sings, then does a full pirouette.

"Show off," I tease. "Can I see your room before we go?" I ask. "There's no reason to rush back to my house."

"Sure!"

We run upstairs. There are still some boxes, but he has shelves up with his books and things. Awe, it's cute. He's got those little Disney Tsum Tsums and a huge sparkly poster of Edward from Twilight on the wall and a pair of pointe shoes for ballet hanging on a hook.

"Really, team Edward?"

"Oh my god, he's the most gorgeous boy alive!" He makes a kiss kiss face at the poster.

"But in that movie, he's not alive. He's a vampire," I correct him. "The books were much better... Actually, The Host by Stephenie Meyer is even better than Twilight and one of my favorite books."

"Can I borrow it?" he asks.

"Of course." I walk over and pick up the pointe shoes.

"Umm... Those are nothing," he blushes.

"Don't do that. Be proud," I say with a fierceness that makes him stiffen.

He flops down on his bed, and pats the spot next to him. I sit next to him and he holds out his hands to me, so I take them.

"Jinny, can I ask you something serious?" He shakes the hair from his eyes.

"Of course, Thomas, you can ask me anything," I reply.

I'm kind of nervous because I don't know where this is going.

"Have you ever imagined doing it with a vampire?" He says it so seriously at first I'm confused, but then I see the spark in his eye.

He laughs and then I start laughing even harder. I play slap at him and then we are practically shouting about what doing it with a vampire would be like versus a werewolf. My sides hurt so hard from laughing, because he's so animated, and making goofy, kissy faces mixed with growls.

"THOMAS! JINNY!" His mom shouts and we both jump.

That's our cue so we rush back down the stairs.

"What mom?" he puts his hand on his hip. "We're kinda busy!"

"Guess what? I just got off the phone with the Miami Fine Arts Academy. They are hosting open auditions on Sunday. I sent them a video of your singing and dancing and they LOVED you! They said it would be tragic if you didn't come to the auditions!" She does a booty shake and squeals and we all laugh.

She puts up her hand to hi-five me. I can't remember the last time an adult tried to hi-five me, but I put my hand up and Sil claps it.

"Woooo! Jinny, thank you so much!" Then she hugs me.

Now it's Thomas's turn to look at me funny. Oh shit, he's mad...

"Jinny, did you have something to do with this?" he asks.

"I just told your mom about the Miami Fine Arts Academy. They are always flexing on TikTok, but you're a million times better... So I just thought..." I explain, but he hugs me before I can say anything else.

"OMG!! Thank you!" He freaks out.

So, he's not mad.

He's happy.

Why do I have such a hard time figuring out people?

"Jinny, do you want to go with us to the audition? I'll take you for ice cream on the way home? Will your mom mind?" Sil asks.

"Yes, I mean, no," I say. Sil looks at me confused. "I mean, yes Sil, I would love to go with you to the audition, but I have homework." I remember I'm supposed to read The Raven Boys this weekend.

Thomas is on his phone texting someone and looks up. "Mom, tomorrow can you drive me and Jinny to the beach to meet up with Ang and Jonelle, the other girls I told you about? At 1 p.m. Please?" he begs.

"I don't know, Thomas. Should you stay home and practice for the audition? This could be huge for you."

She's getting parental.

Damn it.

I really wanted to show him my favorite spot to look for shells.

"We're going to look for seashells. I have the best spot. And we won't even go in the ocean. Could he come just for like an hour?" I plead his case.

Sil thinks about it for a minute. "Okay, just for an hour to look for shells. Now, go have your sleepover and actually SLEEP! Come back tomorrow when you're ready for the beach," she says and hugs Thomas.

We grab his stuff and run out the door, all the way to my house. It feels good to stretch my legs.

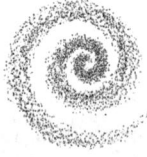

– Chapter Eleven –
It's a g-g-g-ghost!

"Sup turds." Sabrina is on her porch rolling joints for Grann Ruth on a paper plate in her lap. She licks the side of one and seals it tight.

"Really? Out in the open?" I shake my head.

"Shut it, Cheeseburger… Her pain is real bad today. I don't need your mouth." Sabrina gives me a nasty look and sticks her tongue out at me. I stick mine back at her before Thomas and I run upstairs and into my apartment.

"Thomas, I'm so excited about your audition! I can't believe that just happened so fast. Are you nervous?" We throw our bags in my room.

"Yes. No. I don't know! I don't know how good the competition is here. I mean, I've been in dance and singing lessons as long as I can remember, but nothing like this."

I'm so happy for Thomas. But, if I have to admit, I'm a little jealous. I wish my mom cared enough to put me in dance or music.

I've never accomplished anything besides survive.

"I'm sorry I can't go to your audition. I have a lot of homework. Plus, with Mama being gone, I probably shouldn't go to Miami, even for the afternoon."

"It's okay, I understand. I'll call you as soon as it's over and tell you how it goes. BTW, does your mom really leave you like this all the time?" He asks cautiously.

"Yeah, but don't worry about it." I don't really want to talk about it or think about Mama right now. I turn on some music, hoping to lighten the mood again.

"Great song!" He starts dancing.

"Show me how to do that."

"Okay, follow me, and stand like this," he says, putting his hips out and arms up. "Then move like this to the beat, see, one, two, three." He makes it look easy. I stand like him and try.

"YES!" he screams. "One, two, three, repeat, yaaaasssss Jinny, shake those hips, one two three!"

I can't help but laugh. Even Pearl joins in.

Finally, Thomas collapses on the couch and I get us each a tall glass of Diet Coke. I put ice in first and then a lemon wedge. Total Mama move, but I don't care, it tastes better this way.

"You wanna sit on the porch?" Our skin is damp from dancing, but gets extra sweaty from the humidity outside as we collapse on the steps. The cicadas buzz and cars whizz by on the busy road in front of the apartments.

"I can't walk home with you on Wednesdays," I tell Thomas before taking a drink of my Diet Coke. My glass is sweating. God it's hot.

"Why girl, what's up?" he asks.

"Ms. Fleming wants me to start meeting with her. She says I scored higher than all the other students in the entire state of Florida on the stupid FSA's."

"What's an FSA?"

"They're these standardized tests we take every spring. She said it's time I take my life seriously. You know, like college planning. Ms. Fleming thinks she can save me from all this white trash glory."

As if on cue, the Hernandez boys start throwing rocks at the dumpster.

"Jinny, wait, what?! So like, you aren't just in all the accelerated classes, you're like the smartest student in all of Florida? Holy shit! Wait till I tell Mom."

"Yeah, well, I ain't goin' to college." I say in my most slangy kind of way. Just to show off and prove I don't care, I spit across the railing. "Yep, no college for me." I say again.

Thomas sets his glass on the landing and runs down the steps to the sidewalk. He does a high kick, that shouldn't be humanly possible. "Jinny, why are you talking and acting like you're a trashy nobody? Because from where I stand, I'm looking up at someone amazing! What would happen if you let Ms. Fleming help you?"

I frown.

"But, you don't know what my Mama is like…"

"You've spent your entire life with that smart-ass brain in your head, just waiting for a moment to use it. Figure it out! To hell with your Mama!" He does another high kick.

I guess he has a point.

My heart hurts for a moment as I imagine my future if I don't kick my life into gear.

I shiver.

"You wanna get your butt up here and eat candy and watch a movie?" I put my hand on my hip and change the subject. It's getting way too serious.

"Yaaasssss!" Thomas comes running back up the stairs.

We laugh and talk long into the night.

I show him the picture of my Daddy on the porch out in the swamps with all his sisters.

"I think I've been seeing Daddy's ghost in my room at night," I admit.

"Girl, you're just getting second hand high from Sabrina's Grann Ruth," Thomas says and laughs.

"Right? I mean, you smell it too, don't you?"

"Yeah, it's strong!" Then he pulls out his phone and opens a video. "I have an idea, let's watch one of those ghost hunting shows."

By the end, we laugh so hard.

"Y'all, look it's a g-g-g-ghost," he says, making fun of the video and acting twangy as any southerner. My sides hurt and tears shoot out my eyeballs.

"Can I ask you something?" Thomas gets all serious. "Do you really believe in all that mysterious magical stuff out there in the swamps?"

"You know, I guess I do," I whisper.

"Then I do too," he replies and yawns.

Within minutes I hear him breathing heavily. I smile. Then, without warning, a current of warm swampy air whooshes over my bed. The crickets and bullfrogs from the Everglades sing us a sweet lullaby. I get up and turn off my bedroom light, careful not to disturb Thomas. And when I lay back down, the moon is centered outside my bedroom window, casting a warm buttery glow over us. Pearl appears, from wherever she's been hiding, curls up on my chest, and starts to purr. I fall into a perfect dream world snuggled up in bed next to my new best friend.

It's the safest I've ever felt.

When I wake and check my phone, it's 11 a.m. Thomas and Pearl are still sleeping.

Mama sent a text, but I'm too scared to read it. I tiptoe across the hall to Mama's room. She's been here, her stuff has moved around, and there's a pile of dirty clothes in the hamper. She took her flat iron too. Damn it!

I sit on her bed. It smells dusty. Shows how much she's home... Finally, I check my phone to see what she had to say.

MAMA:
Came home at 4am, didn't want
to wake you and the boy up
Left money for food
Be good, text me every day
I love you Jinny! 🐶

She's the biggest asshole in the world. I hate her. I want to move away and never come back. Then she'd have to come home and pay her own damn bills. I go out to see how much money she left me. There's a couple of twenty dollar bills sitting on the kitchen table. That's it? How am I supposed to eat for two weeks on forty bucks?

I want to scream as loud as I can, but I don't want to scare Thomas or Pearl. I can feel the blood pulse in my veins. My chest rises rapidly, up, down, up, down, my heart might explode.

"Are you okay?" Thomas comes out. His dark hair is ruffled, so cute it makes me smile even though I'm still so angry at Mama.

"I'm fine." I shake it off.

Thomas already knows too much about my broken life. I can't let him see me have a complete meltdown, at least not during our first sleepover.

"You ready to hunt seashells at the beach? I checked the tides and it looks like we will have perfect weather." I'm not embarrassed about my seashells around Thomas. He's seen my room.

"I can't wait!" He opens the fridge. "Um, Jinny, you don't have anything to eat... Do you want to walk back to my house?"

I didn't think about having anything here for breakfast.

How embarrassing.

"Don't worry, my mom will fix us lunch before driving us to the beach. Oh, hey, did your mom come home?" He looks around.

I can still smell her stale cigarette smoke and perfume lingering, just enough to rub it in my face she was here. I don't know why, but part of me thought she'd stay. That she would come home and miss me and not leave again.

"Yeah, she came and left again while we were still sleeping," I say while hiding the pain in my voice. "I'll put on my swimsuit and grab my bag."

I run to my room and get my stuff.

"I will use my mom's room, so you can use the bathroom," I holler out at Thomas who's still standing in the kitchen.

I close Mama's door and press my back against it. I slide to the ground and put my hands over my face to muffle the sobs. She's really gone for two weeks and only left me forty dollars. There's nothing here to eat. I'll have to do laundry by myself down at the shitty coin-op, none of the bills are gonna get paid if she doesn't put money into the account. The list of crap keeps piling up in my mind.

Even when she's home, she's not here a lot, but at least I know she's close.

What now? I wipe my face.

"Daddy, what should I do?" I ask.

I wait a minute to see if his ghost might answer. Then I remember the one person I can talk to–Marco. But what do I say? The first thing that pops into my mind.

ME:
Did Mama get fired?

MARCO:
What? Why kiddo?
Whats goin on?

ME:
Nevermind

MARCO:
What happened?
Everything okay Jinny?

No. It's not okay.

"Jinny?" There's a soft knock on the door. I jump and throw on my swimsuit and a pair of shorts as fast as I can before I open the door.

"You ready?" I walk out.

He looks at me and frowns. My bottom lip quivers for a second, so I throw on my sunglasses before shoving a ratty towel and my phone keys into my beach bag.

***

Sil makes amazing food.

I didn't realize how hungry I was for a real meal. All I've eaten in days is that Twix bar and a lot of Diet Coke. She makes the best grilled cheese and tomato soup I've ever had, and I eat every last bite. I'd literally lick my bowl and plate clean right now, but I don't want them to think I'm completely classless.

"Park right there Mom!" Thomas hisses and points when we pull into the 7-11 parking lot across the street from the beach. Jonelle and Ang are waiting for us and run up to the minivan.

Thomas makes introductions and Sil seems thrilled to meet all of his new friends.

"Jinny, are you sure you can't go with us tomorrow?" Sil asks as I'm about to get out.

"I wish I could, but I have an entire book to read before Monday, for my book club."

"Okay, well if you're sure," Sil says with longing in her voice.

"MOM, stop pushing it. Come on, Jinny." Thomas opens the door.

"Wait, I need a picture!" Sil jumps out and makes us all pose together. Jonelle throws her arm around me and Thomas while Ang stands in front and we all laugh. Thomas seems annoyed when she can't get her phone to stop using the flash in the daylight, but it's only because he doesn't know how lucky he is to have a parent who loves him and wants to take a million pictures of him.

I bet Mama doesn't have a single picture of me on her phone.

"Jonelle, Ang, guess what?" Thomas does a run and the highest jump leap I've ever seen. Jonelle pretends to be knocked over by it and Ang claps.

"Boy, that was sick! How'd you learn to jump like that?" Jonelle asks.

"That's what I'm trying to tell you! I have an audition tomorrow at the Miami Fine Arts Academy. Jinny helped me get it," he tells them in his sing-song voice.

"Wow, Thomas, that's amazing," Ang says as we walk across the street to the beach.

Everyone is busy talking and pays me no attention, so I run across at the light while they walk slowly behind me. I head for my usual spot and take off my shoes to feel the soft, silky sand between my toes. The smell of the salty ocean breeze washes over me and helps soothe my hurting soul.

I walk to the wet sand and dig my toes deep down feeling around for shells, like I always do. A flock of seagulls fly near me, hovering low in the breeze, and land just down from where I look for shells. One of the grayish ones cocks its head to the side at me; something about it makes me think of Pearl, the way she looks into my heart with her little eyes, calming me…

I spend my time quietly searching for shells while everyone else is running up and down the beach, being as loud as they possibly can.

- Chapter Twelve -
Where the heck am I?

I wave bye to Thomas when Sil drops me off and rush to my apartment. For a split second, I think maybe Mama will have changed her mind. Maybe she will be home, waiting for me, ready to make me an early dinner and hang out and–

"Mama!" I call out.

But the apartment is painfully empty. Except for Pearl who stares at me from the couch. The quiet is oppressive, even the faint sound of Grann Ruth's afternoon crime show doesn't give me any relief.

My bottom lip shakes and my breathing quickens in fear. She really is gone for two weeks. I'm all alone. My shoulders go limp, and my beach bag slides to the floor in a heap. I walk zombified to my room and crawl into bed.

"You're going to be fine, Jinny," I say.

The tears start.

"Stop it! Stop crying, you big baby." I pull the covers tighter around me. As if they can block out the pain and stop my anxiety.

But a ratty blanket can't stop anything and hot tears weep from my eyes.

I gasp and choke and sob.

"Mama, I fucking hate you!" I scream into my pillow. "I fucking hate you so much." Over and over, I curse Mama until I fall asleep.

"Jinny Buffett, hey girl, come out here," someone yells for me, but I can't place the voice.

I sit up and rub my eyes, half-expecting to see Daddy's ghost again. But he's not there. I crawl out of bed to check things out and my legs tangle in extra fabric. I'm wearing a long, white dress with a necklace full of gator teeth. My hair feels different, so I reach back to find it pulled into a ponytail.

Am I dreaming? It doesn't feel like a dream.

"What the hell is this?"

I'm so confused. As I walk out of my room a swampy mist floats all around me. The sounds of cicadas fill the hot night, chirping fiercely, much louder than I'm used to. I look around, a scream brews in my chest. This can't be real. Whoever is playing this prank can get the fuck out of my apartment.

That's when I realize I'm not in my apartment.

I'm on the porch of Daddy's cabin in the Everglades. The one from the picture. To my right are the same white rocking chairs and side table with a mason jar of moonshine. To my left is a stack of fruit crates filled with old car parts.

"Hello? Is anyone here?"

I know I should be freaking out. I just woke up and I'm inside of a picture. But it's Grann's place and my Daddy's ghost is probably floating around somewhere, so I'm not scared.

"Come here, girl," the voice calls to me again.

I look around, but I can't find the source of the voice. Off in the distance, deeper in the swamp, I see an old lantern. "Daddy? Is that you?" I call out into the night.

I take a step off the porch; the water and muck make sloppy sounds as I trudge through it toward the light. I sink into it with every step I take and I'm not sure I can make it to the light.

"They need you to succeed, build them a bridge, save them, and save yourself."

"Who's there? Who said that?" I spin around, sloshing mud and water.

"Build them a bridge, Jinny," the voice is directly beneath me now.

I look down and there's a giant alligator floating in the swamp water right between my legs. Its eyes are bright yellow, staring at me. Then, it raises one eyebrow at me, then the other one. Wait, do swamp gators have eyebrows?

"Did you just tell me to build a bridge?" I ask the alligator. "And are you waggling your eyes at me?" I try not to laugh.

"George, stop scaring the child. Can't you see she's not ready?" A woman's voice comes up behind me. I spin around, careful not to step on the gator, and see the woman from the picture.

My Grann Lola.

My aunties are behind her, lingering by the house. I don't even know all their names. I know there's Nina, Bonnie, and Esther, but that's all I can remember.

"Hiya, Jinny! Come warm up by the fire," one of my Aunties shouts and waves.

They start building a bonfire. The flames are blue and green and rise up, crackling high in the night air, the smell of smoke filling my nostrils.

"She's ready, Lola. She needs to succeed. She needs to build you a bridge," George says to my Grann.

"George, you really should mind your own business," Grann scolds the gator. I open my mouth to say something, but the words are frozen on my lips.

"Ask him, he knows." George snaps his huge jaw, light reflecting off his gleaming rows of teeth.

I blink and manage to squeak out a sound, a cross between a what and a who.

"Ask Marco!" The gator slides back into the swamp water and disappears into the lily pads. Grann is already walking in the other direction through the reeds and saw grass foliage.

"Wait! Grann!" I scream after her. I'm not ready for her to leave. I have so many questions. I try to chase after her, but I'm stuck in the mud.

"Wake up Jinny."

I sit up in bed, covered in sweat, snot dried to my face, and my swimsuit stuck to my body. My heart pumps from the dream. I reach up to my neck to see if the necklace full of teeth is still there. I swear I can almost feel the weight of those teeth, but all I touch is my own sticky flesh.

I've never had a lucid dream. I've read about them in books, where you're asleep, but awake at the same time. That's what this felt like, because I swear, I was in that swamp with my Grann Lola and her pet gator George. I can still smell the smoke from the bonfire my aunties started. I can still hear the creaking of the rocking chairs on the porch.

Now I'm alone again.

Mama's gone.

My dream family is gone.

What a shitty day!

I quickly change out of my swimsuit into some old baggy sweats and a t-shirt. I wore these when I was Jinny Cheeseburger, now they barely stay on my hips. I wash my sweaty, snotty face and sit on the couch with my phone. My hands shake as I type out the text.

ME:
Does my Daddy's family know
much about me?

MARCO:
Yah girl, I send them pics.
Don't you ever talk to ur Grann Lola?
She prays for you.

ME:
Oh. K.
Does Grann Lola have a
bridge by her house?

MARCO:
Yeah, but it got washed out last
summer. R U okay Jinny?

ME:
Fine. It's nothing.

He doesn't say anything else. So, part of my dream was true! Grann Lola had a bridge by her house, but it washed out. The alligator told me I need to build a bridge. Chills crawl up my spine. I wish I could call my Grann and talk to her. I want to know for myself if she's really a superstitious old bat making moonshine in the swamps or if she actually has magic. I mean, she did send the dream to me, right? I think maybe that's what Daddy's doing– using magic to cross over from wherever he is, to send me messages.

Does that make me some kind of clairvoyant?

My eyes dart over to a worn copy of Stephen King's The Shining, and I get up to hide it under my bed.

I guess I could ask Marco for Grann's number, but, if Mama ever found out I was calling or texting her she'd lose her mind– I shake my head.

I know, I'll write her a letter! But I don't know where I'd send it, so I draft a pretend letter in my head and say it out loud to Pearl who's busy pouncing on my feet.

Dear Grann Lola,

I never met you before because my Mama says you are all a bunch of superstitious hillbillies living out in the swamp. I think she's just scared of you and my Aunties, cause you think she got my Daddy mixed up with drugs and killed for dealing.

They say I'm the smartest student in Florida because of my test scores. But it doesn't matter, cause Mama don't care. This time she's left me here alone for two weeks. You wanna know the truth, Grann? I feel like a broken doll someone threw in the trash.

I just had a dream about you and my aunties. I saw you and Nina and Bonnie and Esther deep in the Everglades. There was a talking Alligator named George that said I have to build you a bridge. But how am I supposed to do that?

I think maybe you used some of your swamp magic to send me the dream, but doesn't that just make me crazy?

K. Bye. Blah, blah, blah....
Love,
  Jinny

After my fake letter to Grann, I get up and drink a huge glass of water to help wash away the fog from my brain.

My body aches. I wish I didn't feel so sorry for myself right now. But I've never been very good at dealing with how I feel. It consumes me...

I decide to read the book Ms. Fleming gave me. The Raven Boys. I like it right away because the main character's name is Blue and she has magical powers and lives with a weird family and she goes to a graveyard and sees ghosts. Like I'm hearing Daddy's ghost and dreaming about Grann Lola and speaking to alligators.

I stay up all night reading. Clasping on to the book makes me long for a home I've never known. The sound of loud bass coming from a car driving around the apartment complex reminds me where I truly am. You always know when it's Saturday night around here because the bass rattles the windows and you can feel it in your lungs. I should put the book down and try to sleep, but there is literally nothing more I love than getting lost in a book, especially this book. It takes me away from who I really am and gives me a glimpse of who I should be.

Maybe I'll read it twice tonight.

– Chapter Thirteen –
Take a picture!

I wish Thomas good luck as soon as I wake up. I know he's gonna get into the Miami Fine Arts Academy. He doesn't need my luck, he's got real talent. But, that's what you're supposed to do right? Tell your new BFF good luck and break a leg and four-leaf clovers and goofy eyed emojis and hearts and stars. I do feel those things for him, because for the first time in my life I feel happy for someone and I want to do something equally amazing. I want someone to send me hearts and stars and tell me I'm gonna rock it.

Then I text Ms. Fleming.

ME:
Can you order the books?

MS. FLEMING:
Did you love it?

ME:
Yes, I stayed up all night and read it twice. It's shit Noah is dead!! But, I suspected it...

MS. FLEMING:
Don't ruin it for the others in Mysterious Magical Book Club. I'll order them right now.

ME:

Obviously! Anything else I should do?

MS. FLEMING:

How about constructing
discussion questions for
your first meeting.
Or an activity...

ME:

Oh. K.
Bye
TY!!!

But, what kind of activities would Jonelle like to do? Or Ang? Or Victor? I don't know! I barely understand people my age at all.

Knock...

Knock, knock...

Who the hell is this? I'm in pajamas. I look through the peephole.

It's a police officer.

Are you kidding me?

"Can I help you?" I yell through the door.

"Yes, we have a report of a minor here with no parents," he says.

I take a deep breath. Of course this is happening. I open the door.

"Hello, are you Jinny Buffett?" He asks and smiles. He doesn't comment on my name, but I know what he's thinking. The lyrics to Margaritaville are probably playing in his head right now.

"That's me." I take a deep breath. I've already prepared the speech in my head for this exact moment. "My mom is at work and I'm in tenth grade so I'm old enough to be home alone," my voice is dry with zero emotion. I leave the door open and go sit on the couch. Pearl arches her back and hisses.

"My name is Officer Riddley." He comes inside and sniffs the air.

"The lady downstairs has cancer," I tell him. He narrows his eyes on me but he knows I'm telling the truth.

"Where does your mom work?" His eyes scan our small apartment. It's clean, probably not what he was expecting.

"She's a waitress at Jimmy Buffett's Margaritaville Resort," I tell him.

"And your name is Jinny Buffett?" He tries not to smile.

"What can I say— my mom is a super fan.".

"So, Jinny Buffett, when was the last time you saw your mom?" Officer Riddley asks.

"Um, yesterday… She works nights, so by the time I got home from the beach she had already left for work, and it's Sunday. She always picks up extra shifts on the weekend. It's busy at her work, vacation season. I just got up… Do you want me to call her?" I hold up my phone. I hope he buys the lie. She really was here yesterday at 4 a.m.

"Hmmm…" he makes a sound. "No, you don't need to bother her at work."

"You wanna look around, make sure I'm safe?"

"Since you are offering," he says and I show him my room, then Mama's, and the bathroom too. He can see I have nothing to hide.

"Jinny, you seem like a smart girl. I hope you know the police are here to help you. If you are ever in a situation you can call this number and ask for me or my partner Officer Garcia." He hands me a card with a number on it. "She's real nice. Has kids about your age. Either one of us would gladly help you out."

Then I do something crazy, I don't know why, but I blurt out, "I'm going to become an engineer and build bridges when I grow up."

Oh, my god. Why did I just say that? But, for some reason, I feel better blurting it out.

"That's real nice, Jinny. Perfect place around here. Lotta waterways in Florida. Lotta messy hurricanes. I served in the Army before joining the force. You ever heard of the Army Corp of Engineers? They help build and maintain the infrastructure during times of emergencies. The Army will even pay for you to go to college," he says. His hard police exterior has softened completely. I sit back down on the couch.

"Thank you," I say and pick up Pearl.

"Jinny, lock the door when I leave and tell your Mom I stopped by to check on you."

He hands me a card before shutting the front door snugly. I put Pearl down and pick up a pillow from the couch and scream bloody murder into it. I do not want social services here today. If Officer Riddley decides to do a follow up and goes to Margaritaville to speak with Mama, he'll figure out she hasn't been there in a week.

I'm anxious and I hate to do it, but I pick up my phone and text Mama.

ME:
Cops were here, someone

told em u left me here ALONE.
I said u picked up 2xwork all
wknd... he believed me....

Nothing.

She says nothing!

I check my phone a thousand times as I pace around the apartment. Nada. Zip. Zilch. I wait for an hour before I curse her.

"Mama, you are such a bitch!" I scream at my phone's blank screen and storm into my room. I cry, big sloppy tears just like yesterday after the beach.

I can't catch my breath and the room feels like it's spinning.

Is it so wrong that I just want to be like everybody else, with parents or grandparents or SOMEONE who cares about them! Is that so much to ask for?

Abandoned minor... Officer Riddley's voice echoes in my head.

"JINNY!" Sabrina is banging on the door. I go and answer it. I don't care that I have snot on my face from crying.

"What do you want?" I snap at her.

"Why were the cops here? Grann's paranoid and makin' me come ask."

"Some turd snitched and told 'em I'm alone. Mama was here yesterday to pick up stuff. She's just in the Keys for work for a couple days. She'll be home soon," I lie to Sabrina.

Well, I half-truth it again. Word will spread fast in our complex of the police sniffing around and I don't want anyone else getting the wrong idea about me being here alone.

"Fuck that! Who you told 'bout your Mama?" She asks and looks from side to side. "What are you lookin' at Terrence?" She shouts across the breezeway. Then she flips him off.

"I didn't tell anyone Sabrina! Like I want to deal with the cops!" I yell at her. "Now get the fuck off my porch. I need to shower and do my homework." I slam the door. I know it was rude. But Sabrina doesn't care. She just wants to peek around and see how my apartment looks and decide if the cops are coming back with social services.

I open the door again quick.

She's already stomped to the bottom of the steps and turned to go under the overhang of our balcony and back into her apartment.

"Sabrina wait! If I give you five bucks will you take me to Walmart after I shower?" I say over the railing.

"For ten you little twat. Don't be so snatchy all the time Jinny. You know I like you." She slams her door rattling the railing. Terrance is still staring from across the way.

"Take a picture Terrance! Jesus Christ you perv!" I yell at him.

I'm ready to pull my hair out.

– Chapter Fourteen –
So YOU'RE the snitch!

Thank god the trip to Walmart with Sabrina is uneventful. We don't speak at all. When I get back, I close the apartment door and lock it. I stomp into the kitchen with my few things. Salad mix. Cheerios. Milk. Toothpaste. I check my phone for the thousandth time. No word from Mama. I'm so angry at her that I don't want to talk to her until she comes home.

I haven't heard from Thomas, but I have no doubt his audition in Miami is going perfectly. There's no way it couldn't. He's amazing.

Like magic, as soon as I think about him, my phone buzzes.

"OMG, OMG, OMG!" he screams as soon as I pick up the phone and say hello.

"Did you get accepted?" I ask, but I already know what he's gonna say.

He's crying and gasping for air, I think I hear a yes in there some-where, and get completely wrapped up in his success and I forget my own woes. I'm crying with him. Tears of joy.

"Boy, I knew it. I knew you were something special. Too special for Hollywood, Florida, that's for sure. You're gonna make it big."

He tells me all about the audition and how they made him wait until the very end for the results and his mom almost passed out. Then she took him for a lobster dinner at a fancy restaurant in Miami, right on the ocean with a million dollar view.

I don't want to ruin his special moment, so I don't tell him the cops were here. Or anything else. He's too good for me anyway.

Too good for dumb ol' fat Jinny Cheeseburger.

He'll make all kinds of new fabulous friends at the Miami Fine Arts Academy. Sil will probably move them to downtown Miami to be close to the school. Why did I think I could have friends? After a week, I'm already losing the best friend I ever had.

"Jinny, I can't tell you how happy I am! Oh, mom needs me to come talk to my grandma on her phone. My family back in Seattle are all freaking out! Love you girl. See you for our walk to school tomorrow," he says and hangs up.

I sit on the couch and pull my knees up to my chest.

I feel more alone right now than I've ever felt in my life. Something has to give. I look on the side table and see the phone number for Officer Riddley. If I called him, what would he do? Call social services and put me in foster care. I know what happens to girls my age in the system.

They get pimped out for cash. Or they have to watch ten other little foster kids end up with serious abuse issues or drug addiction.

I can't call him.

Then I think about what he said about the Army Corps of Engineers. I can't believe I told him I was going to become an engineer and build bridges when I grow up! Like I'm some toddler at a preschool graduation, standing there proclaiming my grown-up aspirations.

But, that stupid swamp alligator George said Gran Lola needed me to build a bridge. I close my eyes to try and remember the other details from the dream, my aunties, the sounds, and smells of the swamp. It all felt so real. And where was Daddy? I reach out with my mind to see if I can find his spirit to give me any guidance.

But he's not there.

My screen flashes with a text. MAMA!

But it's only Ms. Fleming...

MS. FLEMING:
Jinny, can you stop by
my classroom after school
tomorrow? I got the books ordered.
Did you work on the notes for
Mysterious Magical Book Club?

ME:
Yep.

MS. FLEMING:
Perfect! I'm proud of you
Jinny

ME:
I'm nothing to waste
your pride on...

My phone rings. It's Ms. Fleming. I answer it.

"Jinny, are you okay? Why would you say that?" she asks.

"I don't know, because maybe it's true," I whimper.

"That's far from the truth... I hope you know I'm here for you," she says with genuine concern.

Maybe she's the one who called the cops. But how would she know that Mama's gone?

"I'm going to bed. See you at school tomorrow Ms. Fleming." I hang up without waiting for her to say goodnight.

I'm over today.

I get up early, it was an uneventful night for me. No dreams. No visits from my Daddy. No texts either. It really isn't like Mama not to answer me at all, especially after I mentioned the cops being here.

I wash my hair and decide to put some salt spray in it, since Mama took her flat iron. Better to make it look beachy from the humidity.

I call Mama's phone and it goes right to voicemail.

I text and it says undeliverable.

ME:
Marco, Mama's phone goin
to VM!!! She took that other job
in the Keys. Do u know how
to reach her?

MARCO:
I'll ask around.... U OK?

ME:
Not really. Cops came by.
Snitches ratted me 4 bein an
"Abandoned Minor" But I told em
she's @wrk.

MARCO:
Shit... Um. Jinny. This aint
good girl. U wanna come

stay at my place?

ME:
Nah. I got school.
Gotta go. Just find Mama!!

I don't like it at Marco's house. He's a slob and he smokes pot and he has like fifteen cousins that live with him. I'd probably wake up with one of them in bed with me. I know he'd never hurt me. Marco loves me, cause he loved my Daddy. They were like brothers. I could ask him to drive me anywhere or to pick me up any day and he'd always do it. But, staying with him is not an option, ever.

FUCK! What is going on with Mama?

I put on a pair of hot pink jean shorts that I would normally NEVER wear to school. Mama got them on sale at some trashy boutique on first street she likes to hang out at. I put on a sparkly silver tank top and a ton of heavy black waterproof mascara. I don't know why except that I want to be someone else today.

I immediately regret my choice of clothing and make-up the moment I walked out of the apartment, but it's too late now. Thomas's jaw drops when he sees me.

"You look all glitz and glam," he says.

"I feel stupid. I don't know what I was thinking," I admit.

"Own it babes. You look fierce and brave!" He hands me one of his Airpods.

"I'm so happy for you. I want to hear all about the audition," I say to him, hoping not to talk anymore about myself or poor choice of clothing.

He glows like fireworks on the Fourth of July. "Thanks, Jinny!" he says. "You want to see my routine?"

I look around, there isn't anywhere for him to perform. "Where? Here?" I ask.

"No goof! How about in the gym after school?" he asks.

"Yeah, I gotta meet with Ms. Fleming for a while, but I can come after," I explain. "Oh, the idiot cheers use the gym after school… So, be prepared for Shantel and Britney and the gang of evil Barbies."

"I can dance circles around them Jinny! I'm not worried in the slightest." He blows me a kiss and prances up the stairs into the building.

Looks like I don't need to walk with him to class anymore, he has more swag and confidence than ever. Matt and Victor and the footballers aren't around. That's probably a good thing.

Jonelle finds me and says in a hushed somber voice, "I heard the cops were at your place yesterday. You straight?" I know she's had a few run-ins with the cops. Being a big black girl. Living in our part of town, it's a sad reality.

"Word travels fast," I say with a shrug.

Jonelle waits for me to tell her what's up, but in all honesty, I don't think I can. Jonelle's mama took off last year. This will hit too close to home and now is not the time. Ang appears and saves me from getting into all of my Mama drama.

"I gotta go," I say and rush into the building.

"I like your look today Jinny!" Ang shouts after me.

I look over my shoulder to wave and see her and Jonelle whispering. Figures.

I go straight to the library and try to block out the noise in my head and heart. I get so wrapped up in calculus I don't realize, that in an hour, I have done all the work for the entire week of class. I email the teacher and ask if she has any more work I can do. I'm not even thinking, I just hit send. Most kids wouldn't fess up if they did all the work, they'd just take a break the rest of the week. But I need the schoolwork to keep my mind busy. I'll go insane without it.

I see Victor between all my classes, and he keeps giving me a look like he wants to talk. I have nothing to say to him right now, or ever! He might be cute and smart in English class, but I'm not interested in having a boyfriend. Especially one like Victor, who is from a good family and has people who care about him. If Victor really knew about my life and my family he'd run away screaming or tell the cheerleaders and they'd torment me.

At least that's what I keep telling myself. Trying to rid my body of that ache and longing that happens every time Victor is close to me.

God, what is happening to me?

At lunch I eat my salad in silence and listen to Ang complain about her classes and an upcoming science project. Jonelle laughs about a substitute teacher she was harassing. They don't mind me being quiet, but then Ang looks at me, really looks.

"Jinny, what's the matter? You were quiet Saturday at the beach, and you don't seem like yourself now."

Jonelle elbows her.

"What! I just want Jinny to know we are here for her. Anyway, are you excited about the Mysterious Magical Book Club tomorrow? What book are we going to read?" She changes the subject.

I already know Jonelle told her the cops came by my house, but neither of them knows the real reason. It's pretty clear they can see right through my heavy black mascara and into my broken soul.

"I'm fine, Ang."

Lies.

"And yes, I picked a book I think everyone will like. It has magic, plot twists, and murder." I try to smile so they don't ask any more questions.

"Ooooh girl. Sounds like my kind of book," Jonelle says.

She leans in and rubs her shoulder on mine. Of any of my friends, she'd understand the most. But at least she still has a dad to take care of her. If Mama doesn't come home I'll have no one. I'll get shipped to some shitty foster home on the other side of town and won't be able to have a Mysterious Magical Book Club anyway.

The bell rings and we head to our next classes.

"Oh! Thomas is gonna show off his routine from his audition in the gym after school if you can stay," I remember to tell them.

"I'll try." Jonelle nods.

"Me too!" Ang smiles and trots off to her next class.

When I get to Ms. Fleming's room she looks at me funny. I guess my current fashion is out of sync with who she wants me to be. Damn, I hate that look on her face.

"Hey Jinny, you look, different," Victor says.

"Yeah, well, maybe I wanted to be someone different today," I say with as much attitude as I can muster.

My guard is up.

I slide into my seat and pull out my stuff. I already completed the work for our group project. I see Victor hasn't started yet. But that's typical. When I work on group projects, I'm always the first one done, and then I usually end up doing the other person's work for them.

I hand the notebook to Victor, and he looks at all the pages I've written in.

"Wow! You're already done? Jinny, you are so smart," he says.

"The first part's not due for a few weeks. Don't worry. I'll add more to it as we keep working."

He doesn't seem upset, he's well, he's impressed— I think.

I take a copy of The Metamorphosis from the class library and start reading while he works on his part of our journal project.

"Jinny, can you come here for a minute?" Ms. Fleming asks.

I get up and go to her desk. She writes down on a piece of paper so I can read it and points—

Are you being a good partner to Victor by doing all the work ahead of time? I wanted you to work TOGETHER...

I guess she's right. But how was I supposed to know? Maybe she should have let me pick my own partner! I glance at him; he's doing that thing where he's concentrating and pushing out his lip. God, why does he have to be so cute? Okay, so maybe I would like to work with Victor.

I'm just in a bad mood.

I go back to my desk and sigh. "Hey Victor, I'm sorry I did everything ahead of time. We could pick different journal questions and I can work with you if you want."

"Thanks Jinny, but it's alright. I actually like reading everything you wrote and learning how you think. Maybe for the next section we can work together," he suggests. Then he goes right back to his work.

"Yeah, I'd like that," I whisper.

***

After school I find Thomas. "You still want to show me your routine?" He's all smiles.

"Yaaassss!!" He jumps and twirls.

"Okay, I've got to go see Ms. Fleming then I'll meet you in the gym." He does a pirouette then leaps and bounds down the hall toward the gym.

"Hey, Ms. Fleming, am I in trouble?" I ask when I go in.

"Not at all, Jinny. First, I want to show you the books for the Mysterious Magical Book Club arrived and I'm putting them right here. Also, here is a key to my classroom. Please lock up when you are done and don't lose this," she says and hands me a key card with a fuzzy hippo keychain.

I hold it in my hand and play with it, not making eye contact with her.

"Is that all?" I ask. "Thomas is waiting for me in the gym. He's going to show me his routine, the one that got him into Miami Fine Arts Academy for dancing and singing."

"Wow, that's very impressive. Especially just moving here from Seattle. I'm happy to see you've already made some friends this year," she says.

"Yup." I flip the hippo over and over in my hands. I turn to leave, but before I take a step, Ms. Fleming opens her mouth.

"Jinny, wait. I need to talk with you about Officer Riddley," she says.

And BOOM! Just like that, the wind is knocked out of my lungs. How does Ms. Fleming know about Officer Riddley? Did she find out Mama is gone and snitch on me? I will never speak to her again. I hate her.

"Oh, so you're the snitch?" I spit the words. Tears well up in my eyes.

"No, Jinny. I'm not the snitch. Officer Riddley happens to be friends with Principal Guthrie and mentioned it to him. Principal Guthrie called me into his office this morning to ask if I knew what was going on with you. We are all just worried about you."

"I bet," I mumble sarcastically, the heat rising in my face.

"I wish you would tell me the truth. Is your mom at home or is she gone? There are resources and services, Jinny. You don't have to be alone."

"Mind your own business!" I burst into tears, running out of her classroom, and out of the school building, forgetting my promise to meet Thomas.

I sprint all the way home ignoring the sweat and tears in my eyes.

ME:
WHERE ARE U?

ME:
I NEED U!!!

ME:
ARE U STILL ALIVE?

ME:
I HATE U!!!

All of my texts say undeliverable and just keep bouncing back to me even though I keep sending them over and over.

Then I call Thomas.

"Jinny are you okay?" he asks as soon as he answers.

"Sorry I left school without you. There was a family emergency and I had to come home. I'll see you tomorrow." I hang up before he can respond.

I sit on the couch and hold Pearl and try to keep it together. Something bad must have happened to Mama.... She would have tried to call me by now, even if she lost her phone. She could have used the phone at her hotel or at a gas station.

My phone buzzes, but it's not Mama.

JONELLE:
Girl????
I'm here 4 u! U safe?

ANGIE:
Jinny r u k?
Thomas said u have a fmly
emergency. My dad will bring
dinner 2 u if u want...

THOMAS:
Do u wanna stay
@ my house 2nite?
Mom said u can!!

SHIT! Everyone is worried about me. This entire thing is spinning out of control. Mama should have known better. Or I should have. Why did I think I could have friends and people in my life anyway? If I was still dumb Jinny Cheeseburger, no one would care if Mama was gone. No one would notice me. Why did I try to become something I'm not? I'm never gonna do anything with my life and be pretty or skinny or somebody who goes to college or someone who has parents and people who care.

I sob.

My spirit is sad and angry as pain wells up inside of me.

My chest is going to explode.

Pearl rubs her cute wet nose on me and licks my hand with her scratchy tongue. It's the only affection I'll ever have from now on.

Because Ms. Fleming was wrong... I will always be alone.

- Chapter Fifteen -
You are a buffett.

"Think Jinny! Think, think, think…" I say out loud to myself as I pace around the kitchen.

I've stopped crying long enough to drink the last of the Diet Coke. Pearl is pouncing around, lunging at my feet as I go back and forth in the kitchen. She thinks it's a game. "Not now kitty!" I swat her away. She scurries back off to my room and I feel guilty.

"She's gonna call. She's not dead."

If I say it out loud then maybe it will be true.

"She's gonna call. She's not dead."

I say it over and over.

Then, like magic, I hear the metal key in the door. A horrid noise escapes my lips when I see Mama walk in.

"MAMA!!" I croak and hug her as hard as I've ever hugged her in my entire life. She pushes me away from her, surprised, and annoyed.

"Watch the sunburn girl," she snaps. Her skin is the color of my hot pink shorts. Her lip is split and when she lifts up her sunglasses to put them on her head, she has a nasty black eye.

"Jinny, what in God's name are you wearing and why do you have mascara all over your face? You been cryin'? How many times I gotta tell you, men don't like a crier. Go wash up right now and put on pajamas! It's 2 a.m. on a school night," she says, like she fucking cares if I stay up late, and pajamas?

"Mama, what happened to you? I've been trying your phone for days," I say and follow her into her room. She sets her stuff down and lights up a cigarette. I can forgive her smoking in the house if she's going to tell me what the hell is going on. "You know the cops came by! I thought they were gonna take me to foster care."

She rolls her eyes at me.

"Yeah, well, my fucking phone got broken and I lost my Goddamned wallet. I caught a ride home with another girl and–" then she starts crying and slumps down on the edge of her bed.

I sit down next to her and try putting my arm around her, but she recoils.

"I thought you were dead Mama."

All I want is for her to hold me and love me and tell me everything is going to be alright. But, instead, she grabs me by the shoulders and shakes the shit out of me. Her ashes fly all over, singeing my skin.

"Damn it Jinny! You are a Buffett. Death is not an option for us, girl." She pauses and lets me go.

"God Mama." I stand up to get away from her.

"Look at your cute little body." She smiles and wipes her face. She looks terrible.

I can tell she hasn't eaten in days.

"Can I help you clean up?" I ask.

"No, you can't help me fuckin' clean up." Her vibe changes in an instant.

"Sorry, Mama." I sniffle.

"I told you I'd be home in two weeks. I don't know why you have to act all stupid, like I wasn't comin' back." Her pupils are huge. She gets up and starts pacing, lighting up another smoke. "Goddamnit Jinny. Why do you have to make me feel like such shit? I mean, I said I was coming home, didn't I?"

I don't say anything.

"Well, DIDN'T I?"

"Yes Mama."

"So why you gotta start talkin' about foster care?" She flinches.

"Do you want me to get you something for the pain?" I ask, looking for a reason to leave her room. My heart races. I've honestly never seen her this bad before.

She puts the menthol up to her mouth and takes a long, hard drag. I notice all of her pristine manicured nails are broken and jagged. She has hand shaped bruises up and down her arm.

"No, I don't need nothin' for the pain!" She starts laughing.

It's hard to keep track of the emotional rollercoaster ride that is Mama. From sad to happy to angry and back again, all in a matter of seconds.

"I'm just thankful you're home Mama. Please don't go working nights anymore. Stay with me. Don't go," I beg.

Her shoulders relax and she smiles and points to her face.

"Honey, I'm not leaving until this is healed! Oh my, look at the time! You have school in the morning, time for bed."

She follows me to my room and tucks me into bed. Which is not like her at all. She even leans in to kiss me, but then backs away before she actually does and walks out.

I don't want to sleep. I know something is seriously wrong with her, but I'm overwhelmed by exhaustion and the moment I close my eyes, I fall sound asleep.

When I wake up the sun is assaulting me.

My heart sinks. No visits from my dead Daddy while I slept. He's the one person who would make me feel better right now.

I look at my phone and it's 10 a.m. Oh shit! I didn't set my alarm. I've missed all my morning classes. I get ready as fast as I can and grab my bag to leave, but figure I better check on Mama before I go.

I can hear her talking. I wonder if Marco came over. I gently knock and then crack the door.

"Mama, I'm late for school. I have to go. Will you be okay if I leave?" I put my eye up to the crack and peek in. She's on her bed having a conversation, but it's not with Marco. It's no one. She's alone. She looks really strange, and I swallow hard with fear. A pain shoots up the back of my throat into my nostril, like when I accidentally swallow an ice cube.

"Oh, Jinny! Oh no, you're not going to school today. I need you to go to Cricket and buy me a new phone. I stuck some cash in my bra, so not all was lost from my job. Then I need you to order me a Driver's License online and start looking for new apartments for us. Maybe something further north, like in Coconut Creek…"

"But why would we move there? Did you lose your job at Margaritaville?" I ask.

"Just do it Jinny."

"But Mama, I like it here! I don't want to move," I whine. "I'm in the accelerated program. Plus, I have my book club afterschool and—"

Her face twists up.

"Shut up, right now. Let me tell you something, sweetheart. Book club is over. School? You're lucky I let you go. And if you're smart enough for accelerated bullshit, then it won't mean nothin' to go to a new school."

"But Mama!"

"YES, okay, I got fired from Margaritaville. No matter, my friend Sheila owes me a favor. She manages the girls at the Coconut Creek Casino. I can make good money as a cocktail waitress with all them rich, old, retired men who hang out there." She's wild eyed. "What are you waiting for? Go buy me a phone!"

I'm in shock. But I can't stay here and spend another second looking at her.

"Fine. Give me the money." I sneer and she hands me a wad of mostly fives.

I change from my school clothes to my running clothes and take off as fast as I can, out of our apartment and toward the Cricket store. I want to keep running and never look back. I'm so angry at her. Now I regret ever wanting her to come home. The pavement feels good beneath my feet as I circle around the block a few times to get all the rage out of me before going into the store.

I walk inside, anxious to get this over with, but the man behind the counter moves slow, taking his sweet time with another customer. I tap my toe impatiently and clear my throat a few times, but he ignores me.

So, I pull out my phone. Ms. Fleming texted.

MS. FLEMING:
Jinny, are you coming to
school?

ME:
No. Mama won't let me...
she said I can't do book club
she said we're movin!!
IDNKY I even tried
2 make friends this year
or be something, when
I'm nothin...

MS. FLEMING:
Jinny, you are special.
Stay safe. I hope you come to
school tomorrow.

ME:
Yeah...
Can u give the books 2
Jonelle and ask her
2 lead? She's
smarter than she lets on...

MS. FLEMING:

Of course.

I put my phone away and try not to cry. I can't believe I have to miss my first book club meeting. I didn't even want to do this stupid club, and now I got my hopes up. I was excited about it.

"Whatever I can get for fifty bucks," I tell the idiot when it's my turn.

After I pay for the phone, I sit on the floor to open the package and set it up. Mama has no clue how to do it for herself. I use her passwords and check the bank account. Mama withdrew all our money, or someone else did. Whoever stole her wallet. Now I definitely can't pay any of the bills... What the hell!

I get up and pace around.

I know I'm making the salesman nervous, so I walk outside and slump down on a bench.

No money. No school. No Mysterious Magical Book Club. No Thomas. No Victor. No Jonelle. No Ms. Fleming...

"Miss. Are you okay?" A lady puts her hand on my shoulder.

I didn't realize I was shaking until her cool hand makes my skin relax. Tears drip down my face and landing on my legs, rolling off the sides. I feel like I'm four years old again, sitting outside of Chuck E Cheese when Mama used to leave me there. She claimed it was a daycare. She would pull up and drop me off– but without a parent, I couldn't go inside. I'd sit on a bench outside all day waiting for her to come back. She's so fucking stupid.

"Sorry, yes, I'm fine." I get up, wipe my face, and walk down the sidewalk.

I'm not fine though. Nothing about my life is fine right now.

"Miss, wait! Hold on." The lady follows me.

I stop and look at her. My lip quivers and I think my knees might buckle.

"Do you have a mom or dad close by? Do you need me to help you find something?" she asks, the concern clear on her face.

"No. I'm–" I suck in, like I'm going to say more, but instead I walk away. But then, a quote from a book pops into my mind, so I turn back to her, and say, "All that is gold does not glitter, and not all those who wander are lost."

"The Riddle of Strider," she replies.

I nod. I'm surprised she even knew what the hell I was talking about. She pulls a card out of her purse and hands it to me.

"I'm a school guidance counselor in St. Petersburg at Admiral Farragut Academy. I'm here for a conference and had to pick up a new charger for my phone. But I don't believe in coincidence… There's something about you. If you ever need someone to talk to, call me. God bless you."

I take the card from her.

"Thanks. My name is Jinny Buffett."

Before she can say anything else I run toward home. I run as fast, and as hard, as I can. I'm mad at Mama. I'm mad at– I look at the card– Mrs. Lenora Ollena. What kind of name is that anyway? And what the hell is Admiral Farragut Academy? Some kind of fancy school for rich assholes.

When I get home, Mama is on the couch with an ashtray in her lap watching Judge Judy and laughing.

"Here's your stupid phone. I set it up for you and checked the bank account. No money for rent. That's awesome."

"Where's my change?" Mama asks, refusing to look at me.

I drop the remaining ten dollars on the floor and walk to my room.

"AGH!!" I scream as loud as I can into my pillow.

I knew I didn't deserve a real life. Just this strange existence. Not anything special or magical like in my books or like in my dreams about the swamp. There is no spirit helping guide me. There is no mysterious connection between me and my family out in the Everglades. I can't talk to alligators named George.

I am not the smartest student in Florida.

I'm just Jinny fucking Cheeseburger.

***

The rest of the week I'm a zombie. I go through the motions at school. Thomas talks. I listen and nod, but I can't smile. The happiness of making friends and feeling like I could be someone has left me.

I'm back to who I used to be when I was invisible.

When I just drifted around.

Not caring about anyone.

I have my nose in a book all week. If I can just stay lost in another world, maybe all of this will go away.

On Friday, Jonelle is pissed during lunch because Ms. Fleming asked her to be the new leader of Mysterious Magical Book Club.

"Damn it, Jinny! You know I have to watch my littles bros after school…" she whines.

"But you signed up for it. You said you'd come to the club. I'm sorry, my mom is being a real piece of crap this week," I try to explain.

"Yeah, but if I'm the leader, that means I can't miss no meetings, and what if my pops has work or can't get the littles and I can't go?" She slaps her pizza down on the plate.

Sauce squirts out. The cafeteria always serves greasy, nasty pepperoni pizza on Friday. I'm glad I'm only eating salad.

"I can help. So, if you have to miss the club to pick up your little brothers," Ang offers.

"Thanks girl," Jonelle puts her fist up and does the pound and explosion with Ang.

I feel like such a shitty friend.

"Seriously, what's your mom's deal anyway?" Ang asks.

I look at her. I know I should trust her and Jonelle, but my heart and head are struggling to trust anything or anyone. I let all the air out of my lungs.

"Something happened, something bad. I don't want to talk about it here. Maybe we could hang out tonight?" I suggest.

Mama won't be home anyway. She said she was staying with Sheila and picking up some shifts at the casino, but I'm not sure I believe her. This morning I saw her packing her big bag, with the clothes she wears when she's working overnights. Her bruises aren't even healed! None of the tourists will pay for damaged goods... Which means locals.

She can't control herself.

"I know. Can you spend the night with me tonight?" Ang begs with excitement. I've been to her house before, back in elementary school. It would be nice not to be alone.

"Okay. Can I go home with you after school and borrow pajamas?" I ask.

I don't really need anything else. If I go home, I'll have to walk three miles to her house, or beg Sabrina for a ride.

"YES! I'll go ask my dad and I'll text Emily's parents. They won't mind if you come with me to get her from school and play for a while. Jonelle, can you come over at 6 p.m.? Friday is Chinese food at our house! Do you like fried rice and noodles?" Ang's eyes light up.

Jonelle and I look at one another and realize I may have gotten us into more than we bargained for.

"Ang, don't tease me. You know I love fried rice... Get me some egg rolls too. I'm sure Pops can bring me, he ain't workin' this weekend."

She gets up and throws the greasy pizza at the trash can and misses. We all laugh as loud and hard as we can. It feels good to be myself again with my friends, even if just for a second.

The bell rings and we head our separate ways. Ang runs up behind me and pulls on my arm. I stop to look at her, the excitement I felt only minutes before escapes me. I know this is the part where she cancels our plans and tells me how stupid I am.

"Jinny, I'm so happy you want to come over tonight. You know, I worry about you," she says it kind of quiet. I try not to take offense to so many people in my gravity worrying about me.

I change the subject and say, "Would your parents let Thomas stay over tonight too? Since he's gay and all?"

She doesn't even hesitate. "Of course they won't care! They are sort of old-school hippies if you never noticed..."

"Yeah girl, I noticed" I wink at her.

Ang hugs me before running to her next class.

– Chapter Sixteen –
(Un)Predictable Situations

Ms. Fleming faces the board, writing something, while we are all supposed to be taking a test. I literally finish it in two minutes and turn it over on my desk. God, look at everyone else, not even done with the first page. I carefully slide my phone out of my bag and put it under the book I'm reading. It vibrates and I look to make sure no one heard. Then it buzzes again. And again! I cough a few times and Ms. Fleming looks back at me. I pretend to be reading and don't make eye contact with her. I read the texts quick and respond.

ANGIE:
Sleepover approved! my
house @ 6
except Jinny...
U can ride the bus w/me
2 get Emily 😄

THOMAS:
Sleepover??? YASSSSSS
What's ur address?

JONELLE:
Grl, shit. Gonna be wild.
dont 4get muh egg rolls

THOMAS:
Egg rolls?? YAASSSSS

ME:
Lmao! Meet u by the
bus Ang. Thx babes...

I raise my hand. Ms. Fleming is back at her desk and waves me to come up.

"Yes Jinny?" She whispers. "Is everything alright? Do you have a question?"

"Can I go to the bathroom?" I ask. It's like the first thing I've said to her all week.

"Are you done already?"

"Yes, the test was easy." But then I throw her a feel good, since I'm in such a good mood now, "I liked the question about analyzing dialogue in secondary scenes."

She smiles ear to ear. "I can tell you're feeling better, Jinny. And yes, you can go to the bathroom," she whispers.

I roll my eyes at her before walking out of the room, my cell phone hidden in my pocket. As soon as I'm out of the classroom I call Mama.

She picks up on the third ring. "I'm driving to my new job. What's up baby girl?"

She is so nonchalant about it. Like it isn't killing her that she isn't going to her favorite place in the whole world, Margaritaville. Like she isn't dying inside that she can't see Marco and Cheryl and Jesus. But, knowing her, she will convince her "crew" to move to the casino with her. She has that power over people. She can persuade them to do whatever she wants.

But I see past that. Always have.

"I'm going to ride the bus home with Angie and spend the night," I don't ask, I'm telling. I never talk like this to her. "Her parents are getting us Chinese food for dinner. Jonelle and Thomas are coming over too and we are going to watch movies. They will drive me home tomorrow."

I wait for a few seconds...

"See! You still have friends! Looks like you spent the entire week whining and crying for no reason. Oh, Sheila is calling. Have fun, Jinny, gotta go." Then she hangs up.

That's it?

She doesn't ask me any questions. Like does Angie still live at the same house? What's her parent's phone number? Nothing! It makes no difference to her where I am or what I do. Picking up Sheila's call was more important than talking to me.

Most fifteen-year-olds would love this kind of freedom.

But all it says to me is that I don't matter. I'm not important to the one person who is supposed to care about me and my wellbeing. My hands form fists at my side after I put my phone back in my pocket. I have to tell myself not to cry. This is what I wanted! I wanted to go to Ang's house and spend the night. So why am I so upset? Mama's just being who she's always been. Selfish and shitty.

"Jinny? Are you okay?" Victor comes out of the classroom. I guess maybe I should have stood further from the window in the door.

"Hi, um… yeah, I'm fine," I say and wipe the tears that started streaming down my face.

"Are you sure?" He stares at me with those big brown eyes.

"Did Jonelle give you the book for Mysterious Magical Book Club?" I ask. I should have asked earlier this week, but I've been distracted.

"She did. But I haven't had time to read it because of football. Actually, my older sister Andrea saw it and snatched it from my bag." He laughs. "She's been reading it all week. She told me I'm stupid for trying to join your book club and football at the same time."

"Oh yeah." I frown.

"But, then she said maybe, since you picked a good first book it would be worth it."

I smile.

"Well, Ms. Fleming had a hand in it. She suggested The Raven Boys. It is sort of perfect for our first book, mysterious and magical. I read it last weekend, so I'd know what to talk about during book club." I laugh.

"You read a whole book in a weekend? Impressive!" Victor smiles.

I'm not sure how to handle his admiration. I want to turn around so he won't see me blush, but I can't take my eyes off him. My heart thumps.

"Actually, I read it twice," I say softly.

"Jinny, you're so smart," he says.

I know he isn't trying to be hurtful. But it still cuts me because I keep hearing Mama's voice. "Men think smart girls are ugly, Jinny! Stop acting so fucking smart all the time!"

The blush in my cheeks burns angry.

"Yep. So fucking smart. And ugly too?" I spit the words like they will burn my mouth if I keep them in any longer.

"That is not at all what I was thinking! God, why are you so defensive all the time?" He yells back at me.

"Is everything alright out here?" Ms. Fleming opens her door and eyes us.

"Sorry," Victor mumbles.

I don't say anything and walk to my desk.

Well, I've ruined any chance I might have had with Victor after that little display. He has to think I'm the worst– why did I snap like that? Why can't I just accept a compliment? I put my head down on my desk and pray for the bell to ring.

As soon as school is over I run to find Ang, Thomas, and Jonelle. I decide to confess everything that happened with Mama, so my friends will stop worrying about me, and I can stop feeling like I'm lying. I feel lighter already, like I might fly away.

"You ready to go get Emily?" Ang says with a smile.

"Yes, I'm excited to meet her."

Ang has said a lot of nice things about Emily. She's in 5th grade and has Down syndrome, but she has a sense of humor or at least, she makes Ang laugh all the time. You can see it in Ang's eyes when she talks about her.

But as we are about to get on the small handicapped bus that goes to the elementary school, Shantel and her band of cheers walk toward us.

"Oh look, Jinny Cheeseburger and that freak Angie are going on a date. They had to call the Uber for retards!" She laughs and points.

I almost tell her what a hateful stupid cow she is, when her own cheer friend Britney turns on her and says, "Shantel, not cool. My brother has autism spectrum disorder and rides that bus for band practice. The word retard is unacceptable!" Britney is shaking mad. "You're just jealous because Victor has a crush on Jinny and she's tall and skinny and pretty and smart," she screams and runs off.

Several of the cheer girls follow her. Some of the others look lost like they don't know who to follow or what to do. Shantel folds her arms over her chest, and I flip her off. Then I pull Ang by the arm, and we take our seats as the bus pulls out of the parking lot.

"Shantel is such an asshole. Are you okay?" I ask.

Ang's face is beet red. "It's just sad, you know, that girls like her exist."

"Yeah. She might think we are freaks, but at least we have class." I nudge Ang with my shoulder. She looks over at me and smiles.

"Yeah, class!" And then we both laugh.

"So, Emily's parents are cool with me coming along? I just want to make sure. I really don't need any more drama this week."

"They were totally fine with it and said we can take her to the park after school. Emily loves to go to the park," Ang says.

The bus lurches and opens the creaky door at the elementary school.

A few kids get on and find seats.

Ang waves at a girl who's giving me the stink eye. "Emily, come over and sit with us! This is my friend Jinny. She's going to play with us today,"

Ang explains.

I wink at her.

"JINNNNEEEEE," she says very dramatically. "You look nice. Are you nice? Angie is nice," she says and sticks her hand out to me. I take it and shake it.

"Nice to meet you Emily. And yes, I think I'm nice."

The bus starts moving and the driver shouts at us to sit our asses down and buckle up. Ang and Emily, who are sharing a seat, immediately comply. I don't like the driver's attitude. But I buckle up anyway. Safety first.

We don't go far before turning into a nice neighborhood.

"JINNEEEE, get off this bus right now if you are coming with me," Emily says very matter of factly and we pile off the bus.

I recognize Ang's house.

"Are we going to your house first?" I ask.

"No Jinnneeee. We're going to my house. Do you want to come over? Angie, can she come over to play?" Emily asks Ang.

"Yes, Emily, Jinny is gonna come play today. And guess what? I called your parents and they said we can go to the park. Do you want to go to the park?"

"I want to go to the park. I want Jinneeee to push me on the swing."

She's a girl who knows what she wants and isn't afraid to say it. I could take some lessons from Emily.

I take a moment to look around when we get inside. It's really nice, recently remodeled, and smells brand new. It looks like something from a TV show, one with a regular family. The kind who have dinner together every night and share heartfelt moments. It's the kind of place I've never been–

I think about the picture of Daddy's family.

I wonder if they ate dinner around a big oak table and told jokes or played cards.

My heart aches for people I don't know.

For a life I don't have.

"Emily, can I use your bathroom before we walk to the park?" I ask, trying to hide the wave of emotion washing over me.

"Yes. But you have to flush and wash your hands." Emily says and looks at me with intense eyes. It's hard to feel sad when I have those big gray eyes staring at me. "Flush AND wash!" She repeats.

"Got it." I say to her.

Ang giggles and goes to the kitchen. "I'll make snack bags!" she shouts when I go into the bathroom.

My stomach rumbles. I could eat a whole bag of snacks right about now.

"JINNEEEE, are you okay in there? The toilet paper is on the left. Do you see it?" Emily knocks and yells through the door.

"Yes, Emily, I see it. Thank you," I yell back. She's very helpful, that's for sure.

When I come out she looks at me with those eyes again.

"Are you sure you washed for thirty seconds with soap and water?"

"Emily, lay off it. I thought you wanted to go to the park," Ang says with her hand on her hip. She opens the front door. "I've got water and cheddar fish crackers! Come on."

"I better go pee and poop first. I have had to poop all day," Emily says.

Ang shuts the front door and lets out a long sigh.

Emily runs into the bathroom and slams the door.

"We might as well sit down, Emily takes for-ev-er to poop," Ang doesn't laugh, and I respect her more right now than I could ever explain.

My Mama would have laughed thirty times at Emily and said horrible cruel things. Mama's like that, making fun of people in wheelchairs and with disabilities. I think it makes her feel better about herself, like even though we're poor and she sleeps with men for money, she still thinks she's better off.

I look at Ang, she's a genuinely good person.

I need more good people in my life.

"Can I eat those little fishies? I'm starved."

"So, you gonna tell me first or make me wait until tonight?" She holds the baggie up and wags it from side to side.

"You really want to hear my drama twice?" I ask and snatch the fish from her. I pop a couple in my mouth.

"That's what friends are for."

Friends.

Just when I am finally finding people who care enough to listen, Mama goes and pulls the rug out from under me. Well screw that! I can have a friend like Ang, whether Mama moves me far away or not, so I start from the beginning.

"I'm warning you, this story is ugly," I tell Ang.

"I figured," she replies and starts eating her snacks like she's at the movies and I'm about to give her an Oscar winning performance.

"You probably don't know, but my Mama's not just a waitress— she uh, goes on dates with men… for money."

"Like a sex worker?" She asks.

"Yes. And she makes really stupid decisions— like this last job. She went to the Florida Keys with some stranger for two weeks! But she came home all beat up. That's why I missed school and I've been miserable all week."

"Oh Jinny, I'm so sorry," Ang says with a frown.

"Now she wants to move to Coconut Creek. She lost her job at Margaritaville. And the cops were snooping around when she was gone– I think they are on to her. I can't tell them she's at work anymore if she leaves me alone again," I explain.

Emily is out of the bathroom. She's quiet as a mouse.

"How about we walk and talk," Ang suggests.

We pile out the front door for the park, and I'm on such a roll, I don't think I can stop the words from pouring out of me.

"My life just feels out of control! That's why I started running over the summer, to escape these stupid feelings. Not to mention I've been having these dreams about my dead Daddy's family out in the Everglades. I swear, I know it sounds crazy, but I think I'm supposed to build them a bridge. There was a talking gator named George, and he…" I trail off, boy, I sound insane.

"How you gonna do that Jinnneeee?" Emily asks, highly interested in my mania.

"I'm not real sure, Emily. But I met this lady the other day from some fancy boarding school called Admiral Farragut Academy. They have an engineering program and help prepare you for college."

But the thought of college makes me laugh.

Of all the problems in my life, I'm really worried about college?

I laugh harder.

"What's so funny?" Ang asks.

I hear the concern in her voice. She's worried that I'm on the brink of a meltdown. This is how they start right? Maniacal laughing for no apparent reason.

"Mama won't let me go to college, let alone a fancy boarding school all the way on the other side of the state! She hates school. She's said it plenty of times. I'm lucky she even lets me go at all."

Ang and Emily are staring at me. If I was them I would have told me to shut up by now.

Emily puts out her hand and waves a finger at me.

I try not to smile, because I know whatever she's going to say is serious.

"Your mama is not a good person. My Mom says being a good person is better than anything else. You should go to that school and learn to build super bridges." Her waving finger turns into a big swooping arm motion, to prove to me just how big a bridge I outta build. Then she adds, "I don't like gators. Don't bring George to my house."

She spots the swing, forgetting my drama, and climbs on to the black rubber seat. The humid breeze whips her hair. She pumps her legs, swinging all wonky from side to side.

"HELP! PUSH ME!" She screams and waves her arms at me.

I push her gently at first. She's kind of heavy, but I don't mind. Once I get her going fast, she pumps her legs in unison and squeals. Then Ang and I crawl on the swings next to her. We start swinging just as hard and fast as she is, sailing through the sweet afternoon air.

"Emily is right, you know..." Ang says as we pass on the swings and then careen off in opposite directions.

"I won't bring a gator to her house," I agree.

"No stupid," Ang says with a smirk as we pass again on the swing. "Your mom isn't a good person for what she's been doing to you. Leaving you home, making you responsible for paying the bills, and surviving on your own. Then coming home all beat up and leaving again. Something's not right."

I nod.

"Maybe you should call that lady from the Admiral Farragut Academy and ask about going to school there. It's like a boarding school right? Then you wouldn't need your Mama. You know, Emily's mom is a social worker for Palm Beach County. I bet she can help you get placed there."

Emily and Ang are both right. But, reminding me that Emily's mom's a social worker gets under my skin. My chest feels tight, and I can tell I'm getting anxious.

I've been lucky to stay out of the foster care system.

I'm NOT calling a social worker for help. They don't help! Not girls like me. They look at me and think I'm trashy and do drugs and have sex and party all the time. Girls like me get used up in the system. Kids in my complex are always getting yanked from their beds and placed into the foster system, sometimes they come back, and when they do, they're changed.

"Yeah, maybe," I mumble.

Emily starts singing twinkle, twinkle, little star and lies back in the swing. It pulls me from the spiral of self-despair I'm about to drown in.

She screams, "I'm floating!"

"Uhhhh... Emily, don't do that or you'll get sick like last time," Ang says and gets off the swing and kicks into full babysitter mode. I'm impressed.

I've never babysat before.

It's always just been me and Mama.

"Okay, let's head back, your parents will be home soon." Ang tries, unsuccessfully, to get Emily off the swings.

"You can't tell me what to do." Emily's defiant and throws a full fist punch at Ang and I'm taken aback. This isn't the same Emily from a few minutes ago, but Ang stays calm.

"Emily, we have to walk home now. It's time for dinner. Your mom said she's making spaghetti. And Dora the Explorer is on. We need to go now," Ang says. She means business.

"FINE. Bitch." Emily says it and doesn't care.

My eyes are like saucers on my face.

"Whoa, burn," I whisper. Ang shoots me a look, like, don't egg her on. So, I reach my hand out and say, "Emily, will you walk with me?" She takes the bait. And takes my hand.

"Okay! Do you like Dora?" she asks as we walk to her house like nothing happened at all.

"Yes, I love Dora. There's nothing better than exploring and predictable situations," I tell her. She gives me a goofy look.

"Jinneeee, I hope you build your bridge someday."

I squeeze her hand.

I'm happy I met Emily.

Who'd have thought a fifth grader with Down syndrome could give me such commonsense advice.

- Chapter Seventeen -
Swamp magic will take your cat!

"Mrs. Bailey, thanks again for having us over for dinner," I say to Ang's mom.

"Oh sweetheart, call me Connie. And you are very welcome. China One down on First street really does have the best General Tso's Chicken, extra crispy with that spicy sauce everyone loves. I don't know if you remember coming over to play when you were little, but you're always welcome here." Connie gives me a shoulder squeeze and a look.

"Thanks," I reply.

Ang must have told her things about me. I don't know if I like it or not, but Connie is nice, and normal. Way more normal than Mr. Bailey, who is still struggling with his chopsticks and slurping noodles while trying to read two books at the same time.

"Yeah, thanks Connie!" Jonelle and Thomas both echo the sentiment.

Then we all go piling into Ang's room. Jonelle and Thomas mess around with their phones and take pictures and laugh and watch TikTok. Basically, just being silly. I lay on the floor on Ang's fuzzy, pink rug and look up at the ceiling. She hand-painted stars and quotes all over it. I wonder what it feels like to have someplace really feel like home.

All you need is LOVE

Stars can't SHINE without darkness

You're STRONGER than you believe

All shit she probably saw on coffee mugs or t-shirts, but I guess I like it. My cheeks burn when I realize I'm jealous of the permanence of her life, that she has a room she can paint with quotes. I don't like being jealous of other people! Especially Ang.

Ang lies down next to me, and we admire the view together for a while.

"Is everything in your life good, Ang?" I ask. "I haven't been a very good friend the last few days. I only talk about myself." I roll over and look at her. It's freeing to say it out loud. I'm sick of thinking about my own life.

Ang turns and looks at me.

"Did you get your project done in science? The thing with the water table." I ask, remembering that she mentioned it.

She laughs.

"Yes, goof. I told you that today at lunch. But it's okay. I understand your life is messy and it's hard to concentrate when life is messy."

"Messy is right," I say.

"Jinny, don't be so hard on yourself. It's hard to be a good friend under regular circumstances, let alone when you've been going through all that crap with your Mama. But I think you're learning." A big smile creeps across her face.

She laces her fingers through mine. Holding hands feels weird. It's intimate. Although, it's what we should have always done as friends. Why didn't I try harder over the years with Ang? She was right here all along and could have been the support I needed in my life– and I could have been something more to her too! I'm so stupid! Tears escape my eyes and the stars above my head go blurry.

"OH SHIT!" Thomas screams and we both jump up.

"WHAT?" Ang yells and looks around expecting a mouse or a spider.

"I love this song more than life!" He stands on her bed and starts dancing.

"Well, turn it up!" Jonelle shoves him and he jumps down in a very elegant way and fumbles around with Ang's speakers for a minute, then turns the volume all the way up.

Jonelle looks ridiculous trying to keep up with Thomas. Then Ang surprises us by doing a floor drop and shaking her ass.

"Get it girl!" I cheer her on.

"Woot woot!" Thomas is fist pumping the air.

Jonelle lets out one of her loud, hearty laughs and I laugh too. It feels so good to be with my friends tonight. Nothing else matters. I have a full stomach and people who love me. No more tears or sadness. No more pain and feeling depressed.

And this is our entire night! One big party.

Laughing. Snacking. Music. Movies. Dancing. Repeat.

***

"Girls, and Thomas, it's time to wake up! It's noon. I'm sure your parents will want you home at some point today." Connie is so polite and sweet trying to wake us up.

We are a mass of teenagers sleeping piled all over Ang's room. I should go home and make sure Pearl is okay, so I get up first. The others are groggy.

"Thomas, what time is your mom comin'? Do you want me to text her?" I ask and shake his shoulder. He moans. So, I take that as a yes. While we wait for Sil to pick us up, Connie offers me a bowl of cereal or something else to eat. I only take a glass of water and sit at the table and wait.

"Mr. Bailey tells me you've been a topic of discussion at school, Jinny. I had no idea how bright you were. You know, all the private schools have been calling Mr. Guthrie to try and get their hands on you," she says, like I'm supposed to know. I try not to look baffled. What does that even mean?

"Oh?"

"Yes, dear. Well, every private school in the state wants a girl like you! You'll probably invent the cure for cancer or something! Sounds like all of the elite universities will be after you soon. Your mailbox will be full of letters from Harvard, Stanford, MIT, Yale. I hope your mother is proud of you." She sneaks that last part in. I know she doesn't mean to keep cutting me open. But she does. Every word is like a knife or a punch to my gut.

Sil starts honking outside, saving me from further misery.

"THOMAS!" I scream and run out the door as fast as I can. I don't even say goodbye or thank you.

Yale? Harvard? Curing cancer? Mrs. Bailey is a weirdo just like her husband. I don't know how I could have been fooled.

I'm quiet the entire way home. But that's okay because so is Thomas. He's sleeping in the back seat, so I put my head in my hand and close my eyes. The sunshine is hot and angry through the window, but I'm numb.

As soon as Sil pulls up to my apartment I jump out and run up two steps at a time and let myself in.

I already know Mama's not here yet. Her BMW is gone. So, either she came home from the casino this morning and left again, or she hasn't come home at all. Big bag. She took the big bag. It could be days before I see her.

ME:
When ru coming home?

MAMA:
In a few days...
I made $800 last night in tips!
This place is amazing!

They want me
to start work immediately...

ME:
Oh. K. Bye.

MAMA:
Be good. I luv u 🖤

"ARGH!!!!" I scream as loud as I can. Sabrina or Grann Ruth bangs on the floor beneath me, probably with a broom. I stomp my foot in response, but then yell, "SORRY!" because I don't need Sabrina's pizza face rushing up here to scream at me.

I go to my room. It stinks like Grann Ruth's marijuana. Pearl is mad and I'm mad at Pearl for making me find her on the beach that day and making me love her.

That feeling of anger and disgust about myself creeps up again.

What if Mama found a letter in the mailbox from an Ivy League school? How would she react? I have a vision of her smashing plates and screaming and crying and telling me I'm only trying to be smart to make her feel stupid. Then she'll tell me I'm a nobody piece of shit like my Daddy and I'm not even pretty enough to work at Tootsie's like she did when she was sixteen and got kicked out of her parents' house. She'll tell me I'm a fuck up and that even if I go to Yale or Harvard they'll spit in my face because I'm a white trash loser. And she'd be right.

I want to throw up.

I need to get out of here. The walls feel like they are closing in on me and my throat is tightening up.

"Maybe I'll go for a run to clear my head," I say to myself.

With a shaky hand I fill a glass of water and tip it back all the way, chugging down every last drop. Finally feeling some relief.

But I must have drunk it too fast because my head spins and I see smoke rising up from the floor. Wait, smoke? Oh my god, did Grann Ruth set her apartment on fire with one of her joints? I try to remember what you're supposed to do in a fire.

Stop, drop, and roll.

Before I can roll anywhere, I hear voices, and see spirits in the smoke– the glass slips from my hand and smashes on the floor. Shattering into a thousand pieces.

"Whoa, baby girl, watch yourself," drawls a southern voice.

"This is not really happening," I reply.

"Sure it is."

I squeeze my eyes as tight as I can, expecting everything to be normal again when I open them. My lids lift a sliver, and the smoke is gone. I take a deep breath. The air smells like fresh brewed sweet tea. My eyes fly open, and my living room is still full of spirits. The low chirping crickets chime in with someone strumming on a guitar. There's even a harmonica, wailing a sad lowly tune.

It's the Everglades, right here in my tiny apartment. Warm, murky water rises around my ankles and Grann Lola chats with my Auntie's Bonnie, Nina, and Esther. All the women from my dream world. The blood family I've never met in real life. There's other spirit faces too, cousins I guess. I look around to see if Daddy's ghost is with them. But I don't see him anywhere.

Maybe because he's a different kind of spirit, the dead kind. And I think maybe these are the alive kind.

"Grann Lola, what are y'all doing here?" I ask.

"Your Daddy's ghost is so loud; he's been howling at my door day and night tellin' me to come see you. Everyone in the swamp talkin' bout Jinny Buffett, the girl who builds bridges, the girl who's gonna save the world. The girl who has a Mysterious Magical Book Club."

"You know about my book club?"

"Used to have!" Shouts Aunt Bonnie.

"That's right... Used to. Girl you have a terrible Mama. I ain't never liked Crystal Diamond Buffett. She's the most nasty, selfish woman I ever met! Wouldn't marry your Daddy on account she didn't want to change her last name. Always movin' you around, changing her number so I can't find you," Grann Lola says with a thick southern accent.

She looks like she just stepped out of the hot summer sun. Her skin is tan and worn like leather.

"Your Daddy told us you on the edge, Jinny. Like you either gonna be right or wrong. Up or down. Hot or cold. What's it gonna be?" asks Auntie Nina.

"I don't know what you mean?"

The room gets darker and darker as the moon rises over the swamp. Little fireflies blink their neon glow and Grann reaches over and hands me a mason jar.

"Catch yourself a dream girl," she says with a wink. "Go on now, play with your cousins." There's a bunch of kids my age running and laughing and catching fireflies in their own jars. My apartment has morphed into Grann's land in the Everglades.

A string of old twinkle lights flicks on and blinks across the property. There's a lean-to workshop and a bunch of rusty cars to one side. There's a hand painted sign that reads, "Welcome to Alligator Alley" affixed to the side of the shop. My cousins laugh and jump and chase each other back and forth.

"Just do right, child. Be like your old Grann. Drink your tea sweet and keep your attitude salty. Be suspicious of those around you who mean you harm and take care of the ones you love."

"I'll try, Grann! I love my friends and I don't break the rules, unless cursing is breaking the rules," I say.

Grann Lola laughs hard and stomps her feet, splashing the swamp water. Then Auntie Nina joins her and starts stomping and splashing and waving her arms in the air. The beads and fringe on her vest bounce. She reaches her hands out to me.

"Come on Jinny, dance with me," she says and pulls me into a spin.

I swear I can feel her hands in mine. I flash for a moment, thinking about when me and Thomas were dancing around the living room.

"When in Rome, right?" I laugh and dance with my Auntie and Grann and run around splashing.

"When in Rome? Hell, girl, when you in the swamps!"

"SHUT UP! DO YOU HAVE A GODDAMN PARTY UP THERE? IT'S 1PM ASSHOLE!!" Sabrina screams and pounds on the floor.

"Uh, you have to be quiet. My neighbor will be up in a few minutes to see what's going on. I'm not sure how to explain this," I say nervously.

I mean, my living room has turned into a full on swamp, with trees and mucky water and fireflies and everything. I'm not even sure I'm in my living room at all. I mean, I can see Grann's house and their shop.

"You tell her your Mama has abandoned you in your hour of need, and your Grann and Aunties and all your cousins have come to rescue you," Grann Lola says.

I look at all the spirit faces in the room. I want to believe Grann. I want to believe this is real and they are here to rescue me from Mama.

I look down, and Pearl is crying for me, half-soaked in swamp water. I lean to get her, but before I can, Auntie Bonnie's spirit swoops over and scoops her up. Pearl meows once, then disappears, along with Auntie Bonnie. I look around and call out for them.

"PEARL! AUNTIE BONNIE!"

"Don't worry about your kitten. We can use a good mouser on our spread, got a lot of land out here in the Everglades. You should visit us Jinny.

You always got a home here," Auntie Nina says.

"Wait, did she just take Pearl? Like really take her?" I scan the room in a panic. "Pearl, come here kitty, come back." I'm frantic. This whole thing is just a dream! A dream ghost or spirit or whatever my Aunties are can't just take my cat— can they?

"Shhhhh...." Grann Lola pets my head.

Then Auntie Esther hands me a piece of paper. "That's the address to our spread. It's off Old Highway 99 past the town of Jerome in Alligator Alley. Write to us and we'll write back," she says.

I can feel the paper in my hands. It's not a hallucination. It's worn and magical between my fingers, like I'm holding an ancient treasure map.

Sabrina starts banging on the door and the magic of the dream vision starts to fade.

"What am I supposed to do about my life? Mama. School. The bridges. All of it..." My voice weakens with every pound on the door.

"Call the Admiral of course!" Grann Lola starts laughing. All my aunties and cousins laugh too, and I smile, cause I guess that's what family does.

"The Admiral?" I ask.

"OPEN THE DOOR!" Sabrina yells.

I can't wait any longer, so I trudge through the muddy swamp and open the door.

"What the fuck are you doing up here?" Sabrina barges in and looks around. "Sounds like a goddamn Fourth of July party with a bunch of assholes dancing and screaming."

"I don't know what you're talkin' about. Ain't no one here Sabrina. I was in my room reading." I shrug.

She doesn't trust me and gets right up in my face. Her hot Cheeto breath is all over me and I'm about to shove her away from me.

But, then I hear Auntie Nina's words, "You are either gonna be right or wrong." But it's like she was saying, DO RIGHT or DO WRONG.

If I push Sabrina, I'm no better than she is. Plus, she's bigger than me. If I so much as lay a finger on her, she will literally kick my ass.

"Sorry Sabrina. I'll keep it down."

"Yeah you better." Sabrina slams the door as hard as she can, for the trouble of walking up here, I suppose.

"What a day." I rub my head.

My whole life, I've felt the spirit of my dead Daddy. I have longed to know more about him and his family. I've stared at the picture in my shoebox so many times and made-up stories about who my Grann was and what life was like for my Daddy growing up.

Marco always tells me the spirit of the swamp is looking out for me. Maybe this is what he meant!

I want to believe. But it's not like they've been around for the last fifteen years. Maybe I needed them. Maybe I needed someone to love me and protect me when Mama was acting like a fool. But Grann did say that Mama kept changing her phone number. It's not like she'd know how to call me.

I look at my phone.

And a light goes off in my head.

"I GET IT GRANN!" I shout into the air. "Call the Admiral!"

I race to my room and dig through my dresser to find what I'm looking for. I dial the number on the card. It's ringing. My palms are clammy. I sure hope this is what Grann Lola meant for me to do.

"Hello, you've reached Lenora Ollena. Please leave your name, number. and a detailed message and I will return your call within twenty-four hours," says the woman's voice. It's kind and professional at the same time.

"Mrs. Ollena, 'Sometimes you put up walls not to keep people out, but to see who cares enough to break them down'. If you have time to talk, call me back. Oh, this is Jinny Buffett. The girl from the Cricket store in Hollywood. The girl who was crying. You gave me your card. Um. K, bye."

The quote from Socrates, one on Ms. Fleming's wall, staring me in the face. I've been too ignorant to actually listen to the words. I feel like I have to say things to impress Lenora Ollena, but perpetually quoting other people's words is only being a fake, a hack. Using the words others say doesn't mean I'm smart or anything.

I need to make up my own philosophical sayings, like-

Being smart doesn't mean shit if you're already broken without hope

Or better...

Swamp magic will take your cat, to save your heart

Maybe she will call me back. What would I even say? I could ask her about the Admiral Farragut Academy. Grann Lola said to ask the Admiral. That has to be what she meant. Maybe I can tell her what Ang's mom said about the private schools and Harvard and Yale and curing cancer.

Or maybe I just won't pick up if she calls.

– Chapter Eighteen –
Making plans, LOTS of them!

I'm surprisingly calm about what happened. Maybe it's because the apartment is eerily quiet, as if nothing really happened at all. I'm sitting on the couch, trying to wrap my mind around it when I get a message from Thomas.

THOMAS:
Sorry i was soooo tired this
morning on the drive home

ME:
HA, cause u and Jonelle
dancing like all night!!!
😄😆

THOMAS:
Mom wants u 2 come
over 4 dinner

ME:
K. What time?

THOMAS:
6. Can u stay the night?

ME:
Of course! <3
See u @ 6

THOMAS:
YASSSSSS!!!!

ME:
Wait... don't u have practice?

THOMAS:
Starts Monday!
See u soon

I better take a shower if I'm going to have dinner with Thomas and his Mom and spend the night. As I grab some clothes from my room I realize Pearl is truly gone. No pouncing. No little meows. No one to snuggle with me when I sleep... There's an emptiness inside of me, one that's always there, but Pearl helped fill –

A tear rolls down my cheek because I don't want to face the truth. Pearl was never real at all. Another ghost. I smell the faint tangy sweet of Daddy's oranges. Maybe Pearl was his doing.

I check my phone. It's already 5 p.m.!

I go to set it down so I can shower, but it vibrates. It's Victor.

Why is he calling me?

"Hello?" I answer.

"Hey Jinny, are you busy?" he asks.

"Hi Victor. Yeah, kind of. I'm getting ready to go spend the night at Thomas's house," I tell him.

"Your mom lets you spend the night with him?"

"Yeah. So?"

"Oh." He pauses and I can hear him breathing. "I called because I started reading the book for Mysterious Magical Book Club and I wondered if you wanted to talk about it... since neither of us went to the meetings this week, I thought maybe you'd want a partner?" He stumbles over the words repeatedly. Then I hear his mom yelling something at him in the background. "Mom says you can come over tomorrow if you want to do school work." He sounds shy, like inviting me was definitely not the reason he called.

"Ummmm... Yes. But my mom is working in Coconut Creek all weekend. I don't have a ride to your house. Can you pick me up and bring me home?" I ask.

My heart races. I want to stick my hand inside my chest and hold it steady because I know if I don't he's going to hear it through the phone.

"Hold on," he says. "Mom, can you pick up Jinny?" He shouts into another room.

I hear her yell something back.

"Mom says we can pick you up at two and she'll bring you home on her way to yoga. Does that work?"

"Yeah, okay. See you tomorrow at two." I hang up before he can change his mind or say anything else or before my heart explodes.

Today has been the strangest day in my life.

Period.

My phone rings again, and I look, expecting it to be Victor telling me he changed his mind. But instead it's the number I called earlier. The one for Mrs. Lenora Ollena. It's already 5:20. I really don't want to have this conversation with her right at this very moment, but I guess that's what's happening.

"Hello?"

"Jinny? This is Mrs. Ollena. Thank you for calling, I'm sorry I missed your call earlier," she actually sounds happy to hear my voice.

"Oh, hi," I say like some bashful dumb toddler.

"Was there something I could help you with?" she asks. "Or do you just need a sounding board?"

I want to scream. No, I don't need a stupid sounding board. I need a new life. "Yes Ma'am. Well, see, I was at one of my friends' house last night and her dad's a teacher at my school. And see, um… I guess a bunch of private schools have been calling my school and want me to attend. And, uh, well, I scored the highest on the Florida Standard Assessments out of anyone in Florida and now Mr. Bailey told Mrs. Bailey that I'm supposed to go to Harvard, and they think I'm gonna cure cancer. You should probably know my Daddy is dead and my Mama's never around and she hates me going to school anyway, cause she hates that I'm smarter than her." Then I start CRYING!

What is my problem, why am I telling her my entire life?

"Jinny. Jinny… take a deep breath. It sounds like you've been through a lot. I'm very happy you called me. I would love to talk through some of this with you. Can I ask, is your mother home right now?" Her voice is gentle and sincere.

I stop crying and take a deep breath.

"No."

"Is she coming home tonight?"

"No. She's staying in Coconut Creek with some friends and working at a casino for a while," I admit. "But I'm going to Thomas's to spend the night. And tomorrow I'm going to another friend's for our book club." I sniffle and grab some toilet paper to wipe my nose, so I don't drip on my shirt.

"Is Thomas your boyfriend?" she asks.

"Um, no, he's my best friend. He's gay. His mom Silvia is nice and gives me rides," I tell her because I don't want her to get the wrong idea about me and Thomas.

"Okay, Jinny, I'm very happy you have some friends in your life right now to help you this weekend. Would it be okay if I share some of what you've told me tonight with some colleagues of mine and we can come up with a game plan? We have scholarships and resources for students of your academic caliber. Maybe I'll arrange to come visit you next week at school. Who is your favorite teacher? I'll give them a call and coordinate it," she says it the way you would talk to a scared dog in a corner, so you don't get bit.

"Yeah, I guess that would be all right. I, um, you can call Ms. Fleming. Or even Principal Guthrie has been helping me. He got me into advanced calculus II at the college since everything is too easy at my school," I explain.

"Wonderful. I will contact Ms. Fleming and Principal Guthrie and arrange to come visit with you in person this week. Jinny, when do you expect your mother home?" she asks. I know I shouldn't tell her, because she will probably call social services.

But, that nagging voice from Grann Lola, about the Admiral is in my head, so I spill the dirt on Mama. "She didn't say exactly. I can text her and ask if you want. But she just started, so maybe all week. She made $800 in tips yesterday on her first shift. She lost her wallet at her last job, so she's tryin' to make it up because we have rent and stuff."

"No worries. No need to take her away from her job since she is doing so well to earn the necessary funds to care for you," she says.

If I'd been having this conversation with her a week ago, I would have told her to mind her own goddamn business, because that's just what I do. But pushing people away is exhausting. Maybe I need Mrs. Ollena to rescue me. Maybe it's time Jinny Buffett really does get rescued.

"K. I gotta go. I told Thomas I'd be there at six and I'm walking." I grab the overnight bag I packed and start out the front door and lock up the apartment. I hate walking and talking on the phone in the swampy Florida heat, it makes my lungs burn.

Gross. I forgot to shower!

But it's too late now.

"I'll see you soon, Jinny. Have fun with your friends and stay safe," Mrs. Ollena says.

Not even a drop of sarcasm, anger, bitterness, or any other tone I'm used to hearing from Mama. We hang up and I pocket my phone. I'm ready to forget about today and just let Thomas talk and dance and play music for me.

"Stop throwing rocks you little shits!" I yell at the Hernandez boys as I walk past them at the end of the lot. "Someone's gonna call the cops on you. Maybe it will be ME!" I shout and stick my tongue out at them.

"Go eat a cheeseburger, Jinny!" the one with the cross-eyes yells back at me.

His brother flips me off. So, I flip him back off and just keep walking. Turds.

– Chapter Nineteen –
Hot Wings and First Kisses

My night with Thomas is uneventful. We eat like pigs because Sil's home-made chicken enchiladas, and something called Chile rice, is so good. Un-godly amounts fill my shrunken stomach, which is now protesting and pro-truding, as we lie on Thomas's bed. The movie Sleepover is on Netflix, and I fall asleep when the pudgy kid in pajamas shoots lasers out of the mini-van and I dream all night of kids in tents and superhero moms. I wake up, in the middle of the night, feeling anxious, and longing for a mom who loves me and would change her identity to protect me.

The next morning, as soon as the sun begins to glimmer through the curtains, I crawl out of bed. Thomas is still sleeping, and I hate to wake him. So, leave him curled up, grab my bag, and tip-toe downstairs to the kitchen.

"Hey, Sil. I think I'm gonna walk home. I have a study group later, so I should get ready."

"Are you sure honey? You don't want some breakfast?"

"I'm fine." My stomach growls, betraying my answer.

"Is Thomas still sleeping? Oh, that boy can sleep for days!" She smiles and shakes her head. I can see how happy it makes her to talk about Thomas.

I've never seen my Mama look happy talking about me to anyone, except maybe now that I lost weight. I heard her tell the lady at the store how happy she was that she didn't have to buy me Little Debbie Oatmeal Pies anymore. She said it with a big ugly smile. That's the last time we went grocery shopping. It was at least two months ago.

I frown, not at Sil, but she thinks it's at her.

"Oh, I'm sorry. I know if you have to go, I shouldn't beg for you to stay, but I just feel like," she pauses. She wants to say something but doesn't.

I wait.

"Jinny? Does your mother ever come home? Like to feed you or take care of you?"

She tenderly steps over the words and phrases. Like I'm a venomous snake in a basket and she just took off the lid and now she's afraid to look and get snapped in the face. But my cobra hood backs down. I like Sil. I don't wanna hurt her or Thomas.

"Mama works a lot. I can take care of myself," I explain.

"Jinny, hon, I know you can take care of yourself. I wasn't insinuating that you can't. There's just something nice about a mother or a father, for that matter, caring for their child during their formative years," she says.

"If you're worried I'll be a bad influence on Thomas, I'm not like that. I get straight A's and I don't do drugs or drink or anything," I say it nicely, without any sass.

"God no, Jinny, that isn't what I mean at all!" She looks horrified.

"Okay. Well, I better go then. Thanks for dinner last night, it was amazing," I compliment her again. I'm tired of trying to say the right thing to adults. I never seem to say what they want to hear.

"Jinny, wait. Look, if you ever have questions, things you'd ask a mom, things about life… All I was getting at was, you can always ask me." She huffs a bit. There. That wasn't hard now.

So, I hug her because I think that's all she really wants anyway. To feel wanted as a parent, probably like how I want to have a parent. Then I leave and walk home kicking rocks and things along the way.

I regret having told Victor I'd go over today. I'm sick and tired of talking to people.

My apartment is frightfully empty when I turn the key. No Pearl. No Grann Lola or spirit Aunties or dead Daddy.

And no Mama.

Okay, maybe I am happy I'm going over to Victor's house later, because I don't want to be alone. Maybe I should have stayed longer with Thomas to pass the time. I crawl onto my bed and reach under it and pull out the first book I feel. Its cover is worn and loved by a child. I remember the day I found Stargirl half buried in the sand. I sat down and read it while the water lapped against my toes.

There is a knock at the door. I look down, to make sure I'm dressed okay. After I finished reading, I took a long hot shower, and slid on a pair of tight jean shorts and plain white v-neck t-shirt. I use bleach when I do the laundry, so it is bright. I wear my white sandals and have on gold hoop earrings. No make-up though. I can't believe I went overboard like that last week. I'm still embarrassed about it.

"Hi Jinny, you look nice. You ready?" Victor says as soon as I open the door. He didn't even have time to look at me, it must have been a prepared statement. Like he's nervous. We walk down the stairs of the porch and head to his mom's freshly washed black Mercedes. I knew Victor came from money, but not like– my dad drives a Lincoln Navigator XLS Edition, and my mom drives a 700 series Mercedes-Benz money.

"Hi Jinny! I'm Victor's mom Kelsey! Nice to meet you." She's bouncy with perfectly styled honey hair.

"Hello," I whisper.

"Victor talks about you all the time! He said you're the smartest girl in English class." She smiles as she drives.

"Oh?"

"Mom, relax!" Victor hisses.

"Well, what? You do talk about her. I think it's great you kids are working together on a book club. His father and I are always telling him his brain can take him just as far as football, with far less risk of injury."

Victor gasps.

"MOM!" he exclaims. I imagine he's making a face in the back seat. He gave me the front. The luxury of the car is in full effect from this seat.

"Um… Victor is very smart," I assure her. "I'm happy to have a partner like him to work with in class." I am not sure if that's what his mom wants to hear, but it seems to satisfy her. She settles back into her leather seat and puts on her Gucci sunglasses and starts driving. We turn and head the way I like to run to the beach. I stare out the window at the towering palm trees waving in the breeze.

"We just live a few blocks from the beach," she says and blasts the A/C and some kind of mellow jazz music. I didn't know Victor lived so close. She turns down a private driveway that's hidden by a huge Bird of Paradise and clicks a button to a rod iron gate that slides open.

I can hear Victor squirming in his seat like he's nervous for me to see where he lives. Like he's embarrassed for having rich parents, just like I'm embarrassed for having a poor Mama.

"Jinny, have you had lunch? I know it's already two, but I thought I'd make some snacks for your study session, if you're hungry," she says while pulling into the garage of a huge modern aesthetic three-story home made of wood and metal and glass shaped like squares on top of squares.

"I could eat. Thank you." But I'm not sure if I can, realizing the gravity of this moment. I am at Victor Suarez's house! This is insane.

Victor lingers next to me when I get out of the car. He smells nice. He nudges me with his shoulder and smiles.

We walk up three flights of stairs to the top floor where the living room, kitchen, and main floor are located. The entire space is lined with floor to ceiling windows and the view is incredible. You can see the entire Atlantic Ocean.

"WOW, your house is beautiful."

"Thanks, Jinny! Now do you kids want cherry cheesecake bites and hot wings with celery and ranch?" Mrs. Suarez asks from the glowing white marble kitchen where she's already busy puttering around.

"Um, yes please, Ma'am." I say before Victor grabs my hand and pulls me out the glass sliding doors.

I wasn't expecting him to hold my hand. Even if it was just to lead me to the table out on the veranda. My body tingles from his touch.

"Is it okay if we study out here? It's a nice day," he says.

The sunlight makes his dark hair shine.

"Sure," I reply and sit in a chair that probably cost more than all the furniture combined in our dinky apartment.

He pulls his copy of The Raven Boys from his back pocket. We start flipping through it and talking about the story so far.

"I'm at the point when Adam is at Blue's house doing the Tarot reading and pulls the Two of Swords," he tells me and reads the passage.

I smile.

"How do you think he feels?" I ask.

Victor squints up his face to think, and I practically see the wheels turning in his head. I'm actually really surprised he's read so much of the book. I'm impressed.

"I think he's conflicted, because he knows the meaning of the card is true, but he's not sure he believes in the magic."

"I think you're right." I nod.

We talk for a long time about the book, and he has so many interesting ideas on what is going to happen to the characters. It's so easy to talk to Victor. It's like we really are friends. We easily turn the conversation from the book to school and even laugh and joke.

His mom comes out after a while with a platter of food. It smells so good and my stomach growls. I haven't eaten since last night.

"So, Jinny Buffett, has anyone ever commented about how similar your name is to–" she says as I pick up a hot wing and devour it.

"Mmmhmm... Yes Ma'am. All the time," I mumble, but remember I should have manners and I wipe my face and smile. "These are the best hot wings I ever had!"

Victor lets out a little laugh and picks up his third wing in about two minutes.

"Oh, thanks dear. I run the Hollywood Beach Marriott and our chef makes amazing food. I bring a lot home, so I don't have to cook much. The kids aren't fond of my cooking anyway." She laughs at herself, and Victor makes a noise like he's agreeing as he's sucking on a chicken wing.

"My Mama used to work at the Margaritaville and would bring home food too," I say as I help myself to one of the fancy looking cheesecake bites. It bursts with sweet flavor in my mouth and cools the burn from the spicy wings.

"And where does she work now?" She sits down at the table and picks up Victor's book and starts flipping through the pages.

I like her. She's fancy and pretty and Mama would hate her. But, she has kind eyes and is interested in me, and I like her attention. She must be smart too, if she runs an entire hotel like the Marriott and has a husband and family.

"Ooooh this book looks wonderful! Victor, I want to read it when you're done." She puts it back down.

"Uh, she's working at a casino in Coconut Creek now. I think we are moving there," I say softly. Victor looks at me and furrows his brow.

"What? You're moving? No, Jinny, you can't move. I mean, who will I study with? Who will help me in Ms. Fleming's class?" He sounds upset.

"Um. I don't know. I can't make Mama do anything. She might hate it anyway and not keep the job. She's been there all weekend working," I say.

"If she needs a waitress job or housekeeping, I could set up with an interview at my hotel," Mrs. Suarez says rather flippantly.

It's a horrible idea.

I imagine the look on Mama's face if I told her and shiver.

But to be polite I say, "I'll let her know. She should be home in a few days," I immediately regret saying that.

"Are you home alone Jinny?" Mrs. Suarez asks.

"It's okay. I'm old enough. Victor, should we get back to the book?" I try to change the subject.

"Yes, you are old enough for after school, or evenings, but not for long periods of time," she says, going into full parent mode.

I take the book and hold it up to hide my face, then I put it down. Crap. This is why coming here was a bad idea. I've said too much.

"Can I use the bathroom?" I stand up and start walking inside.

"Let me show you," Victor gets up and walks me down the hall.

"Sorry about my mom. She, well, I don't have a lot of girls over. Actually, you're the first one. So, she just doesn't know how to act," he explains it away.

He looks shy and vulnerable all of a sudden as we stand in the doorframe of his very luxurious and expensively decorated guest bathroom. He stands so close to me I can smell the spray he put on for the occasion. I hope I smell okay.

"Oh."

I slowly back into the bathroom and shut the door. I wait a few minutes, so he can't hear me pee. I look at my cell phone, it's already 3:15. He said his mom would take me home at four. I can deal with forty-five more minutes. After I wash my hands and quietly open the bathroom door, I look right and left to see if Victor is lingering. But he's gone back upstairs.

I admire the decor in the hallway and wander in the wrong direction. At the end of the hallway is a large office overlooking the gardens on the opposite side from the ocean. There are models of ships and boats on shelves and anchors and knots of rope and flags mounted to the wall. It looks like a room for the navy or a boat club. Something catches my eye, a diploma that says Admiral Farragut Academy.

No. Way.

"Jinny, whatcha doing?" Victor asks. I jump a foot when I hear his voice.

"Sorry, I guess I went the wrong way."

"This is my dad's office. He was in the Navy. Now he is a private contractor or something," he tells me. "He loves boats. We have a sailboat that we go out on. You should come with us sometime. Have you ever gone sailing?" The words "gone sailing" have never been in my vocabulary, but for some reason they strike a chord. Suddenly all I want in the world is to go sailing with Victor Suarez.

"I'd like that," I say softly. Victor puts his hand on my back, gently, more gently than some stupid teenage boy should know how to do, and turns me around to leave his dad's office.

"That diploma, for the Admiral Farragut Academy, did your dad go to school there?" I ask. I'm being so nosey!

"Yeah, why?" he asks as we walk back outside. His mom has vacated the veranda. Probably off to put on her yoga pants.

"I met the counselor from there. She's real nice. She's coming to see me this week at school," I tell him. I don't know why I tell him. It's none of his business really.

"My parents would LOVE for me to go to school there. You know they have sailing clubs and STEM programs. Almost all the students from Farragut get into Ivy League schools. But it's in St. Petersburg, and you have to live there, away from home and your friends and your life and they don't have real football, just intramural teams."

I can tell it's a point of contention for Victor and his parents.

"Sorry, I don't mean to be the girl who kicked the hornet's nest," I say to him.

He brushes his shoulder, like some invisible hornet is on him. He doesn't get the Stieg Larsson reference, but most kids, most adults, wouldn't. Why is my brain so full of stupid shit?

"You want to see my room?" he asks.

"Okay." We go back inside, and I follow him down to the second level of the house. He leads me to his room. It's what I imagine it will look like. Furniture from Crate & Barrel, expensive sports memorabilia on the walls. But I spot something on the ledge of his oak bookshelf. It's a stone carving of a witch owl. No one else would probably know what it is, but I do.

"Do you believe in this stuff?" I ask and pick up the little figure. It's soft and smooth in my hand.

"What? Owls?" He laughs. "Uh, yeah Jinny, owls are real."

"No goof. This isn't just an owl. It's a witch owl. They are part of the folklore in the Everglades. You know, the mysterious magical stuff. It was what I originally wanted my club to be about."

"Wait, you wanted the book club to be about owls?"

He's cute when he's confused.

"Not exactly. Witch owls are these creatures that are rumored to live in the Everglades– they look like regular people during the day and turn into giant flying owls at night," I explain.

"How do you know that?" He asks.

"I read a lot. And I'm fascinated by otherworldly things, like spirits and ghosts and mythical creatures." I'm embarrassed. He's gonna think I'm such a dork. But instead, he smiles at me.

"My mom's all in-tune to spiritualization and aligning yourself to get what you want in life, using chakra beads, meditation, and yoga to visualize the spirit self. My dad says it's a bunch of nonsense, but sometimes I see him doing meditation and yoga on the deck in the morning," he admits. "She got that at the street fair they have on Ocean Drive every fall. I guess I thought it was just an owl. But it does kind of look ominous doesn't it?"

"Hoo, hoo," I tease and wave the little owl in front of him.

He smiles and steps closer to me. The space between us has evaporated. My senses are suddenly heightened. When did this moment become more than just book club?

"There's a lot more to you than I thought," I say softly. My heart beats faster.

"There's a lot more to you, too." He takes another step closer.

Why does my skin feel tight?

And my throat, is it closing up?

Is that sweat rolling down my back!

I want what he's about to do, more than I can imagine so I say a quick prayer to any swamp spirit who's listening. Let me do this right! Then Victor leans in and puts his arm around me.

"Can I kiss you?" He is inches from my face.

Oh my god. I've never kissed a boy before.

"Yes."

As his lips touch mine I wonder how many girls Victor has kissed and why would he pick me to kiss when any one of those dumb-ass cheerleaders would be slobbering to get their hands on him.

It happens so fast. It's warm and soft and not at all what I expected, and I feel tingly in places I didn't know existed. I want more. So, I lean forward and kiss him again. My eyes are squeezed tight as he pulls me closer into his body. The heat between us is like a sticky humid day. If I could stand here in his arms forever, I just might. We keep kissing, and it changes from soft and gentle to a more urgent and desperate kind of entanglement. He holds me tighter, our bodies pressed completely together.

Just as a moan is about to escape my lips, "VICTOR! JINNY! Time to go!" his mom shouts from upstairs.

We both jump!

I'm embarrassed. I hope he doesn't see me blushing.

"I guess this is goodbye," I say quickly.

UGH… I feel so corny and happy at the same time.

"Bye, Jinny. Thanks for coming over," he says as I walk out of his room.

Mrs. Suarez walks down the stairs towards the garage. Thank god she didn't come into his room and catch us making out! I'm in a daze as we load into her car, and she talks about yoga and how the class she's taking has helped her reach her spirit-self. She even offers to take me to a class sometime if I want. I wonder if she knows I just kissed her son? I wonder if she thinks her son could like a trashy girl like me? I feel sick. I don't belong in their world. Mansions, money, Mercedes.

"Jinny, I hope you come over to study with Victor again soon. Here is my card." She hands me a business card as I'm getting out of the car. "Tell your mom to call me if she'd like an interview."

"Thanks for the ride Mrs. Suarez."

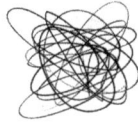

– Chapter Twenty –
The truth is a hard pill!

Monday. Back to real life after a weekend of sleep overs and first kisses. I'm okay with it being a slow day. Jonelle doesn't come to school; she texts that she is watching her little brother who is home sick. Ang is tired and practically sleeps through lunch. Thomas has his first day at the Miami Fine Arts Academy, so I have to walk home alone.

I'm not even a block from school and I'm already lonely.

I miss Thomas shoving his Airpod in my ear and giving me my own private song and dance performance while we walk, talk, and laugh. If you'd have asked me last year if I could have made a bestie like Thomas and that I could miss him so bad it hurts, I'd have told you how crazy stupid you were. But here I am, shuffling down the block to my apartment, feeling emotional for all new reasons.

Then I see Mama's ancient BMW parked in the lot with moving boxes in the back seat. And now I'm emotional for all the same old reasons.

"Are we moving?" I demand as soon as I open up the door to our apartment.

"Heyo, Jinny! My favorite southern belle!" It's Marco. He's dismantling the table in the kitchen and has tools spread out. There are boxes and bubble wrap strewn across the living room.

"Where's Mama?"

"She took my truck up to grab some beers and smokes and to terminate your lease at the main office," he says as he puts down the allen wrench and wipes the sweat off his dark brow. It is unusually hot, so I go to turn the temp down on the A/C and see it's shut off.

"Why's the air off?"

"Your Mama said she don't wanna pay the bill no more," he chuckles. "She's a stubborn, funny woman, ain't she? Said now that she's startin' a new life for you in Coconut Creek, no sense spending money or time here in Hollywood. I'm sure gonna miss you girls. I know it's only like forty-five minutes away, but it won't be the same." He smiles and frowns at the same time, his crooked teeth have bits of chewing tobacco in them.

"I can't believe she made this decision without askin' me or at least talkin' to me about it! I don't want to move. I don't want to go to Coconut Creek! This is the dumbest thing she's ever done." But I remember all the other dumb shit Mama's done; this is typical Crystal Buffett behavior.

"Aw now girl, don't be mad at your pretty Mama. She tryin'. Ain't been easy on her since your Daddy died. God rest his soul. Plus, the kind a woman she is, you know the kinda life she had before you come along… She does her best." He tries to persuade me to believe, but I'm the one who's been living with her.

I know exactly what kind of woman she is.

"Yeah right." I storm past the boxes and into my room. At least she hasn't touched my things. She flung a pile of boxes and tape in on the floor, but that's it. If she expects me to pack up my life tonight, she has another thing coming.

Neither Principal Guthrie nor Ms. Fleming mentioned if they heard from Lenora Ollena at the Admiral Farragut Academy today. I don't know if she can do anything to help me or not. I don't know if anything matters anymore. Because, with just a snap of the fingers, I'm gone.

No friends. No Victor. No Mysterious Magical Book Club.

Mama ruins everything.

I hate her.

I must've fallen asleep from the heat in my room. I wake up sweaty to the smell of cigarette smoke and music and laughing. I hear Mama's voice and Marco and Grann Ruth and Sabrina. Yuck. Of course, Mama invited them up. She doesn't care now that we are moving. They are out there partying in the middle of the living room with the doors and windows wide open.

I wish the cops would show up now. Maybe I should call Officer Riddley myself. I open the top drawer in my dresser. I've been collecting a lot of names and numbers lately; there's a mess of business cards and the paper note from Auntie Nina during the swamp night.

"Look at all these cards and numbers and addresses," I say out loud to Pearl before I remember she magically disappeared with Grann Lola and my Aunties.

I miss my ghost kitten.

Thumbing through the names on the cards of the people who want to help me makes me uncomfortable. They say they want to see me succeed, but they don't really know me. They can't really care about me, can they?

Mama's laughter floats through the door, the one she only has when she's been drinking beer with Marco or smoking pot with Grann Ruth. It's unpredictable and wild and it frightens me. It's minutes away from making bad decisions with horrible consequences. It's a laugh filled with regret and pride. It's a laugh that reminds me of where I came from and how rising above my pathetic life is a joke. I am bound to Mama and her choices. I'm a minor. This is my life.

I flinch.

I'll never get to go sailing with Victor.

I'll never have another sleep over with Thomas.

I'll never get to go to Harvard.

I'll never be more than the trashy daughter of a strung-out prostitute.

"JINNY! Come out and party, I mean pack," Sabrina shouts. She's loaded, I can tell. Mama laughs again. Grann Ruth coughs.

I'm ashamed for thinking my life had hope. It's my own fault, if I had just kept to myself like I used to instead of trying to make friends. My heart hurts and my throat feels tight.

Why do I care? I never used to care. I never let myself care. I just went about life like a feather floating on a hot Florida breeze. I close my eyes, thinking about Ang, Jonelle, Thomas, Victor, Ms. Fleming… The burn in my eyes is real.

"Stop it, Jinny, just stop," I say to myself.

I pick up one of the boxes and put it together. Then I turn up the music on my phone and try not to cry while I go through my things. I open my closet and pull out my shoe box and look at the worn picture of my Daddy, Grann, and Aunties. I rub my thumb over their faces and try to imagine a life with them.

I want to see them again, to ask them to come and take me away. So instead of packing, I curl back up on my bed and pull my hot sweaty blanket over my head and try to drown out the sounds from the living room with my own sniffles and sobs in my pillow until I fall back asleep, praying I'll have another mysterious magical dream about the swamps. Maybe my Aunties will take me to the Everglades like they did with Pearl.

I'll wake up tomorrow far, far away from here.

***

The next morning I open my eyes. It's still dark outside. For a split second, I think I'm in the Everglades, the shadows look like trees, and I smell the air; hoping for the sweet stink of swamp mud. I strain my ears, listening for screech owls and crickets.

But all I smell is stale pot and all I hear is someone snoring. I'm in my room. I didn't dream about Daddy's family, and I wasn't visited by any spirits or ghosts. My heart sinks. I tip-toe out of my room and peer around, looking at the damage. Marco is passed out on the floor snoring like a chainsaw. Mama's phone and keys are on the kitchen counter next to a full ashtray and a weed pipe. She must be in her bedroom.

I carefully go to the bathroom to brush my teeth and hair and change into clean clothes. The only clothes are the shorts and shirt I wore to Victors on Sunday. I don't care, I put them on. Then I walk back out through the apartment, navigating between the piles of shit and boxes. We barely have anything in our apartment, I don't know where all this stuff even came from. I'm emotionally drained and for a second I think I should just go back to bed. But, this is hardly where I want to spend the day.

School is the only option; too bad classes don't start for another couple of hours.

I text Thomas to see if he's up. Maybe he will walk with me.

ME:
I'm walking to school now.
R u ready?

THOMAS:
Sorry babes, just woke up

ME:
K well i'm goin now w/out u

THOMAS:
ayok?

ME:
Nah... tell u later

I don't even get my school bag. Marco is stirring and if I go back to my room, I might wake him. Although I'd like to grab the book I'm reading, When Things Fall Apart, by Pema Chödrön. Seems fitting. I found it on a bench by the beach a few weeks ago.

As tempting as it is to turn around and grab my stuff, I just walk out of the apartment and toward school, and without hesitation I run. The morning dew clings for dear life on the grasses of neatly trimmed lawns at perfect houses that line the road near the school. Everywhere I look there are happy, stupid people getting in their happy, stupid cars going to their happy, stupid jobs. Not packing up their lives to move away.

When I reach the school, there aren't many cars in the parking lot, but I spot the one I'm looking for. Ms. Fleming. She's so young and ambitious, I knew she'd be here early, getting ready to shape and mold young minds like mine.

ME:
Ms. Fleming, I'm at school already. Can I come see you?

MS. FLEMING:
Jinny, are you safe?

Am I safe? That's a loaded question. Of course, I'm not safe. Far from it. But, I don't want to say that on a text.

ME:
I dunno....

MS. FLEMING:
Meet me at the front, I'll let you in the building.

I walk up to the front door of the school and realize how sweaty my pits are from running to school. I should have put on deodorant. I bet Pema Chödrön doesn't wear deodorant. I smile; I'll wear my stench like a coat of armor to protect the softness of my heart.

"Why are you smiling?" Ms. Fleming asks when she opens the door.

"I'm just thinking about a Buddhist nun."

She doesn't even bat an eye at that statement and ushers me into the building and locks the door again. "The janitor will unlock it for everyone else in a while. I've made that mistake before, forgetting to lock it back up when I get here early, had my head bit off," she explains and then takes a long thoughtful drink from her Starbucks.

"Oh." I just stand there. Does she expect me to spill my guts right here?

"Come on, let's go sit in the teacher's lounge, there's a nice sitting area." She turns and walks towards the office.

I follow her.

An itchy feeling is rising up when I realize this might be the last time I walk through these halls. Mama might wake up and come drag my ass outta here to go home and help her finish packing. A noise bubbles up from my throat, a cross between a cry and swamp bullfrog.

"Jinny?" Ms. Fleming looks at me when she flips the lights on in the teacher's lounge. "You look green. Sit." She points at the couch, then goes to the fridge and retrieves a bottle of iced tea and hands it to me.

"Thanks," I say and take a few drinks to quiet down my insides.

She pulls a chair over and sits in front of me. "Now, tell me what the heck is going on!" It's an order, a demand. Any other day I might say something snarky, but I'm tired.

"Mama's packin' us up and we're moving!" I sob.

Ms. Fleming jumps up from her chair and crowds onto the couch next to me and wraps her arms around me. She hugs me like I've never been hugged before. She smells clean and beautiful, like new books in a library. It makes me cry harder and my whole body shakes.

Other teachers start coming in to put their lunches in the fridge and get coffee or whatever teachers do before teaching. Ms. Fleming hisses at them and gets up. She locks the door, from the inside with a loud click.

"Can you do that?" I sniffle.

"I just did," she says. "Jinny, can you start from the beginning?"

So, I do. I start at the beginning. Like the real beginning...

"Mama is a prostitute. She pretends she's not. She usually works as a cocktail waitress— but that's just so she can meet wealthy vacationers looking for a good time."

Ms. Fleming's face remains still.

"She leaves me home alone most of the time. She used to fill up the apartment with junk food and turn on movies for me and then she'd leave all night. That's why everyone called me Jinny Cheeseburger, I was pretty overweight. Food was my comfort."

She nods and strokes my arm.

"I dunno. I mean, I don't know what changed, why suddenly I can't just let this be my life anymore. I guess when you came and told me I scored the highest FSA's in the state it got me thinking. It made me believe that maybe I could be more." I sniffle and reach for a tissue.

I tell her about Mama's latest trip to the Keys and her coming home with a beat-up face and her talking to herself when no one's there and leaving me home alone for days and weeks at a time and not buying food anymore. I tell her about Officer Riddley and Mrs. Lenora Ollena and about Ang's mom.

"I mean, do you think I should go to Yale? Do you think I'm going to cure cancer?" I ask. But I don't wait for her to answer. Instead, I tell her about going to Victor's house and his mom and sailing on boats and everything else I can think of, even the kiss.

I don't know what time it is when I'm done.

A thousand pound weight feels lifted from my chest.

I know I've already been spilling my guts to Thomas and Ang and even Mrs. Ollena.

But, for some reason, telling Ms. Fleming all my drama truly solidifies what I'm going through. It's not just me, complaining and being a whiner. I'm officially waving a white flag and telling someone who can help me. Because if I don't tell her now, then I have to swallow this pill and just take what life is dishing out. I know what's going on in my life is not okay.

I'm smart right? Smartest girl in the entire State of Florida.

But sometimes I feel so stupid.

Useless.

A piece of trash.

There is a knock on the door. Principal Guthrie's face is in the window.

"Hold on for a few minutes, Jinny," Ms. Fleming says and gets up to unlock the door.

She walks out and closes it. I check my phone, it's already 8:45! School started a long time ago. I really hope Ms. Fleming doesn't get in trouble. I close my eyes and lie down on the couch. I really shouldn't be tired, since I slept most of yesterday after school and last night, but I'm mentally drained and want to curl up again on my bed in my apartment and sleep. All I want to do is sleep. So, that's what I do.

"Jinny." Someone is lightly shaking my shoulder.

I crack open my eyes.

"Grann Lola?" I ask.

My view comes into focus, and I sit up.

It's the police.

I'm busted. I knew it! Ms. Fleming is in trouble for locking out the other teachers and she's blamed it on me and now they've called the cops because I'm loitering in the teacher's lounge. Mind is twitching with all the ways I'm in trouble.

"Please don't arrest Ms. Fleming," I say. "It's my fault, I came to school early, I practically forced her to let me in the building early and it's my fault none a them teachers could get in here with their lunches and shit.

I mean stuff. I mean, I was crying, and Ms. Fleming was just being nice. I didn't mean to get anyone in trouble–" but before I can keep bubbling up words in a ridiculous frenzy, the lady officer holds her hand up.

"Jinny, you are not in trouble. My name is Officer Garcia. I think you might know my partner, Officer Riddley," she says.

I nod.

"I'm here to help you. Ms. Fleming and Principal Guthrie called me in to assess your situation at home. They thought this might be a safe space and you'd be able to help me understand what's been going on. Would you be okay answering a few questions?"

I look her up and down. Her hair is pulled back into a severe bun. But I see she has caramel highlights tucked into it. She has just the right amount of make-up on. I sniff the air, she smells nice too, clean and fresh.

"I don't know what you wanna know..." I pull my legs up to my chest and wrap my arms around them and set my chin on my knees.

Officer Garcia sits down on the chair Ms. Fleming was using.

"My job, in this situation, is to determine if a crime is being committed and report it to the correct channels so we can protect you. Jinny, you are a minor. But I've heard from the staff here just how special and very smart you are. I'm sure you understand the living situation you are in is unhealthy at best and extremely dangerous at worst."

She looks genuinely concerned. God I hate when adults think they know my life. But, then she says, "Jinny, can I tell you a story?"

I want to say, I don't know, can you?

But I'm weak.

"There was a girl about your age named Vicki. She lived over in Pinecrest trailers. She was in a very similar situation to yours... meaning, Vicki's Mama was behaving erratically and making bad decisions about drugs, men, and money. Putting Vicki at risk with every bad choice she made."

Hmmm. This sounds familiar.

"Unfortunately, Vicki didn't feel safe enough to tell anyone, because she was afraid they'd call her a snitch. Well, one day, some men came to the trailer, looking for her Mama. But she wasn't home. So those men hurt Vicki, they hurt her real bad, Jinny. They stole something from her that can never be given back. At that point, Vicki was forced to call the police for help." A tear slides out of Officer Garcia's eye.

"Is Vicki okay?" I ask.

I blink hard and fast. I have tears in my eyes too.

"Yes, the police and social services helped Vicki. They got her Mama in rehab and placed Vicki in a temporary foster home with some people who loved her very much and helped her see there was more to life than what she was living," she explains.

I feel happy for Vicki, this mysterious girl, even if it was only a story. She smiles and wipes her eyes.

"I know what you're tryin' to do. Make me believe it will all be okay using some make-believe girl's story about overcoming tragedy. It's nice and all," I say softly. "But, you don't know anything about me."

"Hi Jinny, my name is Vicki Garcia." Officer Garcia puts out her hand to shake mine. "I am the girl from the story. It was NOT something I just made up. I was you; I am you! My temporary foster parents became my forever parents when my Mama realized she couldn't take care of me and herself. My foster parents are amazing people. They're both sheriffs in the Broward County Sheriff's Department and I grew up safe and I went into law enforcement to find and protect girls like me. Like you." She stands up and I curl back up into a ball.

"Sorry," I mumble.

"You have nothing to be sorry for Jinny. You have done nothing wrong. You are a young woman in an unfortunate situation. I want to help you, before something happens, and you end up like…" she pauses. I think she's afraid of saying too much. Like lookin at me makes her feel all those old feelings of what happened to her.

"I can't snitch on Mama to the police," I say. Sure, I can tell my friends and Ms. Fleming, but the police? I shake with fear imagining the rage in Mama's eyes.

"Jinny," Officer Garcia says my name softly.

"You don't know her! She'll scream and cry and break things. She'll grab me and shake me and tell me how stupid I am. She'll throw all my books away! She'll tell me I betrayed her."

I break out in a cold sweat picturing Mama as the police take her away in handcuffs. Then some social worker will come take me to foster care. I won't get nice parents like Vicki. I'll get stuck in some shitty home full of lice and have to babysit ten brats.

I shake my head vigorously. "No. I won't do it." I fold my arms over my chest.

"If your Mama moves you to Coconut Creek, you'll be a long way from the people here who care about you and are ready to help you." Officer Garcia lets out a long breath. "Do you know if she has housing yet? Or will you be staying with her friends? Has she enrolled you in school there? Does this sudden move feel safe and normal to you? Think logically Jinny." She looks me hard in the eye.

I see something deep and under the surface glimmering back at me, it's pain and pride and a lotta mixed up shit, but maybe those are my own emotions reflecting back at me. I hate that I actually like this cop. I think she kinda gets me, like more than any other adult could.

Before I can say anything else, she gets a call on her radio that's attached to her shoulder. She mumbles something into it, cop code, and goes over to the door.

"I'll be right back," she says and walks out of the room.

"JINNY! I'm scared for you and your damaged heart." It's Grann Lola. She's standing there, appearing like magic, right out of thin air. No smoke, no swamp. Just Grann Lola in the flesh.

"Grann! What are you doin' here?" I look around to see if any of my other relatives from the Everglades are gonna magically appear.

"Granddaughter, you are in big stinkin' trouble! I came to warn you. You gotta run. Your Mama's soul is possessed by a nasty dark demon. You gotta get outta here before it's too late. Ask that doe eyed teacher. She'll take ya girl. Tell her to take you far, far away."

"But I can't leave, I'd be a runaway!"

"You should run, far, far away." Grann Lola shakes her head.

I run to her, I want to hug her and never let go. "Grann, I'm scared!" I cry and wrap my arms around her, but it's like holding a squishee pillow that I can't quite grip onto, and her spirit slides through my arms.

"I love you Jinny." She disappears.

The door opens and I'm standing with empty arms.

Just like my heart.

"Jinny, Officer Garcia had to go to an emergency call. I wanted to come ask if you want to go to class or lunch? What do YOU want to do?" Ms. Fleming smiles.

"What I want to do is curl up and go to sleep under a rock, or in the Catskills for a long time."

Ms. Fleming smiles. "I see you haven't lost your touch. Was that a quote from Rip Van Winkle? Jinny, you are such an interesting girl," she says and puts her arm around me.

"My brain is filled with a lot of nonsense." I shrug. "I guess I am kind of hungry."

"Then let's go eat. I took the rest of the day off. Would you like to go to my house and have lunch? I'm sure Principal Guthrie wouldn't mind," she says.

"Um, is that allowed? Like, you aren't my parent or guardian." I step aside, afraid Mama is going to leap out from around the corner with fangs, like in a horror movie. Grann Lola just told me that Mama has a demon in her. The hair on the back of my neck stands up.

"You're right. How about we grab something from the cafeteria and head to my classroom," she suggests.

That sounds nice and the fear clenching my insides subsides and I manage a half smile. That is, until Principal Guthrie comes racing in out of breath, panic stricken.

"We have a bit of a situation. Jinny, can you come to the front office please? Your mother is here to pick you up," he says.

Uh oh. Mama HATES coming to school. She makes a habit of staying far, far away...

This is not gonna be pretty.

I think I'm gonna be sick.

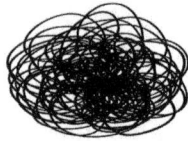

– Chapter Twenty-One –
It's me, Daddy, it's Jinny...

I can hear her screaming at Miss Charmaine before I'm even there.

"I don't give a shit Charmaine; I know SOMEONE here called the cops on me. Go eat another goddamn donut or pumpkin pie or whatever it is you stuff your fat-fucking-face with at night," Mama's voice is a fist throwing punches. Been a long time since this Mama's been out in public.

She's unhinged. Desperate.

Someone called the cops.

Ms. Fleming.

Principal Guthrie.

Or anyone really.

"Mama, what are you doin'?" I ask, using my quiet voice.

"There you are. Jesus. How long does it take to get one scrawny ass kid! I've been here for like twenty minutes!" she exclaims. Her bleached hair is wild. She hasn't showered and she smells like smoke and her make-ups not on point like it usually is. The corner of her mouth looks bloody, and I try not to make a face.

"Are you okay?" I ask her softly.

"No, I'm not OK! You didn't wake me before you left for school. I wanted you to stay home and finish packing your room today. Then, the cops showed up! Askin' about stuff they shouldn't know about. I nearly got myself arrested. Now get that ass over here– we are leaving!" She grabs my arm and pulls me out of the office, digging into my skin with her acrylics, and I whimper.

"Ms. Buffett, um, Crystal," Ms. Fleming runs after us as Mama drags me outta the school.

"What?" Mama snaps. Her grip tightens, she's here, to exert control over me.

"God, Mama, you're hurting me. Get off." I push her hand away.

She shoots me a nasty glare. I start crying, because I'm already a mess, and after Grann Lola's warning, all I see now is the darkness in Mama's eyes. Her soul is being tormented by a demon.

My heart squeezes and I gasp.

I shouldn't, but I feel bad for Mama, because something is really wrong with her.

"I'd be happy to bring Jinny home later, if she could just finish school today." Ms. Fleming is grasping at straws.

"Ms. Fleming, I think Mama needs me. I need to go home and take care of her. I'll talk to you another day. Thanks for everything," I say and wave her off.

Mama walks away without another word.

Silent Mama is dangerous.

Her BMW is parked in the emergency lane. I can feel the tension building in the silence and watch in horror as her shoulders square off. She's trying to decide if she's gonna lay into me here or wait until we get home.

I clench my bladder, so I don't pee my pants.

My breathing quickens.

Then she grabs my face and squeezes it as hard as she can and puts her nose to my nose, her breath is foul like rotting foliage. "Are you fucking kidding me?" She hisses. "I don't need you takin' care of me. I'M the parent. NOT you."

"I'm sorry, Mama." I try to pull my face from her grip.

"Look at me when I'm talking you fucking little shit. Do you think I enjoy coming up here and freaking out?" She says through gritted teeth.

"No Ma'am."

"Don't give me that Ma'am shit. I know your game, Jinny. All perfect and innocent. Your perfect fucking test scores. You're so goddamn smart aren't you, Jinny?"

It takes every ounce of control I have not to start sobbing. I hold my chin up.

"Get your sorry ass in the car."

There's a strong musky male scent.

It's recent.

Once we are inside the car, Mama seems to relax momentarily. "Look, I'm sorry. I'm stressed out. They want me to go work a double tonight at the casino for some exclusive high roller event, they've got men flying in from Tokyo, I could make some serious cash if I play it right. I've got to get my highlights redone and I need a new set of nails." Her voice is shaky. "I shouldn't have had a party last night. Pot and beer always put me in a spiral.

I need you to finish packing. Tomorrow a truck is coming to take everything to storage." She pulls out a cigarette and we aren't even off school property.

"Storage? Wait, I thought we were movin' to a new apartment in Coconut Creek." I'm shocked.

"No, look now, I never said we were moving to a new apartment. We are going to stay in a house with some friends of mine. I owe them some money, an old debt. Nothing you have to worry about. But livin' with them lets me pay the money I would have spent on rent. I'll pay it off faster, see?" she tries to explain her logic. Her voice shifts to the one she uses on people to buy more drinks or add desert to their order. It's charming and pathetic all wrapped up in one.

I feel used and dirty.

"What are you talkin' about?" I yell. "Who do you owe money to? How much? How long do we have to stay with them?" I'm freaking out.

"Not that it's any of your business, but about six month's worth of rent. Listen, before you say any snarky shit to me. I figure, if I pull doubles and you do some baby sitting or that tutoring shit, maybe we can pay it off in half that time and be outta there by Christmas," she explains.

"NO WAY, I am not moving in with strangers!"

She peels out of the school parking lot and is driving like a maniac, passing cars and honking. "Slow down! Jesus Mama, you're gonna kill us!"

She laughs.

"Why don't you just sell the BMW... or take out a loan... or ask Marco or Grann Lola or someone for help! Why would we move in with people who think they own you. That seems really unsafe Mama!" I am so frantic at this point. "And what am I supposed to do when you're workin' overnights and doubles?"

All I keep thinking about is Officer Garcia's story about Vicki.

Vicki was hurt. For her mother's crimes.

I'm Vicki. I'm about to be used as collateral for Mama's debts.

I'm about to be used.

Abused.

She turns down our road without stopping at the stop sign and speeds up, thirty... forty... fifty... sixty... The bile in my stomach works up my throat and I throw-up before I can even stop myself. It's hot and green and stings my nose and eyes. Mama screams and swerves and smacks her BMW right into oncoming traffic.

It's like slow motion, being jerked forward and slamming into air-bags. We lift up as the car goes airborne. The contents of Mama's purse float around– lipstick, cigarettes, loose change.

The sound of breaking glass and crunching metal and fiberglass assaults my ears.

My long dirty hair twists around my face when the car turns on its side and for some reason I can't feel the impact.

What I feel most is the hot, damp Florida air as it floods inside the car and cocoons me through smashed windows.

I shake my head and see stars and little sprinkles of glass cascade over my body.

"Mama?" I croak out the word like a question. Blood oozes from a big gash on her face and she isn't moving.

I think she might be dead.

Everything hurts all at once and I'm really confused. I can't tell if I'm hanging upside down or laying on my side. Was I wearing a seatbelt?

I'm vaguely aware of my door being wrenched open and the bright sunlight hitting my face.

There's a man standing there. A halo of light around him. It must be an angel or a ghost.

"Holy shit," he says.

I try to smile when I realize it might be my Daddy's ghost, but something is wrong with my lips, and they don't want to curl up into a smile.

The rich iron taste of blood fills my mouth.

"Daddy, am I gonna die?" I manage to slur out the words through my broken face. He moves fast and gets me out of the car in one fell swoop and carries me out of the wreckage and to the side of the road and lays me down. I hear sirens and people screaming. I close my eyes and wait to cross over.

"You've been in a car accident. Please, don't fall asleep. You have a head injury. An ambulance will be here soon. Stay with me," the man who is, or isn't, my dead Daddy holds my hand. I wonder if Grann Lola sent him here to help me. I try to open my eyes, but they feel so heavy, like they are glued to my face. What I can see, through lidded slits, is a haze of smoke and dust. Is this what heaven is like?

My face and body throb with pain. Informing me I'm probably not in heaven.

"Come on girl, don't sleep. Can you tell me your name?" the man asks. A strong smell of oranges mixes with the metal tang and oil fumes from the wreckage.

My heart calms.

"It's me, Daddy, it's Jinny…"

Then darkness.

***

"Jinny, you are a very lucky girl," says a female voice.

I open my eyes and look carefully. Where the hell am I? This isn't the afterlife! This is a hospital bed. I'm sore everywhere and I've got needles in my arm and something in my nose. My head is swimming with murky visions. Officer Garcia. Grann Lola. Mama... oh God! Mama. The car wreck. Someone pushes back a curtain, the metal rings making a screeching noise as they slide around.

"Uh...where's Mama?" My mouth feels sandy and salty, like after I've been looking for seashells all day.

"She's in surgery, took a pretty hard hit to her head and has a deep wound on her face," the lady says while inspecting x-rays on a computer screen.

White coat. Must be a doctor.

"My name is Dr. Rosemary Leveau. I'm a general surgeon and I work in the ER here at Memorial Regional Hospital. You were in a car accident, Jinny. Do you remember what happened?" She scrolls through notes on her computer.

"No," I answer. "I can't–"

"JINNY!" screams a familiar voice. It's Thomas. Sil is right behind him. And then there's Jonelle and Ang and Ms. Fleming. They all come rushing into the room.

"Whoa, Jinny, looks like Team Buffett has arrived. Only for a few minutes okay guys? She's been through a lot and needs to rest," Dr. Leveau says and walks out of the room.

"I was so scared when I heard!" Ang says and rushes up and puts her head on my lap.

"Give our girl some space, Ang," laughs Jonelle. "You look like shit Jinny." She says it like it is.

I love the honesty. But I see the glaze in her eyes, she's been crying.

"I thought you were dead," Thomas barely whispers. Then he takes his phone and holds it up to my face.

I squint my eyes and try to figure out what the mangled mess on his screen is. Then it hits me. That's the BMW. That's Mama's car! Holy crap, how did I survive?

"Oh sweetheart! They say most accidents happen within a mile from your home. How true. Thank God you're alive!" Sil says all motherly.

Ms. Fleming is standing quietly in the corner.

Waiting for her turn.

I reach for a cup that has water and a straw, but Ang grabs it up and holds it to my mouth. I sip the water to clear the sandy gritty feeling from my mouth. But I can't really swish it around, even my teeth hurt.

I try to remember what happened. We left the school and Mama was angry and speeding and driving like a maniac.

Oh.

The moving. The storage unit.

The debt and me puking.

I did this.

I caused the wreck.

"Okay, we should give Jinny some space and time to rest, let's go to the cafeteria. I'll buy everyone a cookie. Ms. Fleming, can you stay with her until the doctor comes back. Meet us when you're ready?" Sil ushers my friends out. They say bye and pile out of the room.

"Jinny, I am so sorry. I cannot believe this happened. I feel partially responsible, if, if–" Then Ms. Fleming starts crying.

"It's not your fault. It's my fault. I threw up and she crashed. Something's wrong with her, Ms. Fleming. She's not herself," I try to explain. But, I'm having trouble putting the thoughts in the right order and moving my lips to match.

"Jinny, how much have they told you?" Ms. Fleming asks.

"Nothing. I woke up just before you came in."

"You should be dead. When your mom swerved, she turned so hard, your side of the car took the full impact of the crash, before flipping and landing upside down. A guardian angel was with you today." She pulls up a chair and sits by my bed. She heaves a deep breath.

My own breathing is shallow and labored.

Everything hurts.

"It was my Daddy. He opened the door and pulled me out of the wreckage and kept me awake until the ambulance came. He took care of me." I close my eyes and I can see him again, the sun blazing behind him, the sweet smell of oranges.

"But I don't understand?" Ms. Fleming says.

"I got spirits to protect me, Ms. Fleming," I explain. "Grann Lola, Pearl the ghost kitten, my Aunties, George the gator– and Daddy. I think he watches over me and sends visions of his family to look after me," my voice is crackly cause I'm tired. "Have you seen my phone?" I ask and look around.

"Actually Jinny, you left it on the couch in the teacher's lounge, here you go," she says and pulls it out of her purse and hands it to me. She also pulls out her own Airpods. "You can have these. I never use them; you can listen to music. I'll go buy you a charger in the gift shop."

"Thank you, Ms. Fleming. You're the best teacher I ever had. I wish I wasn't such a disappointment to everyone, I'm sorry. I don't think I can cure cancer or build bridges."

Ms. Fleming turns her head and narrows her eyes at me. She looks sad. "Jinny, my God. You are not a disappointment to any of us. You have so much potential, we are going to help you and if you are meant to cure cancer or build a bridge, then I have no doubt in my mind that's what you'll do!" She walks out of the room, and I see her pull out her phone and call someone when she walks down the hall.

A nurse comes in quietly and checks the whirring machines and my vitals, keying things into a computer. He doesn't say anything to me, and I don't say anything to him. I just fumble with my phone and sync the Airpods to it, but I can't figure out the hospital WIFI and I let out an irritated sound.

"Let me," he says, and takes my phone, does a few things, then hands it back.

"Thanks," I grumble.

"Listen to Livingston," he says and walks out with his laptop.

I feel bratty and try sticking my tongue out at him. But my mouth really hurts. I reach up to feel and there are stitches on the side of my face.

Great.

I'm going to look like the Joker. I want to scream. Instead I turn on some music like the nurse suggested. I close my eyes and try to think about something worthwhile, something that makes me happy. I picture the ocean, with its endless blue waves. Until a storm comes, making my vision dark. My life is a sandcastle crashing down into the foam, sucked out by the riptides.

There's a knock on the door.

It's Officer Riddley and Officer Garcia.

"Hello Jinny," they say in unison.

"Hey," I say.

"How you doing, kid?" Officer Riddley smiles.

Officer Garcia elbows him. "How do you think she's doing George?"

My eyes get big. Did she just call him George?

Then she places her hand on my forehead gently, it's cool and soft. It makes my bottom lip quiver.

"Jinny!" It's Victor's mom. "Hello Officers. My name is Kelsey Suarez, Jinny is friends with my son Victor. I heard what happened, and I know she doesn't really have anyone to advocate for her, and I wanted to speak with the physicians and see if there is anything my family can do for her.

She's a very smart young lady," Mrs. Suarez gushes about me. She's dressed in a suit, different from the relaxed yoga pants, cool mom look. This is the I run a massive multi-million-dollar hotel look. I try to smile.

"Hi Mrs. Suarez," it comes out softly.

"Oh honey. You poor thing." She pats my feet through the hospital blankets.

"We need to get a statement from her, Mrs. Suarez." Officer Riddley says, but he adds, "She's lucky to have you, she could absolutely use an advocate."

"Do you think you're up for it, Jinny?" Mrs. Suarez asks.

I nod.

Officer Riddley retrieves a little notebook from his front pocket.

"Mama said she had a debt to pay, said we had to move in with the people she owed. I... I... got scared! I threw up and we crashed." Each word comes out of me choppy, like a toddler playing a piano one key at a time.

Officer Garcia holds my hand.

It's enough to make the tears slide out and my throat close.

I gasp for air.

Mrs. Suarez rubs my feet and I calm down. "That's it, take a nice deep breath. You're going to be okay."

"Did your Mama say the names of the people she owes this debt to?" Officer Riddley asks.

"No," I shake my head. "Mama keeps secrets. She's been real strange and paranoid lately, since some guy beat her up in the Keys and she got fired from Margaritaville. Ask Marco maybe he knows something... He was over last night, and they got drunk and high."

The idea that Marco could be involved makes me want to laugh. He was Daddy's best friend, but he has chased after Mama like he was in love with her ever since Daddy died.

"Do you have Marco's address?" Officer Garcia asks.

"Um. No. I can give you his number and tell you where he lives, but I don't know the exact house number." I open my phone and read off his phone number and describe which house is his. "It's off 10th Ave, a big two-story house with neon blue shutters. Lots of people live with him. I don't like to go there."

I see their exchanged glances.

Mrs. Suarez notices too.

"I think maybe Jinny should get some rest, what do you say?" She asks.

"Jinny, I'll come back to check on you tomorrow," Officer Garcia says.

For a moment I see a teenage girl like me. I see her as Vicki, the scars she bears from being abused by those men who came looking for her Mama. Then I imagine myself. How thin and gross I look, the cuts on my face, the bruises and the years of abuse I've endured.

"Wait! What happened to the person Mama hit? Are they okay?" I ask.

Officer Riddley looks over his shoulder as they are leaving my room.

"No, actually, the other driver did not survive the crash."

Oh my god.

Mama killed someone.

– Chapter Twenty-Two –
Not my period!

Vehicular homicide. That's what it's called. Mama is criminally negligent because she was going seventy miles an hour in a thirty mile an hour zone. It was an accident, cause I threw up and startled her, so she swerved. But, if she was only going the actual speed limit and had just slowed down or stopped or pulled to the shoulder, then someone else's Grann would still be alive.

And now Mama's going to jail.

"She's in here." A nurse wheels me past an armed guard, into a hospital room like mine. Mama's hooked up to a bunch of IV bags and tubes and wires and has a brace thing on one arm. I can't ask her how she feels.

They said she's unconscious.

I'm glad she can't talk.

If she was awake, I might lose my mind arguing with her.

But maybe I want to tell her I still love her too.

Even after all this shit she's put me through.

"Are you ready to go back to your room?" The nurse turns my wheelchair around and pushes me back to my room. I really don't want to go back, but I have an appointment with a social worker.

She's coming to discuss my options once I get released.

The nurse helps me back into my bed, reconnecting all my monitors and hanging my IV bag back on the stand. I hurt and feel really crampy. They say it's going to take weeks for the pain to go away. Even without any broken bones, I feel shattered.

Just as the nurse leaves, a woman with a scowl on her face barges in. "My name is Julia Miller and I'm your case worker."

I don't like her.

She's an evil witch if I ever saw one, with a hook nose and sneering glare.

"Can you come back later? When Mrs. Suarez gets here? I don't think I should be alone with you," I tell her.

"That's not how this works. The state of Florida has assigned me to manage your case and we need to get through this intake paperwork," she snips and flips open a leather folio with a yellow legal pad inside of it.

"No." I cross my arms over my chest.

"Hmmm. Non-compliant. Girls like you don't go far in the system," she says matter of factly and writes something in her notes. I want to spit on her, but my mouth still doesn't move right.

Girls like me...

I grab my phone and text Mrs. Suarez.

ME:
Help! Social worker showed
up early...

MRS. SUAREZ:
I'm pulling into the parking
garage. Hang tight.

"Mrs. Suarez is my advocate. I refuse to do this until she's here," I say. Then I close my eyes and use the button on my bed to buzz the nurse.

"Now, Jinny, is that necessary? I think we can do this civilly without you getting any of your neighborhood friends involved," she says with an attitude.

"I choose not to respond to that." I buzz the button again. Come on! Save me!

"Do you need something?" The nurse who helped me with the WIFI comes into the room.

"I need to go to the bathroom; can you help with the monitor and drip stand thing?" I point to the metal pole where my IV fluid and heart monitor and oxygen sensor are connected. "And I think I started my period," I admit. My stomach's been cramping all day and this dumb lady Julia Miller, super witch, is making it worse.

"I don't want her here, she's being mean to me," I whisper to the nurse when he leans in to unhook my monitor.

"I'm gonna need you to wait outside," his voice is strong and implies he means business.

I smirk.

Julia Miller looks pissed off but does as she's told.

"Now. Jinny, I want to get you into the bathroom, but I need to know something first." He's typing into his chart on the computer. "How often do you have your menstrual cycle? Is it regular, like once a month? Do you remember the last time you had a cycle?" he asks. God. Why does it matter?

I shrug. "Like three or four times last year and once in the summer…" I try to think, but that must be it.

Then he walks out.

"Wait! I need to pee!" I holler after him. But he returns quickly with Dr. Leveau.

"Hi Jinny, how are you feeling?" Dr. Leveau asks when she enters. She looks concerned. I haven't seen her since the first day I was here. It's been three days. Other doctors have come and gone to check on me, but not her.

"I dunno," I shrug.

"I'm on call today and I'm glad I stopped over to see you. Nurse Damien said you think you may have started your period? I want to help you get into the bathroom to alleviate your bladder, but we are going to put a specimen pan in to collect the urine and any blood that comes out. Then I'll have you lie back down so I can perform an examination. Jinny, menstrual bleeding right after a car accident can indicate internal bleeding. So, I want to take this VERY seriously."

Nurse Damien helps me from the bed to the bathroom. I feel weird peeing with two adults watching me. My pee makes splashy sounds as it hits the collection pan in the toilet.

"Knock, knock," It's Mrs. Suarez. Thank God.

"Hi Mrs. Suarez!" I yell. "I might have internal bleeding, that's why I have an audience in the bathroom."

"Then I'm glad I got here when I did," she says.

"Me too." I finish and Nurse Damien helps me crawl back into bed and connect everything. Dr. Leveau presses on my stomach and makes tapping motions with her hands and listens with her stethoscope.

"Where's the social worker?" Mrs. Suarez asks.

I point out into the hallway.

"That witch. Her name is Julia Miller."

Nurse Damien lets out a laugh. But quickly tries to cover it with a cough.

"Let me go out and speak with her and see what I can do. Oh, I brought you a gift from Victor. He's dying to come see you, but football has run late every day this week." She sets a pretty gift bag on the table next to my bed and walks out to speak with the witch.

There are flowers and balloons and cards in my room from school. But I'm most excited to open a present from Victor.

Dr. Leveau has finished my exam and talks to Nurse Damien in doctor language, I overhear her ordering tests and blood and scans.

I tune them out to focus on my present.

I carefully remove the tissue paper and reach my hand in. First, I take out a sea foam green journal made with soft dyed leather. Next, a pack of rainbow gel rollerball pens, the kind with good ink that glides onto paper. And last, something wrapped with a note taped on it.

Jinny,

I hope you get better real soon... I already miss you.
Victor

P.S. Maybe this would be good for the Mysterious Magical Book Club?

Is my heart supposed to feel like this? Should I tell Dr. Leveau, who's still talking with Nurse Damien at the foot of my bed and looking at the computer and typing things furiously. It's not a pain so much as an aching, a longing, a flutter and bit of hope remembering a kiss on these lips.

I sigh.

The content of the wrapped package is a book, based on Victor's note. I'm anxious to see what he thinks I'd like or that our non-existent book club would like. Maybe I can join again since Mama can't stop me. But maybe I won't be going back to Hollywood Hills High School if I get placed in a foster home outside the district.

I want to frown, but I really can't.

Before I can open the book, Dr. Leveau and Nurse Damien exit the room and shut the door loudly without saying goodbye. Through the glass window, I watch them speak with Mrs. Suarez and that witch.

Julia Miller is angry and waving her pen around and taping it on the folio. Finally, she comes back into my room, grabs her bag, then storms out.

"What's up her butthole?" I ask Nurse Damien when he returns.

"We asked her to come back in a few days," he says, then starts adjusting my bed and machines.

"Are you serious? That's awesome!" I reach out to fist bump Nurse Damien for sending the wicked witch away, but he doesn't put out a fist. He just looks at me.

"Dr. Leveau asked Ms. Miller to leave because you're going for a CT scan and an angiogram up in Radiology to determine how serious this is.

Jinny, internal bleeding is extremely dangerous, depending on the location of the bleed. Rest and fluids might help, but you could be looking at having emergency surgery tonight, based on what the doctors find in your scans." He's serious.

"Oh. Sorry."

"Don't be sorry. And here—" He sticks out his fist now. "You got this and I'm glad the witch is gone too." He winks at me, and I laugh. He pushes the button on the door to keep it open then pops the lock on my bed so the wheels can move. I still have my presents from Victor in my lap.

"Oh, Jinny honey, Dr. Leveau said you are going up to Radiology. I'll be right here when you get back," Mrs. Suarez says.

I hand her the presents and my phone, even though I hate to let them leave my grasp.

"Are you sure? You don't mind waiting? Can you hold these for me?" My hands are shaky. "I'm scared." I admit.

She tries hard to hide the look of fear on her own face, but it's still there. I don't want more tests. I don't want anything else to be wrong with me. I just want to go home, not that I have a home to go home to.

"It's okay to be scared, Jinny. This whole thing has been scary! But remember, you have a lot of people who love you and you are a very strong young woman. You'll get through this, and I know good things are on the horizon for you," she says, like a mother.

Like she knows I need to hear it. For a moment I forget she's the mom of the boy I like. I pretend for a split second that she's actually my mom. My heart calms down.

Nurse Damien wheels me off and I just close my eyes for the ride.

– Chapter Twenty-Three –
Fuzzy Socks

Everything happens fast once the doors of the elevator open and Nurse Damien wheels me down the fourth-floor corridor. Faster than I expected.

"I'll take you back down when they are done," he says and leaves me in a room with crazy-looking machines. My heart still isn't cooperating. Maybe the stress from all this is getting to me. I know I'm mad at Mama, but I wish she was here. I wonder if she's awake now and if they told her what's going on with me. Does she know I might have internal bleeding? Does she know what she's done? That she killed someone.

Does she even care?

When the CT scan is over, I hear Dr. Leveau talking to two other doctors. I lean over and try to see them and catch a glimpse of a tall old doctor who talks with a deep southern voice and a short lady with thick glasses talking super-fast and hyper.

"HELLO! I'm right here!" I yell. I really hate when adults act like they know everything. Dr. Leveau laughs.

"Sorry, Jinny, this is Dr. Bordel and Dr. Sun, we were just discussing your CT scan and what we should do. Fortunately, it doesn't look like there is enough blood that we will need to perform surgery. We are going to set up monitoring and daily scans until your body has reabsorbed the blood that's pooled up inside of you," Dr. Leveau explains.

"Good," I finally let out the breath that feels like I've been holding since we got to the fourth floor. I close my eyes. "Does that mean I can stay here for a while longer? I don't have a home to go to. I'm not sure if you know, but my Mama killed someone in the car accident. They call it Vehicular Homicide. She was negligent because she was driving seventy, in a thirty. I'm pretty sure her parental rights have been terminated. Or will be. So, I guess Memorial Regional is my home for now." I should shut up. But I guess my nerves are making me chatty. Ugh.

The three doctors look at one another then at me.

"Looks like we will see you for daily visits, Jinny! Nice to meet you. If we can do anything to make your stay in our lovely establishment any more enjoyable, just tell Dr. Bordel, he's super hospitable," Dr. Sun says with a giggle. She made "hospitable" sound like "hospital", and she makes Dr. Bordel look dreadfully annoyed. I like her right away.

"I see what you did there, clever." I'd smile if I could.

"We do what we can in Radiology," she says.

Dr. Bordel walks over to me. "Yes. What Dr. Sun said, we will see you every day for scans. And as long as you never lie to us, we will get along well," he says with his deep smooth southern voice. I can see he is smirking and Dr. Leveau rolls her eyes.

"Why? Cause you'll see right through it?" I ask.

"You didn't tell us she was so smart Rosemary!" he gasps. "No one usually gets that joke." He chuckles to himself then pushes the button for the door to open. Nurse Damien is standing outside waiting for me.

"Good news?" he asks.

"You can take her back to her room," Dr. Leveau says and then goes back to Dr. Sun and Dr. Bordel.

I like that they ignored my outburst about Mama. I regretted saying it the moment it came out of my mouth. It's true though. I don't have any place else to go. Maybe I shouldn't have been so rude to Julia Miller. I guess it's her job to figure out what to do with me. But a foster home isn't a real home and based on what I know from kids who've been in and out of the system, they can get moved without warning, sometimes in the middle of the night. I wonder what happens to their stuff? Do they even have any stuff? I wonder if I'll be allowed to go home and get a suitcase and my things.

Not that there's a home left.

I bet another family has already moved into our old apartment.

"Jinny, you're awfully quiet," Nurse Damien says as we ride the elevator.

"Yeah, just wondering where my stuff at home will go if the landlord didn't already throw it in the dumpster... It's nothing much. It's mostly books I find that people leave by the trash and my seashell collection," I tell him.

It sounds dumb. Bunch of worthless crap. But it's my crap. It's all I've got, besides the shoe box with Daddy's pictures and Dolphins shirt in my closet. My heart can't take thinking about it. I blink back a sneaky tear.

"If you need books, I can get you books. My girlfriend works at the public library. People donate paperbacks all the time and the library gives them away. Back into the community. What do you like to read? I'll message her." We get back to my room and he pushes the bed into place and rehooks all my cords and IVs.

"Wow, you know, you're pretty cool."

"Yeah I know," he says and walks out. He comes back with a pen and paper. "Make me a list. Authors you like and your favorite genres. I'll grab the list from you before I get off tonight." Then he walks out.

My wrapped present from Victor is sitting on the side table, right where Mrs. Suarez left it with my phone. I don't know if she went home already or if she lingers around somewhere. I don't know how long I was in Radiology. Time went fast, and it's dark outside my window, the kind of dark at night that makes my skin itch cause I'm too tired to still be awake.

But I am in an overly lit hospital room.

Did you know they never turn off all the lights in a hospital?

It's always a strange hour here.

I look at my phone. I have a ton of missed texts. But, I really am tired, my guts hurt, so I don't want to talk to anyone. I pick up the wrapped book from Victor and clutch it tightly in my arms. I'm scared to open it. What if it's something I've already read twenty times? What if it's the best book I've ever read and nothing else I read will ever compare to this book? I close my eyes and imagine the various possibilities.

My phone buzzes and wakes me up. I didn't even know I fell asleep. Clutching my present from Victor, a boy who might be my boyfriend. I don't recognize the phone number. But I decide to answer it anyway.

"Hello?" My voice is cracked and dusted with sleep.

"Jinny? This is Principal Guthrie, I was just calling to check on you. How are you doing? I'm sorry, did I wake you?" he asks.

"I have internal bleeding. My mouth is sewn weird, and I can't smile or frown. My Mama's been charged with vehicular homicide, and I've been assigned a social worker who hates me. Besides that, everything is okay."

"Do you want my pity or my help?" he asks.

"Help. Never pity."

He restarts the conversation. "Jinny, this is Principal Guthrie. How can I help you?"

"Hi Principal Guthrie. Can you have my homework and a laptop sent to the hospital? Also, could you find out if I can get into Admiral Farragut Academy on scholarship and live there? It's like a college prep boarding school. Then maybe I wouldn't have to go into foster care," I respond this time.

"Yes to the laptop and homework. I'll make some calls regarding Admiral Farragut Academy. And Ms. Fleming and I will swing by tomorrow. Would you like anything else Jinny?" he asks.

"Fuzzy socks. My feet are cold... thank you." I hang up the phone.

"Jinny, you got the list of books?" Nurse Damien walks in. I scribble down something on the paper and hand it to him. He reads it and nods, then looks off, out the dark window of my room. It's raining. "You're a pretty special kid. Good things are coming your way. Just hold on a little longer." He leaves the door cracked as he walks down the hall.

My hunger for knowledge is mysterious and magical. I consume all books.

The words I scribbled on the paper. Maybe he's right. Maybe good things are coming my way. Maybe not.

Now that I'm alone, I decide I can't wait any longer to unwrap the book from Victor. I need to know what it is! The paper anxiously comes undone when I pull at the tape. I look at the cover and smile. I'll Give You the Sun by Jandy Nelson. I read the first line. "We are all headed on a collision course, no matter what."

I'd laugh at the irony of it all, if I wasn't a complete mess of a human.

Before I start reading the book my phone buzzes.

THOMAS:
U awake? How you doin?

ME:
OK. I miss u! 😈

THOMAS:
Girl, you don't even know!

ME:
How is school?

THOMAS:
Shantel and the cheers asked
me 2 try out!!

ME:
WTF!?!

THOMAS:
Don't worry! I told them
NO WAY

ME:
😆

THOMAS:
I miss our sleepovers
Come home soon
Nite   🩶

– Chapter Twenty-Four –
All HELL breaks loose!

"I think she's asleep," Ms. Fleming says.

I hear quiet whispers and crack open my eyes in a snake-like slit. I watch as Principal Guthrie sets down a purple and blue backpack and puts something pink on top, like a cherry on an ice cream sundae.

"Oooohhhh… Are those my socks?" I ask, my voice creepy like a ghost.

"Jinny! You startled me!" Ms. Fleming's face makes me want to laugh. The side of my lip finally feels like it's healing and her eyes light up when she sees me smile. "Principal Guthrie stopped at three stores to find fuzzy socks for you."

"Well, he's the one who asked if there was anything else besides homework that I needed," I smirk. "My feet are cold and hospital socks sucks. And I don't have any parents to do nice things for me, like get me fuzzy socks. So, thank you."

"I'm happy to do it for you Jinny." Principal Guthrie smiles at me, then the smile fades into a serious expression. "Now, regarding that other item on your list. I've been in close contact with Mrs. Lenora Ollena this week. She is fully aware of what's happened, and she was pleasantly surprised when I told her you would like to attend the academy." His smile comes back.

I'm holding my breath.

"We are going to work with your social worker, Ms. Miller, and see what arrangements can be made, considering your situation. I'm going to speak with a judge friend of mine tomorrow and see what he thinks."

I see what looks like pride on his face. For me. For him. For feeling like he's making a difference in the life of a troubled teen.

The old Jinny would scoff at such a display. She would say something shitty to push him away, to guard herself. But, I'm not that girl anymore. I am beginning to realize people aren't as bad as Mama has always said…

I'm temporarily pulled back in time, to a conversation I had with Mama, when I was in fifth grade.

"Jinny, you wouldn't believe the bullshit I dealt with last night. These snobs stayin' at the resort think they are God's gift to humanity! Their husbands tip like the world gonna end and hire me for a little after-hours fun. So, I smile and take their shit. Those bitches can suck it. I can buy the same damn jeans they wear too! Remember, people with money think they own you, but they don't. YOU make your OWN way, Jinny."

She was supposed to take me to the craft store to buy supplies for a diorama book report. I was doing mine on the Iliad by Homer. All the other kids in my class picked flimsy chapter books from the teachers shelf, like Jumaji and James and the Giant Peach.

Books I read when I was in kindergarten.

But instead of shopping for popsicle sticks to make a Trojan horse, I was standing in some boutique downtown while Mama was trying on Gucci jeans and giving me advice on how to handle rich snobs and their husbands.

The memory, the way it made me feel that day and the anxiety it caused me for years, reminds me of how I ended up in this hospital bed.

Mama.

Too proud to be my mom.

I never questioned where she got the money for those jeans and why she didn't have any money for my school project, or dinner that night.

"Jinny?" Ms. Fleming's voice brings me back to reality. Back to the scratchy hospital sheets. Back to my cold feet. Back to feeling like I'm never gonna be good enough. But that burning inside of my belly, the excess blood trying to absorb, it's forcing me to figure out how to be good enough.

"Sorry, I'm just anxious to find out what can be done, I don't want to be in foster care, I don't want to be invisible," I explain and beg my bottom lip not to quiver.

"We are going to do everything we can to help you, Jinny. You will NEVER be invisible." Principal Guthrie takes my hand and squeezes it. "I bookmarked a few websites on the laptop I brought you. I'd like you to go online and register then do some of the work. I'll count it as extra credit," he says.

"What kind of work?" I ask, not that I care. Anything to keep my mind busy.

"Some stuff one of my buddies from MIT sent me. I think you'll find it opens up your mind and allows you to focus some of your energy while you're here healing," he says.

"Okay." I shrug.

"Victor's mom, Mrs. Suarez and I have been in close contact. She's got a lot of pull in the community," Ms. Fleming says. "She's a great person to have on your side. We will be working on the scholarships for you. Is that okay?"

I nod. I'm overwhelmed by the amount of support and kindness.

"Time to take Jinny for her scan upstairs. You're welcome to wait or come back later. They are pretty backed up, so it might be an hour." A mousy nurse I've never seen before comes in and taps her foot on the floor impatiently.

"Okay, we can get going. Jinny, we'll be in touch." Principal Guthrie waves and heads out. Ms. Fleming comes over and gives me a hug. Then she slips the fuzzy socks on my feet for me. Good thing, cause I can't really lean over all that well.

After my scan, the same mousy nurse comes to get me and take me back to my room.

I wonder where Nurse Damien is? Maybe it's his day off. I wonder if he'll bring me books like he promised. I guess I can work on homework now that I have a school computer. I'm busy thinking of what assignments I might have when the nurse stops pushing my bed and walks over to look at me.

"Your Mama been askin' about you," she says. Something about the way she says it– has me on high alert.

"Yeah, you her nurse too?" I easily slide into my usual neighborhood slang voice.

"Yep... You want me to take you to see her?" Her pupils are dilated and they dart right, then left. She's shifty.

"No. Take me to my room." I lift my chin up.

"Are you sure?" There's something strange in her voice and she slides back behind my bed and starts pushing me, fast.

"Did I stutter? Take me to my room!" I spit out the words. My senses are going crazy. Everything is screaming at me that I'm headed for danger, not Mama, but danger.

"Well, aren't you a little bitch."

My heart pounds. She just called me a bitch!

"Where is Nurse Damien?"

She doesn't answer.

She's wheeling me down the wrong hallway.

Tell her to STOP, Grann Lola's voice screams in my head and I look around to see if her spirit is here. But I can't see her, I only feel her presence. My heart is in my throat and that bile feeling is creeping up ready to burst.

"STOP! What are you doing?" I scream.

She doesn't stop. She pushes my gurney faster and harder than should be possible for a weasely little waif.

My arm has a needle with tubing and IV bag connected to it and I've got sticky heart monitors on my chest, but I am not helpless. My adrenaline kicks in and I swallow down the vomit.

I have to defend myself.

"THIS WAY!" yells a huge scary orderly I've never seen before. He's holding the automatic button to keep a pair of double doors open and he's waving and shouting, "HURRY GOD DAMNIT, THIS WAY!!"

"I'm coming Tallon, SHUT UP!" the nurse screams back.

Jinny, girl, for the love of all that's southern, you got to run! Auntie Bonnie's voice is ringing in my ears. I don't see her, but I know she's somewhere using swamp magic with Grann Lola to help me in my time of need.

Meow!

Pearl's cute kitten meow and soft fur rubs against my arm. I look down and see my little ghost kitten. She's chewing on the IV in my arm.

I know what to do.

In one fast movement I rip the IV out of my arm, the other plugs and connections will snap the moment I run.

I fling myself up and over the cold metal guardrail on my hospital bed.

My legs are weak and I flop when I hit the floor.

The squeaky nurse is taken by surprise, because she's pushing the bed so fast, she keeps going with it right past the big orderly. He has a tattoo of a tear beneath his left eye, I am so close I can see it. That can only mean one thing– he's a very dangerous man and I don't want to be anywhere near him.

It takes half a second for my legs to flood with energy, that same feeling I always have before I go running. I take one step forward and my foot grips the floor! My new fuzzy socks have anti-slip rubber on the bottom. Thank God!

"STOP, you little bitch!"

"Grab her, Josie! That twat is our meal ticket!" the tattooed beast shouts.

"FUCK YOU!" I scream as loud as I can and run back the way we came. "HELP! HELP! HELP! HELP!" I keep screaming as I run down the hallway. My hospital gown flaps wildly. The IV tube floats and drops of fluid leak out. I'm going so fast that it feels like I'm in slow motion.

People come out of rooms. Nurses and doctors are materializing out of nowhere. Everyone is frozen with confusion. I'm literally being chased through the hospital by criminals, and no one is doing a damn thing.

Then, I spot a familiar dark hair as Nurse Damien comes around the corner. He's carrying at least twenty books in his arms.

I don't stop. I don't slow down.

I just run straight into him.

"Jinny!" he screams before we collide and fall to the floor. Books fly everywhere. In the air, on the floor, smacking the walls. I hear Josie the nurse slip and fall behind me, I can tell because of her squeak.

"What is going on!" A doctor screams at the chaos.

"That nurse and orderly are trying–" I pant, "to kidnap me!" I'm hyperventilating. "They called me a bitch and a twat and said I'm their meal ticket."

"Call the police!" Nurse Damien screams.

"Radio hospital security!" Someone else shouts.

"YOU, STOP!" A doctor is shouting at Josie the nurse, if that's really what she is.

I watch as at least three or four people start chasing Josie and Tallon the fake orderly in the other direction.

Nurse Damien is up off the floor and barking orders. When he realizes I'm still splayed-out whimpering, he scoops me up into his arms and carries me into an empty room.

"Jesus, Jinny, are you okay?" he asks and places me gently on a bed. His face contorts and the blood vessel in the side of his neck bulges.

"No, I'm not okay!" Tears stream down my face.

"You did the right thing. You are a brave girl," he goes into nurse mode, even though he's wearing street clothes, and starts hooking me up to new monitors and machines. He calls in another nurse and she helps get a new IV line placed in my arm.

Dr. Leveau comes flying into the room. "Holy shit!" She looks wild.

I bet potential kidnappings don't happen very often.

I laugh nervously to keep from crying.

"Well, I'm glad you can laugh Jinny. But Jesus, I don't know what is going on around this place. I cannot believe this!" She puts her stethoscope on my belly and listens. Then she puts her hands on my stomach and does a tapping thing.

I want my phone. I want my backpack of homework. I want to close my eyes and make all of this go away! I want to stop crying in front of Damien and Dr. Leveau and this other dumb nurse. I want to go home. Or away. Anywhere but here.

"Can we go back to my room?" I ask.

There's a clatter of metal when the nurse drops a piece of equipment, startled by the person who's walked into my makeshift hospital room.

Mama.

She's dressed in jeans and a gray t-shirt, her hair up in a ponytail, and has on a pair of oversized black sunglasses. I can still see the gash on her cheek from our accident, angry and red. Her bandages are gone and the brace is off her arm.

She's so cool and collected, pointing a gun into the room.

It's not flashy and shiny, announcing its presence. It's compact and flat black. The sight of it sucks every drop of oxygen from my lungs.

I gasp and choke.

Mama steps further into the room. The hospital ID bracelet on her wrist seems out of place.

"Jinny." Her voice is a knife stabbing my heart.

This cannot be happening.

"Come on, Jinny. Get your goddamn ass out of that bed. You are coming with me right now. No one is going to stop us. Marco has a car waiting out back," she says as calmly as she can muster.

I know that voice. It's the one she uses right before she loses all control. Right before she does something she regrets. I reach to my arm and I pull out the IV. She's serious. I know it. If I don't go, she's gonna kill someone. This time on purpose.

"Jinny, don't move another muscle," Nurse Damien says.

If she didn't have a gun, I'd listen to him. I'd tell Mama the cops are coming and she should give herself up. But, that black thing in her hand, it's powerful.

"You can stop talking. My daughter will do exactly what I say or you'll be the first to go."

Dr. Leveau's body tenses as Mama comes closer with the gun.

"Mama, I don't know what game you're playing, but just put the gun down. I'll go with you," I say and crawl out of the bed. "It's okay. I'm comin', Mama. It's okay." I take a few steps forward. There is no other option, I have to go. I don't want these people to get hurt trying to protect me.

"If you had just gone with Josie and Tallon, I wouldn't have to do this." Her voice quivers as I walk toward her. "I told you before the crash. I told you! I don't know why you didn't just listen!" She urges me to understand. But, I don't know what she means... I mean not really. I mean, maybe I do. Maybe I understand.

"Just put the gun down, Mama. You'll shoot me. Then what will happen?" I keep walking forward. God, my stomach hurts. My body doesn't know if it should make more adrenaline or make me fall to my knees. I urge my legs to move. Don't betray me now!

"Jinny..." Nurse Damien's voice is ragged.

"I'm going to go with Mama."

When I reach her, she grabs me, and puts the cold black metal gun to my head. Of course, I'm her collateral to get out of here. I'm her escape plan.

Oh Mama. What have you done...

– Chapter Twenty-Five –
Eyes Wide Open

My mind is jumbled as Mama pushes me through the sterile hospital. Down this hall, down stairs, through a kitchen. Mama screams she's gonna shoot me and blow my brains out if anyone gets in our way. Doors open and a blast of humid air hits me in the face. She walks me out the back service entrance of the hospital.

I hear sirens.

Cops.

Ambulances.

Fire trucks.

Mama looks around for Marco, but there's no car, he's not waiting to take us away.

This is bad.

"MARCO!" She screams, ripping off her sunglasses and looks up and down the rain soaked street. "Where the hell is he? That pathetic piece of shit."

She should have known better. Marco loves me, he wouldn't help her kidnap me and betray the ghost of my Daddy.

"MAMA, put the gun down." My voice cracks.

"Shut up, Jinny. I'm not going to shoot you," she says, but doesn't move the gun from my throbbing temple.

"Pathetic," I whisper.

"I'm not pathetic! I'm a survivor! I've been a survivor my entire life. YOU know nothing about me JINNY. The struggles I've faced as a single mom of a fucking smart-ass know-it-all! You think it's been easy for me, knowing my own flesh and blood has been smarter than me since she was three?"

I struggle but she just digs the barrel harder.

"Ouch, Mama."

"You think it's been easy for me knowing I'm the one who sent your Daddy on that last deal that got him killed? You don't know a fucking thing!" She screams. "If you really loved me, you'd just shut the hell up and help me. Help me JINNY! I'm gonna go to prison for the rest of my fucking life for this shit!"

I don't say a word, afraid of what might come out of my mouth. Mama drags me across the wet pavement. It's warm on my soggy, fuzzy feet. The smell of gasoline is heavy in the air. We reach the busy Washington Street intersection and cars honk and swerve to avoid us. People shout out their windows and pull over to film us on their cell phones.

Mama with her gun pressed to my head.

The sirens are loud, approaching us from all sides.

"WE HAVE YOU SURROUNDED. PUT DOWN THE GUN."

That's Officer Riddley's voice.

"Please Mama!"

"I didn't mean to crash and kill that woman! I wasn't thinkin' clearly! I'm not thinkin' straight. I've been off my meds. FUCK!" Mama screams.

"Please," I beg.

Officer Riddley's voice comes over the speaker again, "DROP THE WEAPON!"

But we keep walking.

"Mama, put the gun down."

"Do you hear her begging?" Mama asks and laughs. "Oh poor, Jinny. How about poor Crystal!" She tightens her grip around me. My stomach is cramping so bad and my knees are doing everything they can not to buckle and fall out from under me.

"You are supposed to love me. That's what Mama's do! Not this." My body shakes like an earthquake and sweat rolls down my back. Everything around me seems to stop and I turn, ignoring the gun and I look Mama square in the eyes. "I love you Mama."

"What would you know about love, Jinny?"

My heart breaks.

I loved you, Jinny. I still love you. Wherever I am– I'll always be in your heart… It's Daddy.

"Daddy loved me," I tell her. "And Thomas loves me and Jonelle and Ang love me. And there's Grann Lola and my aunties and Pearl and–" Mama slaps my face.

"Just shut up!" She screams.

"DROP THE WEAPON! LET JINNY GO!"

"Shoot me then! End this! Because, you're already going to jail." My voice is horse from yelling. "You blame me for your shit life Mama, but it's not like I wanted Daddy to get killed and to leave you alone as a single parent." My chest heaves. "I have tried my hardest to take care of myself, to take care of you."

"SHUT UP JINNY!" She cries.

I'm reeling. I don't know what the fuck to do!

"I'll try harder. I'll get a job to pay the bills." My tears drown me. "I just want to go to college and learn how to change the world. I'll make it a better place for you Mama!"

Mama stops.

"Don't you think I wanted those same things when I was your age?" She pushes the gun hard against my head and taps it, trying to drill it into my skull. "Look at me. LOOK AT ME! I'm a fucking junkie and a prostitute!" She screams.

My body finally betrays me and my knees slip.

The trigger clicks.

My eyes are closed. But really, they are wide open.

– Chapter Twenty-Six –
Take a deep breath!

"Jinny, thank you for coming to our session today. When we met last week you were pretty upset," Dr. Jaeger says.

"Yep."

I take a seat on the big blue couch in Dr. Jaeger's office.

I've been coming here twice a week for six weeks. Ever since I arrived. My new school wants to make sure the "incident" with Mama doesn't affect me permanently.

How could it not?

Since the incident at the hospital, I've learned Mama was using illegal prescription drugs to self-medicate her bi-polar disorder. Josie and Tallon were her dealers. Thankfully, they've been apprehended and are awaiting a trial. The cops uncovered a huge network up and down South Florida. Josie and Tallon were foot soldiers, stealing meds and supplies from hospitals and selling them in low-income neighborhoods to people like Mama. And since she owed them money, they hadn't been giving her the pills and they were trying to extort her, and sell me into a sex trafficking ring.

Thinking about how close I was to it makes my skin crawl.

I still can't believe Mama managed to hide her illness from me my entire life. I feel guilty that I didn't recognize it sooner. The extreme highs, the utter lows, and everything in-between. It was our life. I thought it was normal. I know I shouldn't feel like it was my fault… but that's easier said than done.

"I just don't understand why she didn't get health insurance and a regular prescription to manage her illness, or see a psychiatrist," I complain.

"Well Jinny, why do you think she might have avoided those things?" Dr. Jaeger asks.

"Her line of work? Not wanting to admit she actually had a problem? Like, if she didn't get a real diagnosis, then maybe it would go away, like if she self-medicated it could stay her secret," I suggest my best guess.

"Those are all reasonable assumptions, and at the end of the day, what Crystal chose to do was her decision. All we can do now is move forward and make sure you receive the proper treatment and medication you need to help you cope and be successful. PTSD and anxiety are common in situations like these."

"Oh, are situations like mine common?" I say it more forcefully than I mean to.

"Now Jinny–" Dr. Jaeger protests.

I fold my arms over my chest and look out the window at the waving palm trees. I take a few deep breaths, like Dr. Jaeger says I'm supposed to, when my anxiety starts to take over my emotions. Yeah right, like some deep breathing is really gonna work!

Doesn't she get it?

***

"It's nothing to be ashamed of!" Victor scoots closer to me on his bed.

I've spent the last three days staying at Ms. Flemings house, for the arraignment hearing, and she dropped me off to see Victor before his Mom drives me back to school.

"Yeah right," I put my head down on my knees.

"Jinny Buffett! You are the smartest, prettiest, most interesting girl I've ever met. I'd never trade anything about you away, even having PTSD and taking anxiety meds. Just keep going to therapy so you can learn to manage how you feel," Victor says.

"But, what if it turns into more? What if I can't escape this pain I'm feeling?" I sit up and look at him.

That's part of what's so frustrating about PTSD.

It's a panic attack for no reason. It's fear of leaving my room. It's being afraid to let new people in, or to try new things. It's pain that even the strongest pain pills can't touch.

"You gotta kinda feel sorry for your mom. I mean, she had no one to help her and look what happened."

"Yeah, I guess." I shrug it off. I know he means well, but I don't really wanna talk about it anymore.

"Come here." He pulls me closer to him.

I told myself I wasn't gonna cry. So instead I lean in and kiss him. His lips are soft and tender against mine. Every part of me longs to be closer, to hold him tighter. It helps with the pain.

It's magic being with Victor.

So how can I leave him? How can I just leave the only boy I've ever had feelings, like this, for? But, this is what I wanted, right? To go to the Admiral Farragut Academy and get a good education and finally be challenged. I'm the one who wanted to be at a place I feel safe because if I stay in Hollywood, and go into foster care. What chance will I ever have to rise up and do better than my dead drug-dealing Daddy and imprisoned bi-polar Mama?

Standing outside in his driveway, Victor holds me tight. He tucks my hair behind my ear and looks deep into my eyes. Then he gives me the softest goodbye kiss. One I will never forget. Etched into my heart, forever a part of my soul.

"Don't cry," he says, more to himself than me. Then he kisses me again, hard and urgent. "I love you Jinny Buffett," he whispers.

"I love you too," I reply quietly.

Then I climb into his mom's car.

***

"Do you want to start by telling me how school has been since the hearing last week? I'm sure it stirred up some deep emotions. I want to know if that had any impact on your classwork or ability to concentrate," Dr. Jaeger asks. She clicks on her mini tape recorder. I'm shocked people still use those things.

"Is that really what you want to know?" I ask. I can feel myself getting irritated.

"It's a starting point." She writes something down on the yellow legal pad she has in her lap. Then she adjusts her tortoise shell glasses.

I sit quietly.

Contemplating what kind of mood I'm in. Finally I take a deep breath.

"School was actually really good this week. I love it here."

"Jinny, that's wonderful. Can you tell me what you love about it?" She writes down so many notes. What's the point of that ridiculous mini-tape recorder?

"Well, I love that I can stay in my room and study or read all night long without Mama yelling at me," I tell her. "And, I worked up the courage to join the sailing team. But what I love most is that my classes are challenging."

"Do you feel like you can relate to the other students?" She shifts our conversation.

"How so?"

"Well, most of our students come from stronger family backgrounds," she says honestly.

"Hmmm. Does that matter?" I ask. I hadn't given it any thought until now.

"Do you think it matters Jinny?" She answers me with a question. I really hate it when she does that.

"I don't think so. I think my background allows me to have a deep appreciation for the opportunities that I'm being given here at school. The full-ride scholarship, the paid dorm, the computer, all of it. Nothing in my life has been easy. Even speaking to you, without using slang, is hard for me," I try to explain.

Dr. Jaeger writes something on her pad and nods. I know when she does that it means she wants me to keep going.

"I know I'm lucky." She looks up. "I mean, most kids in my shoes wouldn't have this opportunity. Like you said, I don't come from a strong family background... in Hollywood." I'm not prepared to tell her about my family in the Everglades who tried, in their mysterious way, to help me as much as they could. "I was lucky to have people like Ms. Fleming who saw my potential. She saw beyond my crappy home life and my emotional ups and downs."

"And?"

"And what?" I get defensive.

"And does that make you fit in with your peers?"

"I don't know! Do I have to? Is that a requirement or something? I guess they learned from an early age how to be successful, part of their happy suburban home life, so it's built into who they are. But I was raised by a Mama who hated school, mistrusted authority, cut corners, and didn't want me to be somebody because it made her feel worthless."

"Good. Keep going." She urges.

"I have issues! I HAVE to prove I'm more than just the daughter of a dead drug-dealer who's not going to end up a prostitute with a homicide rap in prison like their Mama." I'm practically shouting.

"Yes, you have a lot to prove," she says as she writes something down again.

My face starts to burn. I really don't think she gets it! And I swear to God, if she writes one more thing on that pad, I'm going to lose my mind. But then I realize what's happening. And a lightbulb goes off inside of my brain. "I don't have to let the world happen to me. I can be in control!"

"You're right, Jinny. You can be in control of your own life and when you focus, you have a lovely way of articulating yourself. You should feel proud of how far you've come," she says with a smile.

"Really? I thought you were going to tell me how stupid I am."

"Why on Earth would I tell you that?" She sounds annoyed.

"Because, you think I really don't belong here, right? I don't fit in. I don't have the same background as everyone else. Isn't that what you meant? That I'm just some piece of white trash." I'm pushing her buttons and I know it.

"Let's not backslide, Jinny. I've told you before, you are not allowed to assume you know what I am thinking or to judge our sessions by the questions I ask you. My job is to help keep you moving forward and to provide you a safe place to explore the emotional turmoil you have faced."

"Fine. Sorry." I mumble.

"There's an exercise I want you to work on over the weekend. I want you to text your friends and teachers from Hollywood. Ask them if they think you are trashy." She's dead serious. "I'd like you to come back next week prepared to share their answers with me."

"That's not fair. No one is gonna be truthful. No one ever tells the truth." I argue.

She can't make me. I look around the room for someone or something to help me. But, these are closed sessions. I'm alone with Dr. Jaeger. Her office has nothing remotely interesting in it.

"Life is not fair Jinny. You have a lot of issues to work through if you want to be successful at Admiral Farragut Academy and in life. I've seen your scores. I've read your essays. I know how brilliant you are. But, many brilliant people have ended up living disappointed lives filled with tragedy, too afraid to face their demons or challenge themselves to get outside of their own head. It is my job to help you, to guide you so you can manage your trauma and grow up to use your gifts, rather than becoming self-destructive," she says. It's not the first time she's preached to me.

"FINE!" I snap. I get up and walk out and slam the door.

I don't get far before I break down. I hate myself for crying. I shouldn't have let Dr. Jaeger get under my skin. Things have been going so well here. She's right, I can't back slide. But, now I have to do her stupid assignment. I slump in the chair sitting at the end of the hallway atrium. I'm not ready to face the golden sunshine outside. I pull my phone out of my bag and realize what time it is. So, I take out one of my anti-anxiety pills and a water bottle.

Learning to manage my meds has been high on my list of must-haves in my new life. I will NOT turn out like Mama. I'm done crying, but still feeling pathetic, so I text Thomas.

Might as well get this assignment over with.

ME:
Do u think I'm trash?
Like my Mama...

THOMAS:
U are NOT defined by ur
parents. If that were true, I'd
be a homophobic bigot
like my dad!

ME:
Sorry... my shrink is
forcing me to face my fear
makin me ask my friends if
they think i'm trash

THOMAS:
Tell ur shrink to lay off!
We all love you!
Guess what?
mom said u can spend
Christmas break w/us!! 😊

ME:
OMG YASSSSS!!!!

THOMAS:
I feel a dance party
coming on!

ME:
How is dance? BTW

THOMAS:
AMAZING. I won the lead

for the big holiday production.
U'll be in the front row!

ME:
OMG Thomas!
I can't wait!! I'm so proud
of U Boy!!

THOMAS:
Thank you!!
Okay, gotta go to practice!
Bye girl.
I love you 🤍

Okay, so maybe I'm not trash. Thomas is right.

I decide not to message Jonelle or Ang. It would only hurt them. Being my friend is roller coaster enough without me asking people if I'm trash... But, maybe that was the point of Dr. Jaeger's assignment, to make me realize how stupid and pathetic I sound when I revert back into the old Jinny. Everyone has shit, everyone has their own drama and trauma. I'm here on scholarship because I'm smart. I better start proving it.

I get up from the chair with new energy. I step outside into the sun and let its rays wash the anxiety and pain off of me. I take a deep breath. "You can do this," I say to myself. I smile and start the walk across campus to my dorm room. The air is sweet, drifting between the buildings. The campus is a mixture of new and old architecture, southern charm meets modern and cutting edge. Everything about it makes me happy.

I'm determined more than ever to hold on to my happiness and never let go.

"Hey Jinny!" yells Marianna from bio-chem.

I smile and wave. Then a group of juniors walk by. One of the girls fist pumps me as I pass. I don't know her, but that's just the vibe here. I look around at the different groups of students, laughing and talking and studying. I realize it doesn't matter where any of them have come from, who their parents are, or what their background is.

So why should it matter for me?

I'm not going to be ashamed of my past, it's made me who I am. I won't let anything get in my way. Not fear. Not failure. Not my anxiety. I'm going to work harder and be stronger than I thought was possible. A tickle of wind and the smell of the Everglades blows past my face. My Daddy's spirit, always close by, reminding me I'm heading in the right direction.

I hang up my keys and put my bag away when I get back to my room. I turn some music on and lie on my bed. This room has become my sanctuary, a sacred place. Decorated to reflect who I am. There is a very full bookshelf including The Raven Boys and I'll Give You the Sun. There's a poem Victor wrote for me pinned up on the wall, along with the picture of Daddy, Grann Lola and all my Aunties on that big porch in the swamp. My beloved seashell collection is on the shelf by the window, a surprise from Officer Garcia. She went back and saved them from the dumpster at my old apartment.

Then, I look up at the ceiling. The paint is still fresh.

All you need is LOVE

Stars can't SHINE without darkness

You're STRONGER than you believe

I remember lying on the floor with Ang. Listening to Jonelle and Thomas singing and laughing and dancing. That night was so many months ago. An eternity ago, but forever close to me. I think that was the night I realized I had to take control.

"Knock, knock Jinny!" Selina opens my door. "I think you must be the most popular girl at school, you get so many letters!" She walks in and hands me a stack of mail.

I thumb through the huge bundle of envelopes, some covered in interesting looking stamps. I see a big yellow one written in crayon, must be from Emily.

"Thanks for bringing my mail Selina. I'm still in a book club back at my old school, so we write letters back and forth about the books and life in Hollywood. Some of the teachers write to me, too. Oh, my Grann and aunties in the Everglades, they love to write letters," I explain.

"You know we have a book club here, right? You should join! We are reading The Fountainhead by Ayn Rand. You're going into engineering and architecture right? You'll probably enjoy the nuance and complexity of it. I'll bring by my copy later so you can start reading tonight. We can get you your own copy in class tomorrow," Selina says thoughtfully. She doesn't give me a chance to say no.

But, I don't want to decline. I want to join their book club.

"That sounds great. I'd love to join. What's it called?" I ask.

"The Fountainhead." She repeats the name of the book.

"No, not the book. The club. What's the name of the book club here?" I laugh.

"Um... just book club I guess... Why? What was it called at your old school?" she asks with a half-smile.

"The Mysterious Magical Book Club."

The End

Thank You!

This book has been on a magical journey since I sat down one hot, humid, Florida September day to write Jinny's story. One I wouldn't trade, but it wasn't easy, that's for sure! There are many people I'd like to thank for your love, encouragement, support and friendship along the way.

First, I have to thank my loving husband and children for supporting me during my long nights and weekends of writing, revising, and editing. You inspire me and you are my reason. I swear, if it's the last thing I do, I'll give you all that 'Celebration Life' we've all been dreaming of. ;)

To my Daddy… who's been encouraging me to write and create for as long as I can remember. I love you more than all the stars, because they go on forever and ever.

To Abigail Wild for taking a chance on a poor, self-loathing, girl who couldn't see her worth– sometimes it was hard to separate me from the characters, but your guidance got me there.

To Brittany McMunn for your editing genius! Your ability is astounding and your love for my characters makes me cry.

To Amy Nielsen, my writing bestie & cheerleader extraordinaire, thank you a thousand times over.

To Ginny Myers Sain, my swamp sister, your words of wisdom when I was stuck is what allowed me to push this book to what it is today.

To Theresa Green and the entire Writer's Workout gang, you've taught me more about writing than I'll ever be able to thank you for! I love you.

To my #WantYaNeedYA Twitter Crew, y'all, for real!!! So many tweets, so much encouragement, all the feels and friendships. Thank you.

And for all the girls like Jinny. I see you. You can build a bridge… It might be the hardest thing you ever do, to rise up, to ask for help, but believe me– you can do this.

Resources

Jinny suffered far longer than she had to, because she was scared.

Please ask for help.

If you or someone you love is the victim of human trafficking or is suffering from PTSD, there is help and I promise, there are people who care.

Please call 9-1-1 if you are in immediate danger!

Childhelp National Child Abuse Hotline
Call or text 1-800-4-A-CHILD (1800-422-4453)

For Information about Sex Trafficking, please see:

National Human Trafficking Hotline
1-888-373-7888
humantraffickinghotline.org/en/type-trafficking/sex

National Center on Sexual Exploitation
endsexualexploitation.org/

She's Somebody's Daughter
shessomebodysdaughter.org

For Information About Substance Abuse and Mental Health, please see:

SAMSHA
www.samhsa.gov
1-800-662-HELP (4357)
Or text your zip code to: 435748 (HELP4U)

If you are a teen who is struggling with depresssion, addiction, and/or self injury, please reach out to:

To Write Love On Her Arms
twloha.com
Or Text TWLOHA to 741741 (from the U.S. and Canada)

About S.E. Reed

S.E. has spent the last 20 years of her life moving around all five-regions of the United States which gives her a unique American perspective. Many of her pieces have a strong Southern theme, but she also dabbles in the strange, bizarre and fantastical.

Her work has been featured by Wild Ink Publishing, Parhelion Lit, The Writer's Workout, Tempered Rune's Press and Survival Guide for the 21st Century. She has won several YA writing contests and actively participates as a delegate for YA Hub on Twitter.

S.E. resides in Florida with her family– nestled between the swamps of the Everglades and the salt of the Atlantic Ocean. This summer she'll be sitting in a lawn chair, working on her next novel and listening to EDM… (Ask her about her days as a DJ). Or she'll be in the pool begging her kids not to get her hair wet.

Find out more about S.E. Reed by visiting her website
www.writingwithreed.com
and by visiting wild-ink-publishing.com/s-e-reed/

Watch for S.E. Reed's upcoming novel

Old Palmetto Drive
Coming in August 2024

Teen socialite Rian Callusa's privileged NY life is over! Following her parent's nasty divorce, and the death of her aunt & uncle, Rian's mom drags her kicking and screaming all the way to Everglades City. Who cares if her new home is a mansion when it's in the middle of nowhere without a nail salon or shopping mall in sight? And friends? Hell might as well freeze over before Rian would hang out with her hillbilly cousins. The news that her Dad won't be returning to New York after his job abroad crushes any hope Rian had of moving back to the Big Apple. So without a plan B, Rian explores the swamp and learns her cousins aren't as backward as they first appeared. She even falls head over heels for a cute vintage-loving local girl. Now that she thinks about it, this might turn out to be the best summer of Rian's life! Until her cousin Travis gets drunk at a party and confesses the dark truth about what really happened on Old Palmetto Drive, sending Rian into a tailspin of fear and self-doubt.

To find more exciting Wild Ink books visit wild-ink-publishing.com

Diagnostic Testing in Advanced Biology

Diagnostic Testing in Advanced Biology

R. E. LISTER B.Sc., F.I.Biol.,

Formerly Chief Examiner in Nuffield Advanced Level Biology,
Senior Lecturer in Biological Science,
University of London Institute of Education.

HODDER AND STOUGHTON
LONDON SYDNEY AUCKLAND TORONTO

Acknowledgements

My thanks are due for the essential contributions of Mr A.J.Jennings (University of London Institute of Education), Mr D.J.Mallett (Spencer Park School), Mr B.Taylor (Westminster City School) and Mr H.T.Stewart (Stretford Grammar School for Boys). The sound advice given by Professor J.F.Eggleston (University of Nottingham School of Education) was invaluable in organizing the book. A number of schools contributed to the improvement of the material by trials with students and providing useful comments and information for item analysis. Any errors or areas of doubt will, I hope, be treated with tolerance and reported to me for future amendment.

British Library Cataloguing in Publication Data

Lister, R E
Diagnostic testing in advanced biology.–
(Diagnostic notes).
Test Vol.
1. Biology
I. Title   II. Series
574   QH308.7
ISBN 0–340–21226–8

Complete Vol.
ISBN 0–340–21227–6

First Printed 1978, Reprinted 1978

Printed in Great Britain for Hodder and Stoughton Educational, a division of Hodder and Stoughton Ltd, Mill Road, Dunton Green, Sevenoaks, Kent, by J. W. Arrowsmith Ltd., Bristol BS3 2NT.

Computer Typesetting by Print Origination, Bootle L20 6NS, Merseyside.

Contents

Preface

The items and diagnostic notes in the Complete Volume are intended for use in teaching situations as stimulus material for students and as feedback material for teachers. The use of selected items at appropriate places in a course can provide the basis for class discussion, self checking or further study. With these aims in view, the items have been written at a level of difficulty which is likely to stretch the capabilities of students. If the items are incorporated in the conventional objective tests of student achievement, they should be selected carefully and possibly included with other items which reflect the current course or the special requirements of a particular examination syllabus.

In a book of this size, it is not possible to provide more than a selection of the possible topics in biology. The diagnostic notes on each item bear a title which indicates the intellectual skill which is likely to be employed in answering the question. Any earlier encounter with a situation similar to that in the item inevitably leads to the employment of recalled knowledge in answering it. Teachers must therefore take into account the previous experiences of students in judging whether the skill suggested is likely to be used in an item. A record of the achievements of students in the various skills which have been tested across the various topics would provide the information for building up student profiles assessed throughout the course. The categories used are related to Bloom's Taxonomy of Educational Objectives in so far as these can be applied in multiple choice items. They can be set out as follows.

Knowledge— of facts, terms, principles, sequences, processes and procedures

Comprehension—of principles, relationships, experimental procedure and design, translation and interpretation of information

Application— of principles to new situations, of numerical and non-numerical data, of graphical information and the making of predictions

Evaluation— of relationships between principles and situations and of experimental design

The skills of synthesis and logical coherence in expressing various aspects of biological knowledge and the ability to solve problems requiring analysis and a series of steps are also essential. For testing these, structured problems and exercises in continuous prose should be used.

I Understanding of Biological Science

1 Which statement represents the main aim of biology?

    A   to collect observations on living organisms
    B   to explain observations on living organisms in terms of principles and theories
    C   to collect facts about living organisms
    D   to provide man with powers of control of the living environment

2 Mendel's first law of segregation, when applied to the results of a genetics experiment, is a

    A   rule to which the design of the experiment must conform.
    B   description of the relationships which affect the results.
    C   prediction of the results.
    D   method for testing a hypothesis.

3 An hypothesis is

    A   an assumption to account for something not fully understood.
    B   a suggestion of how an experiment might be carried out.
    C   a complete explanation of the cause of the phenomenon.
    D   factual evidence which explains the phenomenon.

4 Which statement about progress in science is true?

    A   It depends upon putting hypotheses forward and then setting out to show that they could be false.
    B   It is impeded if an experiment fails to show that an hypothesis is true.
    C   It is promoted more by observation than by hypothesis.
    D   It is maintained by the verification of theories.

5 Which one of the following questions could be answered from the results of a single experimental procedure?

    A   What is the effect of varying the light intensity on the phototropic responses of a plant?
    B   What is the effect of the direction of light on the direction of growth of a shoot?
    C   What is the mechanism for the reception of light by a shoot?
    D   How does light from a certain direction cause curvature of the shoot?

6 Which statement is a proper expression of cause and effect?

    A   Water is absorbed by plants to maintain the turgor of cells.
    B   The water requirements of plants lead to the growth of roots towards suitably moist regions of soil.
    C   The need for protection of the young in mammals has led to the evolution of maternal care.
    D   The incubation of birds' eggs promotes embryonic development.

7 The graph illustrates a mathematical relationship between an environmental factor and a biological characteristic.

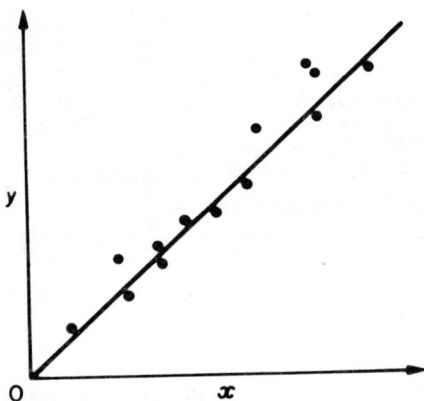

Which should represent the dependent variable?

A the x axis
B the y axis
C the points representing pairs of observations
D the line drawn through the scatter of points

8 The relationship between the fluid output from a species of fresh water protozoan and the concentration of the surrounding medium was investigated by placing individuals in different concentrations. The following results were obtained.

Concentration of the medium	Fluid output of the vacuole (arbitrary units)
Tap water	6.5
2% sea water	4.0
4% sea water	0.5

What is the correct conclusion from this data?

A Vacuole activity is inversely related to increase in concentration of the external medium.
B Increase in osmotic pressure of the external medium decreases the rate of inflow of water into the animal.
C Vacuole activity is regulated by osmotic pressure.
D Higher concentrations of sea water would cause vacuole activity to cease.

9 Which activity related to the study of ecology provides the most opportunities for experiencing the processes of science?

A study of an aspect of a single species in relation to the variation of a single environmental factor
B quantitative recording of the distribution of organisms and of environmental factors in an ecosystem
C correlation of the distribution of a species with an environmental factor
D recording of a succession of organisms in a particular environment over a period of time

II Basic Chemistry

1 The pH scale of 1 to 14 uses a mathematical device which expresses hydrogen ion concentrations as

    A an arithmetical increase.
    B a logarithmic increase.
    C a logarithmic decrease.
    D an arithmetical ratio of the concentration of H ions to OH ions.

2 Which expression is true for all reactions in which oxidation occurs?

    A transfer of electrons or protons
    B transfer of electrons only
    C gain in oxygen
    D loss of hydrogen

3 Which one of the following chemical processes does *not* involve the elimination of the elements of water between two molecules?

    A condensation
    B hydrolysis
    C esterification
    D phosphorylation

4 The structure of the glucose molecule is most accurately represented by

    A $C_6H_{12}O_6$
    B a linear arrangement of six carbon atoms with the other atoms attached.
    C a symmetrical ring of six carbon atoms with the other atoms attached in a regular pattern.
    D an asymmetrical ring of five carbon atoms and another atom with the other atoms attached.

5 Using an appropriate enzyme, which substrate could be used for the artificial synthesis of starch?

    A glucose
    B glucose–1–phosphate
    C maltose
    D sucrose

6 Which attribute identifies the molecule of an unsaturated fat?

    A a low proportion by weight of oxygen
    B the presence of some carbon atoms which do not have valency bonds linked with hydrogen atoms
    C the incorporation of straight-chain fatty acids of the stearic series
    D an ester formed by a fatty acid with an alcohol other than glycerol

7 Which type of molecular association is responsible for the α helix configuration of polypeptide chains?

    A   linkages between amino groups and carboxyl groups with the removal of the elements of water

    B   bridges formed by H bonds established within the molecule between the NH group of each amino acid residue and the CO group of another

    C   intrachain bridges formed by disulphide groups of the same chain

    D   interchain bridges between different polypeptides held together mainly by H bonds

8 Which type of substance could be most easily separated from an enzyme?

    A   co-enzyme
    B   activator
    C   prosthetic group
    D   a protein substrate

9 Enzymes promote reactions because

    A   reacting substances are brought into highly specific relations with each other.
    B   energy is added to the system.
    C   molecules of the reactants are speeded up so that random encounters are increased.
    D   products of the reaction are removed so that the reaction proceeds in one direction.

10 The diagram represents the energy levels involved in a biochemical reaction in which molecules x and y combine to give the molecule xy.

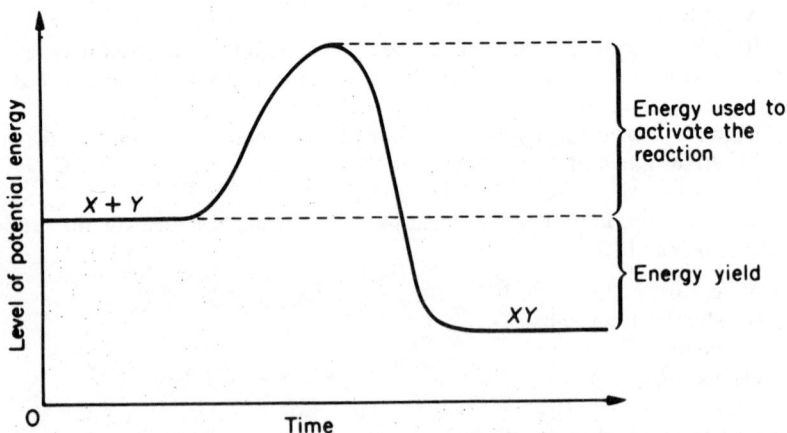

Select the correct statement concerning the effect of an enzyme on the reaction.

    A   Without an enzyme, there would be no initial peak on the curve.
    B   An enzyme would affect neither the energy required to activate the reaction nor the energy yield.
    C   An enzyme would decrease the energy used to activate the reaction but not the final energy level.

D An enzyme would increase the energy used for the reaction and the final energy yield.

11 Which one of the following curves represents the most usual relationship between temperature and enzyme activity when the temperature is raised steadily from 0 - 70° C over a period of three hours?

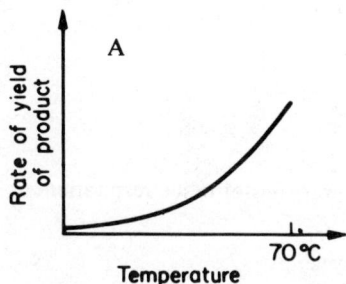

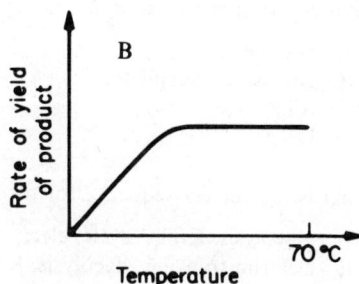

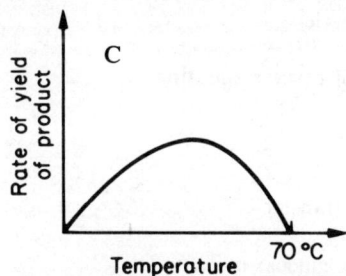

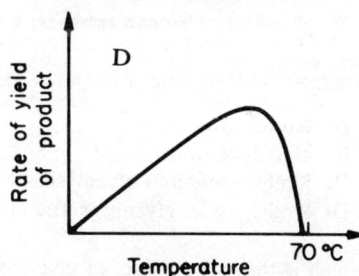

12 In the operon theory of enzyme induction proposed by Jacobs and Monod, the presence of the substrate induces the production of an enzyme in the cell by acting on the

A regulator gene.
B regulator substance.
C operator gene.
D structural gene.

13 Which property makes it possible to use heavy isotopes of elements as tracers in biochemical reactions?

A chemical reactivity different from the more usual isotope
B unreactivity in chemical processes
C radioactivity
D some physical property which is different from the more usual isotope

III Organization of Cells

1 The most common intermediate substance which is utilized in a wide range of energy-requiring processes in living organisms is

   A glucose.
   B glucose-1-phosphate.
   C ATP
   D DNA

2 What is the correct sequence for the main processes of tissue respiration?

   A glycolysis, Krebs' cycle, electron transfer
   B electron transfer, glycolysis, Krebs' cycle
   C Krebs' cycle, electron transfer, glycolysis
   D glycolysis, electron transfer, Krebs' cycle

3 Where is ATP produced in the processes of tissue respiration?

   A Krebs' cycle only
   B glycolysis only
   C Krebs' cycle and glycolysis
   D Krebs' cycle, glycolysis and electron transfer

4 Which is the end product of glycolysis of a glucose molecule?

   A fructose diphosphate
   B phosphoglyceraldehyde
   C pyruvate and ATP
   D NAD and ADP

5 Which reaction in tissue respiration requires the uptake of energy?

   A glucose-6-phosphate → fructose diphosphate
   B phosphoglyceraldehyde → phosphoenol pyruvate
   C NAD → FAD
   D cytochrome B → cytochrome C

6 Which intermediate product is found in all three of the following processes?

          anaerobic respiration
          aerobic respiration
          photosynthesis

   A succinic acid
   B lactic acid
   C phosphoglyceric acid
   D ribulose diphosphate

7 Material containing mitochondria was extracted from germinating mung beans for use in an experiment in which succinic acid was oxidised to fumaric acid and DCIP used as a hydrogen acceptor. The effective agent was the enzyme succinic dehydrogenase in the mitochondria. During the procedure, a sucrose/phosphate mixture was added. The purpose of this was to

A   act as a reducing agent.
B   provide energy for the reaction.
C   protect the mitochondria from changes in the reaction mixture.
D   preserve the material until the DCIP was added.

8 Which cell structures are most likely to be abundant at sites of active transport?

A   lysosomes
B   mitochondria
C   rough endoplasmic reticulum
D   Golgi apparatus

9 In which animal cells would Golgi apparatus be most abundant?

A   voluntary muscle
B   red blood cells
C   gland cells
D   unfertilized egg cells

10 In which cell structures would multiple layers of electron donors and acceptors be found?

A   the inner folded membranes of mitochondria
B   grana of chloroplasts
C   muscle fibrils
D   non-myelinated axons of neurons

11 Which reaction is characteristic of a bacterium which is a photosynthetic autotroph?

A $2NH_3 + 3O_2 \rightarrow 2HNO_2 + 2H_2O$
B $4H_2 + H_2SO_4 \rightarrow 4H_2O + H_2S$
C $4H_2 + CO_2 \rightarrow 2H_2O + CH_4$
D $2H_2S + CO_2 \rightarrow (CH_2O) + 2S + H_2O$

12 Which one of the following general equations for respiration in various microorganisms represents fermentation?

A $C_6H_{12}O_6 \rightarrow 2C_2H_5OH + 2CO_2$
B $C_2H_5OH + O_2 \rightarrow CH_3COOH + H_2O$
C $C_6H_{12}O_6 + 12HNO_3 \rightarrow 6CO_2 + 6H_2O + 12HNO_2$
D $2C_2H_5OH + CO_2 \rightarrow 2CH_3COOH + CH_4$

13 Which one of the stab cultures of bacteria would represent the distribution of a population of facultative anaerobes?

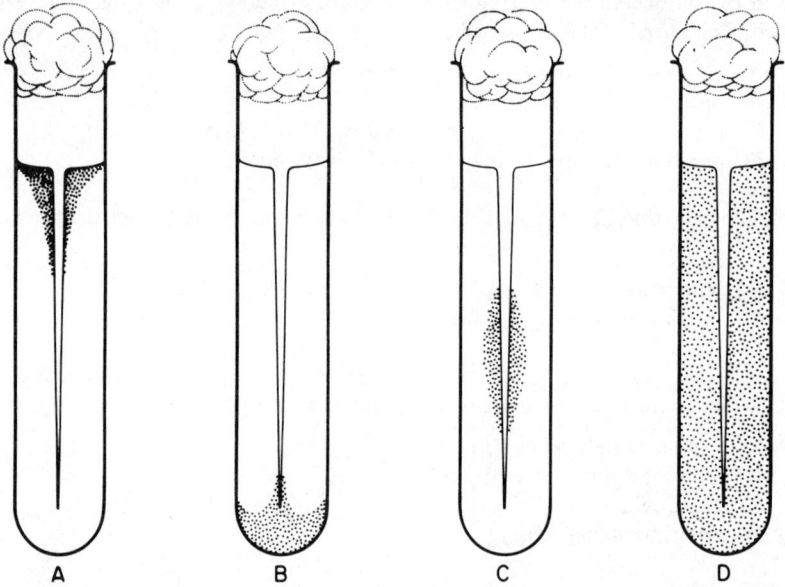

14 Gram's stain is often used in identifying bacteria. The following substances are added in succession for this technique; gentian violet, iodine solution, alcohol 100% carbol fuchsin (a red stain). A Gram positive species will show the effect of

    A   a violet colour from the gentian violet stain.
    B   a colour due to a reaction between gentian violet and iodine.
    C   a colour due to the effect of combination of gentian violet and carbol fuchsin.
    D   a red colour from the carbol fuchsin.

IV Genetics

1 Which process of cell division is essential if Mendel's first law of Segregation is to be fulfilled?

   A   division of the centromere
   B   duplication of chromosomes
   C   pairing of homologous chromosomes
   D   formation of chiasmata

2 Which process of meiosis is *least* directly related to Mendel's second law of Independent Assortment?

   A   the specific pairing of homologous chromosomes
   B   the reciprocal exchange of corresponding segments between non-sister chromatids in the paired associations
   C   randomly orientated separation of the double chromosomes of each associated pair
   D   randomly orientated division of the chromosomes in each daughter nucleus to give four single-stranded chromosomes

3 In a breeding experiment between a parental type showing the dominant phenotype and a parental type showing the recessive phenotype, the offspring showed equal proportions of the dominant and recessive phenotypes. Which one of the following statements must be true?

   A   Both parents had equal numbers of genes for the characters.
   B   Both parents carried recessive genes.
   C   The parents were pure strains.
   D   Half of the parents carried recessive genes.

4 For which genetical investigation would you use a breeding experiment which involved making a dihybrid cross, followed by a back-cross?

   A   determining the genotype of a parent generation of an observed phenotype
   B   investigating coupling or repulsion of genes
   C   finding if a gene were recessive and lethal
   D   confirming characters as alleles

5 It was found that a certain strain of dwarf mice was infertile. To obtain a supply of this dwarf it is necessary to arrange matings between heterozygotes for the gene. Which of the following procedures should be used to identify the required heterozygotes?

   A   cross them with normal homozygotes
   B   cross them with known heterozgotes
   C   cross them with dwarf homozygotes
   D   cross normal homozygotes with dwarf homozygotes

6 When a mouse with white fur was crossed with a mouse with black fur, the F_1 generation had grey fur. What ratios of phenotypes could be expected in the F_2 generation?

A 75% white, 25% black
B all grey
C 50% black, 50% white
D 50% grey, 25% black, 25% white

7 In a human family, the gene for right-handedness (R) was dominant to the gene for left-handedness. The descent over three generations is shown.

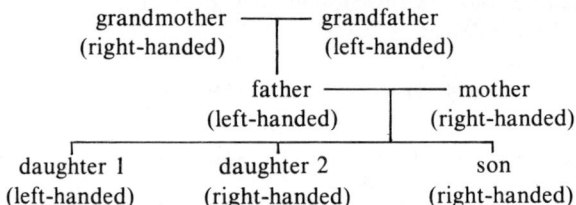

grandmother ——┬—— grandfather
(right-handed)   │   (left-handed)

father ———————┬——— mother
(left-handed)   │   (right-handed)

daughter 1   daughter 2   son
(left-handed)   (right-handed)   (right-handed)

Which is the correct expression of the genotypes of the three individuals shown in the table?

	grandmother	mother	daughter 1
A	Rr	Rr	RR
B	Rr	RR	rr
C	RR	Rr	rr
D	Rr	Rr	rr

8 How many different genotypes could be derived in one generation from a dihybrid cross between two organisms which were heterozygous for both characters?

A 4
B 8
C 9
D 16

9 What is the greatest number of homozygous genotypes which could be derived by a series of crosses from an organism which was heterozygous for the four alleles Pp Qq Rr Ss?

A 2
B 4
C 8
D 16

10 Which is the main disadvantage in using *Drosophila* for breeding experiments?

A small size of the imago
B short life cycle
C large numbers of eggs produced
D occurrence of mating soon after emergence from the pupa

10

11 Which of the following breeding experiments with the garden pea *Pisum sativum* would require the simplest procedure?

    A producing an F_1 hybrid generation by a monohybrid cross between homozygous strains of tall and dwarf plants

    B finding the ratios of the genotypes in the dominant phenotype in the F_2 generation of a monohybrid cross

    C testing a dominant phenotype for smooth seeds by a back-cross with a recessive phenotype for wrinkled seeds

    D finding the ratios of the F_2 phenotypes derived from the F_1 generation of a dihybrid cross between smooth green and yellow wrinkled parent seeds

12 Haemophilia is a condition in which human blood will clot only very slowly. It is produced by a recessive sex-linked gene and appears in males, but rarely in females. It can be transmitted by females which do not show the condition and also by affected males. Which offspring could be produced by a normal female and a haemophiliac male parent?

    A haemophiliac males and carrier females

    B normal males and carrier females

    C haemophiliac and normal males and carrier females

    D normal males and normal females

13 In *Drosophila*, the male sex is determined by the chromosomes XY and the female by XX. A recessive mutation in the X chromosome of a male was produced by exposure to radiation. The effect of this mutation could appear in the phenotype of a

    A female in the F_1 generation.

    B male in the F_1 generation.

    C female in the F_2 generation.

    D male in the F_2 generation.

14 In the magpie moth *Abraxas*, the female is the heterogametic sex and the gene for wing colour is sex-linked. From a cross between a normal coloured male and a pale coloured female, the F_1 offspring consisted of all normal coloured individuals with the two sexes in equal proportions. Which ratio would be obtained in an F_2 generation produced from these?

    A normal coloured males to normal females 1:1

    B normal coloured males and females to pale females 3:1

    C normal coloured males and females to pale males and females 1:1

    D normal coloured males to pale coloured females 1:1

15 In a heterozygous diploid organism, the genes P and Q were carried on one chromosome and their alleles p and q were carried on the homologous chromosome as shown below.

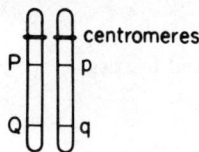

centromeres

P   p

Q   q

Which diagram would represent the arrangement of the genes at the end of meiosis I with one chiasma between the genes?

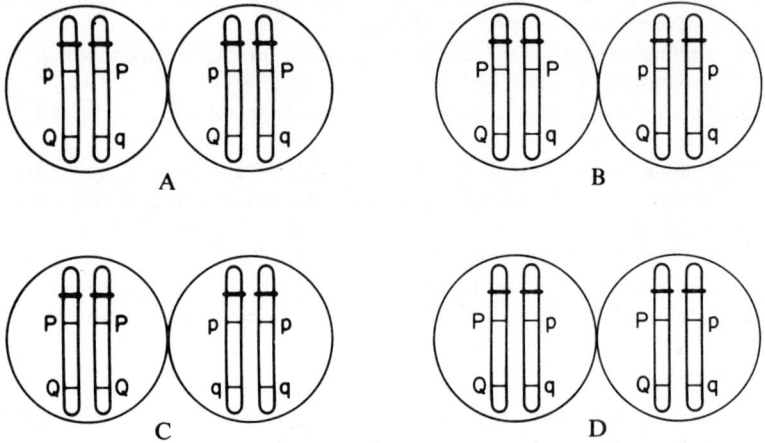

A

B

C

D

16 The cross-over value between two gene loci is

A the distance in map units between two genes.
B a measure of the importance of chiasmata in producing new combinations of characters upon which natural selection can act.
C the number of chiasmata that form on an average between a given pair of homologous chromosomes at meiotic division.
D the percentage obtained experimentally from the number of recombination types found in a given number of offspring.

17 The table shows the locus of certain genes in *Drosophila* which occur on chromosomes I and III.

Character controlled by the gene	Chromosome	Locus
Cut wings	I	20
body stripe	III	62
vermillion eye	I	33
rough eye	III	91
pink eye	III	48
forked bristles	I	57

Which would be the best examples to use to illustrate a high percentage of crossing-over?

A cut wings and rough eye
B body stripe and rough eye
C pink eye and rough eye
D vermillion eye and forked bristles

18 For four genes on a homologous pair of chromosomes, the following crosses between heterozygotes and homozygous recessives produced the percentage of recombinant phenotypes shown in the table.

Parents	Percentages of recombinants
AaBb and aabb	10
CcDd and ccdd	7
DdBb and ddbb	35
AaCc and aacc	32

Which diagram would most nearly represent a linkage map of the genes?

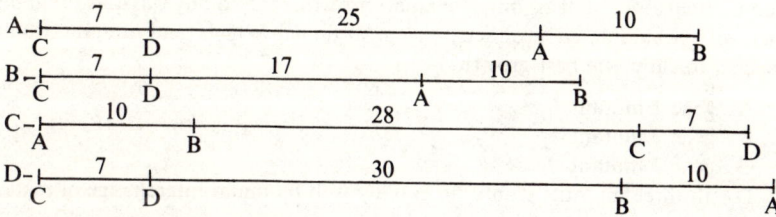

A ⊢——7——+——————25——————+——————10——————⊣
   C   D   A   B

B ⊢——7——+——————17——————+————10————⊣
   C   D   A   B

C ⊢——10——+——————28——————+————7————⊣
   A   B   C   D

D ⊢——7——+——————30——————+————10————⊣
   C   D   B   A

19 Each of the following expressions gives some attribute of a mutation. Which one provides the best general definition?

A the change in chemical structure of a gene that causes a different character to be expressed

B the rearrangement of atoms in a molecule of DNA

C a change in the expression of a character which occurs as a result of a change in the hereditary material

D a change in a gamete which is expressed in the phenotype of the next generation

20 The diagram illustrates some of the intermediate substances involved in the synthesis of the amino acid tryptophane in the haploid fungus *Neurospora*. The steps controlled by the genes A and B are indicated.

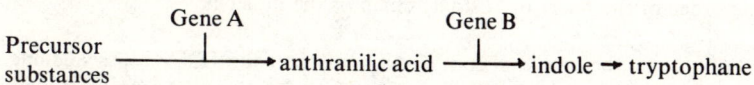

```
              Gene A                Gene B
                |                      |
Precursor  ————————→ anthranilic acid ————→ indole → tryptophane
substances
```

A mutant form fails to form tryptophane unless *either* anthranilic acid *or* indole are provided in the culture medium. If the mutant genes are a and b, this mutant form of Neurospora must be expressed as

A   Ab
B   aB
C   ab
D   AaBb

13

21 Inability to synthesize the essential amino acid arginine was found to exist in three different biochemical mutants of the bacterium *Escherichia coli*. Their respective mutations are expressed in the diagram.

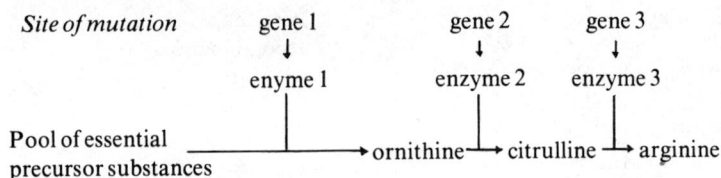

Site of mutation   gene 1   gene 2   gene 3
          ↓   ↓   ↓

         enyme 1   enzyme 2 enzyme 3

Pool of essential   → ornithine → citrulline → arginine
precursor substances

When grown together as neighbouring colony streaks on a solid nutrient medium with a subminimal amount of arginine to initiate growth, each colony was able to supply the other with accumulated products, except arginine. Which gene mutant would be expected to show the best growth?

 A gene 1 mutant
 B gene 2 mutant
 C gene 3 mutant
 D all three mutants would do equally well by mutal interchange of materials.

22 The amount of DNA found in the interphase nucleus of tissues showing active mitosis in animals may be twice or four times the amount found in gametes. This suggests that DNA synthesis occurs during

 A prophase of mitosis.
 B metaphase of mitosis
 C prophase of meiosis I.
 D interphase.

23 Which is an irregular feature of the DNA molecule?

 A the arrangement of sugar-phosphate groups
 B the pattern of the helix structure
 C the pairing of adenine with thymine and of guanine with cytosine
 D the order of the bases on a single chain of the molecule

24 Which would be the smallest combination of the four DNA bases adenine, thymine, cytosine and guanine to give a sufficient number of codes to represent the range of amino acids necessary for protein synthesis?

 A the single bases
 B bases in pairs
 C bases in threes
 D bases in fours

25 In the cell, polypeptide synthesis proceeds through the linking together of amino acids. The base sequence of messenger RNA defines the primary structure of the polypeptides because

    A it determines the order of alignment of amino acid-charged transfer RNA molecules.

    B there is a one to one coding relationship between each base on the messenger RNA and each amino acid.

    C each amino acid is defined by a pair of bases on the messenger RNA.

    D amino acid molecules align directly on the polynucleotides of the messenger RNA.

26 Which group of processes is most closely associated with the greater development of cell organelles in eukaryotes when compared with prokaryotes?

    A intermolecular interactions of metabolism not involving sequence coding

    B control of processes concerned with the selection and movement of substances

    C replication of DNA or RNA

    D polymer synthesis involving sequence coding

27 In eukaryotes, DNA may be found in

    A nuclei.

    B mitochondria.

    C chloroplasts.

    D all of these.

28 Unattached viruses always possess

    A DNA.

    B RNA.

    C enzymes.

    D proteins.

29 Which type of bacterial activity is most likely to be a two-way process by which genetic material is gained and lost?

    A mutation

    B transformation

    C transduction

    D genetic transfer

V Population Genetics

1 Continuous inbreeding in an isolated population leads to

    A increase in variation.
    B decrease in variation.
    C increase in mutation rate.
    D extinction of the population.

2 In a gene pool with equal proportions of a dominant and a recessive genotype, the removal of the recessive phenotypes in each generation would

    A make no difference to the proportions of the genotypes.
    B decrease the proportion of the recessive genotypes.
    C lead to the disappearance of the recessive phenotypes.
    D lead to the disappearance of the recessive genotypes.

3 A species of insect was found to have developed resistance to a commonly used insecticide. Which one of the following explanations is most likely?

    A The insect population was evolving towards resistance to the insecticide.
    B The original gene pool included genes which determined resistance to the insecticide.
    C The insecticide stimulated development of resistance in certain individuals and this was inherited.
    D The insecticide caused a mutation which was favourable to resistance and this was inherited.

4 Which one of the following examples of polymorphism in a population is initiated in each generation by the influence of the environment?

    A workers and queens in the honey bee
    B drones and workers in the honey bee
    C heterostyly in certain *Primula* Species
    D industrial melanism in the peppered moth

5 The genotype frequencies among the progeny of a random-mating population can be determined by finding the frequencies of the different types of gametes and

    A dividing their numbers by half.
    B adding them together.
    C finding which combinations are possible by constructing a table.
    D finding the product of the combined frequencies.

6 The frequency of each genotype in a randomly breeding population can be found by using the Hardy-Weinberg equation

$$p^2 + 2pq + q^2 = 1$$

Its use indicates that

A the dominant phenotype tends to increase in each generation.
B the results of breeding through several generations can be predicted.
C changes in the proportions of genes in a population when new mating types are introduced can be taken into account.
D the proportion of dominant phenotypes to recessive phenotypes is 3 to 1.

7 Which one of the following populations is in Hardy-Weinberg equilibrium?

	A'A'	A'A"	A"A"
A	0.49	0.42	0.09
B	0.64	0.68	0.04
C	0.64	0.16	0.04
D	0.36	0.15	0.49

8 To find the frequency of an allele in a population by using the Hardy-Weinberg equation we would only need to know the frequency of the

A heterozygote.
B dominant phenotype.
C recessive phenotype.
D dominant and recessive phenotypes.

9 84% of a human population were able to taste the substance phenylthiourea. The gene concerned with this has only two known alleles T and t. The non-tasters are recessive homozygotes. What was the frequency of the recessive allele in the population?

A 0.04
B 0.16
C 0.40
D 0.80

VI Life Cycles and Development in Animals

1 Which reproductive process in a protozoon is likely to produce the most genetic variation?

    A syngamy in *Paramecium*
    B autogamy in *Paramecium*
    C multiple fission in *Amoeba*
    D sporogeny in *Plasmodium*

2 Which part of a protozoon is most comparable to the soma of a metazoan animal?

    A residual cytoplasm of *Amoeba* undergoing multiple fission
    B residual cytoplasm of *Monocystis* gametocyte which has formed gametes
    C meganucleus of *Paramecium*
    D the three aborting nuclei formed from the micronucleus of *Paramecium* during the production of a gametic nucleus

3 The life cycle of *Obelia* differs from that of *Hydra* in displaying

    A polymorphism.
    B alternation between a sexual and an asexual generation.
    C a haploid generation
    D oogamy

4 Which animal can reproduce by parthenogenesis as a normal process?

    A *Hydra*
    B the tapeworm
    C the earthworm
    D the honey bee

5 Which example shows metameric segmentation?

    A formation of proglottides in a tapeworm
    B division of the body of an insect into head, thorax and abdomen
    C development of spinal nerves in a vertebrate
    D origin of the notochord in the embryo of a vertebrate

6 Where would imaginal buds be found in an insect?

    A nymph of cockroach
    B body of a caterpillar
    C corpora allata of a fly maggot
    D imago of a mosquito

7 Which factor determines sex in the honey bee?

    A queen substance
    B a chromosome mechanism
    C feeding of the larvae
    D type of comb cell in which larvae and pupae develop

8 In order to make an estimate of the size of a small, growing organism it was necessary to find the diameter of the visible field of a microscope under high power. With a magnification of 50X the field diameter was 1.2 mm. With the high power objective in use the magnification was 300X. The field diameter would then be

A 0.2 mm
B 1.2 mm
C 3.6 mm
D 7.2 mm

9 Which statement is true concerning the control of development of the tissues in a multicellular organism?

A For its development, each tissue depends solely upon the genetic expression of its own cells.
B The genetic code is modified by the environment.
C The development of a tissue depends upon interaction between genetic expression and the environment.
D Co-ordination of tissue development depends upon uniform genetic expression throughout the organism.

10 An investigation was set up into the effects of adding various concentrations of a dissolved substance on the rate of metamorphosis of amphibian tadpoles. At each concentration, the volume of solution and the number of tadpoles used was the same. The most important reason for this procedure was, that, at each concentration,

A interactions between the tadpoles would be the same as in any other concentration.
B the tadpoles would be likely to receive comparable doses of the substance.
C there would be less variation between the results for different individuals.
D a definite growth response could be expected from which valid comparisons of numerical results could be made.

11 Which has the greatest effect on the formation of the presumptive areas of the early frog embryo?

A migration of cytoplasmic material as a result of fertilization
B different rates of cell division caused by the presence of yolk
C the organizing influence of one tissue on another
D the expression of genetic influences from the zygote nucleus

12 During gastrulation in the frog, which cells do *not* migrate inwards through the blastopore lips?

A notochord
B roof of the archenteron
C lateral plate mesoderm
D neural plate

13 Which mesodermal component in the frog embryo is *not* segmented?

    A   myotome

    B   sclerotome

    C   pronephros

    D   lateral plate

14 Which feature in the development of the frog is a general characteristic of amphibia and not of other vertebrates?

    A   the almost entire replacement of the notochord by vertebrae

    B   the formation of gill pouches and lungs from the anterior part of the gut

    C   the formation of external gills

    D   the breakdown of tail tissues at metamorphosis

15 In the development of the chick, cleavage of the zygote is

    A   more regular than in the frog.

    B   replaced by the formation of the germinal disc (blastodisc).

    C   completed after gastrulation.

    D   never completed.

16 The addition of a harmless stain along the sides of a living 36 hour chick embryo helps to show the

    A   convergence of external cells towards the mid-dorsal line.

    B   spread of peripheral tissues to form the yolk sac.

    C   separation of notochord from the gut roof.

    D   origin of the endoderm by inward migration of cells.

17 Of the chick embryonic membranes, which is lined internally with ectoderm?

    A   amnion

    B   allantois

    C   yolk sac

    D   chorion

18 Which is the site of respiratory exchange between the chick embryo and the environment?

    A   allantois

    B   allanto-chorion

    C   sero-amniotic connection

    D   amnion

19 In experiments on inductive relationships in chick development, limb buds of three-day-old embryos were removed and grafted on to the flank of host embryos. The following results were obtained.

		Result
1	Separate grafts of limb-bud ectoderm and of limb-bud mesoderm.	No limb developed
2	Limb-bud ectoderm and non-limb-bud mesoderm grafted together	No limb developed
3	Non-limb-bud ectoderm and limb-bud mesoderm grafted together	No limb developed
4	Wing-bud ectoderm and leg-bud mesoderm grafted together	A leg developed
5	Leg-bud ectoderm and wing-bud mesoderm grafted together	A wing developed

These results indicate that the type of limb developed is determined by

    A mesoderm only.
    B the area of the embryo from which both tissues are derived.
    C ectoderm acting on mesoderm.
    D mesoderm when interacting with ectoderm.

20 In which cell of the female mammal does the nucleus undergo reduction division?

    A oogonium
    B primary oocyte
    C secondary oocyte
    D first polar body

21 Similarity between the embryo of the chick and mammal is most apparent in

    A the process of cleavage.
    B the process of gastrulation.
    C the completed gastrula.
    D the process of forming the embryonic membranes.

22 In the mammalian embryo, the first structure to develop a relationship with the wall of the uterus is

    A the amnion.
    B the chorion.
    C the allantois.
    D the trophoblast.

23 In the development of the rabbit placenta, which tissue remains intact?

    A uterine epithelium
    B uterine blood capillaries
    C foetal capillaries
    D foetal connective tissue

24 Which one of the following exchanges between foetal and maternal blood through the placenta of a mammal is non-selective?

    A absorption of foods
    B passage of hormones
    C exchange of oxygen and carbon dioxide
    D exchange of A and B blood group antigens

25 The diagram is a schematic respresentation of the circulation of the foetal and maternal blood in opposite directions at the sites of exchange in the mammalian placenta. The transport of oxygen from maternal to foetal blood takes place through the thin membrane.

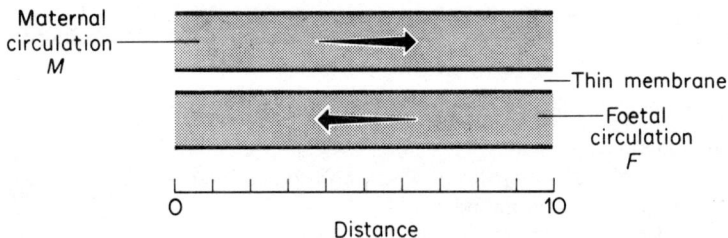

Which graph illustrates the counter-flow principle which promotes the intake of oxygen by the foetal blood?

M = maternal circulation
F = foetal circulation

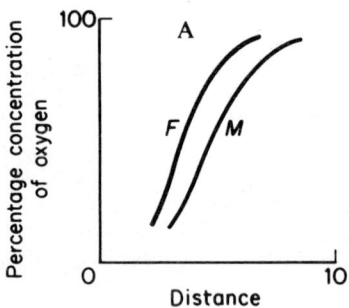

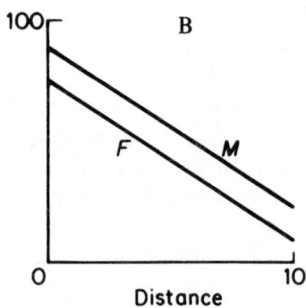

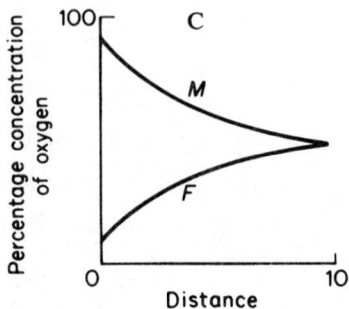

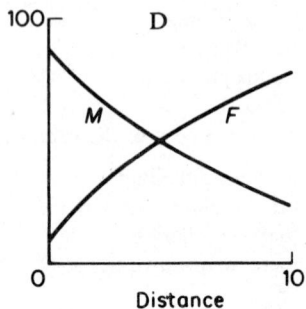

26 The diagram shows part of the human foetal circulation

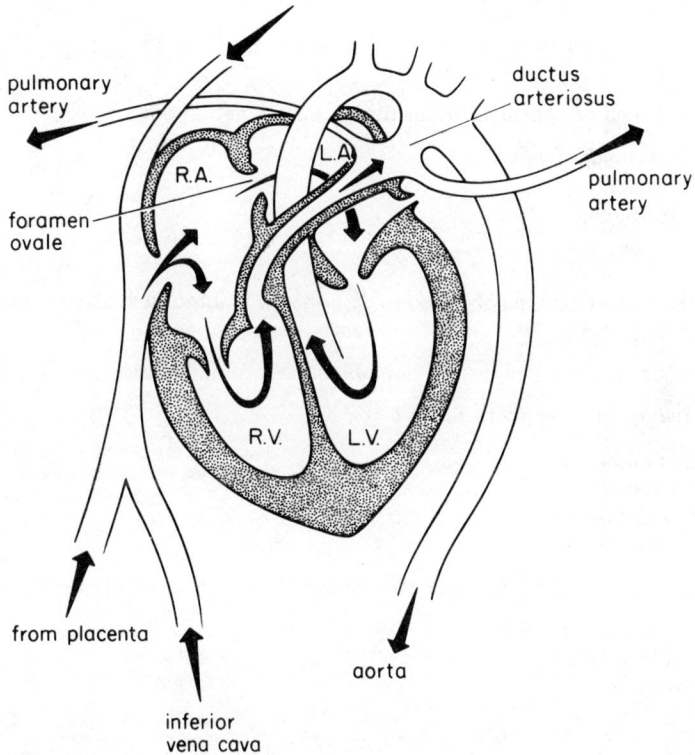

The function of the ductus arteriosus is to

    A allow blood to bypass the lung circulation.
    B provide the pulmonary arteries with oxygenated blood.
    C allow oxygenated blood to reach the aorta.
    D expand the lungs at birth.

VII Life Cycles and Development in Plants

1 In which alga does meiosis occur during the formation of gametes?

    A *Chlamydomonas*
    B *Volvox*
    C *Spirogyra*
    D *Fucus*

2 The following terms may be used to describe the status of sexual development and life history in algae;

i oogamous, ii anisogamous, iii haplobiontic, iv diplobiontic

Which two of these apply to *Fucus*?

    A i and iii
    B i and iv
    C ii and iii
    D ii and iv

3 Which plant produces the greatest number of meioses in its life cycle?

    A a haplobiont alga
    B a liverwort
    C a moss
    D a fern

4 Which was the first development in plants which eventually led to life on land?

    A development of a vascular system
    B retention of the egg in the archegonium for fertilization
    C development of a foot on the sporophyte
    D formation of a tube for fertilization by male gametes

5. Which group of plants has the most highly developed gametophyte?

    A liverworts
    B mosses
    C ferns
    D seed plants

6 Which type of plant does *not* reproduce by vegetative means?

    A thallus of *Pellia*
    B protonema of *Funaria*
    C sporophyte of *Funaria*
    D sporophyte of *Dryopteris*

7 In which respect is the fern *Dryopteris* more advanced than *Selaginella*?

A possessing large leaves and foliar gaps in the stele
B bearing spores on the vegetative leaves
C having one kind of spore
D having a gametophyte which lives independently

8 Which structure in non-flowering plants corresponds to the ovule of a flowering plant?

A scale of a female cone of a gymnosperm
B sporangium of a fern
C archegonium of a bryophyte
D egg cell of a bryophyte

9 Which structure is found in angiosperms but not in gymnosperms?

A carpel
B stigma
C pollen tube
D ovule integument

10 In the flowering plant, which one of the following is produced as a direct result of meiosis?

A pollen mother cells
B male nuclei in a developing pollen tube
C the ovule
D the embryo sac

11 Which part of the developing seed of a flowering plant is derived from the female parent only?

A testa
B endosperm
C radicle
D suspensor

12 Which tissue is triploid?

A endosperm of gymnosperms
B endosperm of angiosperms
C nucellus of angiosperms
D pro-embryo of angiosperms

13 Growth ceases in a mature flower. Its renewal, leading to fruit formation, is initiated by

A fusion of the male nucleus and the egg nucleus.
B cell division in the embryonic seed.
C a hormone produced by the embryonic seed.
D a hormone produced in the pollen grain.

14 By which process is water first absorbed by a germinating seed?

    A osmosis
    B hydrolysis
    C imbibition
    D translocation

15 Which combination of tissues acts together to provide the support of the hypocotyl of a cress seedling?

    A epidermis and collenchyma
    B xylem and parenchyma
    C epidermis and parenchyma
    D xylem and phloem fibres

16 In epigeal seedlings, which factor is mainly responsible for the emergence of cotyledons above the soil surface?

    A elongation of the hypocotyl
    B elongation of the plumule
    C the presence of endosperm
    D the absence of endosperm

17 The diagram illustrates an experiment on the interaction of the embryo E and the aleurone layer L of germinating barley to produce an enzyme which hydrolyses starch in the endosperm. The dialysing membrane M is impervious to proteins.

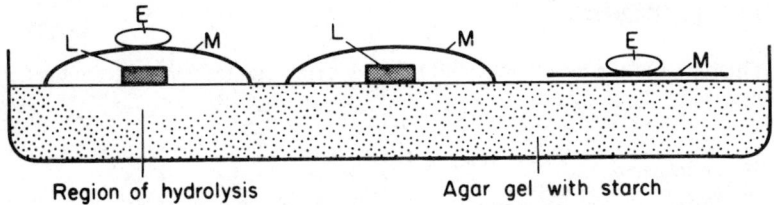

Region of hydrolysis   Agar gel with starch

Which conclusion can be drawn from this result?

    A The embryo is stimulated by the aleurone to produce the enzyme.
    B Aleurone produces a co-enzyme necessary for the activity of an enzyme produced by the embryo.
    C The embryo produces a substance which stimulates the aleurone to produce the enzyme.
    D The embryo produces an enzyme which cannot pass through the membrane. A substance from the aleurone breaks the enzyme down so that it can pass through the membrane.

18 A growing plant stem was marked in zones as shown in the diagram.

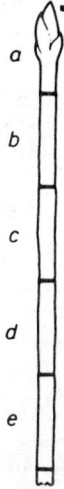

If the zones were measured at intervals of one week, which form would be expected for the curves on a graph recording growth?

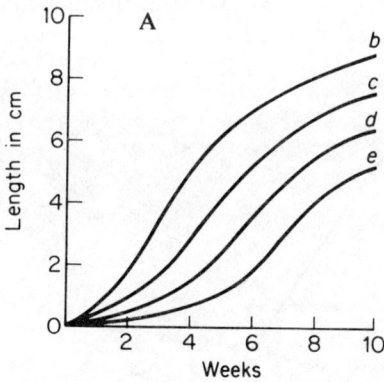

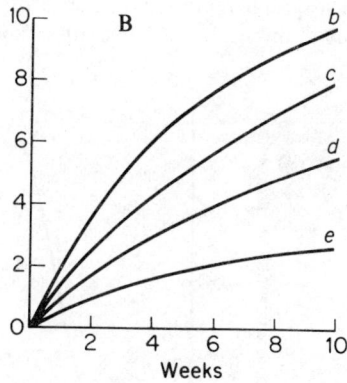

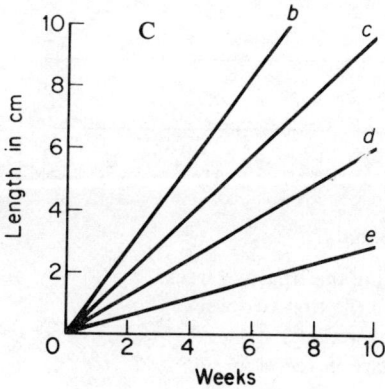

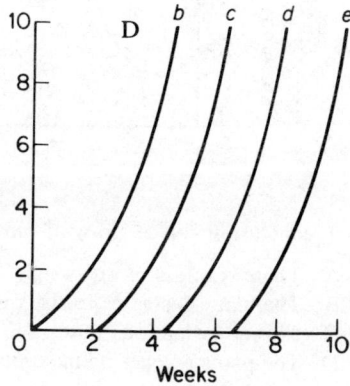

19 In what way is the growth of a herbaceous plant most different from the growth of a mammal?

    A Parts of the organism grow at different rates.

    B The growth of one part may be controlled by another part.

    C The total mass of the organism remains relatively constant once maturity is reached.

    D Growth tends to become confined to special groups of cells.

20 Which tissue of a dicotyledon stem is of secondary origin?

    A phellogen of the stem

    B calyptrogen of the root

    C fascicular cambium of the stem

    D metaxylem of the stem

21 Inverse correlation of terminal growth and the development of lateral shoots in plants is most directly dependent on

    A the direction in which food materials are supplied for growth.

    B the distribution of auxins such as indole-3-acetic acid (IAA).

    C the direct effect of the environment on each of these parts.

    D genetical factors which determine the order of development.

22 The graph represents the rate of growth of an annual plant from the time of germination until some time after flowering.

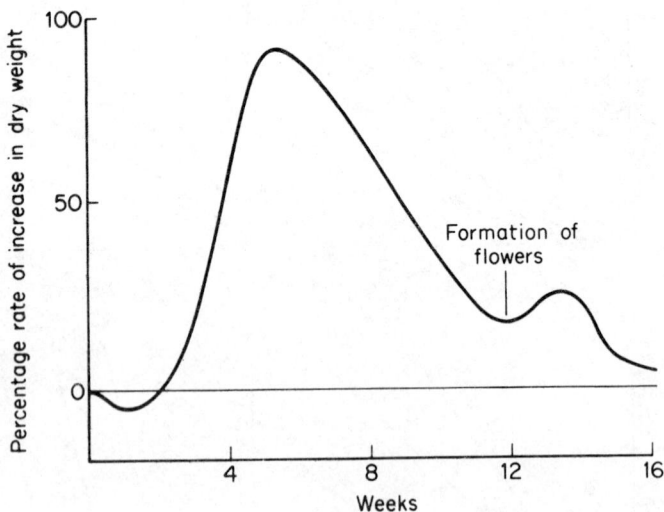

Which conclusion can be drawn from this data?

    A There is a loss of dry weight during the first two weeks.

    B The plant decreases in size during the first two weeks.

    C Flower formation causes a loss of weight.

    D The plant reaches its maximum size in five weeks.

23 The zone of maximum elongation in a root is characterized by

    A   replication of DNA.
    B   cell division.
    C   formation of cell vacuoles.
    D   differentation of cells.

24 In angiosperms, which type of organ is most likely to grow from the renewed division of apparently mature internal tissue?

    A   leaves
    B   flowers
    C   branch stems from a main stem
    D   branch roots from a main root

25 The graph summarizes the growth responses of standard lengths of root and stem of a plant when placed in a range of concentrations of a certain auxin.

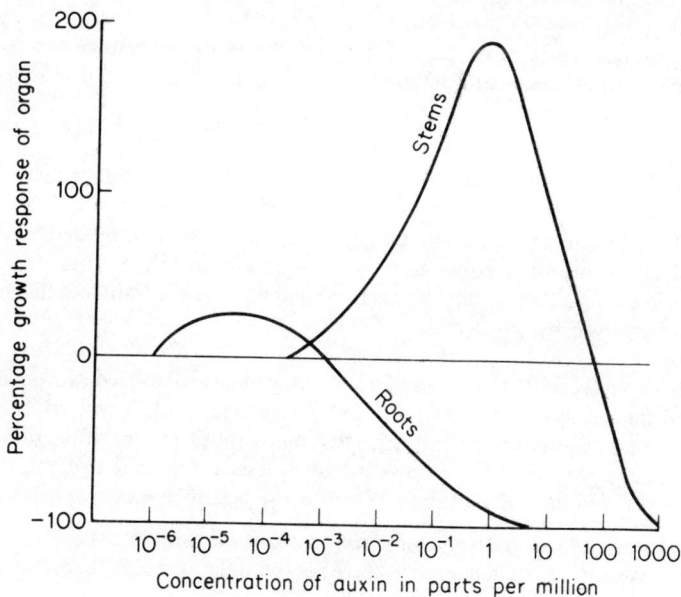

Which conclusion can be drawn from the graph?

    A   Roots are less sensitive than stems in their growth response to the auxin.
    B   Roots are more sensitive than stems in their growth response to the auxin.
    C   The presence of the auxin in the stems can repress the growth of roots.
    D   Roots do not require the auxin for growth.

26 The main effect of gibberellins is to promote

    A   bending in tropic movements.
    B   internodal growth.
    C   growth of lateral buds.
    D   growth of main roots.

27 Which would be the best treatment of tobacco plants in order to produce the large thin leaves required for cigar wrappers?

    A grow in lightly shaded conditions
    B feed liberally with nitrogenous fertilizer
    C plant well apart to give maximum exposure to light and air
    D spray with 0.1% gibberellic acid.

28 The climbing movement of the stem of a twining plant is preceded by

    A a regular movement of the stem tip.
    B a positive phototropic response of the stem tip.
    C an elongation of the cells closest to the support.
    D growth of the leaves.

29 Which treatment will break the dormancy of the seeds of some species of plants but have the opposite effect on others?

    A abrasion of the seed coat
    B illumination with far red light
    C generous watering of the soil in which the seeds are planted
    D maintaining seeds at a temperature between $0°$ C and $5°$ C for a week

30 Which one of the following statements is *untrue*?

    A Etiolation of the stem of a plant is stimulated by far-red light and inhibited by red light.
    B Lateral root growth is stimulated by far-red light and inhibited by red light.
    C Leaf expansion is stimulated by red light and inhibited by far-red light.
    D Flowering in 'short-day' plants is inhibited by far-red light and the inhibition is removed by red light.

31 When all parts except the leaves of a short-day plant are covered with a light-proof cover and then subjected to short-day light/dark treatment, it will produce flower buds. When a portion of this plant is grafted on to another plant of the same species which has been prevented from flowering by excessive exposure to light, this latter plant will also produce flower buds. Which is the best inference from this result?

    A Hormones can transmit information to all parts of plants.
    B Leaves are more sensitive to the photoperiodic stimulus than other parts of the plant.
    C The photoperiodic stimulus is received by the leaves and transmitted by a hormone.
    D The photoperiodic stimulus is received by all parts of the shoot and transmitted by a hormone.

32 The relation of flowering to the lengths of exposure to alternating periods of light and darkness in a species of plant was investigated by two experiments. In one experiment, the plants were subjected to dark periods of various lengths while the light periods were kept at 4 hours. In the second experiment, plants were kept in dark periods of various lengths while the light periods were kept at 16 hours. The number of inflorescences formed in relation to these periods is shown in the table.

Dark periods	Inflorescences formed in experimental light periods	
hours	4 hours	16 hours
8	0	0
10	0	0
12	4	6
14	5	7
16	5	8

These results indicate that flowering

A   requires long days.
B   is initiated by a long light period.
C   is due to short light periods.
D   requires a minimum dark period.

33 Which arrangement of an agar block on an oat coleoptile would result in the most IAA collecting in the agar?

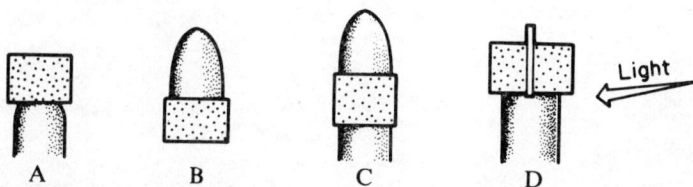

34 In an experiment on abscission at the base of the petiole of *Coleus*, leaves on a growing plant were treated in four different ways. The treatment and results are shown in the table.

Treatment	Results
(i) Leaf and petiole left intact	No abscission
(ii) Leaf cut off, petiole remaining attached to the stem	Abscission
(iii) Treated as in (ii) but the cut ends of the petioles treated with 0.1% IAA in lanolin	No abscission
(iv) Treated as in (ii) but the cut ends of the petioles treated with lanolin only	Abscission

The best inference from the results is that IAA is produced by the

A   petiole and accelerates abscission.
B   petiole and inhibits abscission.
C   leaf blade and accelerates abscission.
D   leaf blade and inhibits abscission.

35 The formation of adventitious roots in a stem cutting may be accelerated by applying

   A   indolylacetic acid.
   B   gibberellic acid.
   C   kinetin.
   D   2.4-dichlorophenoxyacetic acid (2,4-D)

VIII Water Relations in Plants

1 The first part of a procedure for the extraction of the green colour from leaves is to plunge them into boiling water. Why is this done?

    A to cause chlorophyll to break down to smaller molecules for subsequent diffusion from the cells

    B to denature the cell membranes so that they become permeable

    C to cause plasmolysis so that the cells can take up a solvent

    D to fix the cell contents for subsequent treatment

2 The osmotic pressure of a solution is proportional to

    A the number of particles in true solution.

    B the molecular weight of the solute.

    C the hydrostatic pressure of the solution.

    D that of another solution separated from it by a semi-permeable membrane.

3 Strips of a standard length from the epidermis of a plant were immersed in sucrose solutions of different molarities. After 30 minutes, the lengths of the strips were measured and compared with the original length. The results are shown on the graph.

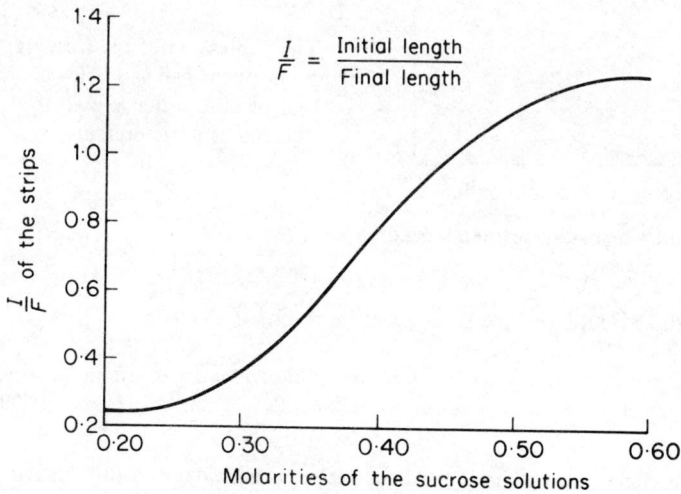

What molarity of sucrose solution would be approximately equal in osmotic pressure to the cell sap in the plant tissue?

    A 0.45

    B 0.50

    C 0.60

    D 1.20

4 The osmotic pressure of molar sucrose at 12° C is 23.3 atmospheres. If the sap of a plant cell had an osmotic pressure equal to that of 0.4 molar sucrose solution, what would be its osmotic pressure in atmospheres?

A 0.9
B 5.6
C 9.3
D 11.1

5 Four methods are indicated for finding the osmotic pressure of the cell sap of plant tissue.

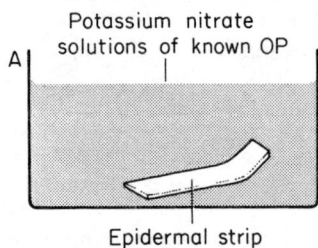

Potassium nitrate solutions of known OP

A

Epidermal strip

Find when 50% of the cells show plasmolysis

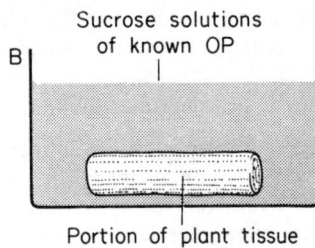

Sucrose solutions of known OP

B

Portion of plant tissue

Find when there is neither loss nor gain in weight

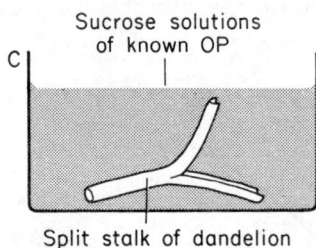

Sucrose solutions of known OP

C

Split stalk of dandelion

Find when stalk segments become straight

D

The depression of the freezing point of the cell sap below that of pure water is used to find the osmotic pressure.

Which method would give the most accurate result?

6 When the concentration of potassium ions in equivalents per litre in sea water was 0.012, the concentration of potassium ions in the cells of a marine plant was 0.509. This is evidence of

A the effect of an osmotic gradient between sea water and the cell sap of the plant.
B the physical diffusion of the potassium ions.
C control of the movement of the ions by metabolic activity.
D a cell sap which is hypertonic to sea water.

34

7 The graph represents the water relations of a model plant cell.

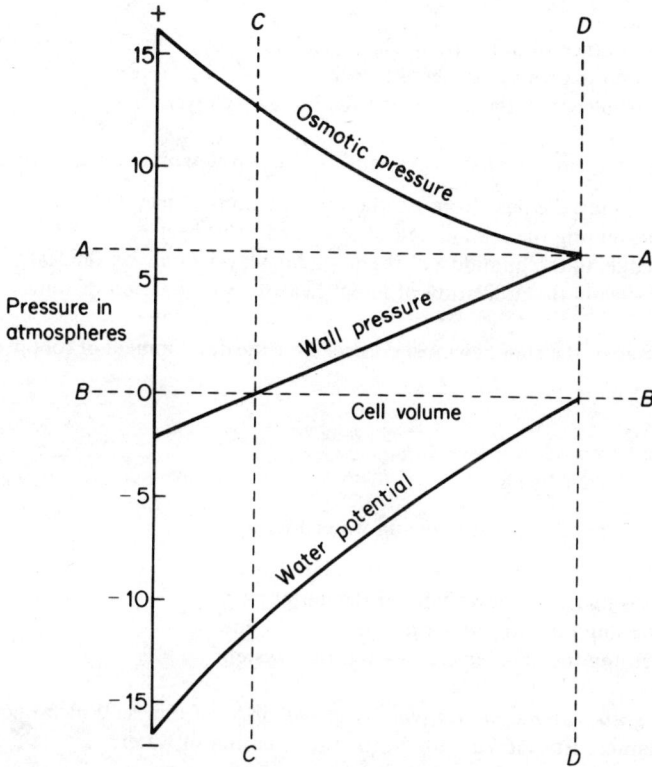

Which one of the four coordinates would best indicate that the cell was just turgid?

A   A – A
B   B – B
C   C – C
D   D – D

8 If plant cells with an osmotic pressure of +7 atmospheres and a water potential of –3 atmospheres were placed in a solution with an osmotic pressure of +5 atmospheres, what would happen to the cells?

A lose water and plasmolysis would take place
B lose water but there would be no plasmolysis
C take in water until an equilibrium below full turgidity was reached
D take in water until full turgidity was reached

9 The rate of transpiration in plants is most dependent upon

A metabolic control of diffusion by the leaf cells.
B metabolic control of the passage of water up the xylem.
C physical conditions of the surrounding atmosphere.
D physical conditions of water availability in the soil.

10 Which factor in transpiration decreases as wind speed increases?

A the rate of diffusion of water in the vapour phase in the intercellular spaces of the leaf
B the resistance to diffusion of the boundary layer of air on the leaf surface
C the osmotic pressure of the leaf cells
D the turbulence of the air outside the boundary layer

11 How could the closure of stomata cause a rise in the temperature of a leaf?

A by trapping the heat from exothermic reactions of metabolism
B by preventing the re-emission of absorbed solar heat
C by reducing the humidity of the boundary layer of air on the leaf
D by reducing the utilization of latent heat for vaporization of water

12 Which tissue of the root has most control over the development of root pressure?

A root hair
B cortex
C endodermis
D xylem parenchyma

13 Xerophytes are adapted to reducing water loss by

A decreasing the surface area of the plant.
B increasing the tissue volume of the aerial parts.
C decreasing the ratio of surface area to volume.
D increasing the area covered by the root system.

14 Marram grass (*Ammophila arenaria*) grows on sand dunes. Which one of the following characteristics is *least* useful for the retention of water?

A large thin walled epidermal cells at the base of grooves on the upper surface of the leaves
B stomata on the sides of the grooves on the upper surface, but absent from the lower surface
C hairs on the ridges between the grooves on the upper surface of the leaves
D extensive branching rhizomes

15 Which piece of evidence supports another view besides the cohesion theory on the ascent of sap in vascular plants?

A water being drawn in rather than exuded when borings are made in the trunks of trees
B stems decreasing in diameter during the day and increasing in diameter at night
C water receding into the xylem vessels when twigs are suddenly snapped
D water exuding from stumps when plants are cut off just above ground level

16 The upward movement of water in the xylem of plant stems is mainly caused by

A the high cohesive force of water under tension and confined to small tubes.
B a free energy gradient resulting from the evaporation of water.
C activated diffusion controlled by xylem parenchyma.
D positive pressure developed by roots.

IX Nutrition in Plants

1 In actively growing young plants, the best data to use for estimating the rate of photosynthesis would be

    A ratio of oxygen evolved to carbon dioxide absorbed.
    B increase in fresh weight.
    C increase in dry weight.
    D increase in carbohydrate.

2 The rate of photosynthesis in a submerged water plant was measured by collecting the gas which was given off in a standard period of time. With light as the limiting factor, all other conditions were kept constant. The volume of the gas produced with the light source 5 cm from the plant was 20 cm³. Assuming that the gas contained a constant proportion of oxygen, what would be the expected volume in cm³ if the light were 10 cm from the plant?

    A 5
    B 10
    C 15
    D 40

3 Under conditions of constant illumination, the compensation period for a whole aquarium would be of infinite length when

    A the biomass of animals equals the biomass of plants.
    B the respiratory exchanges of the animals are equal to the photosynthetic exchanges of the plants.
    C the oxygen intake of the animals equals the oxygen output of photosynthesis.
    D the carbon dioxide output of the animals and plants equals the photosynthetic intake of the plants.

4 The graph records an effect of light intensity on photosynthetic production.

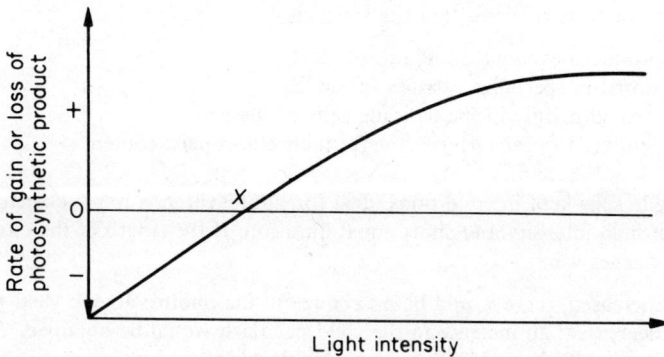

At point X the volume of oxygen used would be

    A   the same as the volume of carbon dioxide produced.
    B   less than the volume of oxygen produced.
    C   greater than the volume of oxygen produced.
    D   less than the volume of carbon dioxide produced.

5 Which one of the following would lead to stomatal closure?

    A   decrease in carbon dioxide concentration in the intercellular spaces of the leaf
    B   active photosynthesis in the stomatal guard cells
    C   conversion of sugar to starch in the stomatal guard cells
    D   increase in pH in the stomatal guard cells

6 A starch test of a variegated leaf which had been exposed to the light showed that starch was present in the green parts but not in the original pale parts of the leaf. Which statement should *not* be made from this result?

    A   This shows that chlorophyll is necessary for starch formation.
    B   The notion that starch is formed in the green parts of the leaf is supported.
    C   An enzyme which destroys starch in the pale parts of the leaf may be present.
    D   Carbohydrates may be transported from the pale parts to the green parts of the leaf.

7 The scattergram records the correlation between the distribution of starch and chloroplasts in a typical dicotyledon leaf.

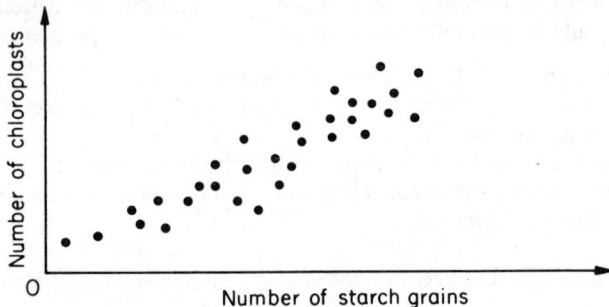

This data supports the view that the starch is

    A   produced evenly throughout the leaf.
    B   stored in specialized tissues in the leaf.
    C   located mainly in the palisade cells of the leaf.
    D   produced in cells irrespective of their chloroplast content.

8 Chlorella cells kept in conditions ideal for photosynthesis were subjected to light flashes of high intensity and short equal duration. If the length of the dark periods between flashes were

    A   increased, there would be no change in the photosynthetic yield per flash.
    B   decreased, an increase in the yield per flash would be obtained.
    C   increased, the yield per flash would decrease.
    D   increased, an increase in the yield per flash up to a maximum would be obtained.

9 In an investigation of photosynthesis in a suspension of *Chlorella*, the isotope of oxygen ^{18}O was supplied in one experiment in water molecules and in the other experiment in bicarbonate ions. What would be the relation expected between the proportion of ^{18}O supplied and the proportion of ^{18}O evolved by *Chlorella*?

    A   approximately the same in the case of the bicarbonate ions only
    B   approximately the same in the case of the water molecules only
    C   approximately the same for both A and B
    D   independent of the amount of ^{18}O supplied

10 A suspension of *Chlorella* cells previously kept in the light was supplied with the radioactive isotope of carbon in $^{14}CO_2$ at the moment the light was switched off. The accumulation of $^{14}CO_2$ in the phosphoglyceric acid (PGA) which then resulted is shown by the curve.

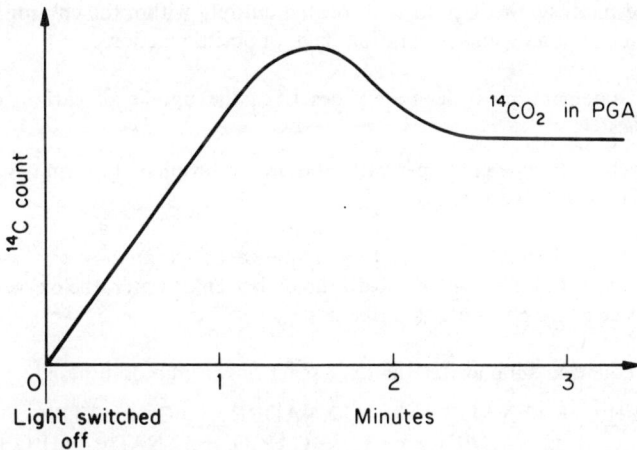

Which statement is supported by this data?

    A   Light inhibits the formation of PGA.
    B   The light reactions are slower than the dark reactions.
    C   A carbon dioxide acceptor is formed in the dark only.
    D   Light is required for the further conversion of PGA.

11 A plant was supplied with carbon dioxide which incorporated an amount of the radioisotope ^{14}C which was small enough to cause no interference with metabolism, but sufficient to be subsequently traced. After a period of photosynthesis, some of the leaves were removed and stored without their petioles for several days. Parts of each leaf were then found to be dead and these showed greater radioactivity than those parts which had remained alive. Which is the most likely explanation?

    A   In the living parts the carbohydrate had been removed by translocation through the phloem.
    B   The brown parts had absorbed more $^{14}CO_2$ and had been killed.
    C   Respiration in the living parts had led to the evolution of $^{14}CO_2$ which had escaped.
    D   The green parts had detected ^{14}C in the carbon dioxide supplied and protected themselves by closing the stomata.

12 The re-emission of light (fluorescence) which is seen from illuminated chlorophyll extracts does not occur from intact chloroplasts because

    A the light energy is being used to break down water to oxygen and hydrogen.
    B the light energy is being used to bring about the formation of ATP.
    C the cyclic system of carbon dioxide fixation absorbs the light.
    D transference of energy between closely arranged pigment particles is possible.

13 In the 'Hill reaction', in the presence of light, a suspension of chloroplasts extracted from leaf cells causes the reduction of the blue substance DCIP to a colourless condition. This provides evidence that, in photosynthesis,

    A an electron donor/acceptor system can be made to work independently of dark processes.
    B oxygen is derived from the water and not from carbon dioxide.
    C the photosynthetic process is located entirely within the chloroplasts.
    D photosynthesis and respiration have opposite reactions.

14 Which statement most accurately describes the uptake of carbon dioxide in photosynthesis?

    A Carbon dioxide combines with ribulose diphosphate to form two molecules of phosphoglyceric acid.
    B Carbon dioxide combines with co-enzyme A to form acetyl co-enzyme A.
    C Carbon dioxide is reduced to a simple carbohydrate.
    D Carbon dioxide combines with the hydrogen of water, the oxygen from the water being given off as a free gas.

15 Which equation summarizes the dark reactions in photosynthesis?

    A $12 H_2O + 12 NADP + nP \rightarrow 12 NADPH_2 + 6O_2 + nATP$
    B $6 CO_2 + 12 NADPH_2 + nATP \rightarrow C_6H_{12}O_6 + 12 NADP + 6H_2O + nADP + nP$
    C $12 NADPH_2 + 6O_2 + nATP \rightarrow 12H_2O + 12 NADP + nADP + nP$
    D $6 CO_2 + 12H_2O + nATP \rightarrow C_6H_{12}O_6 + 6O_2 + 6H_2O + nADP + nP$

16 Which is the direct source of high-energy electrons in the light reactions of photosynthesis?

    A water
    B hydroxyl ions
    C $NADPH_2$
    D ATP

17 Which one of the following factors is usually the most important in the uptake of mineral ions by root hairs?
    A rate of transpiration
    B proportion of minerals in the soil
    C rate of physical diffusion of the ions into the root hairs
    D oxygen available to the root

18 In which case of mineral deficiency would signs first appear in the younger parts of a vascular plant? Deficiency in

A calcium
B nitrogen
C phosphorus
D potassium

19 Which one of the following is *not* a symptom of iron deficiency in plants?

A reduced rate of respiration
B reduced root growth
C long thin internodes
D little starch present in leaf tissue

20 The table shows the percentages of protein and simpler nitrogenous compounds found in detached young leaves before and after they have been floated on two different aqueous media for two days.

	Fresh leaves	Detached leaves in darkness	
		On water	On 2.5% glucose solution
Protein	85%	59%	72%
Simple nitrogen compounds	15%	41%	28%

Which is the best hypothesis to explain the differences between these results?

A The protein is breaking down to simpler nitrogenous compounds.
B Protein is used as an energy source.
C Proteins and glucose are both used for metabolic processes.
D The breakdown of protein for metabolism is delayed by the presence of glucose which can replace it to some extent.

21 In vascular plants, which substance is restricted to one direction of translocation?

A sucrose in sieve tubes
B auxins in growing tissues
C reserve amino acids in germinating seedlings
D gibberellins in growing tissues

X Nutrition in Animals

1 The conversion of the milk protein caseinogen to paracasein which is precipitated to a calcium salt in the stomach

    A   provides small particles which are readily digested by pepsin.
    B   assists the movement of milk protein to the duodenum.
    C   delays the movement of milk protein to the duodenum.
    D   facilitates the break-down of terminal peptide bonds.

2 Which sequence of values represents the best approximation to the optimum pH for the action of the enzymes in the human digestive system?

    A   6.7,   1.8,   8.0,   7.0
    B   1.8,   6.7,   7.0,   8.0
    C   7.0,   8.0,   1.8,   6.7
    D   1.8,   7.0,   6.7,   8.0

3 Which substance, produced in the human digestive system, contains enzymes capable of promoting hydrolysis of whole protein molecules?

    A   secretion of the pyloric glands
    B   pancreatic juice
    C   chyle
    D   intestinal juice (succus entericus)

4 Which muscular movements of the internal parts of the digestive system are activated by sympathetic nerves?

    A   peristalsis
    B   pendular movements
    C   segmentation
    D   sphincter contraction

5 A wave of peristaltic contraction in the mammalian intestine can be stimulated by the presence of a mass of food. Co-ordination of this movement is controlled by the

    A   parasympathetic supply from the vagus nerve.
    B   sympathetic supply from the splanchnic nerve.
    C   intrinsic nerve nets in the plexus of Auerbach.
    D   direct contractile response of the muscles when stretched.

6 In the deamination of an amino acid in the liver, which could be an initial product?

    A   a keto acid
    B   urea
    C   glucose
    D   glycogen

7 The liver can make protein available as a source of energy by utilizing

    A non-essential amino acids for the ornithine-arginine cycle.
    B organic acids from amino acids for the Krebs' cycle.
    C the haem portion of haemoglobin.
    D reabsorbed bile salts.

8 In the digestive process of a mammal, the secretion of the hormone gastrin causes

    A an increase in secretion from the oxyntic cells.
    B an increased flow of bile.
    C inhibition of contractions of the stomach.
    D an increase in the sodium bicarbonate content of the pancreatic juice.

9 In an experiment with a dog, an operation brought the oesophagus to open at the neck so that, although food could be ingested, it did not reach the stomach. Gastric juice was secreted when the food was ingested. Which intermediary was operating to produce this effect?

    A gastrin produced by the walls of the pylorus
    B secretin produced by the walls of the duodenum
    C enterogastrone produced by the walls of the duodenum
    D transmission by the vagus nerve

10 Which feature of the cells of the intestinal villi most strongly indicates that the intake of food molecules is an active process?

    A The presence of the brush border of the columnar cells
    B the enzyme phosphatase in the columnar cells
    C the presence of goblet cells
    D Golgi apparatus in both kinds of cells

11 Which is the best general explanation of the important effects of minute quantities of vitamins on the functions of the mammalian body?

    A They contain essential trace metals which have their effects enhanced by incorporation in large organic molecules.
    B They activate specific hormones.
    C They are amines necessary for forming proteins.
    D They are essential constituents of certain enzymes.

12 The vitamin deficiency disease associated with the accumulation of pyruvic acid is

    A beri beri.
    B pellagra.
    C scurvy.
    D night blindness.

13 The effect of the intake of excessive vitamin D on a mammal would be to increase

    A the secretion of parathormone.
    B the deposition of calcium in the bones.
    C fractures of the bones.
    D the level of blood calcium.

14 The diagram summarizes the clotting sequence in mammalian blood. Which letter indicates the part played by vitamin K?

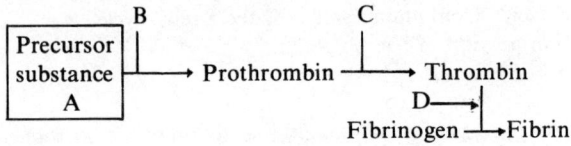

15 In an experiment on the effects of vitamin C and protein in the diet on the growth of a group of test animals, the data was set out as follows.

	Mean weight of N animals	
	Low vitamin	High vitamin
Low protein	a	b
High protein	c	d

Which combination of values would represent the mean effect of the vitamin level on growth?

A $\dfrac{a+b+c+d}{4}$

B $\dfrac{(a+c)-(b+d)}{2}$

C $\dfrac{(a+b)-(c+d)}{2}$

D $\dfrac{(a+d)-(b+c)}{2}$

XI Respiration

1 A moist surface is necessary for gas exchange between organisms and the environment because

    A gases diffuse more rapidly through water than through air.
    B moist membranes can be kept alive.
    C gases diffuse through membranes in solution.
    D living organisms first evolved in water.

2 The diagram illustrates a simple form of respirometer.

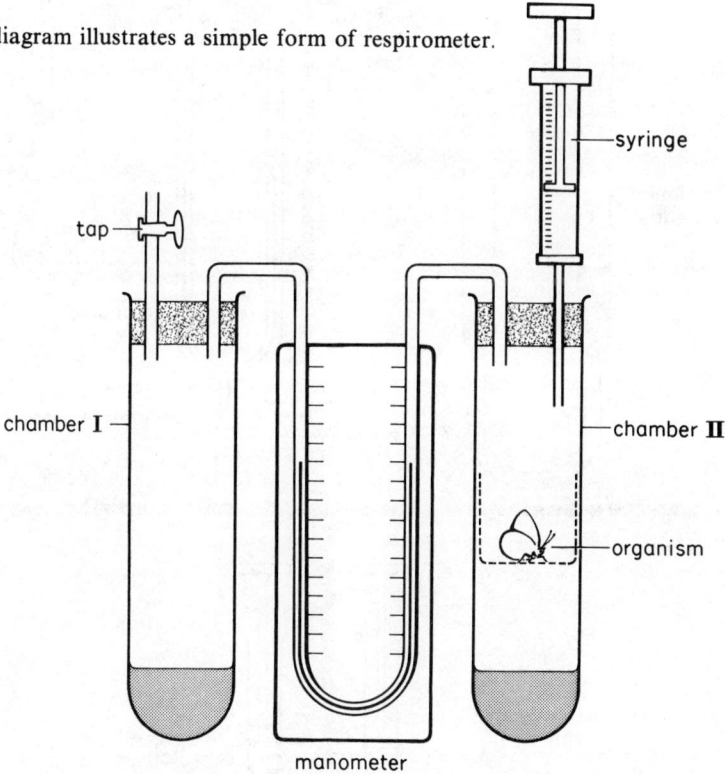

To measure the oxygen uptake of the organism in chamber II, it would be best to

    A place alkaline pyrogallol solution in the bottom of chamber II, use the syringe to adjust the manometer at the start and record changes in the manometer levels.
    B place potassium hydroxide solution in the bottom of chamber II, use the syringe to maintain constant manometer levels throughout the experiment and record changes in the position of the syringe piston.
    C place potassium hydroxide solution in the bottom of chamber II, open the tap on chamber I at the beginning and end of the experiment and note the changes in the piston level of the syringe required to level the manometer.
    D carry out the procedure as in B but first using water instead of potassium hydroxide solution and then repeating the procedure using potassium hydroxide solution.

3 The diagrams illustrate four types of respirometer. In each case the water bath which controls temperature of the working chamber has been omitted. Which one operates by recording changes of pressure?

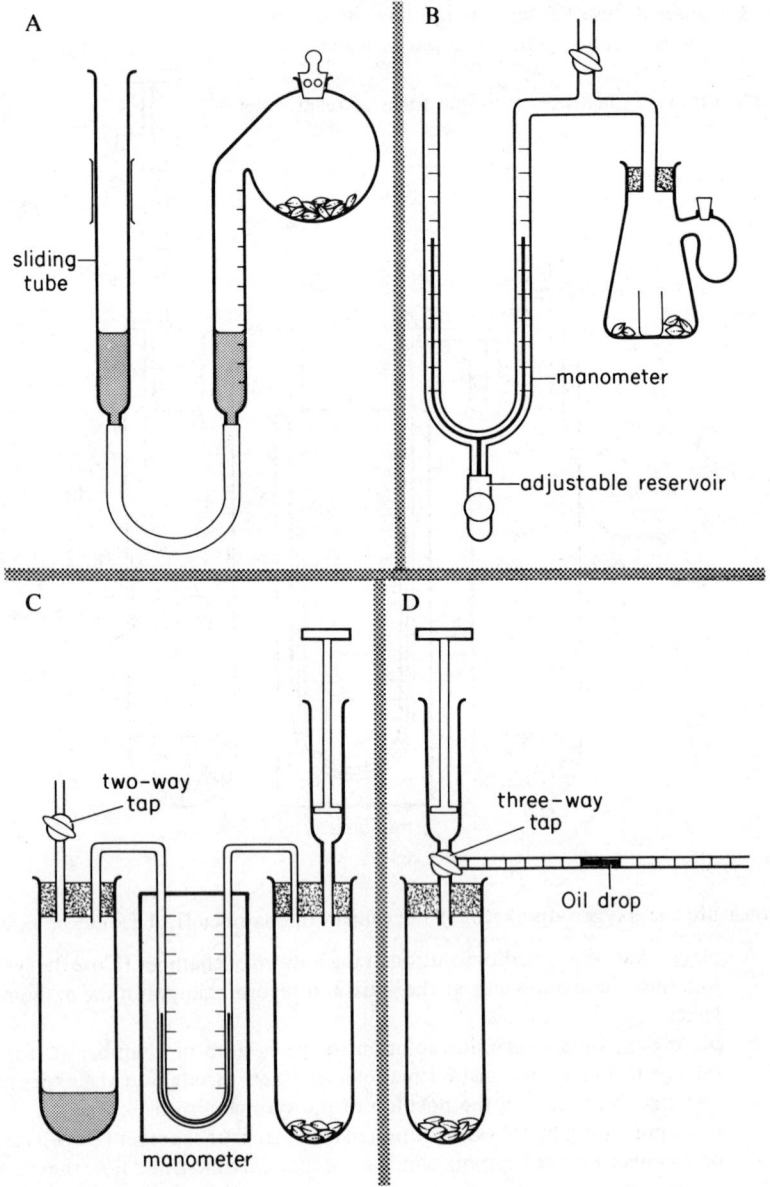

A

sliding tube

B

manometer

adjustable reservoir

C

two-way tap

manometer

D

three-way tap

Oil drop

4 An animal which weighed 4 grams consumed 2 cm³ of oxygen in 10 minutes. Which figure expresses the respiratory rate in volume of oxygen used per gram of body weight per minute?

   A 0.01
   B 0.05
   C 0.1
   D 1.0

5 Which is the best model of energy release in respiration in biological systems?

   A a cascade of electrons through a series of compounds
   B a gain of electrons by a series of acceptors
   C the formation of high energy compounds at certain stages of the respiratory pathway
   D the total transfer of electrons from hydrogen to oxygen

6 Acquiring an oxygen debt is evidence that

   A lactic acid can be converted into glycogen.
   B oxygen cannot be stored in the tissues.
   C anaerobic processes are slower than aerobic processes.
   D aerobic respiration is more complex than glycolysis.

7 Anaerobic respiration in yeast must release less energy than aerobic respiration because

   A energy from oxygen is not available.
   B much carbon dioxide is produced.
   C less energy is required by yeast.
   D ethyl alcohol contains potential energy.

8 Which respiratory quotient would indicate anaerobic respiration in a plant?

   A 2.0 to 7.0
   B 1.0
   C 0.7
   D below 0.5

9 In an experiment on the rate of oxygen consumption of a batch of germinating seeds, a series of replicates was carried out with the aim of providing a reliable mean average result. The reliability would best be expressed by

   A stating the range of values obtained.
   B finding the mean deviation.
   C finding the standard deviation.
   D finding the median of the values obtained.

10 In an animal which is respiring aerobically, which is the most reliable method of estimating the general metabolic activity?

   A finding the calorific value of the foods consumed
   B measuring the uptake of oxygen
   C finding the respiratory quotient
   D finding the temperature of the body surface

11 Which animal takes air most directly to its tissues?

    A   *Amoeba*
    B   a fish
    C   an insect
    D   an earthworm

12 Which is the correct explanation of the advantage of water flowing over the gills of a fish in the opposite direction to the flow of blood in the gill capillaries?

    A   It enables the blood to first meet water with the highest oxygen content.
    B   It allows oxygen and carbon dioxide to replace each other.
    C   It maintains differences in concentration of the dissolved gases between water and the blood along the length of the capillaries.
    D   It produces an increasing difference between oxygen concentration in the blood and oxygen concentration in the water.

13 The rate of gas exchange through the surfaces of the lung in a mammal is largely controlled by the rate of breathing. This is because

    A   the mass flow of air past respiratory surfaces maintains a good diffusion gradient.
    B   it influences the differences in concentration between the gases of the air and of the blood.
    C   the concentration of oxygen at the lung surfaces controls the rate of active transport through the cells of the alveoli.
    D   the saturation of the blood with oxygen and carbon dioxide depends upon the combined partial pressure of these gases.

14 The most favourable feature for a man lifting a weight which required an energy output of 1,000 joules would be a high

    A   tidal volume of the lungs.
    B   heart output when at rest.
    C   blood glucose level.
    D   capacity for oxygen debt.

15 Which volume of the human lungs would be impossible to find by using a simple spirometer only?

    A   inspiratory reserve volume
    B   expiratory reserve volume
    C   residual volume
    D   vital capacity

16 Which volume would most likely represent the residual air in adult human lungs in cubic centimetres?

    A   4500
    B   2000
    C   1000
    D   500

17 The diagram is a simplified representation of the nervous control of breathing in a mammal.

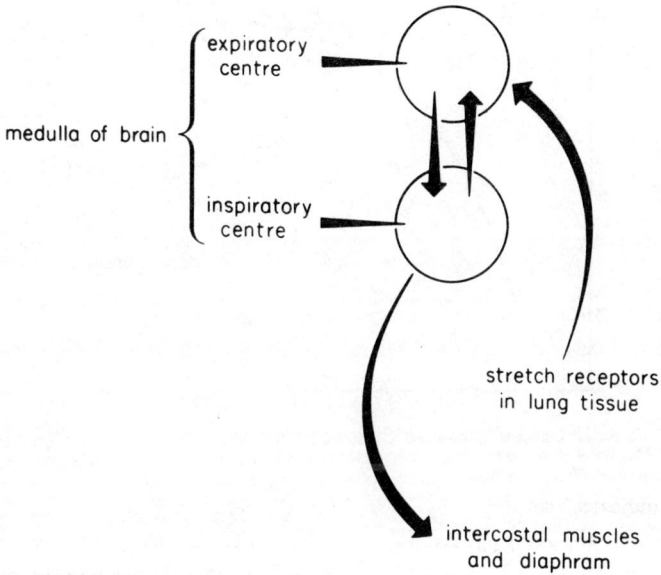

Which term best describes the action of this system?

    A   reflex arc
    B   oscillating negative feedback
    C   positive feedback
    D   homeostasis

18 The ascent of high mountains may cause altitude sickness in man. Which is the prime cause of this condition?

    A   excess carbon dioxide in the blood
    B   decreased efficiency of haemoglobin
    C   decreased partial pressure of oxygen
    D   decreased proportion of oxygen in the air

19 The diagram shows a dissociation curve for oxyhaemoglobin in human blood.

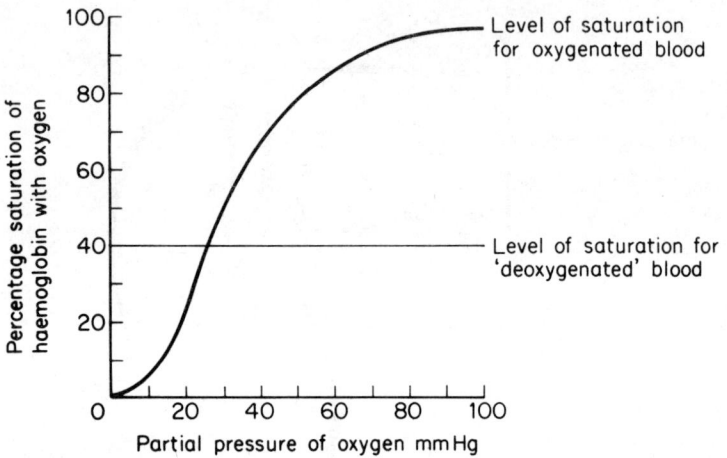

The curve indicates that

A   the blood is fully saturated with oxygen at the lungs.
B   small variations in oxygen pressure in the alveolar air will have little effect on loading the haemoglobin with oxygen.
C   small variations in the oxygen demands of the tissues will have little effect on the unloading of oxygen from the haemoglobin.
D   the affinity of haemoglobin for oxygen decreases at higher partial pressures of oxygen.

20 An increase in carbon dioxide in human blood shifts the oxyhaemoglobin dissociation curve to the right. This is because

A   diffusion of gases between lung alveoli and blood capillaries depends upon their partial pressures.
B   the greater solubility of carbon dioxide allows it to displace oxygen.
C   lowering the pH decreases the oxygen carrying capacity of the blood.
D   an increase in carbon dioxide in the blood increases the ventilation rate.

XII Circulation and Blood

1 Which blood vessel in a mammal will contain the most completely mixed deoxygenated blood?

   A posterior vena cava
   B pulmonary vein
   C pulmonary artery
   D hepatic portal vein

2 Which statement best describes factors associated with the pulse wave in the blood system of a mammal?

   A The rate at which the pulse wave travels depends upon the heart rate and the velocity of the blood in the arteries.
   B The absence of a pulse wave in veins indicates that the blood is propelled in them by some factor other than the heart beat.
   C The energy of each pulse is temporarily stored in the elastic walls of the arteries.
   D A decrease in capillary resistance would increase the pressure, amplitude and velocity of the pulse wave.

3 Which procedure would provide the best evidence of the origin of the excitation wave for the heart beat in a mammal?

   A heating and cooling the sinu-atrial node
   B clamping the right and left bundles of the Purkinje fibres
   C applying electrical stimuli to the cardiac branch of the vagus nerve
   D applying electrical stimuli to the sympathetic nerves to the heart

4 Which is the correct sequence of the following events which occur in the conduction of the excitation wave from the pace maker in the mammalian heart?

   1 Purkinje fibres conduct the wave from the auriculo-ventricular node.
   2 Atrial muscle fibres contract as the wave reaches them.
   3 There is a time delay at the auriculo-ventricular node.
   4 The ventricular muscle fibres contract as the wave reaches them.

   A 2 3 4 1
   B 3 1 2 4
   C 2 3 1 4
   D 1 2 3 4

5 Stimulation of the vagus nerve in a mammal would effect the circulation by

   A increasing the arterial pressure.
   B decreasing the amount of acetyl choline liberated in the heart.
   C increasing the conductivity of the auriculo-ventricular bundle.
   D increasing the venous pressure.

6 The diagram indicates the relative volumes and linear velocities in successive parts of the systemic circulation in a mammal.

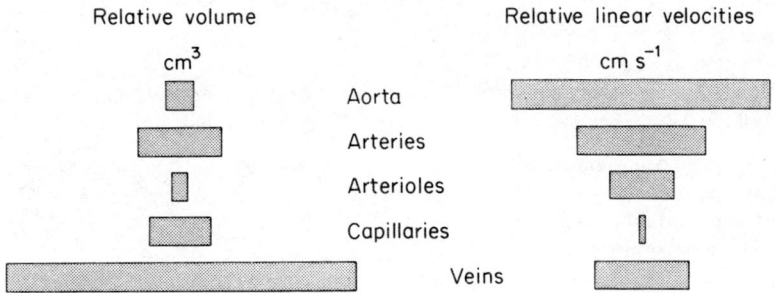

Relative volume cm^3 / Relative linear velocities cm s^{-1} — Aorta, Arteries, Arterioles, Capillaries, Veins

Bearing in mind, that, apart from fluctuations due to the pulse wave, the circulation is maintained by a steady fall of pressure throughout the system; where is the greatest resistance to the flow of blood?

A   aorta
B   arteries
C   arterioles
D   capillaries

7 In a capillary blood vessel, the following pressure relationships were found between the vessel and the surrounding tissue.

	mm Hg
Capillary blood	
hydrostatic pressure	30
osmotic pressure	25
Tissue fluid	
hydrostatic pressure	8
osmotic pressure	10

What is the effective filtration pressure in mm Hg?

A   22
B   15
C   7
D   3

8 The main flow of lymph along lymphatic vessels is due to

A   intermittent pressure of the surrounding muscles and a system of valves.
B   the action of the lymph nodes.
C   pressure of plasma passing from blood capillaries to lymphatic vessels.
D   negative pressure in the veins of the neck into which the thoracic lymph duct opens.

9 Which condition promotes activity of the lymph nodes?

  A local infection
  B absorption of fats
  C loss of blood
  D stress conditions which stimulate the secretions of the adrenal cortex

10 Which one of the following homeostatic properties of the blood is inherited?

  A oxygen carrying capacity
  B speed of circulation
  C resistance to infection
  D capacity for clotting

11 Haemoglobin is released from red blood cells when they are placed in a solution of sodium chloride which is at a lower concentration than that of the solutes in the interior of the cells. This is caused by

  A diffusion of the cell solutes down a concentration gradient.
  B exosmosis of substances from the cells.
  C endosomosis causing rupture of the cell membranes.
  D increased permeability of the cell membranes caused by sodium chloride.

12 Which substance increases in the blood plasma when there is an uptake of carbon dioxide?

  A carbonic acid
  B potassium bicarbonate
  C sodium bicarbonate
  D sodium chloride

13 Which treatment of a sample of blood would increase its intake of oxygen from atmospheric air?

  A raising the temperature
  B decreasing the carbon dioxide content
  C raising the atmospheric pressure
  D lowering the pH value

14 When blood from a donor is incompatible with that of the recipient, agglutination is due to

  A antibodies in the red cells attacking antigens.
  B antigens of the red cells attacking antibodies of the donor.
  C antigens of the donor's red cells attacking other antibodies.
  D antibodies of the recipient reacting with antigens of the donor.

15 In which instance would a blood transfusion be inadvisable?

	Donor	Recipient
A	A	AB
B	B	AB
C	AB	A
D	O	A

16 It has been suggested that there is an exchange of antigenic material between maternal blood and the foetus in a mammal. If this is true, which would be the best explanation of the maintenance of placental union?

A There is a temporary suspension of the maternal immunological response.
B The two kinds of antigenic material do not react because of their similar genetic origins.
C The placental tissues are largely of embryonic origin and therefore tolerate embryonic antigens.
D Differences in the blood groups prevent interaction of antigens.

17 Which statement concerning the rhesus factor in human blood is *untrue?*

A There is no naturally occuring antibody to the rhesus factor.
B Antibodies to the rhesus antigen develop in the mother's blood during pregnancy if she is rhesus negative.
C The rhesus factor is inherited as a dominant gene.
D A transfusion of Rh positive blood to an Rh negative woman would protect an Rh positive foetus.

18 What is the most likely effect of a second innoculation of a mammal with an antigen when it is given a few weeks after a first innoculation?

A Corresponding antibodies are not produced while the original ones are still present.
B The animal acquires sensitivity to the antigen and fails to produce more antibody
C Antibodies are produced in smaller quantities than the first time.
D Antibodies are produced in larger quantities than the first time.

19 A small mammal P was given a skin graft from another individual Q of the same species. The graft was rejected. Skin grafts from other individuals R and S were then tried on P with the following results.

    graft from R; soon rejected
    graft from S; rejected much later

The choice of a donor for a graft for individual Q would be

A R because it was most readily rejected by P.
B S because it is more likely to be accepted by Q.
C neither R nor S because they are both ultimately rejected by P.
D neither R nor S because the results relate to P and not to Q.

20 Biochemical evidence of relationship between species may be obtained by injecting a rabbit with a specific substance derived from a species X. The blood of the rabbit reacts by forming a matching antibody. If this antibody is extracted from the blood, it will form an insoluble compound when mixed with the substance from species X. This also occurs when the antibody is mixed with a corresponding substance from a related species Y. What is the special name for this type of antibody formed in the rabbit blood?

A   antitoxin
B   agglutinin
C   complement
D   precipitin

XIII Osmoregulation and Excretion in Animals

1 When certain marine organisms were placed in fresh water, they eventually died. Which could be the most likely explanation?

A loss of water from the tissues
B excess of water in the tissues
C loss of salts
D loss of permeability of the external membranes

2 In slightly diluted sea water, the marine flatworm *Gunda* swells when deprived of oxygen and shrinks to normal size when the oxygen supply is restored. Which is the most likely explanation?

A Metabolic activity which opposes the effect of osmosis is influenced by the oxygen supply.
B Waste products accumulate when oxidative anabolism is incomplete.
C Permeability of the surface of the organism is decreased by lack of oxygen.
D The animal is able to increase its surface area to compensate for the lower oxygen intake per unit area.

3 The water balance in the mammalian body is controlled by

A the amount of water absorbed by the gut.
B certain hormones.
C glomerular filtration by the kidneys.
D the activity of the sweat glands.

4 The table shows three of the nitrogen compounds excreted by four species of animals.

Species	Percentage of nitrogen excreted		
	Urea	Uric acid	Ammonia
A	0.2	80.8	3.0
B	3.0	0.7	68.0
C	9.9	0.0	73.3
D	85.0	2.2	3.5

Which species shows the best adaptation to water conservation?

5 Urea is directly produced in mammals from

A ammonia released by oxidative deamination.
B oxidative deamination of purines.
C breakdown of ornithine.
D breakdown of arginine.

6 The table shows the proportions of solutes and water in a sample of human blood plasma and a sample of urine.

	Percentage in arterial blood plasma	Percentage in urine
(a) proteins	7.5 to 9.0	0
(b) chloride	0.37	0.6
(c) urea	0.03	2.0
(d) sugar	0.1	0
(e) uric acid	0.003	0.05
(f) hippuric acid	0	0.07
(g) creatinine	0.001	0.1
(h) ammonium salts	0.001	0.04
(i) water	90.0	96.0

Use this data and your knowledge of kidney function to indicate which substances are excreted from the blood.

A c e f g
B b c g i
C c e g h
D b c f i

7 The pressure available for effective filtration in the glomeruli of the mammalian kidney is reduced by

A resorption of the filtrate by the tubules.
B the size of protein molecules in the plasma.
C the osmotic potential of the plasma protein.
D peripheral resistance of the capillaries in the body.

8 Evidence that ultrafiltration occurs at the glomeruli of the kidney could be obtained by comparing the size of the molecules present in the glomerular exudate in the Bowman's capsules with those in the

A lymph.
B plasma.
C urine.
D materials resorbed by the tubules.

9 Which feature enables the mammalian kidney to concentrate urine in the medullary region?

A maintaining a high osmotic pressure in the tissue between the tubules
B rapid removal of sodium ions from the medullary tissues
C rapid flow of blood through the medulla
D high oxidative metabolism of medullary cells

10 The diagram illustrates the essential principle of an artificial kidney machine.

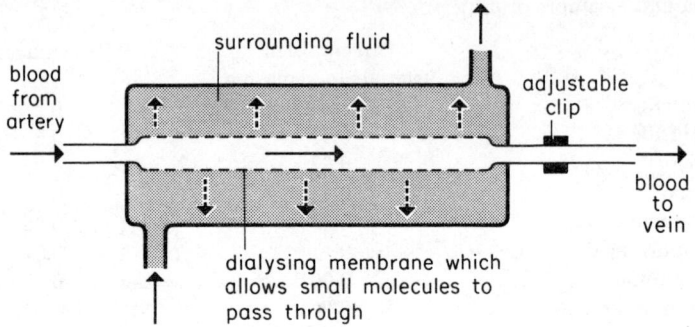

Some of the conditions necessary for the operation of the machine are given. Which one is required for the removal of sufficient water from the blood?

A The surrounding fluid contains salts in the same concentrations as the blood plasma.
B The pressure of the blood in the machine is maintained by adjusting the clip.
C The surrounding fluid contains 1% to 2% dextrose.
D Fresh surrounding fluid is circulated around the dialysing membrane.

11 The antidiuretic hormone (ADH) is secreted by the posterior pituitary gland in response to a need to conserve water. This hormone acts by increasing the permeability of

A the glomerulus.
B the proximal tubules.
C the loop of Henlé.
D the distal tubules and collecting ducts.

12 The diagram illustrates a scheme for the renal control of sodium reabsorption by the kidney.

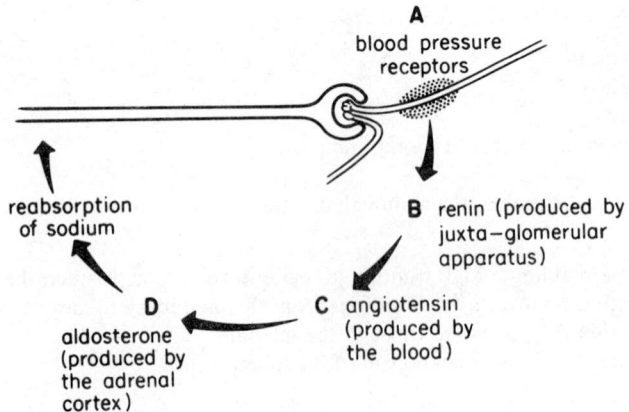

Give the letter to indicate the stage at which the anterior pituitary hormone ACTH can intervene in the system.

XIV Endocrine Control

1 Which one of the following conditions in man is caused by underactivity of the thyroid gland in infancy?

A cretinism
B nervous excitability with enlarged thyroid
C enlarged thyroid which is underactive
D myxoedema

2 Which of the following substances *is not* a secretion of the thyroid gland?

A calcitonin
B thyroxin
C triiodothyronine
D thyrotrophin

3 The effect of excess parathormone is to promote

A excretion of calcium from the kidneys
B release of calcium from the bones
C retention of phosphate by the kidneys
D deposition of calcium and phosphate in the bones

4 The following hormones affect the level of blood glucose in the mammal.

    1 insulin
    2 somatotropin
    3 glucagon
    4 thyroxin
    5 adrenalin

Which numbers represent opposing control factors?

A 3 and 4
B 4 and 5
C 1 and 3
D 2 and 3

5 The diagram illustrates the relationship between a form of inherited dwarfism in mice and the endocrine control mechanism.

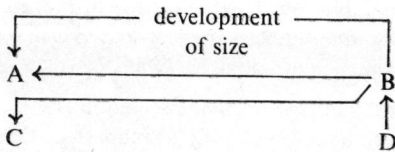

Which letter would best represent the pituitary gland?

6 Which one of the following sites is a target organ of the anterior pituitary gland?

A   parathyroid glands
B   islets of Langerhans
C   thyroid gland
D   hypothalamus

7 Which one of the following pituitary secretions *does not* have as its target organ another endocrine gland?

A   follicle stimulating hormone
B   adrenocorticotrophic hormone (ACTH)
C   somatotrophic hormone
D   luteinizing hormone

8 In an experiment to determine the role of the gonadotrophins secreted by the anterior pituitary gland, follicle stimulating hormone (FSH) was administered to a hamster which had the pituitary gland removed, and also to normal hamsters. Subsequent to this, all of the following events occurred in the normal hamsters. Which of these *would not* occur in the experimental animal?

A   growth of the Graafian follicles
B   ovulation
C   build-up of oestrogen levels in the blood
D   repair of the uterine wall

9 The anterior lobe of the human pituitary gland in the female secretes follicle stimulating hormone (FSH) just after menstruation. This stimulates the growth of the Graafian follicle and the secretion of oestrogen. Which of the following *is not* a function of oestrogen?

A   repair of the uterine wall
B   inhibition of FSH secretion
C   stimulation of luteinizing hormone secretion (LH)
D   formation of the corpus luteum

10 Which one of the following effects *is not* brought about by the secretion of luteinizing hormone (LH)

A   ovulation
B   oestrogen secretion
C   progesterone secretion
D   testosterone secretion

11 In the contraceptive pill, use has been made of progesterone which inhibits the development of the Graafian follicles in the ovary. Which one of the following events *would not* be a consequence of taking these pills?

A   inhibition of luteinizing hormone secretion (LH)
B   inhibition of follicle stimulating hormone secretion (FSH)
C   build-up of oestrogen levels in the body
D   prevention of menstruation

XV Nervous System and Sense Organs

1 The myelin sheath of an axon is formed from

    A Schwann cells.
    B Nissl's granules.
    C nodes of Ranvier.
    D deposits of fat.

2 Which one of the following is *not* a component of a sensory nerve system?

    A axoplasm
    B node of Ranvier
    C end plate
    D synapse

3 An experiment was set up to investigate the effects of repeated stimulations of a sensory cell on the neurons running from it. The arrangement is illustrated below.

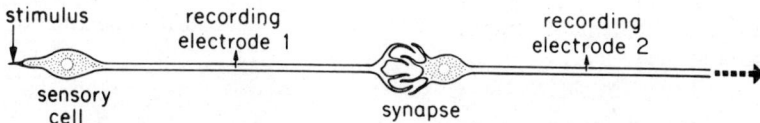

The following traces were obtained from each recorder. S on the time base indicates when each stimulus was applied.

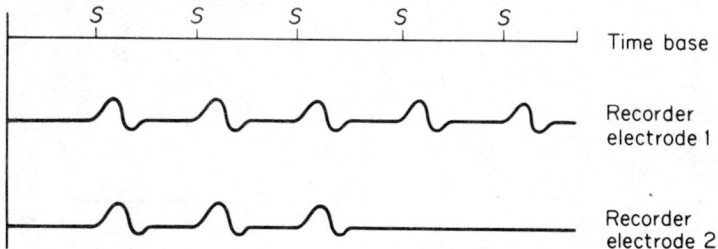

Which one of the following phenomena is occuring at the synapse?

    A inhibition of nerve action
    B development of a latent period
    C accommodation of the impulse
    D facilitation of the impulse

4 The velocity of transmission of an impulse along a neuron pathway would be decreased by

    A myelination of the axons of the neurons.
    B decrease in the number of synapses in the pathway.
    C increase in temperature within physiological limits.
    D decrease in the cross-sectional area of the neurons.

5 Which tissue has the longest refractory period in relation to its period of response?

    A myelinated nerve
    B non-myelinated nerve
    C cardiac muscle
    D striated (voluntary) muscle

6 A nerve axon would be ready to transmit a nerve impulse when

    A sodium ions are moving outwards through the cell membrane.
    B potassium ions are moving inwards through the cell membrane.
    C there is an internal electrical potential which is negative in relation to the external fluid.
    D there is an internal electrical potential which is positive in relation to the outside fluid.

7 The diagram represents a trace produced by a single maximal stimulation of the neuron of a squid.

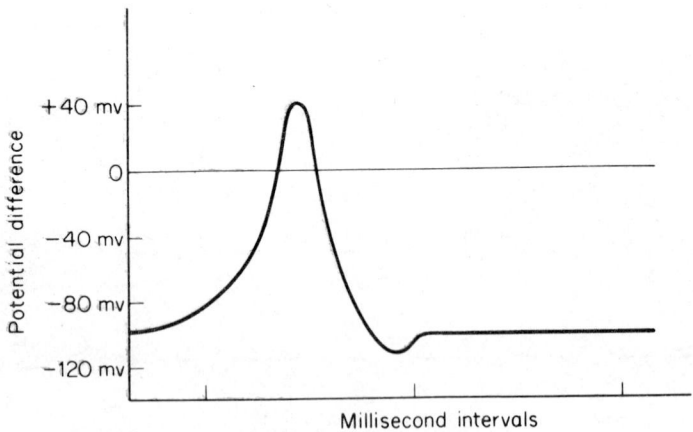

Millisecond intervals

What is the action potential of the neuron in millivolts?

    A   40
    B   50
    C   90
    D 130

8 With a change in the external concentration of sodium ions, the action potential of a neuron would show

    A no change.
    B an increase as the external solution became weaker.
    C a maximum when the external solution was isotonic.
    D an increase as the external solution became stronger.

9 Isolated squid neurons were immersed in a solution which contained labelled sodium ions. The concentration of these ions in the axon was recorded after stimulation under different conditions. Between times X and Y on the graph a non-persistent metabolic poison was applied. A stimulus was applied at the times represented by S.

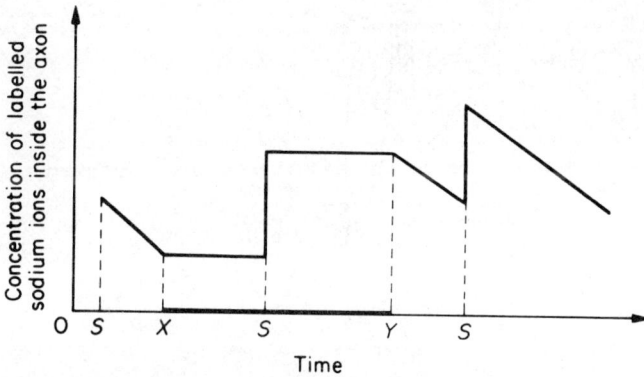

The most likely explanation of the results is that

    A sodium ions normally pass freely out of the axon.
    B axons accumulate sodium ions.
    C stimulation releases sodium ions from the axon.
    D the removal of sodium ions from the axon requires energy.

10 The diagram represents a motor neuron.

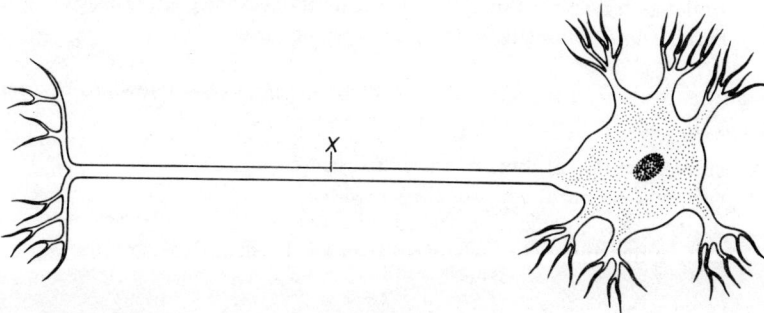

Stimulation by an electrode at point X would cause

    A no flow of an electric current along the axon.
    B an impulse in the direction of the cell body.
    C an impulse in the direction of the motor end plates.
    D an impulse in both directions.

11 The diagram illustrates the relationships between neurons and two muscles in the arm.

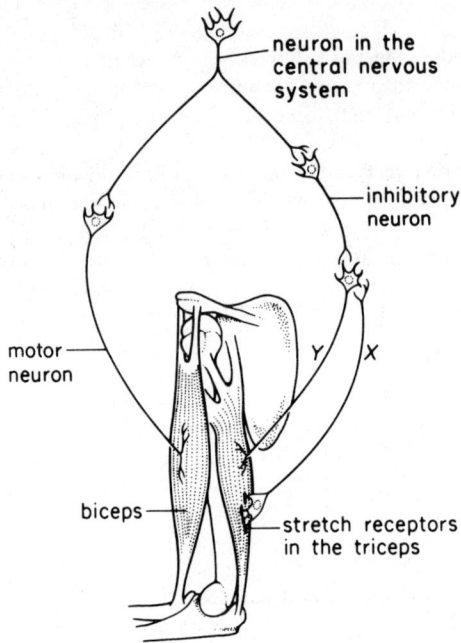

What happens in neuron X and Y when the biceps contracts and the triceps is passively stretched?

    A   Nerve impulses pass along X but not Y because impulses also reach Y from the inhibitory neuron.

    B   Impulses do not travel along X or Y because they are blocked by the inhibitory neuron.

    C   Impulses from Y pass along X and stimulate the stretch receptors.

    D   Impulses travelling along X and Y cannot reach the central nervous system because of impulses from the inhibitory neuron.

12 In a frog, the movement of the leg away from a pin prick is known to be a reflex action. Which one of the following will *not* inhibit this reflex?

    A   cutting the dorsal roots of the spinal nerves

    B   cutting the ventral roots of the spinal nerves

    C   destroying the ganglia on the dorsal roots of the spinal nerves

    D   cutting the spinal cord where it leaves the brain

13 The root of a spinal nerve is cut at X.

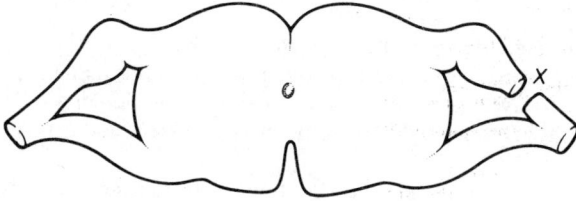

Electrical stimulation at the

    A proximal stump will cause skin stimulation and muscle twitch.
    B distal stump will cause no skin stimulation or muscle twitch.
    C proximal stump will cause muscle twitch only.
    D distal stump will cause muscle twitch only.

14 A generalized discharge of impulses through the network of the mammalian sympathetic nervous system produces

    A contraction of the radial muscles of the iris of the eyes.
    B relaxation of the sphincters of the gut.
    C contraction of the coronary arteries of the heart.
    D conversion of glucose into glycogen in the liver.

15 The terminals of the post-ganglionic fibres of the parasympathetic system produce

    A adrenaline.
    B nor-adrenaline.
    C acetycholine.
    D cholinesterase.

16 Which effect would be expected if the corpus callosum of the mammal brain were severed?

    A loss of sensory input to the cerebral hemispheres
    B failure to co-ordinate the right and left sides of the body
    C over-activity of the posterior pituitary
    D loss of control of the motor responses of the body

17 Sensory data supplied to the cerebellum is used to

    A initiate voluntary movement.
    B regulate motor movement.
    C provide conscious information on muscular movement.
    D control reflexes of the gut and blood system.

18 Which part of the auditory system of the mammal is most concerned with concentrating the force of sound?

    A auditory pinna
    B external auditory meatus
    C auditory ossicles
    D fenestra rotunda

19 Which of the following properties is most important in the operation of the hearing mechanism of the ear?

    A Watery liquids are relatively incompressible.

    B Low pitched sounds travel further through liquids than high pitched sounds.

    C Sound travels faster through air than through liquids.

    D Sound waves are reflected from curved surfaces and can be focussed.

20 Which part of the cochlea of the ear vibrates *least* in response to sound vibrations?

    A tectorial membrane

    B basilar membrane

    C Reissner's membrane

    D cells of the organ of Corti

21 Which organs of the mammalian ear are sensitive to turning movements of the head?

    A macula of the utricle

    B crista acoustica of the ampullae

    C semicircular canals

    D organ of Corti

22 In the human eye, when the ciliary muscles relax,

    A the lens becomes more spherical.

    B the tension of the suspensory ligaments decreases.

    C the pressure of the aqueous and vitreous humours increases.

    D the tension of the choroid is transmitted to the suspensory ligaments.

23 Which action takes place when the eye is used for viewing distant objects?

    A The radial ciliary muscles are contracted and the circular ciliary muscles are relaxed.

    B The radial ciliary muscles are relaxed and the circular ciliary muscles are contracted.

    C Both sets of ciliary muscles are contracted.

    D The tension of the suspensory ligaments is reduced and the pupil is contracted.

24 In the mammalian eye, which feature of retinal function is responsible for acute vision?

    A limited interaction between the cones

    B high threshold of stimulation of the cones

    C low threshold of stimulation of the rods

    D summative interaction between the rods

25 In very low light intensities objects may be seen better by not looking directly at them. Which is the correct explanation of this effect?

    A Light passing through the lens at a wide angle is more sharply focussed.

    B Light entering the eye at a wide angle is subjected to more internal reflection.

    C There is a greater concentration of rods around the periphery of the retina.

    D There is a greater nerve supply to the periphery of the retina.

26 The cones of the human retina are sensitive to colour. Which is the best explanation of this?

A Different wavelengths of light affect a light-sensitive substance to different extents.

B Different colours of the spectrum break down a light-sensitive substance to different products.

C Different colours of the spectrum decolourize a single light-sensitive substance in different types of cone.

D Red, blue and green light affect three different light-sensitive substances in three different types of cone.

XVI Effectors

1 Which theory of amoeboid movement shows a feature similar to a theory of muscular contraction?

    A The plasmagel solates and the inner plasmasol flows into this region by turgor pressure of the cell.

    B Fixed molecules on the inner face of the plasmagel become attached to plasmasol molecules in succession, causing them to move forwards.

    C The plasmasol gelates at the tip of a pseudopodium and attracts plasmasol towards it.

    D A gelating tube of cortical material forms at the sides of the pseudopodium and this contracts to force more plasmasol forwards.

2 The following diagrams represent various features in the structure of voluntary muscle.

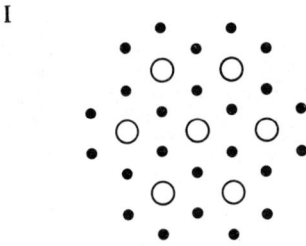

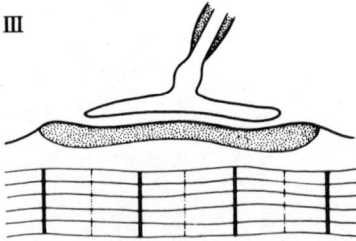

Which is the correct descending order of magnitude?

    A II III I IV

    B IV II III I

    C III I II IV

    D I III IV II

3 The diagram shows part of a muscle fibril.

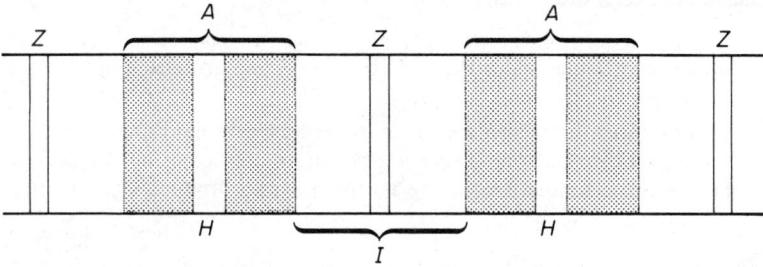

During contraction, the

A *I* zone will decrease in length.
B *A* zone will decrease in length.
C *Z* zone will decrease in length.
D *H* zone will remain the same length.

4 Various kymograph tracings obtained by electrical stimulation of the gastrocnemius muscle of a frog are represented below. The points at which the muscle was stimulated are indicated by *S* on the horizontal axis.

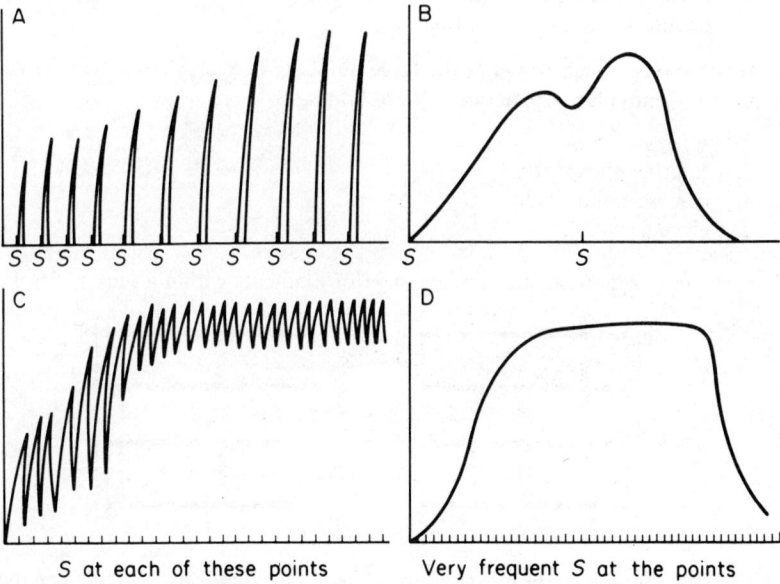

Which one of the traces most clearly illustrates summation?

5 If repeated stimuli were applied to comparable nerve-muscle preparations, in which instance would failure to respond occur first?

A direct electrical stimulation of the muscle to produce a contraction
B direct stimulation of the muscle by injecting acetylcholine into the blood supply to produce a contraction
C electrical stimulation applied at one place on the motor nerve and a response shown by a recorded nerve impulse at another place on the same nerve
D electrical stimulation of the motor nerve to produce a contraction of the muscle

6 Which is a characteristic of isometric muscle contraction?

A There is a change in length of the muscle fibres.
B It is typical of plain (unstriated) muscle.
C External work is done.
D Internal friction is less than in isotonic contraction.

7 If the tendon of a skeletal muscle is cut, the muscle becomes completely flaccid. This is because

A muscle stretch receptors are no longer stimulated.
B sustained isometric contraction is no longer possible.
C motor nerves must have been destroyed.
D tetanus is no longer possible.

8 The substance which provides the large amounts of energy which can be rapidly supplied for muscular contraction in vertebrates is

A ATP
B creatine phosphate.
C glucose-l-phosphate
D glycogen

9 The diagram represents the arrangement of filaments within a muscle fibril.

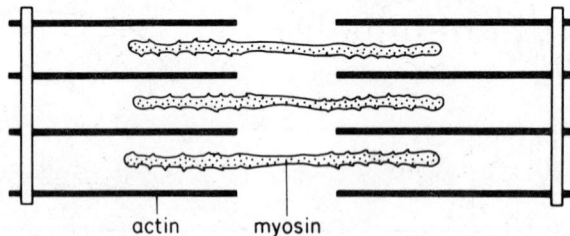

actin   myosin

Which event is thought to be most closely related to the sliding process between the two types of filament which brings about contraction of the fibril?

A the liberation of acetyl choline at the end plates
B splitting of an ATP-myosin complex
C the influx of sodium ions through the sarcolemma
D binding of calcium ions

10 Oxygen debt could be most readily removed from a muscle during and immediately after severe exercise by increasing

    A   the rate of disposal of pyruvic acid in the muscle.
    B   the oxygen supply to the muscle.
    C   the circulation of the blood through the muscle.
    D   the supply of phosphate to the muscle.

11 Which is likely to be the most important means of heat loss by a man sunbathing on a hot day?

    A   convection of air currents
    B   radiation from the skin
    C   evaporation of water
    D   secretion of sweat

12 In very cold weather, the pinna of the human ear may be very cold while the skin behind the ear is warm. Which is the best explanation of this?

    A   More heat is lost per unit area of surface from the ear pinna.
    B   Blood tends to be shunted through a vessel as superficial vessels are constricted.
    C   The metabolic activity of the tissue of the pinna is lower.
    D   A larger amount of water is evaporated from the surface of the pinna.

13 The latent heat of vapourization of water is approximately 2.5 joules per cm^3. If 800 cm^3 of water is vapourized from the lungs and skin per day, what is the approximate heat loss of a man by this process?

    A   320 J
    B   600 J
    C   2000 J
    D   4000 J

14 The hypothalamus of the brain controls body temperature in man by

    A   causing sweat glands to produce bradykinin which dilates skin arterioles.
    B   responding to hormones which increase metabolism.
    C   responding to impulses from skin receptors.
    D   responding to the temperature of the blood.

15 The body temperature of an animal and the temperature of the environment were measured over a period of time when the air temperature was steadily falling. The results are shown on the graph

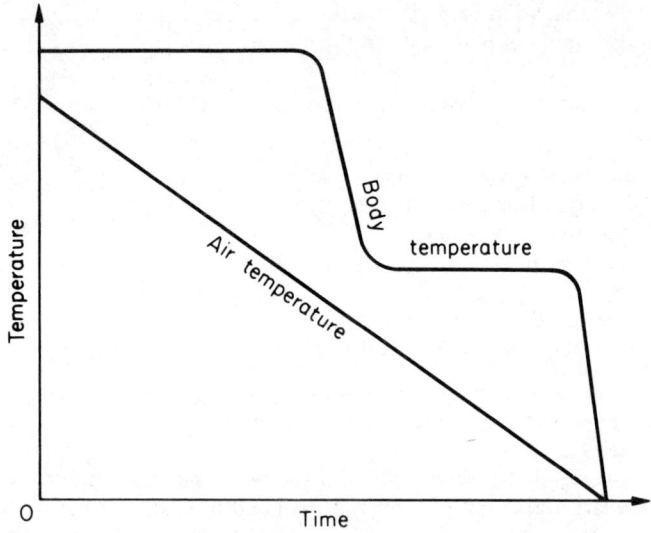

Which type of animal would show this response?

A   a hibernating endotherm (homoiotherm)
B   a non-hibernating endotherm
C   a hibernating ectotherm (poikilotherm)
D   a non-hibernating ectotherm

XVII Animal Behaviour

1 In using a choice chamber, which procedure would enable you to decide whether a response of an animal to two different light intensities were a taxis or a kinesis?

  A Record the pathway of each animal.
  B Count the number of individuals in each chamber at intervals.
  C Count the numbers of individuals moving and stationary at intervals.
  D Record the positions of individuals with eyes covered and with eyes uncovered at intervals.

2 Planarian flatworms change direction of movement more frequently in the light than in the dark. When placed in a dish, half of which is in the light and half in the dark, they gather in the dark portion. The most likely explanation from this evidence is that the flatworms

  A move more slowly in the dark.
  B turn less frequently in the dark.
  C actively seek to avoid light.
  D move in relation to the direction of the light and dark areas.

3 When a third instar *Calliphora* larva is exposed to a light stimulus from a single source, it moves away from the light. If another beam of light is directed across this path, the larva turns away from the second source. In moving away from both sources it swings the anterior end from side to side as if testing the light on each side. Which is the best term for this type of behaviour?

  A telotaxis
  B klinotaxis
  C phobotaxis
  D tropotaxis

4 What type of behaviour is shown when a parent herring gull gives an alarm call and the young birds respond by hiding?

  A taxis
  B kinesis
  C reaction to a sign stimulus
  D displacement activity

5 Which one of the following situations showed displacement activity?

  A During courtship behaviour, a male finch ceased its display and wiped its beak on its perch as it does after feeding.
  B An experienced dog made a detour round an obstacle to obtain food.
  C Migrating birds flew in the original compass direction when captured in one latitude and released in another.
  D Bees returned from gathering food and indicated the horizontal direction of the food source by a dance on the vertical combs of the hive.

73

6 In an investigation of the withdrawl response of a species of snail, an individual was allowed to move on a board. A known weight was repeatedly dropped from a fixed height on to the board. At first, the snail responded by withdrawing into the shell. With repetition of the stimulus the withdrawal response became less until there was little or no response. If a change was made in the weight or the height used, the response was restored. Which is the best term for this behaviour?

    A sensory fatigue
    B classical conditioning
    C habituation
    D imprinting

7 Operant conditioning differs from classical conditioning in that

    A one stimulus is substituted for another.
    B the behaviour is initially spontaneous.
    C the behaviour can be reinforced by reward.
    D it does not involve learning.

8 Which one of the following forms of learning is shown when a hungry animal in a cage learns to move a lever to obtain food?

    A habituation
    B conditioning
    C operant conditioning
    D imprinting

9 A dog normally shows reflex production of saliva when a weak acid is introduced into the mouth. In an investigation of the development of a conditioned reflex salivation, a weak acid was administered and two other substances which normally do not cause salivation were presented as odours in the following treatments.
First treatment Acid was added to the mouth and, after 5 seconds, vanillin odour was presented. After 427 repetitions of this, vanillin odour alone gave no response.
Second treatment Amyl acetate odour was presented and, after 5 seconds, acid was added to the mouth. After 20 repetitions of this, amyl acetate odour alone caused salivation.
Which conclusion can be drawn from these results?

    A Vanillin and amyl acetate odours are both neutral stimuli.
    B Vanillin odour is a neutral stimulus but amyl acetate odour is not.
    C The time at which the conditioning stimulus is given determines its effectiveness.
    D Amyl acetate odour is associated with the unconditioned stimulus when it is given before it.

10 A conditioned reflex was developed in a sheep by first applying an electric current to the foot which caused a flexion of the leg. This stimulus was associated by repetition with the sound of a ticking metronome which preceded the electric stimulus. The following record shows the result after a long period of this treatment.

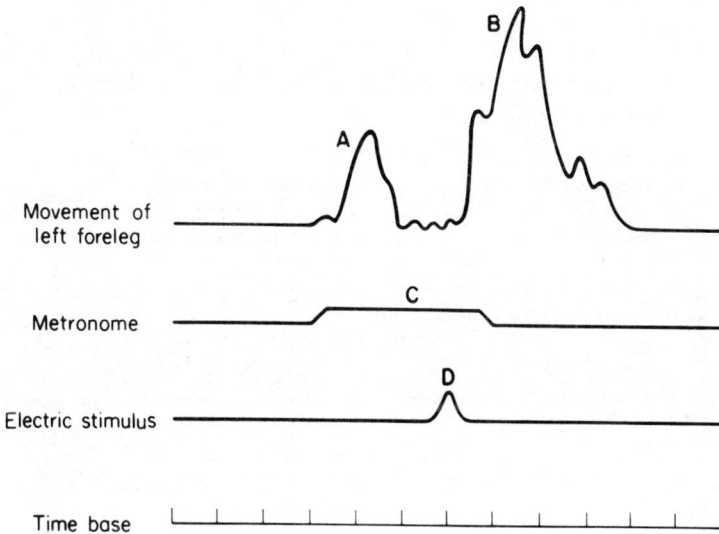

Which letter represents the conditioned reflex?

11 Developing a manual skill in man requires

   A initial feed back of information from the sensory to the motor parts of the nervous system.
   B the development of conditioned reflexes.
   C trial and error with a reduction of randomness.
   D neural facilitation.

12 Which type of learning behaviour is promoted by the achievement of correct answers to items in this book?

   A conditioning
   B trial and error learning
   C perception
   D insight

13 In a colony of honey bees, the dominance of the queen is maintained by the

   A provision of royal jelly for the queen larva.
   B secretion of pheromones by the queen.
   C provision of eggs by the queen.
   D suppression of sexual development of the workers.

14 Which type of social organization was being studied when contests between members of a herd of cattle were being recorded?

    A   caste system
    B   territorial system
    C   leadership
    D   social hierarchy

15 The letters represent individuals in a flock of hens in which one bird predominates over the other in the pairs by pecking.

X pecked U U pecked Z
V pecked X X pecked T
Y pecked V Z pecked W
T pecked W V pecked Z

Which was the second most dominant bird?

    A X
    B Z
    C V
    D Y

XVIII Interactions in Ecology

1 In an ecological study of a species of woodlouse, account was taken of the edaphic factors, microclimate, food preferences, reproductive habits and organisms in competition with it. Which aspect of ecology was being studied?

A environment
B ecosystem
C ecological niche
D synecology

2 For a pyramid of numbers, which of the following groups of pond organisms would show a progressive decrease in the ascending trophic levels?

1. Primary producer	*2. Primary consumer*	*3. Secondary consumer*
A Planktonic algae in late summer	Planktonic animals	Fish
B Higher plants	Larvae of a beetle which feeds on the roots of the plants	Dragonfly nymphs
C Unicellular green algae	Pond snails	Rediae of a fluke which infests the snails
D Unicellullar green algae	Chironomid midge larvae	Leeches

3 In a pyramid of numbers, which one of the following conditions is always related to a decrease in the number of organisms at each successive trophic level?

A increase in the size of the organisms
B loss of energy
C decrease in the mortality rate
D increase in the difficulty of obtaining food

4 In which of the following conditions might an inverted pyramid of numbers be expected?

A when primary producers are small in size
B when primary producers are large in size
C when primary producers are increasing
D when secondary consumers are dying off

5 The pyramid of energy tends to diminish at ascending trophic levels. This is because, at each successive level,

A the organisms become smaller.
B energy is stored and therefore less is passed on to the next level.
C energy is concentrated in fewer larger organisms.
D heat is lost.

6 Which one of the following would *not* be essential in setting up an artificial ecosystem which was self-sufficient in material?

    A producers
    B primary consumers
    C decomposers
    D an energy source

7 The diagram represents the direction in which material is passed between groups of organisms in a food web.

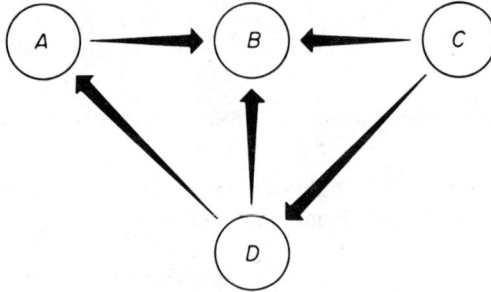

Which letter indicates the decomposers?

8 The biological factor which best accounts for the stability of a mature ecosystem such as a deciduous forest is the

    A complexity of the food chains.
    B rapid adjustment to changes of the environment.
    C high rate of production of the producer organisms.
    D low rate of release of nutrients by the decomposer organisms.

9 An increase in crop production by the use of fertilisers is mainly due to

    A a change in the amount of energy available in the ecosystem.
    B an increase in the complexity of the food web.
    C a change to a more effective food web.
    D an increase in the number of decomposers.

10 Which action would promote stability in an ecosystem?

    A reducing predators and parasites
    B equalising the numbers of producers and consumers
    C increasing the number of species
    D restricting the development of a succession of seres

11 Which diagram illustrates the result of competition for the same source of reasonably abundant food between a successful species and an unsuccessful species of animal?

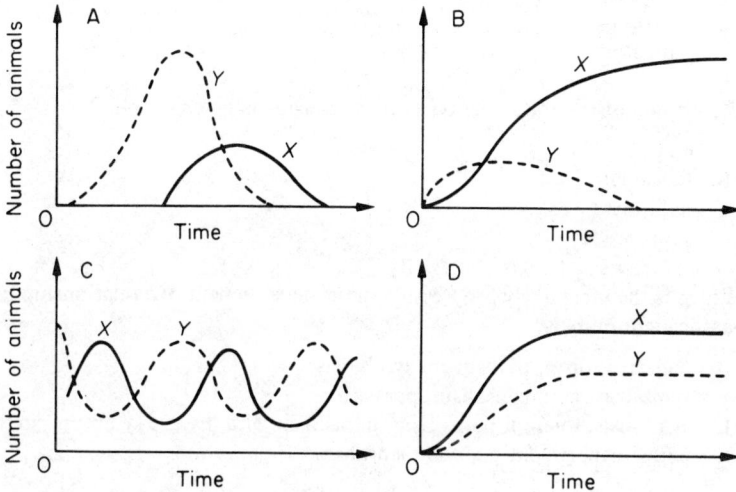

12 Which activity is carried out by denitrifying bacteria?

A decay of organic material in anaerobic conditions
B reduction of nitrates to atmospheric nitrogen
C the use of atmospheric nitrogen to form organic nitrogeneous materials
D production of ammonia from organic nitrogenous materials

13 Which sequence is a correct expression of a part of the nitrogen cycle?

$$\text{A} \quad \text{ammonium ions} \xrightarrow{\text{Nitrosomonas}} \text{nitrite ions}$$

$$\text{B} \quad \text{ammonium ions} \xrightarrow{\text{Nitrobacter}} \text{nitrate ions}$$

$$\text{C} \quad \text{nitrate ions} \xrightarrow{\text{Azotobacter}} \text{atmospheric nitrogen}$$

$$\text{D} \quad \text{atmospheric nitrogen} \xrightarrow{\text{Clostridium}} \text{ammonium ions}$$

14 The beneficial effect of including a leguminous crop in a farming rotation is derived from the symbiotic nitrogen-fixing bacteria in the root nodules. How is this effect transmitted to the other crops in the rotation?

A by the action of saprophytes on the leguminous plant material
B by diffusion of nitrates from the root nodules to the soil
C by infection of the other crops from the root nodules of the leguminous crop
D by fixing nitrogen in the soil by released symbiotic bacteria

15 Which type of nutrition increases the amount of organic carbon compounds in nature?

    A holophytic
    B holozoic
    C saprophytic
    D parasitic

16 Which one of the following types of organisms is heterotrophic?

    A epiphyte
    B holophyte
    C halophyte
    D saprophyte

17 Which is the most likely progression in the development of a relationship between two associated animals?

    A commensalism, parasitism, symbiosis
    B symbiosis, commensalism, parasitism
    C symbiosis, tolerant parasitism, parasitism with disease symptoms in the host
    D parasitism, predation, commensalism

18 The table indicates a necessary growth factor and a substance synthesized by two micro-organisms.

Organism	Growth factor which must be supplied	Substance synthesized and released
Rhodotorula rubra	pyrimidine	thiazole
Mucor ramannianus	thiazole	pyrimidine

Which would be the most likely relationship if they were grown together in the same culture?

    A competition
    B incompatibility
    C independent growth
    D symbiosis

XIX Pollution

1 At which trophic level is contamination from persistent agricultural insecticides most likely to accumulate?

    A   producers (plants)
    B   primary consumers (herbivores)
    C   secondary consumers (carnivores)
    D   detritus feeders

2 Which is the best definition of polluted water?

    A   It is unfit for some use to which it could be put in its natural state.
    B   It has a high biochemical oxygen demand.
    C   It contains waste material produced by human activity.
    D   It is unfit to drink.

3 In which aquatic environment are suspended solids most likely to be a pollution problem?

    A   a rapid stream
    B   a slow flowing river
    C   a pond or lake
    D   an estuary

4 Which is the main advantage of using living organisms as indicators of pollution in streams?

    A   Their presence or absence can be related to specific environmental factors.
    B   They have been affected by the total environment for a period of time.
    C   They are more easily identified than chemical or physical factors.
    D   Their numbers increase as pollution decreases.

5 The best organisms to use as indicators of aquatic pollution are those which are

    A   very mobile.
    B   very stationary.
    C   long living.
    D   short living.

6 In a stream badly polluted by an outfall containing organic matter, which animal population is most likely to be highest in the presence of 'sewage fungi'?

    A   chironomid larvae
    B   tubificid worms
    C   *Asellus* (isopods)
    D   *Gammarus* (amphipods)

7 Three of the curves on the graph represent typical changes in the oxygen, nitrate and ammonia content of a stream polluted by organic matter.

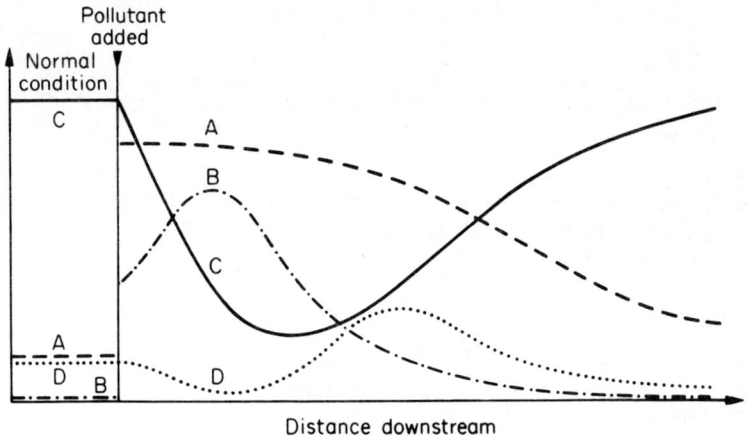

Distance downstream

Identify the fourth curve which represents the biochemical oxygen demand (B.O.D.).

8 The aeration of liquid sewage by sprinkler systems and filter beds promotes purification by

A   aiding the respiration of putrefactive bacteria.
B   direct oxidation of organic material by atmospheric oxygen.
C   indirect oxidation of organic material by nitrifying bacteria.
D   stimulating competition between harmless and harmful organisms.

9 The effect of organic pollution on a long established lake is to produce conditions which are

A   eutrophic.
B   more eutrophic than before.
C   less eutrophic than before.
D   oligotrophic.

10 Which type of organism would be most likely to survive in an organically polluted pond?

A   an insect with tracheal gills
B   an insect utilizing a physical gill consisting of a transported bubble of air
C   an insect with a form of haemoglobin in the blood
D   a crustacean with haemocyanin in the blood

11 In coal smoke, the material which has the most common harmful effect on growing plants is

A   sulphur dioxide.
B   carbon monoxide.
C   carbon particles.
D   tarry deposits.

12 Which product from motor vehicle exhaust fumes causes the most immediately dangerous effects on the human body?

    A   lead products
    B   oxidised hydrocarbon aerosols
    C   carbon monoxide
    D   3:4-benzpyrene

XX Populations

1 A record of a population requires a statement of the number of individuals and

    A no other information.
    B the time of the recording.
    C the area of distribution of the population.
    D both B and C

2 Which is the best method of sampling the population of a species of plant in a grass field?

    A samples obtained from a regular pattern imposed on the field
    B making numbered co-ordinates of the field and using random numbers for selecting samples
    C using samples obtained by throwing a ring
    D obtain samples as in C, but only using those large enough to include at least one organism of the species being counted

3 In an investigation of the size of a population of animals in a defined habitat by the method of capturing, marking, releasing and subsequent recapturing,
P is the number of animals captured and marked on a first occasion and then released,
Q is the number of animals captured from the population on a second occasion,
R is the number of animals in this second capture which show the original marking.
Which is the correct formula for calculating the size of the population?

    A $\dfrac{PQ}{R}$

    B $\dfrac{R}{PQ}$

    C $\dfrac{PR}{Q}$

    D $\dfrac{Q}{PR}$

4 The scatter diagram shows the results of observations of the concentration of dissolved silicates in a lake and the population density of a species of alga.

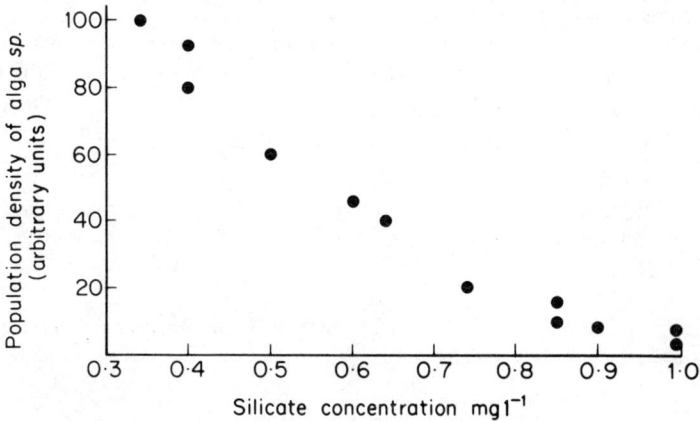

Which statement is justified from this evidence?
Silicate concentration and the growth of the algal population indicate

    A   a negative correlation.
    B   a positive correlation.
    C   that algae use up silicate.
    D   that silicate inhibits algal growth.

5 The net increase of a population could be found by

    A   adding births and deaths and subtracting emigration and immigration.
    B   adding births and immigration and subtracting deaths and emigration.
    C   adding births and emigration and subtracting deaths and immigration.
    D   adding deaths and immigration and subtracting births and emigration.

6 It is assumed that a mated pair of Large White butterflies produce an average of 80 fertilized eggs and the sexes occur in equal numbers. If there were no mortality, how many butterflies would be expected as a second filial generation from a single mated pair?

    A   1600
    B   3200
    C   12800
    D 128000

7 A pure culture of bacteria in a liquid medium is diluted with sterile water and plated out on nutrient agar as follows;

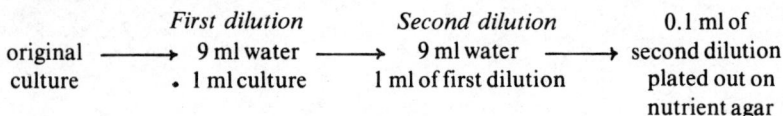

	First dilution	Second dilution	0.1 ml of
original →	9 ml water	9 ml water →	second dilution
culture	• 1 ml culture	1 ml of first dilution	plated out on
			nutrient agar

150 colonies developed on the agar.
The number of bacteria per ml in the original culture was at least

    A   1 500
    B   15 000
    C   150 000
    D 1 500 000

8 In the growth of a population of cells by binary fission, starting with one cell, after n generations, the number of cells would be

    A n
    B $2 \times n$
    C 2^n
    D $1 + n$

9 In the S shaped curve which represents the growth of a population, the exponential or logarithmic phase is due to a progressive

    A increase in the generation time.
    B decrease in the generation time.
    C increase in the number of parents.
    D increase in the number of offspring for each parent.

10 If N represents the number of organisms in a population and a and b are constants, the stationary phase of growth would best be represented by

    A $N(a - b)$
    B $N(a - bN)$
    C $N - N(a + b)$
    D $Na - Nb$

11 The logarithmic growth of a fungal population infecting a crop would be most likely in

    A dry conditions with maximum dispersal and low temperature
    B dry conditions with local dispersal and high temperature
    C moist conditions with maximum dispersal and low temperature
    D moist conditions with local dispersal and high temperature

12 The graph shows the number of larvae produced per day by pairs of adults of the flour beetle *Tribolium confusum*.

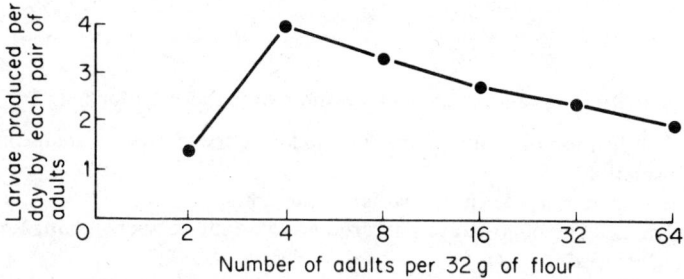

Which interpretation of the graph is correct?

    A   There is a logarithmic (exponential) decrease in numbers of larvae when there are more adults.

    B   When the numbers of larvae and adults become equal, the numbers of larvae subsequently decline.

    C   Above a population density of four adults per 32g of flour, the total number of larvae declines.

    D   A logarithmic (exponential) increase in adults is followed by an arithmetical decrease in the rate of larvae produced.

13 Each of the following pyramids represents a human population structure. The levels represent the proportions of numbers in 10-year age groups. Which pyramid represents the *least* likely population?

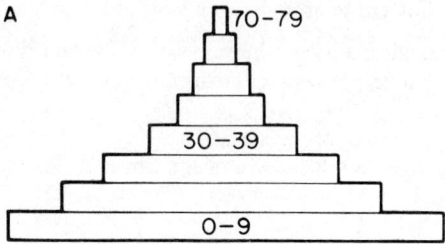

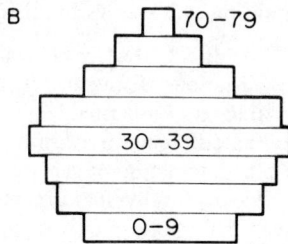

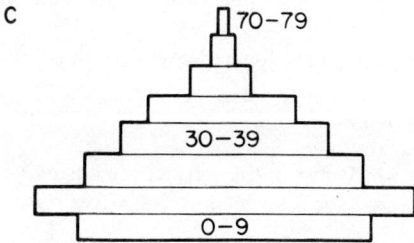

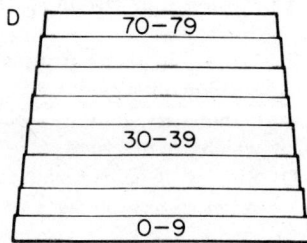

XXI Evolution

1 Which activity in taxonomy contributes most to modern biology?

    A identification of evolutionary units and the effect of the environment in their formation

    B descriptions of the species within communities

    C arrangement of organisms in groups according to their resemblances and differences

    D establishment of an internationally agreed code of names

2 The most successful variation within a species with respect to a characteristic such as size would be represented on a frequency curve by the

    A maximum recorded size

    B mode.

    C mean.

    D median.

3 Variability in a species is most likely to be increased by

    A changing environmental conditions.

    B outbreeding between different populations.

    C mutation within a population.

    D selection for specific characteristics in different populations.

4 Adaptation of a species to an environment is brought about by

    A the direct effect of environmental factors on the genes of the germ cells.

    B variations arising in individuals in response to the environment which become fixed and inherited.

    C the different survival rates of varieties of the species.

    D the interaction of genetical factors and the environment during the development of individual organisms.

5 Which one of the following cases has the *least* significance in the study of evolution?

    A Melanism in certain species of moths is more prevalent in sooty industrial districts.

    B Dandelion plants growing in long grass have longer leaves than those grown on mown lawns.

    C Gamma irradiation of barley seedlings can produce pigment abnormalities which are inherited.

    D Species of hares (genus *Lepus*) which live in the warmer regions of North America have longer ears than those species which live in colder regions.

6 After observation of two plants of the same species which showed certain differences, four different explanations were proposed.

    A They had a common ancestry but they have bred in isolation from each other.
    B They show the effects of different environments on development.
    C The differences between them are the results of somatic mutations.
    D They represent two different points in a continuous range of variation.

In which explanation would the phenotypic differences be *least* related to the genotype?

7 Which one of the following does *not* provide evidence for evolutionary relationships?

    A karyotypes
    B homologous structures
    C vestigial structures
    D analogous structures

8 Which evidence on evolution is most directly provided by fossils?

    A time taken for evolutionary change
    B cause of evolutionary change
    C relationship between species
    D sequence of organisms in time

9 Which one of the following statements is related to the principle of adaptive radiation in evolution?

    A Unrelated organisms living in similar environments may tend to resemble each other.
    B Related organisms living in different environments show modifications of an underlying unity of pattern.
    C Selection in a constant environment tends to maintain the most frequently occuring variety of a species.
    D Species evolve by selection altering the gene frequencies in interbreeding populations.

10 Which factor would be a restraint on evolutionary change in a species of flowering plant?

    A development of a specialized pollination mechanism
    B high productivity
    C the presence of geographical barriers to seed dispersal
    D an annual rather than a perennial habit

11 The theory of evolution originated from

    A the assembly of certain laws which enable prediction to be made in terms of a covering theory.
    B deductive reasoning concerning a hypothesis.
    C inductive reasoning from evidence leading towards the creation of an hypothesis.
    D proof of an hypothesis from the evidence.

12 Which factor is now taken into account when considering the original theory of evolution by natural selection?

    A Mutation can produce discontinuous variation.
    B Food supplies can limit a population.
    C Competition can occur within a species as well as between species.
    D Characters acquired during the lifetime of an individual can be inherited.

13 Which one of the following factors would be most favourable for the continued survival of the human species during the next thousand years?

    A Because of the highly developed nervous system, human behaviour is more adaptable than that of any other species.
    B Human intelligence is capable of exploiting new resources of energy and food.
    C Human evolution has been extremely rapid and there is reason to think that this continues.
    D The selective effect of competition within the human species which has operated in the past will continue to operate in favour of human survival.

Diagnostic Notes

Contents

I Understanding of Biological Science

1 Answer **B**   *Comprehension of the main aim of biological science*
Collecting observations and facts are only steps in the processes of science and not the main aim. The development of principles and theories represents growth of the current structure of a science. Controlling living organisms may be part of an experimental procedure or technology but it does not express the essential intellectual aim in developing science.

2 Answer **B**   *Comprehension of a law*
The term 'law' in this case is the utilization of the simplest mathematical proposition which can explain Mendelian inheritance. It is purely descriptive and does not represent a prerequisite rule to which the experiment must conform. The prediction of results cannot be made in a particular experiment from applying the law. The 'law itself is merely a strong version of a working hypothesis and cannot be used to confirm another hypothesis.

3 Answer **A**   *Comprehension of the nature of an hypothesis*
The essentially tentative nature of an hypothesis is indicated by **A** and contradicted by **C** and **D**. Experiments may be designed to test hypotheses but an hypothesis is not a plan for an experiment.

4 Answer **A**   *Comprehension of the nature of science*
The view of Popper that science progresses by attempting to falsify hypotheses is implied in **A** and contradicted by **B** and **D**. The advancement of science owes more to putting forward new hypotheses than the mere accumulation of observations suggested in **C**.

5 Answer **B**   *Comprehension of Design of an experiment*
This deals with the selection of a single factor and a single effect. **A** is concerned with too many factors. **C** and **D** require complex investigations of physiological details.

6 Answer **D**   *Avoidance of teleology*
Teleology is a common pitfall in biological explanations in which the ultimate 'needs' of an organism are suggested as influencing preceding processes. The expressions in **A, B** and **C** such as 'to maintain', 'requirements' and 'the need for' are often found in teleological expressions. The true scientific explanation requires a cause leading to an effect as in **D**.

7 Answer **B**   *Comprehension of graphical representation*
The x axis is used for the environmental factor which is the independent variable. If x changes, y may be changed, but a change in y will not produce a change in x. Hence y is the dependent variable. The recorded points form a scatter diagram of factual observations which may or may not indicate a causal relationship between the variables. The line through the scatter of points may represent a hypothesis derived from the position of the points or it may be drawn from some independent hypothesis.

8 Answer **A**   *Application of data to express a conclusion*

A conclusion expresses actual results in relation to the condition of the experiment. **B** makes a causal assumption on inflow which is not directly shown by the data. **C** is a hypothesis to explain the results and depends upon **A** and **B**. **D** is a prediction which is made by extrapolation of the data, but is not actually shown by the results.

9 Answer **A**   *Comprehension of science processes in an investigation*

The restricted nature of **A** to a single factor in relation to a single variable provides the conditions for the design of a controlled experiment to test a hypothesis from which results could be obtained and tested statistically. In **B**, however detailed the quantitative methods used, the work is essentially descriptive. The correlation suggested in **C** is essentially a mathematical relationship which does not explain phenomena although it may lead to testable hypotheses. **D** is also descriptive and involves a multiplicity of factors which would require a range of distinct investigations.

II Basic Chemistry

1 Answer **C**   *Interpretion of pH values*
pH expresses the negative logarithm to the base 10 of the hydrogen ion concentration and therefore an increase on the scale represents a logarithmic decrease. **A**
and **B** are therefore incorrect. In **D**, although the pH can be used as an approximation of the proportions of H and OH ion concentrations, the relationship is
logarithmic not arithmetical.

2 Answer **A**   *Comprehension of oxidation*
All of the statements can relate to oxidation, but **A** is the most comprehensive. For
example, the transfer of hydrogen involves the transfer of an electron plus a
proton. In oxidation by atmospheric oxygen, the oxygen acts directly as the
hydrogen acceptor. In many biochemical oxidations, intermediate compounds act
as hydrogen or electron acceptors before hydrogen is finally combined with
atmospheric oxygen to give water.

3 Answer **B**   *Knowledge of chemical processes involving water*
Hydrolysis involves the addition of the elements of water to a larger molecule in
the process of splitting it to smaller molecules. Condensation is a general term for
the combination of smaller molecules to form larger ones with the removal of
water. Esterification is a form of condensation which is the counterpart of
inorganic salt formation. It occurs when an alcohol is linked with an acid with the
elimination of water. Phosphorylation is a special case of esterification when a
sugar is linked with orthophosphoric acid to form sugar phosphate.

4 Answer **D**   *Knowledge of expressions of molecular structure of glucose*
The empirical formula given in **A** does not represent the arrangement of atoms in
the glucose molecule. It could equally be used for fructose which has a different
arrangement. The ring structure of glucose is most nearly represented in **D** where
the asymmetrical nature of the molecule give the dextrorotatory property to D-
glucose. The symmetrical ring expressed in **C** does not exist in nature because all
naturally occuring glucose is related to the D- form of the three-carbon sugar
triose. In certain chemical reactions, the glucose molecule behaves as if the ring
opens out to form a six-carbon chain as in **B**. This change is characteristic of
reducing sugars such as glucose, fructose and maltose which give a positive result
with Fehling's test.

5 Answer **B**   *Knowledge of energy provision in starch synthesis*
The condensation to starch from glucose units requires the production of the high-
energy complex uridine diphosphate glucose which promotes the addition of
successive glucose molecules to the starch helix. In the living cell, the energy is
available from respiratory processes and alternatives **A** or **C** could apply. In an
artificial synthesis however, a phosphorylated sugar is necessary to provide the
energy. Glucose-1-phospate is an intermediate product of respiration which
provides a convenient starting material. Neither maltose nor sucrose would
provide the necessary energy and sucrose incorporates fructose which is not
required.

6 Answer **B** *Knowledge of saturation in fats*

Saturation refers to the condition when all available valency bonds of the carbon atoms have been taken up by hydrogen atoms in fatty acids. The straight-chain fatty acids of the stearic series are in this condition so that **C** is incorrect. The oleic series, on the other hand, are unsaturated. Alternative **A** is generally true of all fats, the consequent high energy yield on oxidation making them important storage substances. Glycerol is the only alcohol incorporated in fats so that **D** refers to other esters.

7 Answer **B** *Knowledge of protein structures*

A represents the essential linkage which forms polypeptide chains by linking amino acids in a linear series. The formation of H bonds between groups in the same polypeptide chain twists it into a regular helix which is a secondary structure. In **C**, the formation of disulphide bridges can occur as a tertiary structure when cysteine residues of a folded chain are able to provide the necessary links. The formation of quaternary structures between different chains as indicated in **D** is characteristic of large protein molecules such as haemoglobin.

8 Answer **B** *Knowledge of enzyme-related substances*

Activators are inorganic ions and therefore readily separated from the colloidal enzyme by dialysis. Co-enzymes are complex organic compounds which are necessary for the working of certain enzymes: for example, many vitamins are co-enzymes and would not be separable by simple dialysis. Enzyme proteins may be firmly attached to prosthetic groups which are essentially conjugated proteins as in NAD and NADP. The separation of these or of the substrate protein in **D** could not be readily achieved. Chromatography is suitable for amino acid separation but not for whole proteins. Other methods of protein separation such as electrophoresis, precipitations or ultracentrifuging can hardly be classed as easy separations.

9 Answer **A** *Comprehension of enzyme function in reactions*

The effectiveness of an enzyme lies essentially in reducing randomness in molecular encounters. Thus **C** is incorrect. Substrate and enzyme form a complex so that there is an increased probability of a reaction occuring. This speeds the attainment of an equilibrium state. **B** is incorrect because the enzyme does not add energy to the system. **D** is incorrect because an enzyme may catalyse a reversible reaction. The removal of a product by further reaction, change of solubility or translocation may promote the reaction in one direction, but this is not due directly to the enzyme.

Comprehension of the effect of an enzyme on the energy
10 Answer **C** *levels of a reaction*

To bring the reactants together, energy has to be expended. This can be provided by raising the temperature or pressure of the system. The initial peak of the curve represents this energy. The presence of an enzyme decreases the randomness of molecular association, thus less energy is required and the initial peak is lower. The enzyme molecule itself is not involved in the energy transaction, hence **C** is correct and **A** is incorrect. This first part of **B** is incorrect, but the latter part is true. **D** is incorrect in both parts.

11 Answer **C**
The rate of reaction increases with temperature until the effect of denaturing the
enzyme protein decreases the amount of available enzyme. At this slow rise in
temperature this effect influences the reaction steadily with a consequent low
optimum rate as in **C**. At a more rapid rise in temperature much of the enzyme
activity would be promoted before denaturing affected the reaction with a
consequent high optimum rate as in **D**, but with a rapid falling off, **B** would
indicate the operation of some limiting factor above a certain temperature, but in
any case, some falling off would occur at the upper part of the temperature range.
Curve **A** indicates the increase in reaction rate with temperature such as might
occur with an inorganic catalyst with no denaturing.

12 Answer **B**   *Knowledge of the feedback mechanism in the operon theory*
The operator gene controls the active production of the enzyme by one or more
structural genes. The regulator gene inhibits the action of the operator gene by
means of a regulator substance. The theory supposes that the inducing substrate
reacts with the regulator substance to prevent it from repressing the operator gene,
thus allowing the operon (operator gene+ structural genes) to function freely. This
is a simplified version of the feed-back mechanism whereby the presence of the
substrate promotes processes for its own removal.

13 Answer **D**
For acting as tracers, heavy isotopes must react chemically in the same way as the
more usual isotopes of the elements. Thus alternatives **A** and **B** cannot be fulfilled.
Although certain heavy isotopes revert at an appreciable rate to more stable forms
by radioactive emission, this is not true for all of them. Thus ^{15}N and ^{18}O are stable
and are detected by physical means such as differences of density or refractive
index. Thus alternative **D** also includes **C**.

III Organization of Cells

1 Answer **C**   *Knowledge of ATP as a medium for energy exchange*
Although they are widely distributed in living organisms and much involved in carbohydrate respiration, neither glucose nor glucose-l-phosphate are involved in such a comprehensive range of processes as ATP. The synthesis and breakdown of ATP has been compared with the 'small change' of an energy currency which is utilized in the various steps of respiration and biochemical synthesis. ATP is also produced during photophophorylation in photosynthesis when some of the light energy is turned into bond energy of ATP. The DNA molecule embodies a conservative code rather than an interchange energy system, whereas energy transactions take place at various sites in the cytoplasm, in mitochondria and in chloroplasts.

2 Answer **A**   *Knowledge of tissue respiration sequence*
Glycolysis starts with glucose and results in the formation of pyruvate with a net gain of 2 ATP molecules for each glucose molecule. The Krebs or tricarboxylic cycle continues from pyruvate and results in the removal of carbon dioxide and hydrogen and the formation of 15 molecules of ATP from each pyruvate molecule. The hydrogen is passed into the electron transfer system by a sequence of carriers to eventually combine with atmospheric oxygen and the formation of further ATP to give a total of 38 ATP molecules for each molecule of glucose.

3 Answer **D**   *Knowledge of ATP production in tissue respiration*
ATP is formed in glycolysis as PGA is transformed to phosphoenol pyruvate and also when this is transformed to pyruvate. In the Krebs cycle ATP is formed when ketoglutarate releases energy on breakdown to carbon dioxide, succinate and hydrogen. ATP is also formed as energy becomes available at stages of electron transfer as from NAD to FAD, cytochrome B to cytochrome C and when cytochrome A releases hydrogen to form water with molecular oxygen.

4 Answer **C**   *Knowledge of the end-product of glycolysis*
The sequence in glycolysis is glucose, glucose-6-phosphate, fructose diphosphate, phosphoglyceraldehyde, phosphoenol pyruvate, pyruvate and 2 ATP molecules.

5 Answer **A**   *Knowledge of a reaction in respiration which requires energy*
Glucose-6-phosphate utilizes energy and phosphate provided through ATP to form fructose diphosphate. The other reactions provide energy for generating ATP at various stages of tissue respiration.

6 Answer **C**   *Knowledge of the involvement of PGA in various processes*
Phosphoglyceric acid (PGA) is formed in the anaerobic stage of carbohydrate respiration from phosphoglyceraldehyde by oxidation in which NAD is the hydrogen acceptor. This PGA is eventually converted into pyruvic acid. This process is also a necessary precursor to the Krebs' cycle in aerobic respiration. In the dark stage of photosynthesis, carbon dioxide is fixed in combination with ribulose diphosphate as a cyclic process, leading to the formation of a transient

six-carbon molecule which breaks down to two three-carbon PGA molecules. Succinic acid in alternative **A** is part of the aerobic Krebs' cycle while lactic acid in alternative **B** is formed by the reduction of pyruvic acid by $NADH_2$ in the absence of oxygen.

Comprehension of an experimental procedure involving
7 Answer **C**   *mitochondria*
The sucrose solution is of a suitable osmotic pressure to prevent mitochondria bursting and the phosphate acts as a buffer to maintain a suitable pH. Sucrose is not a reducing sugar. In this experiment it is the succinic acid which is the reducing agent which becomes oxidised by losing hydrogen to DCIP. The sucrose is not a suitable substrate to provide energy for this reaction. The preservation of the material to prevent other reactions before the experiment is started is accomplished by the provision of a low temperature during extraction.

8 Answer **B**   *Knowledge of mitochondria as sites of energy release*
The cristae of the mitochondria offer the large surface required for the reactions which release energy in respiratory processes. This is required for active transport. In **A**, the lysosomes produce enzymes which can destroy cell structures or whole cells. The rough endoplasmic reticulum is the site of numerous ribosomes on which protein synthesis occurs and the Golgi apparatus offers sites at which proteins and carbohydrates conjugate to form glycoproteins which are then secreted.

9 Answer **C**   *Knowledge of secretory function of Golgi apparatus*
The Golgi apparatus is concerned with the production of secretory substances which might be expected as the main activity of gland cells. Both red blood cells and egg cells are relatively passive and voluntary muscle is mainly concerned with energy conversion which requires abundant mitochondria and arranged fibrils.

Comprehension of the multiplying effect of layered grana in
10 Answer **B**   *chloroplasts*
The grana are thought to be composed of layers of chlorophyll molecules lying between layers of electron donors and acceptors. Photons of light energy activate the donors which pass on electrons to the acceptors, leading to the synthesis of $NADPH_2$ and ATP as the end products of the light phase of photosynthesis. This layered structure gives the necessary multiplying effect for obtaining sufficient energy. The membranes of mitochondria are double and provide sites for related respiratory reactions. The cell membrane of axons is concerned with electron changes which accompany changes of permeability during the transmission of a nerve impulse. Muscle fibrils contain myosin and actin filaments, not layers.

Comprehension of the distinction between a photosynthetic
11 Answer **D**   *process and oxidative processes*
The photochemical splitting of hydrogen sulphide by the purple and green sulphur bacteria is analogous to the splitting of water in the photosynthesis of higher plants, with the liberation of sulphur compared with the evolution of oxygen. Energy derived from light is added on the right hand side of the equation. The first three examples show oxidative activities of various chemosynthetic autotrophs. In **A** *Nitrosomonas* oxidizes ammonia to nitrous acid, using atmospheric oxygen. In **B** and **C** sulphate ions and carbon dioxide are used to oxidize hydrogen to hydrogen sulphide and to methane respectively.

12 Answer **A**
This expresses the fermentation of a monosaccharide sugar to ethyl alcohol and carbon dioxide by yeast. The essential feature is that atmospheric oxygen is not involved as the ultimate hydrogen acceptor but an organic substance, ethyl alcohol, which allows a proportion of the carbon to be oxidized to carbon dioxide. **B** represents incomplete aerobic respiration of ethyl alcohol to acetic acid. **C** and **D** are both examples of anaerobic respiration which differs from fermentation in the use of an inorganic hydrogen acceptor. In **C**, which is the initial stage of denitrification, the acceptor is oxygen derived from the nitric acid which is thereby reduced to nitrous acid. In **D**, carbon is reduced to methane as it accepts hydrogen.

13 Answer **D**
The solid culture medium enables a pattern of distribution of the population to be established which is characteristic in relation to the oxygen requirements. In **D**, the bacteria are evenly distributed because they possess the faculty of tolerating both aerobic and anaerobic conditions. The distribution in **A** represents an aerobe which is obligatory in its dependence upon a supply of atmospheric oxygen. **B** is the opposite of this, an obligatory anaerobe which can only grow in a position furthest from the oxygen supply. **C** is microaerophilous, requiring small amounts of oxygen.

14 Answer **A**   *Interpretation of a Gram positive result*
In the Gram positive species, gentian violet is not removed by washing with iodine and alcohol and any red colour due to carbol fuchsin is not revealed. Thus **C** is incorrect because both stains do not show together. **B** is incorrect as the only effect of iodine solution is to remove gentian violet from Gram negative species. **D** represents the red colour shown by Gram negative bacteria.

IV Genetics

1 Answer **C**

Comprehension of the relationship between a cell process and Mendel's first law

Pairing of the homologous chromosomes is a prerequisite of meiosis I the result of which is that genes of an allele are separated (segregated). Both **A** and **B** are concerned with the mitotic cyle only. **D** is related to Mendel's second law of independent assortment which refers to unrelated interchange of alleles which is promoted by chiasma formation.

2 Answer **A**

Comprehension of relationships between meiotic processes and Mendel's second law

The specific pairing of homologous chromosomes as in **A** is not necessarily followed by independent assortment of alleles although it can be a preliminary to this. Independent assortment is most usually expressed as in **B**, but it can also occur between two pairs of alleles which are on different chromosome pairs as in the cases of **C** and **D**.

3 Answer **B**   *Application of mendelian principles to make a conclusion*

The 50:50 result is typical of a back-cross of a heterozygote with a recessive, therefore both parents carry the recessive. Equal numbers of genes as in **A** would imply that both parents were heterozygotes which would only show the dominant phenotype; so also would the the homozygous dominant and recessive parents proposed in **C**. **D** would not give any recessive phenotypes in the offspring.

4 Answer **B**

Application of an experimental design to an investigation in genetics

Coupling or repulsion would involve more than one allele, thus indicating the use of a dihybrid cross with the backcross to test whether the genes remained associated or not. In **C**, recessive and lethal genes are investigated by breeding from heterozygous parents. Determining the genotype of a parent generation as in **A** is best done by employing a simple back-cross. Confirming characters as alleles in **D** requires a simple monohybrid cross only.

5 Answer **B**   *Application of a procedure for identifying heterozygotes*

This would give the usual 3:1 dominant to recessive ratio in the offspring. The back-cross with the recessive as suggested in **C** to give the more definite 1:1 ratio is not possible because of the infertility of the homozygous dwarfs. Alternative **A** would not reveal the recessive dwarf genotype in any of the offspring. **D** is both impossible and irrelevant to the problem of the question.

6 Answer **D**   *Prediction of F_2 ratios from F_1 results*

As dominance is not an essential feature of mendelian inheritance, the grey heterozygote in the F_1 generation does not affect the monohybrid pattern. Therfore **D** is the correct answer. **A** assumes white to be dominant but the grey F_1 phenotypes show this to be false. **B** would imply that the grey heterozygote bred true without fulfilling Mendel's first law of segregation. The equal proportions of **C** would require a most unlikely form of selective fertilization.

101

7 Answer **D**   *Analysis of data to find genotypes*
As daughter 1 is left-handed and this is recessive, alternative **A** is eliminated. If the mother were homozygous for right-handedness no recessive phenotypes could appear in the F_2 generation, therefore she is heterozygous, eliminating alternative **B**. The father must be a double recessive which could only arise if the grandmother were heterozygous.

8 Answer **C**   *Analysis of dihybrid ratios*
If the usual dihybrid table showing combinations of gametes between two dihybrid parents, the usual 9:3:3:1 ratio of phenotypes is produced by 9 combinations of genotypes.

9 Answer **D**   *Synthesis of genotypes from four alleles*
The homozygous pairs could be dominant or recessive in various combinations up to 16.

                          Comprehension of the relationship between life cycle and
10 Answer **D**   *breeding experiments in Drosophila*
Females required for breeding experiments must be removed from the initial culture before random matings occur. **A**, **B** and **C** are all advantages in giving easily managed cultures which produce rapid results in sufficient numbers for statistical treatment.

11 Answer **D**   *Comprehension of procedures in pea breeding experiments*
As the garden pea is self-pollinating, finding the ratios of the F_2 phenotypes of the dihybrid cross would merely entail planting and growing the F_1 seeds and counting the various phenotypes of the seed yield obtained. In **A**, it would be necessary to remove stamens from the plants which were used for the female parents to prevent self-pollination then to artificially cross pollinate the parents and grow their seeds for a further generation. In **B**, the ratios of the genotypes of the dominant phenotype could be found either by the back-cross as in **C** (again requiring the cross-pollination procedure) or by growing a suitable sample of the seeds of each plant for a further generation to see if they all breed true or yield a proportion of recessive phenotypes.

12 Answer **B**   *Comprehension of sex linkage*
The Y chromosome is shorter than the X, lacking the terminal portion which carries the gene controlling this blood condition. If X represents the normal gene and x the gene for haemophilia, the normal female would be represented by XX and the haemophiliac male by xY. The possibilities of a cross between a normal female and a haemophiliac male are represented thus;

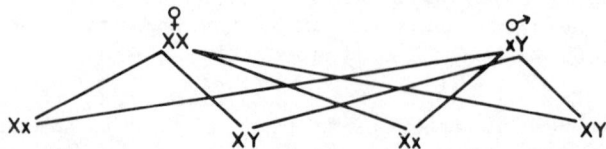

Thus only carrier females and normal males could be produced and no haemophilia would appear in the phenotypes. It would appear in the males of the following generation from the transmitter females and so an alternating cycle would continue.

13 Answer **D**   *Application of sex linkage to a problem*
As the parental female provides an X chromosome for both sexes in the F_1 generation, the recessive mutation could not appear but females could carry it. In the F_2 generation, however, males could show the mutation but females could not.

14 Answer **B**   *Application of sex linkage to a problem*
The normal and pale colours are allelemorphs with normal dominant. If the female is heterogametic it must carry the XY chromosomes and the male the XX. To produce an F_1 generation of all normal colour, the parent male must have been homozygous for normal colour and the F_1 accordingly heterozygous for this so that in each sex one X chromosome carried a normal colour. A cross between these heterozygotes would produce the usual 3:1 ratio for a monohybrid cross but the recessive gene for pale colour could only show in the heterogametic female with the single X chromosome. Thus the males could be homozygous or heterozygous normal coloured and the females either normal coloured or pale coloured in equal proportions. These four possibilities give the ratio in alternative **B**.

15 Answer **B**   *Interpretation of results showing crossing-over*
For one chiasma, only two of the chromatids are altered while the other two retain their original constitution as in **B**. **A** represents crossing-over on both chromatids which would involve two chiasmata. **C** shows no crossing-over. **D** represents the result of crossing-over by a chiasma which is not between the two genes.

                    Comprehension of the relationship between cross-over value
16 Answer **D**   *and experimential data*
The cross-over value is a measure of the frequency of crossing-over which can only be found from experimental data as in **D**. It assumes that the gametes in the experiment are characteristic of the whole population of gametes produced by the line under investigation. Its further use in mapping as in **A**, makes the assumption that crossing over could occur randomly so that frequency of crossing over in a segment of a chromatid is a function of its length. This is not always true. Thus a region of high chiasma frequency will occupy a longer length of a linkage map than a segment of equal physical length from a region where chiasma formation is less frequent. **C** indicates an attempt to summarize all the information which could be obtained from a complete series of experiments on cross-over values to give a complete chromosome map. Moreover, in general, the cross-over value is half the mean chiasma frequency when this is low. **B** goes beyond the definition to much wider evolutionary considerations.

17 Answer **C**   *Interpretation of data on crossing-over*
This provides the greatest difference between the loci which would allow the highest percentage of crossing-over. The differences in **B** and **D** are less than this and **A** refers to genes on different chromosomes where crossing-over could not take place.

18 Answer **A**   *Relating data on recombination to linkage maps*
The calculation has been simplified by making one parent a homozygous double recessive in each case. The correct answer is found by reading off the proposed distances on the map and comparing them with the data. The main task is to find if the overlapping values are compatible. This is not so for the incorrect alternatives.

103

19 Answer **C**   *Comprehension of mutation*
This covers all three of the other expressions. Both **A** and **B** suggest a point mutation which involves a fundamental change in a gene. These could occur in any cell, so that mutations may be somatic or genetic. Alternative **D** refers to the latter. Besides the expressions used in the item, chromosome mutations can occur. These may be related to visible numerical or structural changes. Such rearrangements of chromosome material may have little effect on the phenotype when compared with the effects of point mutations.

Application of the one gene-one enzyme theory to identify a
20 Answer **B**   *mutant*
The problem depends upon the hypothesis that each enzyme in such a sequence is produced by the operation of a particular gene. This example demonstrates epistasis in which the operation or non-operation of gene B depends upon the operation of gene A. (If the sequence were not known, the two genes could only be called complementary). If the mutant form is aB it can produce indole if supplied with anthranilic acid and if it is supplied with indole, anthranilic acid is unnecessary. Genotype Ab would be able to form anthranilic acid but be unable to utilize it to form indole. However, it would grow if indole were supplied. Genotype ab would be unable to synthesize or utilize anthranilic acid but it could grow if supplied with indole. In alternative **D**, the genotype of *Neurospora* is incorrectly expressed as a diploid. The haploid nature of this micro-organism has the advantage of allowing a mutation to be readily expressed in the phenotype.

Application of the one gene-one enzyme theory to predict an
21 Answer **A**   *experimental result*
Growth would depend essentially on cross-feeding between the mutant strains. Ornithine and citrulline accumulate in gene mutants 2 and 3 respectively when further synthesis is blocked. These substances diffuse into the medium and become available to gene mutant 1 for conversion into arginine. Gene mutant 2 will grow to some extent, utilizing citrulline accumulated by gene mutant 3. This latter, however, is unable to utilize the products of the other two mutants and will only be able to accumulate citrulline.

Comprehension of the relationship between the nuclear cycle
22 Answer **D**   *and DNA synthesis*
The process of mitosis is concerned with the distribution of DNA already replicated during interphase. The prophase of meiosis I is concerned with processes preliminary to reduction division which results in the smaller amounts of DNA in gametes. Thus DNA and chromosomes show some similarity of behaviour during the cell cycle.

23 Answer **D**   *Knowledge of DNA structure*
The sugar-phosphate groups in A form the regular structure which imposes the regular pattern of the helix in B. Hydrogen bonding is only possible between the purine adenine and the pyrimidine thymine, and similarly between guanine and cytosine, so that their pairing is regular. Variation in the order of the bases on one single chain as in **D** specifies the sequence on the partner chain of the double helix, thus providing the basis for self-replication.

24 Answer **C**
Comprehension of the relationship between triplet coding and amino acid synthesis

Twenty amino acids have to be represented by separate codes. **A** could only represent four codes. **B** could represent 4^2 combinations, that is 16 codes. **C** could form 4^3 combinations, that is 64 codes which is more than sufficient. The excess codes allow some amino acids to be represented by more than one code ('degenerate' coding). Thus glycine is represented by GGC, GGU, GGA and GGG. Some of the codes are also available to signal the commencement and termination of sequences of amino acids in forming polypeptide chains. **D** represents 4^4 combinations which would be excessive.

25 Answer **A**
Comprehension of the relationship between messenger RNA and polypeptide synthesis

As there are 20 common amino acids but only four kinds of bases, the one to one relationship in **B** is impossible. Similarly, in **C**, pairs of such bases would only provide 16 code words (codons). Bases in threes, however, can provide 64 different combinations, so that an excess of codons is available for representing 20 amino acids. The triplets are represented on the transfer RNA molecules which carry the individual amino acids, as in **A**. These find the corresponding triplets in sequence on the messenger RNA molecule. The transfer RNA is thus a necessary intermediary because the amino acids themselves carry no structure capable of recognising the coding on the messenger RNA, hence **D** is not possible.

26 Answer **B**
Knowledge of the localisation of functions of selection on cell organelles.

A, **C** and **D** are common to prokaryotes and eukaryotes. The study of them in bacteria has illuminated our knowledge of similar processes in eukaryotes. Ribosomes are found in both groups, and although smaller in size in bacteria, are the sites of polymer synthesis. The organelles of eukaryotes possess membranes which localise processes or control diffusion. This applies to the structure of the definitive nucleus, plastids, vacuoles, Golgi apparatus, lysosomes as well as the elaborated endoplasmic reticulum.

27 Answer **D**   *Knowledge of the distribution of DNA in eukaryotes*

The distribution of DNA in organelles such as chloroplasts and mitochondria suggests the possibility of extra-chromosomal inheritance. This is supported by the formation of new organelles only from the division of pre-existing ones. A further theory that such organelles in eukaryotes were derived from symbiotic micro-organisms has been developed from this.

28 Answer **D**   *Knowledge of a characteristic common to all viruses*

One or the other type of nucleic acid is present in a virus, but neither is universally present. Thus either DNA or RNA performs the genetic function. **C** is incorrect because although protein is always present, only in some cases does this include enzymes required for penetration of the host cell. More usually, synthesis of enzymes involves utilization of the metabolic systems of the host. Viral proteins, although not the genetic material, can be shown by serological tests to be highly specific.

29 Answer **B**   *Knowledge of two-way genetic transfer in bacteria*

Transformation is the passive transfer of a portion of DNA which then replaces a corresponding allelic character in the recipient. The DNA may be contributed from a disintegrated cell. Thus, heat-killed, smooth virulent pneumococci can pass virulence to living, rough-coated, non-virulent strains. Exchanges in the reciprocal sense are also possible. Thus, two strains with biochemical blocks represented in different places on the DNA may have DNA added from each other to overcome the deficiency. Mutation is fairly common in bacteria. It is generally regarded as irreversible as the chances of a back mutation are very small because of the great precision which would be required to restore the original condition. Transduction concerns the active introduction of a segment of DNA by a bacteriophage into a bacterial cell. This is usually DNA of the bacteriophage, but a part of it may be derived from a previous bacterial host. Unidirectional genetic transfer of a part or the whole of a bacterial chromosome from a donor to a recipient cell results in a temporary diploid from which the haploid condition is rapidly resumed by reduction division.

V Population Genetics

Comprehension of the effect of inbreeding on an isolated
1 Answer **B** *population*
Continuous inbreeding decreases genetic variation. The effect of isolation is to provide a restricted environment so that genes controlling characteristics not well adapted to it tend to be lost. Natural selection thus has a conservative effect. The mutation rate is unaffected by isolation. The population will only become extinct if the death rate exceeds the birth rate for a sufficient length of time.

Comprehension of the effect of removing recessive pheno-
2 Answer **B** *types from a population*
As recessive phenotypes must be double recessive genotypes, removal of each recessive phenotype will remove two recessive genes from the gene pool. Thus **B** is correct and **A** could not be true. **C** and **D** are both incorrect because some recessive genes would still be present in the heterozygotes and could give rise to a proportion of recessive phenotypes.

Comprehension of the effect of gene selection on a
3 Answer **B** *population*
The rapid effect of the insecticide strongly suggests that a gene for resistance already existed which had survival value in the conditions of high mortality. Alternative **A** is unacceptable because it is a teleological statement which implies that evolution had an 'aim'. **C** is a typical statement of the inheritance of an acquired character which has little credence in neo-Darwinian theory. Any mutations occuring in **D** would be of a non-directional type with very remote chances of being effective for resisting the factor which caused it.

4 Answer **A** *Comprehension of non-genetic and genetic polymorphism*
The polymorphism between workers and queens in the honey bee is induced by the differences in the treatment of the developing individuals, producing a caste difference between these two types of females. In **B**, the difference between drones and workers is a sexual dimorphism due to chromosome differences and this is also true of heterostyly in **C**. In the peppered moth, the polymorphs also have a genetical basis which is then selected by the environment.

5 Answer **D** *Comprehension of the Hardy-Weinberg principle*
This would give the basis of the Hardy-Weinberg equation thus

	pA'	qA''
pA'	$p^2A'A'$	$pqA'A''$
qA''	$pqA'A''$	$q^2A''A''$

C incorrectly suggests using the table to find the possible combinations of gametes as in a mendelian ratio problem. **A** confuses the actual numbers of offspring which would occur if all gametes fused in pairs and the genotype frequencies. **B** begs the question as the frequencies of gametes do not give the genotypes by simple addition. The problem is worked out by first finding the number of homozygous recessives which are readily counted as phenotypes.

6 Answer **B**   *Comprehension of the Hardy-Weinberg equation*
The application of the Hardy-Weinberg equation refutes the notion that the dominant phenotypes tend to increase. Thus A is false and **B** is true. **C** indicates a condition in which the equation cannot be applied as it can only be used for a population unaffected by immigration, emigration or mutation. **D** represents a confusion between the equation and the outcome of a monhybrid mendelian cross in the F_2 generation.

7 Answer **A**   *Application of the Hardy-Weinberg equation*
This is found to fulfil the formula $p^2 + 2pq + q^2 = 1$ as the values given add up to 1.0. In further detail, $p = 0.7$ and $q = 0.3$ which also add up to 1.0. $2PQ = 0.7 \times 0.3 \times 2 = 0.42$. None of the other groups work out in this way.

8 Answer **C**   *Application of the Hardy-Weinberg equation*
Only the recessive phenotype will have a known genetical constitution. From this, the Hardy-Weinberg equation can be applied to find the proportions of the homozygous dominant genotypes and the heterozygotes.

9 Answer **C**   *Application of the Hardy-Weinberg equation*
The frequency of the homozygous recessive phenotype tt for non-tasters must be 16% or 0.16. This can be expressed as $(1-q)^2 = 0.16$. Therefore the frequency of the allele $t = (1-q) = \sqrt{0.16} = 0.40$. (The frequency of the dominant allele T must then be 0.60.)

VI Life Cycles and Development in Animals

1 Answer **A**

Comprehension of the likely effects of reproductive processes in protozoa on variation

Syngamy in *Paramecium* concerns the fusion of nuclei between two conjugating individuals which may be of different strains. As in sexual reproduction in metazoan animals, this provides possibilities for gene recombination. In **B**, **C** and **D** reproduction is from a single individual which makes variation unlikely. In autogamy of *Paramecium* there is a fusion of identical nuclei within one individual. In multiple fission in *Amoeba* and sporogeny in *Plasmodium* the effect is to rapidly increase the number of individuals preparatory to a change in the environment.

2 Answer **C**

Comprehension of the principle of a soma

The polyploid meganucleus of *Paramecium* takes no part in conjugation. Its subsequent disintegration makes it comparable to the somatic cell nuclei of metazoans. The aborting nuclei in **D** are more comparable to polar bodies formed during oogenesis in metazoans. Residual protoplasm, whether from the non-sexual process in *Amoeba* or gamete formation in *Monocystis* does not directly involve the fate of nuclei. Thus the contrast between heritable and non-heritable nuclear material is not present.

3 Answer **A**

Comprehension of a difference between the life cycle of Hydra and Obelia

Polymorphism in *Obelia* is shown by the three types of zoid which are produced, namely, hydranths, blastostyles and medusae. The latter do not represent a separate sexual generation because the gametes in them are formed in the first instance in the ectoderm of the blastostyle. They then migrate into the medusa bud. Oogamy refers to the well-marked differentiation between ovum and spermatozoon which is seen in both *Obelia* and *Hydra*. **C** is incorrect because apart from the gametes themselves, all forms of *Obelia* are diploid.

4 Answer **D**

Comprehension of parthenogenesis and hermaphroditism

Parthenogenesis is the development of an unfertilized egg. This occurs in the honey bee as a normal means of producing haplont males, either from the queen, which can withold sperm from contact with the egg, or occasionally from a worker. The other three organisms are hermaphrodite. The tapeworm shows self-fertilization as an adaptation to a solitary existence in the mammalian gut. *Hydra* and the earthworm both ensure cross-fertilization by protandry.

5 Answer **C**

Knowledge of metameric segmentation

The spinal nerves of a vertebrate are related to the succession of mesodermal somites which represent true metameric segmentation in the Chordates. The budding of proglottides from the scolex of a tapeworm represent a form of budding which continues throughout life and in which all three germ layers are represented. Thus proglottides could be regarded as individuals of a colony in successive stages of development. True metameres, on the other hand, are formed between the anterior and posterior ends of a complete body and they tend to attain a complete maturity with the complete growth of the animal. The nervous system is not segmented in the first place, but the somites impose a segmental pattern on their nerve supply and this is clearly indicated by the spinal nerves of vertebrates. The three body regions of an insect represent functional groups of elements as a pattern superimposed on the original segmentation. In **D**, the notochord originates from the mid-dorsal region of the endoderm of the vertebrate embryo before segmentation of the mesoderm is established.

6 Answer **B**   *Knowledge of imaginal buds in insects*
Imaginal buds are internal groups of cells which survive tissue breakdown in the pupa of a holometabolous insect. The organs of the imago develop from them. **A** is incorrect as the cockroach, which is hemimetabolous, shows incomplete metamorphosis with the progressive development of the wings by external buds. The corpora allata of a larva are endocrine glands situated near the cerebral ganglia which produce a juvenile hormone. This suppresses the development of the imaginal discs for the duration of the larval stage, thus ensuring the holometabolous life history. The imago is the ultimate product of the imaginal buds.

7 Answer **B**   *Knowledge of sex determination in the honey bee*
Females develop from fertilized eggs and males from unfertilized eggs. Thus the former are diploid and the latter haploid. Queen substance is produced by an active queen and it appears to promote the normal activities of the hive. In **C** and **D**, both factors are related to the development of sexuality which has been determined in the first place by the chromosome mechanism. Thus royal jelly, produced by workers, is fed to female larvae in the larger queen cells to produce fully sexual queens, while workers develop in smaller cells on a different diet to become less fully developed females.

Application of magnification to find the diameter of a
8 Answer **A**   *microscope field*
The high power objective gives 6 times the magnification of the low power. The field diameter is therefore six times smaller, that is, 0.2mm.

Knowledge of factors controlling development in a
9 Answer **C**   *multicellular organism*
The genetic code is expressed selectively by each type of cell to produce a characteristic tissue. However, numerous experiments with plants and animals show that this is not an immutable process. Tissues and organs influence the development of adjacent cells. This potency diminishes during development. In plants, the development of lateral buds is influenced by the terminal bud and the development of flowering tissues is affected by external and internal factors. Thus **C** is a more correct statement than **A**. **B** represents a possible influence of the environment in producing a mutation. This is not a normal feature of development and the expression of a mutation is not as an adaptation to its causative agent. **D** is incorrect because the non-uniform expression of the genetic code is the basis of tissue differentiation and co-ordination between cells and tissues depends on forms of cell communication such as 'organizers' and hormones.

10 Answer **B**
A is incorrect as there are no indications that interactions between the tadpoles would remain the same. Thus, if metamorphosis is affected, things such as behaviour and excretory products would change. Any variation as suggested in **C** is likely to be due to individual responses by the tadpoles, not to the concentration used. A definite growth response as in **D** may not occur in all concentrations. **B** gives the most feasible method of controlling dose rate so that comparisons could be made between those concentrations which were found to be critical.

11 Answer **A**
The point of entry of the sperm into the egg determines the symmetry of the embryo. Fertilization also causes cytoplasmic movements with differentiation of the peripheral layers into regions which can be traced to the main organ rudiments. The rates of cell cleavage in **B** do not determine these regions but express the development of some parts of them. The organizing influence of tissues in **C** is a later development which awaits the formation of germ layers and further organs. The genetic influences of the zygote nucleus also await replication of the nuclear material from the blastula onwards when differentiation can be expressed by tissue development.

12 Answer **D**   *Knowledge of neural plate migration in the frog embryo*
A, **B** and **C** represent organs which enter by the dorsal and lateral lips of the blastopore. Initially, the neural plate is furthest from this region and as the blastopore becomes progressively reduced in size, inward migration diminishes. The neural plate is enclosed by its own neural folds, but its relationship to the other tissues is shown by the temporary existence of the neurenteric canal.

13 Answer **D**   *Knowledge of mesodermal segmentaion in the frog embryo*
The mesoderm of the lateral plate is the most ventral part of this layer and is apparently most strongly under the influence of the gut which is not segmented. It splits to give somatopleur next to the ectoderm and splanchnopleur next to the endoderm, forming the main coelomic cavity between. **A**, **B** and **C** all originate from the more dorsal somites which are formed in sequence from the anterior to give the basic segmentation of the vertebrate.

14 Answer **C**   *Knowledge of a special feature in frog development*
Both **A** and **B** are characteristic of vertebrates in general and provide evidence of their common relationship on the basis of von Baer's fourth 'law'. The formation of external gills is characteristic of amphibian larvae only, representing an adaptation for respiration before the essential passages and musculature for internal gills are developed. The reduction of the tail by phagocytosis and the peculiarly short vertebral column is a special feature of the Anura.

15 Answer **D**   *Knowledge of gastrulation in the chick embryo*
The effect of the large amount of yolk is to make cleavage irregular and to slow down the cell division. It is thus confined to the yolk-free germinal disc (already present in the zygote), resulting in the formation of the blastoderm. Thus **A** and **B** are incorrect. Gastrulation in the chick is completed without enclosure of the main mass of yolk which remains non-cellular, thus **C** is not true and **D** is correct.

16 Answer **A**   *Knowledge of cell movement in chick gastrulation*
The convergence of cells to form the primitive streak, their entrance and subsequent lateral spread to form mesoderm can be followed. **B** is untrue as the yolk sac is formed internally by the outward spread of endoderm and its overlying layer of splanchnic mesoderm. At 36 hours the gut roof is already internal by a separate cell migration, so **D** is untrue. The notochord does not separate from the gut roof as suggested in **C**, but is formed as part of the inward migration by the primitive streak.

17 Answer **A**   *Knowledge of amnion structure of the chick embryo*
The amnion arises from folds of the extra embryonic ectoderm and somatopleur (mesoderm). The inner side of the folds form the amnion and is consequently lined with ectoderm. The outer side of the folds forms chorion which has layers in the reverse order. The yolk sac and allantois are both gut extensions and consequently lined with endoderm.

18 Answer **B**   *Knowledge of the respiratory organ of the chick embryo*
The vascular fusion of the allantois with the chorion provides a respiratory organ which is in contact with the non-embryonic egg membranes. The allantois is the inner component of this structure. The amnion is internal to the chorion and consequently not available for respiratory exchange. The sero-amniotic connection is a last connection between ambion and chorion which remains as a result of their common origin from the amniotic folds.

                                           Application of data to make an inference on limb
19 Answer **D**   *development in the chick embryo*
The necessity for interactions is shown by experiments 2 and 3. Experiment 1 shows **A** to be untrue and experiments 4 and 5 show **B** to be untrue. None of the experiments support alternative **C**

20 Answer **B**   *Knowledge of oogenesis*
The primary oocyte represents a growth of an oogonium. When released from the ovary, it undergoes maturation by a meiotic division I to form a secondary oocyte and the first polar body. This is followed by a meiosis II division to form a further polar body from the secondary oocyte and two polar bodies from the first polar body.

                                           Comprehension of a similarity between the embryo of a
21 Answer **C**   *chick and a mammal*
The processes of cleavage and gastrulation in mammal are very different from chick from the outset. The derivation of the mammal from a large-yolked ancestor has produced modifications of these processes, while the subsequent reduction in the amount of yolk and the requirements of implantation have led to further changes. Nevertheless, although the processes in **A** and **B** represent much modified routes of development, the eventual completion of gastrulation results in a stage which is strikingly similar to the chick. In **D**, again the processes by which embryonic membranes form differ widely from the chick and between different mammals although their relationships are eventually comparable to the chick when fully formed. They show, of course, the characteristic adaptations to intrauterine life.

22 Answer **D**

Knowledge of the early origin of the trophoblast of a mammalian embryo

The precocious development of the trophoblast is the equivalent of the ectoderm of the chorion. It enables implantation of the blastocyst to take place, penetrating the uterine wall to some extent and forming trophoblastic villi. The structures **A, B** and **C** are the result of later development.

23 Answer **C**

Knowledge of placental structure in the rabbit

The rabbit placenta is of the haemo-endothelial type. The uterine epithelium is eroded early in the formation of the placenta and maternal and foetal capillaries become closely associated. The breakdown of maternal blood capillaries allows blood to circulate through a series of spaces in the placenta into which the villi of the allanto-chorion develop. The covering of foetal connective tissue on these disappears, leaving only an endothelium separating foetal from maternal blood.

24 Answer **C**

Knowledge of non-selective respiratory exchange in the mammalian placenta

The respiratory exchanges follow the concentration gradients on the principle of physical diffusion. Foetal blood has a greater affinity for oxygen than maternal blood and this reinforces the process. **A** and **B** are selective processes according to foetal requirements. The strict control of hormones is particularly important as the two organisms are in very different stages of development. The placenta itself produces certain hormones in large quantitiies especially concerned with maintaining relationships between the maternal system and the foetus. Antigens cannot be exchanged because they are on the surfaces of red blood cells.

25 Answer **B**

Application of the counter-flow principle to placental exchanges

The counter-flow principle is exemplified by the circulation of the blood in opposite directions, separated only by a membrane permeable to oxygen which moves down a concentration gradient from maternal to foetal blood. The initial high concentration in the maternal blood is higher than that of the loaded foetal blood. As oxygen is lost by the maternal blood it still remains at a higher concentration than the oxygen-deficient foetal blood which is arriving at the site of exchange. Thus **B** illustrates the differences of concentration which are maintained. These are also shown in **A**, but in the reverse order in relation to the distance and to each other. Such curves resemble the dissociation curves for these types of blood rather than the counter-flow principle. **C** represents the type of exchange which would be expected in a parallel flow system in which both circulations move in the same direction with a diminishing concentration gradient between them. The opposing curves of **D** could not operate on purely physical principles.

26 Answer **A**

Knowledge of the function of the ductus arteriosus in the human foetus

The collapsed state of the lungs does not permit a large pulmonary circulation and the bypass ensures that most of the blood entering the pulmonary artery can pass directly to the aorta. **B** is incorrect as the pulmonary arteries already receive oxygenated blood from the right ventricle and their pressure is higher than that of the aorta. **C** is incorrect as the aorta receives oxygenated blood which has passed from the right to the left atrium through the foramen ovale and through the left ventricle. **D** is the opposite statement to the correct answer. The ductus arteriosus relieves pressure of blood on the unexpanded lungs. At birth, the ductus arteriosus closes and the lung blood pressure then rises as this bypass no longer operates.

VII Life Cycles and Development in Plants

1 Answer **D** *Knowledge of algal life cycles*
In **A**, **B** and **C** the alga is a haplont and gametes are formed without meiosis. This then occurs soon after the formation of the zygote, restoring the haplont condition. In *Fucus* the thallus is a diplont and meiosis occurs on gamete formation so that sexual fusion restores the diplont condition.

2 Answer **A** *Comprehension of terms related to the life cycle of Fucus*
The advanced state of differentiation of the gametes taken *Fucus* beyond the anisogamous condition which merely indicates some visible difference such as size. Oogamy on the other hand, indicates a non-motile female gamete. *Fucus* exists in one vegetative form only for which the term haplobiontic is used. The diplobiontic condition indicates that there are two types of plant body which exist in a regular alternation of generations.

3 Answer **D** *Knowledge of life cycles of cryptogams*
The haplobiont algae undergo meiosis immediately on division of the zygote. Thus they can have only one such division. In liverworts and mosses, meiosis takes place on spore formation which although abundant, is limited to a single terminal sporangium. The production of many sporangia on the laterally developed leaves of ferns which also have perennial sporophytes produces far greater numbers of meioses with consequent increased chances of variation.

4 Answer **B** *Comprehension of a sequence of processes related to terrestrial adaptation by plants*
Retention of the egg in the archegonium led to the development of the foot on the retained sporophyte. The vascular system of the sporophyte solved the problem of water loss from well developed sub-aerial organs. The development of pollen tubes is a relatively advanced condition found only in Gymnosperms and Angiosperms.

5 Answer **B** *Comprehension of an order of complexity in gametophytes*
Liverworts represent a more primitive condition in which the gametophyte is less well adapted to life on land. Mosses show the greatest elaboration of this generation. The gametophyte in Pteridophytes and in seed plants shows a progressive reduction in its vegetative structure.

6 Answer **C** *Knowledge of the life cycles of archegoniates*
In these examples, vegetative reproduction depends upon the capacity for continued apical growth. This is present in the dichotomous thallus of *Pellia* and in the rhizomes of *Dryopteris* which can form separate plants as the old parts die off. Budding of the protonema of *Funaria* is a normal method of producing several moss plants. The sporophyte of *Funaria* has a single axis in which growth is terminated by the formation of the spore capsule.

7 Answer **A**   *Knowledge of sporophyte structure in two pteridophytes*
In the fern, the foliar gaps consequent on the large vascular supply to the leaves results in a dictyostele which represents a wider departure from the primitive stele than in the case of *Selaginella*. **B, C** and **D** are less specialized than the conditions found in *Selaginella*.

Comprehension of a relationship between a fern sporangium
8 Answer **B**   *and the ovule in a flowering plant.*
The ovule of a flowering plant represents a megasporangium which retains its large spore as the embryo sac. The carpels on which the ovules are borne represent special reproductive leaves so that comparison with fern sporangia on fern leaves is valid. The scale of the female cone in a gymnosperm is a carpel. Alternatives **C** and **D** represent the female reproductive apparatus of bryophytes which is borne on the gametophyte whereas the sporangia of ferns and ovules of seed plants are borne on the sporophyte.

Comprehension of the relationship of the stigma to the
9 Answer **B**   *angiospermous condition*
The enclosure of the ovules by carpels in angiosperms necessitates the development of a stigmatic surface for the reception of pollen, whereas in gymnosperms pollen is deposited directly at the micropyle of the exposed ovule. A pollen tube is present in both classes although the more primitive gymnosperms release motile antherozoids from it.

10 Answer **D**   *Knowledge of meiosis in the life cycle of the flowering plant*
The embryo sac represents the retained female gametophyte which is formed from a cell of the ovule by meiosis. The rest of the ovular tissue, as in **C**, is sporophyte tissue and therefore, diploid. Pollen mother cells in **A** subsequently divide by meiosis to produce pollen grains, from which further divisions form the male gametophyte, as for example, in **B** where the n number of chromosomes is already present.

11 Answer **A**   *Knowledge of the origin of the testa*
The testa develops from the integument of the ovule which is entirely derived from the female parent. The double fertilization which gives rise to the seed forms on the one hand a proembryo which forms the suspensor and embryo, including the radicle, and also the endosperm tissue by fusion of the other male nucleus with the fusion nucleus of the embryo sac.

12 Answer **B**   *Knowledge of the nuclear condition of ovules*
The angiosperm endosperm develops as a result of a triple fusion of the two haploid polar nuclei and one of the two male nuclei. The endosperm of gymnosperms is haploid, representing female gametophyte tissue. The nucellus of the angiosperm is diploid tissue of the parent sporangium and the pro-embryo is a diploid filament developed from the zygote which gives rise to the embryo from its terminal cell.

Knowledge of the initiation of fruit development by a
13 Answer **D**   ·   *hormone*
The pollen grain carries a hormone which stimulates the development of the carpellary wall to form the pericarp. Pollen extracts have been used to stimulate

the development of parthenocarpic fruits. The processes in **A, B** and **C** then follow as normal fertilization proceeds. Further hormones are probably produced as a result, but pollination is the initiating influence.

14 **Answer C**   *Knowledge of water absorption by a seed*
The initial uptake of water is due to imbibition by colloidal materials in the testa. The water activates enzymes which then hydrolyse storage materials, increasing the concentration of solute molecules and enabling osmosis to take place. The soluble products of hydrolysis are translocated to the growing regions.

15 **Answer C**   *Knowledge of tissue support in a seedling*
Rigidity depends mainly upon turgor pressure within the parenchyma which also produces some tension on the epidermis. In **A**, collemchyma have not developed, and in **B** and **D** the early xylem is for conduction only. Phloem fibres in **D** would not be significant at this stage.

16 **Answer A**   *Knowledge of the cause of epigeal germination*
The hypocotyl is below the cotyledons so that its elongation bears them above the soil. In **B**, the plumule is above the cotyledons so that its elongation does not change their position. In **C** and **D**, the presence or absence of endosperm does not affect the emergence of the cotyledons as endospermic seeds may show epigeal germination as in castor oil seedlings or, more rarely, hypogeal germination. Non-endospermic seeds may produce hypogeal seedlings as in the broad bean, or epigeal seedlings as in cress.

Drawing a conclusion from an experiment on enzyme
17 **Answer C**   *production by barley embryos*
The dialysing membrane prevents the passage of enzymes as these are proteins. Thus any enzyme produced by the embryo alone cannot reach the gel. Thus **A** is false. Hydrolysis of the starch in the gel takes place when a diffusible substance produced by the embryo (in this case, gibberellic acid) passes through the membrane to stimulate enzyme production by the aleurone. This is stated in **C**.
· The statement in **B** is almost the same as A, but suggests that enzyme production by the embryo is incomplete without a co-enzyme, but again, the diffusion barrier shows this to be untrue. The statement in **D** would imply that a breakdown of the enzyme goes on. This would result in a denaturing of the enzyme protein which would then be inactive.

Application of a principle of stem growth to make
18 **Answer B**   *prediction*
This graph shows that zone **B** is already growing most rapidly when recording commences and slows in growth to some extent during the period. The other zones are at progressively later stages of similar curves as each passes through the grand period of growth. Graph A could represent the shape of a complete growth curve commencing at the tip of the stem with an initial lag phase before cell elongation becomes effective in producing longitudinal growth of the stem. This cannot be true for these zones which are some distance below the apical zone. C indicates a uniform but different growth rate for each zone which could show no transition from one to the other. **D** would indicate that each zone grows in succession at different times at exponentially increasing rates as they become older, which is impossible.

19 Answer **D**   *growth*

After the embryonic phase, the indeterminate growth of plants is characterized by the production of new cells in certain zones which remain active. As cells leave the zone, they cease to divide. Both multicellular plants and animals show differential growth as parts develop. The growth of one part is controlled by another part in both cases through the mediation of growth hormones. In both plants and animals, the mature organism remains relatively constant in size, although slow growth may continue in perennial plants

20 Answer **A**   *Knowledge of a plant tissue of secondary origin*

The phellogen is secondary cambium which forms the periderm of the secondary stem. It can originate from the the the renewed division of cells at various depths, from the epidermis, the cortex or the pericycle according to the species. The calyptrogen is a special region of the primary meristem at the apex of the root which forms the root cap. The fascicular cambium of the stem has a lineage derived in continuity from the primary apical meristem. The metaxylem is also a feature of the primary stem, being formed immediately after the protoxylem and centrifugal to it.

21 Answer **B**   *Knowledge of the influence of IAA on the growth of shoots*

The apparently competitive development of terminal and lateral growth is not due to the direction of movement of food resources but to the diffusion of IAA produced in the terminal shoot which suppresses the growth of the lateral shoots. This in its turn is controlled by the interaction of the factors in **C** and **D**.

Interpretation of a graph showing rate of increase in dry
22 Answer **A**   *weight*

The first part of the curve drops below 0, indicating a negative rate of increase. **B** is unjustified by merely considering loss of dry weight as growth utilizes plant reserves but also involves considerable tissue extension by the intake of water. The depression of the curve during flowering indicates a decrease in the rate of increase but not an actual loss as the values are still positive. Similarly, the peak of the curve to be considered in **D** represents only a maximum rate of increase, not actual size.

23 Answer **C**   *Knowledge of the effect of cell extension on plant growth*

Replication of DNA takes place during interphase and is therefore not directly concerned with elongation. **B** is incorrect because the immediate products of cell division in the meristematic zone are small and cell enlargement is slight. Increase in cell volume accounts for most of the elongation in which turgor pressure may increase this volume up to thirty-fold, with especial extension of the longitudinal walls. **C** thus indicates the immediately essential factor. The subsequent differentiation in **D** is accompanied by changes in cell walls which tend to limit further elongation.

24 Answer **D**   *Knowledge of the origin of branch roots*

Both leaf and branch stem initials can be seen as protruberances of the primary meristem of the apex of a main stem. These are also represented in the lateral buds which are derived from the original apex as persistent meristem. Flowers likewise have their origin from primary meristems and are usually characterised by their effect in terminating any further apical growth. The endogenous origin of branch roots in **D** is from cells of the pericycle opposite each xylem group. These cells become meristematic as a secondary feature.

25 Answer **B**   *Interpretation of a graph showing growth rates*
The growth of both roots and stems show at first a positive response in growth to increasing concentrations of the auxin. The rate of response falls off and eventually becomes negative. This takes place at lower concentrations for roots than for stems, indicating that roots are more sensitive. **A** is the opposite of this answer and **D** is an overstatement. **C** is an unjustified conclusion from an experiment with detached portions of the organs.

26 Answer **B**   *Knowledge of the effect of gibberellins on growth*
Gibberellins play no part in tropic movements. They promote the growth of internodes and inhibit the growth of lateral buds and main roots.

27 Answer **A**   *Knowledge of the effects of the environment on leaf growth*
Shading would lower the light intensity while increasing atmospheric humidity, thus reducing the rate of transpiration. These factors would promote the growth of a thin lamina with small veins. Alternative **B** would be unsuitable as the effect of nitrogenous fertilizer would be to produce thicker leaves as the extra material promoted growth. Further exposure of the leaves suggested in **C** would produce a general 'hardening' of the leaves, with increased mechanical tissue and cuticle without a corresponding increase in leaf area. Treatment with gibberellic acid in **D** would cause elongation of the axis with little or no increase in leaf area.

28 Answer **A**   *Knowledge of twining in plant stems*
The regular rotation of the horizontal terminal portion of the stem until a support is reached determines the direction of twining. **B** is incorrect as the movement is a nutation which is independent of light. The effect of cell elongation given in **C** would have the opposite effect to twining. **D** would also interfere with twining and in such plants it is usual to find that leaf expansion is retarded until twining of the relevant part of the stem has been established.

29 Answer **B**   *Application of the phytochrome theory*
The operation of the phytochrome system in plants relates to intensities and wavelengths of light. Different species show different responses to the phytochrome products and this applies to the effects of light on germination. The factors in **A**, **C** and **D** operate in promoting germination in a wide range of plants, but generally do not inhibit germination in those plants for which they are unimportant.

30 Answer **D**   *Comprehension of the phytochrome theory*
According to the phytochrome theory, P665 absorbs red light and is rapidly converted to P725. P725 can absorb far-red light and be converted into P665. This also takes place more slowly in darkness. These photoreceptor pigments can either promote or inhibit growth according to the organ and species of plant involved. Far-red light promotes the growth of stems and lateral roots while red light inhibits their growth. Red light stimulates leaf growth and far-red light inhibits this. Flowering in short-day plants is inhibited by red light and this inhibition is removed by far-red light. Thus these plants will only flower when they are exposed to light for less than a critical period which varies with the species.

31 Answer **C**

The first sentence of the stem suggests that the photoperiodic stimulus is received by the leaves. The second sentence suggests that a substance (i.e. hormone) passes from the plant which has flowered to the grafted plant. **A, B** and **D** may be true but cannot be inferred from these results.

32 Answer **D**

No flowering is shown below a dark period of 12 hours. This minimal requirement is typical of a short day plant, thus **A** is incorrect. Flowering is better with the longer light periods but is not initiated by them, hence **B** is incorrect. **C** is also incorrect as the 12 hour dark period is the lowest shown to be associated with flowering and longer dark periods appear to promote flowering.

33 Answer **B**

IAA is formed in the tip and shows a strong polarity in its direction of downward movement. Thus **B** would show the most accumulation of IAA, **A** and **D** show arrangements for passing IAA into decapitated coleoptiles from agar blocks already containing IAA. In **C**, IAA would tend to pass through the block although some would be retained.

34 Answer **D** *Interpretation of evidence on the abscission of leaves*

Auxin is produced in the leaf blade. While this is abundant, the abscission zone does not develop, but as the leaf becomes old, the auxin supply is diminished and abscission develops, resulting in leaf fall by detachment at the base of the petiole. Thus treatment (iii) is a substitute for treatment (i), and treatment (iv) is a control of treatment (iii).

35 Answer **A** *Knowledge of the effects of IAA on root formation*

Indolylacetic acid promotes cell division and also affects co-ordination of growth by its distribution. In stems, this inhibits development of lateral shoots, but adventitious production of roots from the base of cut stems is promoted. Kinetin also promotes cell division but is local in its effect. Gibberellic acid promotes stem elongation but not lateral development. The effects of 2,4-D include toxicity to many dicotyledons, causing abnormal growth. It is therefore unsuitable for general application to root cuttings.

VIII Water Relations in Plants

1 Answer **B**
Knowledge of the effect of denaturing on the permeability of the cell membrane

Because of their orientated lipoprotein structure, cell membranes are relatively impermeable to many reagents. Denaturing by heat destroys their organization and increases permeability. Alternative **A** is not a main effect as the removal of chlorophyll derivatives requires another solvent. Plasmolysis in **C** is not possible as the cell membranes are no longer operating as semipermeable structures. Although hot water might coagulate certain proteins, other substances would be hydrolysed and thus become mobile. Thus the suggestion in **D** is unacceptable.

2 Answer **A**
Comprehension of the relationship of osmotic pressure to other properties of a solution

The total concentration of a solution is expressed as the number of particles of solute present in a litre of solution. The unit used is the mole. This is the number of grams of a substance corresponding to its molecular weight. This relates directly to the osmotic pressure of a solution irrespective of the molecular weight of the solute. Thus the higher the molecular weight of a solute, the smaller is its osmotic pressure. Thus **A** is correct and **B** is incorrect. Osmotic pressure is thus the property of a solution whether it is being employed to exert a hydrostatic pressure or not. For this reason it may be preferable to use the term osmotic potential. **C** and **D** are both incorrect because any hydrostatic pressure will depend upon the arrangements under which the osmotic effects are operating and the osmotic pressure of one solution does not depend upon another.

3 Answer **A**
Interpretation of a graph relating experimental results to molarity and osmotic pressure

When there has been no change in the length of the strip, the water potential is zero. This is because the cells would neither take in nor lose water and thus show neither stretching nor reduction in volume. This condition would occur if the osmotic pressures of the cell sap and the external solution were the same. Thus 1.0 on the y axis corresponds to 4.5 on the x axis.

4 Answer **C**
Application of molarity to derive osmotic pressure

If the osmotic pressure of molar sucrose at 12° C is 23.3 atmospheres, the molarity of the sucrose is multiplied by this figure to give its osmotic pressure which then corresponds to that of the cell sap. Thus $23.3 \times 0.4 = 9.3$ atmospheres.

5 Answer **D**
Evaluation of procedures for finding osmotic pressure

Investigations which use plant cells as in **A, B** and **C** assume that purely physical factors are involved. This is not strictly true although it gives a convenient approximation. Method **D** is purely physical, depending upon the direct proportional relationship between the absolute temperature of an aqueous solution and its osmotic pressure. In **A**, the potassium nitrate is an electrolyte in which a proportion becomes dissociated to give ions which act individually in producing osmotic pressure so that the osmotic pressure is greater than that of a non-electrolyte of the same molecular concentration. It would therefore be necessary to apply a dissociation factor in order to find the osmotic pressure of this solution. In **B**, the method is sound in principle but could be subject to a number of slight experimental errors in blotting and weighing before and after immersion and in the penetration of the solutions. **C** depends upon tissue tension of the epidermis which is released when the stalk is split. It would be necessary to find the solution in which there is no change in curvature, not that in which the segments become straight.

Interpretation of evidence on metabolic control of ion
6 Answer **C**   *movement*
This is the most likely explanation, the other being dependent on physical factors. Thus **B** is not possible because physical diffusion would tend to produce an equilibrium of concentrations. **A** would work against the concentrations as osmotic entry of water would progressively dilute the cell sap. **D** is based on insufficient evidence as the osmotic potential of the cell sap would depend on the total concentrations of the solutes.

Comprehension of a graph on water relationships of a plant
7 Answer **C**   *cell*
Coordinate **C** represents a zero wall pressure which implies that the cell volume is barely maintained while its intersections with the curve for negative water potential and high positive osmotic pressure indicate a large capacity for taking in water. Coordinate **D** intersects these curves at maximum wall pressure and when zero water potential indicates that the cell will not accept any further water with increase of cell volume. Any further increase of wall pressure will not lead to increase of cell volume but to exudation of water or rupture of the cell. The portions of the curves to the left of **C** represent wilting as the eell volume decreases, wall pressure becomes negative and water potential becomes even more negative, indicating an even greater capacity for taking in water.
Coordinate **A** intersects osmotic pressure when this is balanced by wall pressure at maximum turgor and does not relate this to water potential.
Coordinate **B** indicates zero wall pressure when the cell is just turgid and zero water potential at maxiumum turgor. Neither of these values is related to osmotic pressure nor is the single value required by the answer shown.

Application of data to make a prediction on water relations
8 Answer **C**   *of plant cells*
The water potential of a cell bathed in an external solution is given by the equation. Water potential $= OP_1 - OP_2 - TP$ where OP_1 is the osmotic pressure of the external solution, OP_2 is the osmotic pressure of the cell sap and TP is the turgor pressure. For the given values the equation is $-3 = 5 - 7 - 1$. Thus the turgor pressure is 1 which represents an equilibrium below full turgidity because this is insufficient to completely cancel the negative value of the water potential. Alternative **D** would occur if the two solutions were of equal osmotic pressure when the water potential could be completely cancelled by the turgor pressure. Alternatives **A** and **B** would require the osmotic pressure of the external solution to be higher than the cell sap.

9 Answer **C**   *Knowledge of factors controlling transpiration*
Atmospheric conditions such as humidity, temperature and wind mainly determine transpiration rate. These in their turn can affect the state of guard cells, but usually only in conditions of drought and wilting. Cuticular transpiration may also be appreciable. The metabolic state of leaf cells or the special carbohydrate transformations within guard cells are not directly utilized for transpiration control. The passage of water up the xylem appears to be mainly due to physical factors, of which transpiration itself is the main component. The physical conditions of the soil have little effect except in extreme instances such as drought when the water holding properties of a soil may limit the intake of the last fraction of water by the root system.

                                   Knowledge of a trend in transpiration in relation to wind
10 Answer **B**   *speed*
The boundary layer tends to be removed as wind speed increases so that its effective resistance becomes smaller. The increase in turbulence effectively removes water molecules from the thinner boundary layer. This enhances the concentration gradient which governs the rate of gaseous diffusion from the intercellular spaces. The removal of water from leaf cells tends to concentrate the cell solutions thus raising osmotic pressure.

                                   Application of physical principles influencing leaf
11 Answer **D**   *temperature*
The heating effect of solar radiation is counteracted by the loss of latent heat used in the vaporization of water from cell surfaces to the intercellular spaces. Water already in the vapour phase in the boundary layer will not take up further heat for its removal, therefore **C** does not affect the process. The energy released by metabolism in the leaf is too small to build up an appreciable rise in temperature. The re-emission of solar heat takes place directly through the leaf surface and not through any stomatal exchange.

12 Answer **C**   *Knowledge of the function of the endodermis in roots*
The passage of water across the root is affected by differences in osmotic pressure between the soil solution, the root hairs and the successive cells of the cortex through which the water progresses inwards. Thus all the tissues may be concerned. However, water may traverse the root tissues by passing along the cell walls and through intercellular spaces as vapour. The impermeable casparian strip on the endodermis cells of dicotyledons and the passage cells of monocotyledons confer an active control function on the endodermis cells through which water must pass, allowing hydrostatic pressure to be developed within the vascular cylinder.

13 Answer **C**   *Knowledge of a factor which reduces water loss in plants*
The crucial factor is the surface area-volume ratio. Reduction of the surface area or increasing the tissue volume in A and B respectively are not necessarily related to each other and therefore may not affect the ratio. Increase in root area is a compensating development in some xerophytes to make good water loss but it does not reduce it.

14 Answer **D**   *Knowledge of factors which reduce water loss in Ammophila*
When transpiration rate exceeds water absorption rate, the large thin walled cells
at the base of the grooves lose water, become flaccid, causing the leaf to roll. The
lower surface has a thick cuticle so that the rolling encloses the upper surface and
reduces transpiration. The sunken stomata and the hairs both increase the
boundary layer thickness by decreasing diffusion. The rhizomes have little effect
on retention of water but they increase the rhizosphere from which water may be
absorbed.

                          Comprehension of root pressure as a factor separate from
15 Answer **D**   *the cohesion theory*
This is evidence of a positive pressure generated from the root system. The
cohesion theory depends upon the existence of columns of water under tension in
the xylem. This tension can cause a reduction in diameter of the vessels and this
effect may be detected in the changes in stem diameter when transpiration pull is
most active in the daytime. Both **A** and **C** indicate the effect of columns under
tension receding when the negative pressure is released.

                          Knowledge of the derivation of the motive force for the
16 Answer **B**   *transpiration stream*
The force which raises water through the xylem is derived from the evaporation of
water from the surface of mesophyll cells. The cohesive force in **A** is also derived
from this. Activated diffusion is not considered to be a factor in xylem transport.
(It is a theory concerned with translocation in the phloem.). Root pressure in **D** is
insufficient to have an appreciable effect on water movement in the stems of most
plants.

IX Nutrition in Plants

1 Answer **C**

In young plants, an appreciable proportion of the photosynthetic product is utilized in protein synthesis. Thus dry weight, which includes both protein and carbohydrate, would be a better approximation than the increase in carbohydrate only. Absorbed mineral ions form a negligible proportion of the dry weight as they are rapidly incorporated in organic substances in young plants. In **B**, increase in fresh weight would include water which is abundantly used in cell extension in the young plant. **A** is an expression of the photosynthetic quotient which gives no indication of the rate. In the case of young plants it would be somewhat above unity as a proportion of protein is being produced.

2 Answer **A**

Application of a physical principle to estimate a photosynthetic rate

The inverse square law states that the intensity of light from a source varies inversely with the square of the distance. Thus at 10 cm from the plant (twice the distance) the light energy received would be four times less and the photosynthetic yield of oxygen would be $\frac{20}{4} = 5$ cm^3.

3 Answer **D**   *Comprehension of the compensation period*

D expresses the balance which must be achieved to maintain the state of compensation. In **A**, biomass gives no indication of the rate of the exchanges. **B** and **C** both take no account of the respiratory exchanges of the plants which are involved in the total situation.

4 Answer **A**   *Interpretation of the compensation point on a graph*

The point x is the compensation point at which there is no gain or loss of carbon dioxide. This is related to a balance in the gas exchanges of photosynthesis and respiration in the plant. The other three alternatives express an unbalanced exchange.

5 Answer **C**   *Knowledge of factors affecting stomatal movement*

Stomata are opened and closed by changes in turgidity of the guard cells. An increase in osmotic pressure of the cell sap increases the water potential between the the guard cells and the surrounding cells. This causes an increase in turgor of the guard cells and leads to the opening of the stomata. Option **B** is likely to have this effect by increasing the amount of available sugars, whereas **C** would be the opposite. **A** would take place with active photosynthesis and thus give the same effect as **B**. **D** could be associated with a decrease in carbon dioxide, giving the same result as **A**. There is also evidence of the direct effect of pH on enzyme activity controlling the starch-sugar changes in the guard cells.

6 Answer **A**

Interpretation of evidence on chlorophyl and starch distribution in a leaf

This commonly used demonstration is used to support an assertion, but it is not a proof. The three statements **B, C** and **D** are all possible interpretations of the result.

7 Answer **C**

Application of biological knowledge to interpret a graph on starch and chlorophyll distribution in a leaf

The greatest density of chloroplasts is in the palisade cells. The scattergram indicates a positive correlation, thus alternative **A** is incorrect. There is no evidence of specialised storage tissue mentioned in **B. D** would produce a complete scatter of points indicating zero correlation.

8 Answer **D**

Comprehension of the effects of light and dark periods on photosynthesis

The dark reactions take place more slowly than the light reactions. Hence products of the light reactions can accumulate during the light periods and be used during the subsequent dark periods. The yield per unit flash will depend upon how long it takes to use up the excess product of the light reaction. A certain length of dark period would allow all of the product of the light period to be used. Beyond a maximum dark period there would be no further increase, thus **D** is correct. **A** is incorrect for dark periods below this maximum, but would be true above the maximum dark periods. Both **B** and **C** are the opposite of the true answer.

9 Answer **B**

Application of knowledge of photosynthesis to results from an experiment with ^{18}O

The proportion of ^{18}O in the gas evolved should relate to the proportion of ^{18}O in the source used. Since oxygen is liberated by the photolysis of water, the proportion of ^{18}O will be related to the proportion of ^{18}O in the water. The bicarbonate ions are a source of carbon for photosynthesis and would not show any direct relationship with respect to ^{18}O. This eliminates options **A** and **C. D** is incorrect as the evolution of ^{18}O is a dependent variable.

10 Answer **D**

Application of graphical data showing the influence of light on PGA formation

The light reactions are faster than the dark reactions, thus **B** is incorrect. The initial rapid incorporation of ^{14}C during the dark period implies the existence of a previously formed acceptor substance which must have been present in the light. The falling off shown by the curve indictes that such an acceptor then becomes less abundant while the final level indicates the accumulation of PGA which is no longer being converted into a further substance because of the lack of light. 'A is incorrect as the initial limitation in PGA formation is the lack of carbon dioxide. **C** is incorrect because PGA production falls off at 1½ minutes.

11 Answer **C** *Inference from data on radioisotope distribution in a leaf*

A is not possible as detached leaves would be unable to remove carbohydrate by translocation. **C** involves a biological process which is likely to operate, the evolution of carbon dioxide being related to the availablity of the carbohydrate which incorporated $^{14}CO_2$. Experiments using a radioactive tracer make the assumption that organisms are unable to distinguish the radioactive from the non-radioactive isotope of an element, so that **B** and **D** are not acceptable.

12 Answer **D** *Knowledge of transfer of energy in chloroplasts*
The pigment particles in the lamellae of the grana on the intact chloroplasts are closely arranged thus allowing energy to be readily transferred. This spatial arrangement is destroyed in making extracts. **A** and **B** are both true but are not directly related to the question. In **C**, carbon dioxide fixation is not directly concerned with light.

13 Answer **A** *Comprehension of a result from the 'Hill reaction'*
In the limited conditions of this version of the 'Hill reaction', only the practical effects of light on chloroplasts is shown by providing DCIP as an electron acceptor. The immediate result is the release of a hydrogen atom from each molecule of water which then reduces the DCIP. The oxygen is not immediately released in the intact cell, but it can be demonstrated in the 'Hill reaction' by further sensitive techniques such as the oxidation of myoglobin. Thus **B** is not the answer to this limited experiment, and, in any case would require a different experiment with labelled oxygen ($^{18}O_2$). **C** is incorrect because the whole photosynthetic process has not been demonstrated. **D** may be regarded as a generally true statement, but in this particular experiment, the reduction of DCIP is similar to the effect obtained when succinic acid is oxidised in the presence of the enzyme succinic dehydrogenase in mitochondria. In both cases, one component is oxidised while the other must be reduced. It is therefore necessary for the chloroplast suspension to be free of mitochondria or the decolorization may be due to both reactions.

14 Answer **A** *Knowledge of a part of the carbon pathway in photosynthesis*
Phosphoglyceric acid formation has been shown to fall off rapidly when the carbon dioxide supply is removed, while at the same time, ribulose diphosphate rapidly increases, thus supporting **A**. The co-enzymes in **B** are concerned with the TCA cycle. Answers **C** and **D** represent simplified views of carbon dioxide uptake before the Calvin cycle was elucidated.

15 Answer **B** *Knowledge of dark reactions in photosynthesis*
The light reactions are summarized in **A**. In these, high energy electrons become available to produce ATP and provide sufficient energy for NADP to act as a hydrogen acceptor on the splitting of the water molecule. In **B**, the dark reactions which reduce carbon dioxide to carbohydrate are summarized. The high energy electrons carried by $NADPH_2$ are transferred for forming carbohydrate. Equation **C** does not involve carbon dioxide or a carbohydrate and incorporates oxygen in forming water. Equation **D** involves the splitting of both carbon dioxide and water in the dark stage whereas they take place in the light and the dark stage as shown in **A** and **B**.

16 Answer **B** *Knowledge of the source of high-energy electrons in the light reactions in photosynthesis*
The water is split by light into hydrogen and hydroxyl ions. The hydroxyl ions release high energy electrons, thus,

$$\text{light energy} + 20H \rightarrow H_2O + \tfrac{1}{2}O_2 = 2\overset{*}{\epsilon}$$

These are utilized in the formation of $NADPH_2$ and ATP which are electron acceptors at this stage. They transfer this energy for further reactions.

127

17 Answer **D**
The selective uptake of ions involves metabolic activity which is reflected by the utilization of oxygen. Alternative **A** may be partly true as there is some evidence which suggests passive intake of ions with the water absorbed from the soil. **B** is untrue as selective absorption leads to internal concentrations of ions which do not reflect the concentrations in the soil solution. **C** is untrue because the process of physical diffusion would agree with **B** and contradict **D**.

18 Answer **A**   *Knowledge of the mobility of elements between plant tissues*
Calcium is not mobile and would remain in the older parts while the younger parts would show deficiency. In **B, C** and **D**, the elements are readily re-exported from older tissues to growing regions. Deficiency would consequently show first in the older leaves.

19 Answer **C**   *Knowledge of symptoms of iron deficiency in plants*
In iron deficiency, respiration is decreased and chlorophyll formation is inhibited. Thus both energy release and processes of synthesis are impaired and **A, B** and **D** are consequences. Long thin internodes in **C** are the result of etiolation which in other respects may resemble iron deficiency because of the failure to produce chlorophyll.

20 Answer **D**
Selection of an hypothesis to explain results of an experiment on the nitrogen content of young leaves
A and **B** may be true but they make insufficient use of the data. **C** is a more perceptive statement, but the hypothesis can go further in its use of the data as in **D**.

21 Answer **B**   *Knowledge of polarity of distribution of auxins in plants*
The polar distribution of auxins has been shown by numerous experiments. For example, when detached sections of coleoptiles have an agar block placed at each end, auxin accumulates in the block applied to the original lower end, irrespective of the effect of gravity. In **A** and **C**, the direction of movement of the substances is related to the prevailing requirements of the various parts of the plants. In **D**, gibberellins, which stimulate cell extension in shoots, differ from auxins in not being influenced in their translocation by the polarity of the plant.

X Nutrition in Animals

1 Answer **C**   *Knowledge of the effect of paracasein*
The calcium salt forms a relatively insoluble curd which remains in the stomach while pepsin acts on it. Both **A** and **B** suggest that stomach action would be speeded up, which is not true. The breaking down of terminal peptide bonds in **D** is the final process of hydrolysis carried out by the enzymes of the small intestine.

2 Answer **A**   *Knowledge of trends in pH in human digestion*
These optimum pH values show a relation to the pH of the region of the gut in which they act and to the pH of the secretion in which they are found. The actual secretions may not be at the optimum pH in every instance. For example, the pH of the gastric juice may vary from 1.5 to 2.0

3 Answer **C**   *Knowledge of the protein-digesting components in chyle*
Chyle is the watery fluid which is formed in the small intestine. It contains the various products of digestion, including the protein-splitting enzyme trypsin. The secretion of the pyloric glands of the stomach contains no enzymes. The pancreatic juice contains the inactive substances trypsinogen and chymotrypsinogen. The intestinal juice is the secretion of the crypts of Lieberkühn and Brunner's glands. It contains a series of peptidases which only hydrolyse polypeptides. In addition it provides the activating substance enterokinase which converts trypsinogen into trypsin and this in turn activates chymotrypsinogen in the chyle.

4 Answer **D**   *Knowledge of nervous control of gut movements*
Parasympathetic impulses stimulate the contractions which cause **A**, **B** and **C** and also relax the sphincters. Such a combination promotes active movement of the contents of the digestive system. Conversely, sympathetic impulses contract the sphincters while relaxing the circular and longitudinal muscles responsible for **A**, **B** and **C**.

5 Answer **C**   *Knowledge of co-ordination of peristalsis*
The peristaltic wave stimulated by the presence of food depends upon local co-ordination which requires the local transmission of impulses from the site of stimulation to a region immediately behind the food mass. This causes the muscular contraction which drives the mass forwards. The parasympathetic supply in **A** can stimulate peristalsis, but this is initiation, not co-ordination. The sympathetic supply in **B** has the opposite effect. Alternative **D** would be too local to have the necessary co-ordination of muscles at a short distance from the site of the stimulus.

6 Answer **A**   *Knowledge of an initial product of deamination*
Deamination is a process of nitrogen removal which may, in the first phase, be represented by ammonia. This then enters the ornithine cycle to produce urea by way of arginine. Thus urea in **B** is only indirectly produced. The type of keto acid varies but some may enter the carbohydrate metabolism to give rise indirectly to glucose and glycogen.

7 Answer **B**   *Knowledge of a pathway for deriving energy from proteins*
The ornithine-arginine cycle involves taking up the amino acids to produce urea, and it is the organic acids which remain which can be utilized as a source of energy in the Krebs' cycle. In **C**, the haem of haemoglobin is excreted as bile pigments and the circulation of bile salts between liver and intestine in **D** is concerned with fat digestion.

8 Answer **A**   *Knowledge of the function of gastrin*
Gastrin is produced by the mucosa of the pyloric region of the stomach and it stimulates the production of a gastric juice which is richer in acid than in pepsin. Bile secretion, in **B**, is increased by cholecystokinin produced by the duodenal mucosa. Inhibition of stomach activities in **C** is probably caused by enterogastrone. Increased sodium bicarbonate content of the pancreatic juice in **D** is stimulated by secretin.

9 Answer **D**   *Inference from an experiment on gastric secretion*
A, **B** and **C** refer to hormones which require the presence of food in the organ in which they are produced. Gastrin would stimulate the production of the gastric secretion if food were to reach the stomach. Enterogastrone inhibits stomach activity and secretin stimulates the pancreatic secretion of sodium bicarbonate and of bile by the liver. Thus, stimulation of gastric secretion is, in the first instance, under nervous control.

10 Answer **B**   *Comprehension of evidence of active absorption by villi*
Phosphatase is probably part of the system for making the energy available for active absorption. The brush border indicated in **A** increases the surface area and this probably promotes absorption. Although this could increase the sites available for the active process of pinocytosis, it could be equally valid for promoting physical diffusion. **C** and **D** are both concerned with secretion.

11 Answer **D**   *Knowledge of a general characteristic of vitamins*
Vitamins are parts of certain enzymes involved in metabolism which have to be supplied in the diet. They include a variety of chemical substances, thus 'amines' in alternative **C** represents an early erroneous view which led to the term 'vitamine'. Hormones, which have various effects, have no special relationships to vitamins. Few vitamins contain trace metals although cobalamine is one.

                    Knowledge of the disease associated with the accumulation
12 Answer **A**   *of pyruvic acid*
Vitamin B_1 or thiamine plays a part in forming the co-carboxylase which is a co-enzyme concerned with the decarboxylation of pyruvic acid. If this accumulates, the poisonous effects cause the paralysis of beri beri. Pellagra is associated with the deficiency of nicotinic acid which is necessary for the co-enzymes NAD and NADP which operate in another part of the carbohydrate metabolism. Scurvy is due to a deficiency of ascorbic acid which is concerned with a variety of cell functions. Night blindness is due to a deficiency of vitamin A which is essential for the regeneration of rhodopsin in the retina.

13 Answer **B**

Comprehension of the relationship between vitamin D and a hormone function

Abnormal deposition of calcium in the bones can be caused by excessive vitamin D. This is accompanied by its rapid removal from the blood; thus **C** and **D** are untrue. Parathormone secreted by the parathyroid glands has the opposite effect to vitamin D. Its secretion is stimulated by calcium deficiency and causes the release of calcium from the bones.

14 Answer **B** *Knowledge of the function of vitamin K*

Vitamin K is necessary for the formation of prothrombin but does not form part of it therefore its inclusion in the precursor substance in **A** is incorrect. **C** represents the thromboplastic factors liberated by damaged cells and platelets which initiate the clotting sequence. **D** represents the effect of the thrombin in promoting the formation of fibrin from fibrinogen.

15 Answer **B** *Use of data from an experiment on feeding animals with vitamin C and protein*

This illustrates the design of a factorial experiment with four combinations of treatments. All four expressions shown in the alternatives are independent of each other, providing different information from the experiment. **A** represents the mean for all four treatments and provides the least information. **B** shows the difference between the mean for the low vitamin and the high vitamin treatments. **C** represents the difference between the mean for low protein and high protein treatments. **D** represents the interaction effect of vitamin and protein. This last expression can be subjected to further investigation. For instance, if the interactive effect is zero, the effects of the two factors are independent. This is uncommon. For example, in this experiment the increase in vitamin might promote the uptake of protein.

XI Respiration

1 Answer **C** *Knowledge of gaseous exchange by diffusion in solution*
The rate of gaseous exchange is limited by the rate of diffusion of gases in solution
through the surface membranes. **A** is untrue and therefore it is efficient to keep the
diffusion pathway while in solution as short as possible. **B** is true but represents a
problem to be solved in those organisms which breathe atmospheric air. **D** does
not offer a valid explanation of the physical necessity for a moist surface although
it may be true and have some bearing on the continued use of moist membranes
throughout evolution.

2 Answer **B** *Knowledge of procedure in using a respirometer*
By absorbing the carbon dioxide given out, the reduction in volume shown on the
syringe indicates the oxygen absorbed. **A** is incorrect as the pyrogallol would
remove oxygen from the system. The manometer is used to monitor pressures
between the working chamber II and the thermobarometer chamber I. Procedure
C would eliminate the thermobarometer effect and give poor control of manometer levels and for reading volume changes. Procedure **D** is used for finding
respiratory quotient in which

$$RQ = \frac{\text{volume carbon dioxide given out}}{\text{volume of oxygen absorbed}}$$

3 Answer **B** *Knowledge of the working principles of respirometers*
In the Warburg respirometer at **B**, the volume is kept constant by adjustment of
the reservoir and the readings on the open side of the manometer indicate the
pressure change required to maintain this volume. The constant for each flask
must be known in order to convert the pressure reading to volume. In the Ganong
respirometer at **A**, the experiment is started at atmospheric pressure and the
sliding tube is used to adjust the level in the graduated tube before closing the
stopper. In both **A** and **B** a control respirometer is required using water in place of
the respiring material to allow for changes in temperature and pressure due to the
thermobarometer effect. The simplified Barcroft respirometer at **C** has a compensating chamber to allow for this. The syringe is used to adjust manometer levels
before the apparatus is closed. The differences in manometer levels indicate
change in volume, or the movement of the syringe can be used to record volume
change after equilibrating the manometer. **D** is a smaller apparatus which works at
atmospheric pressure and is suitable for short runs. The syringe is used to move the
oil drop indicator to a suitable starting position.

4 Answer **B** *Comprehension of a respiratory rate from data*
In 10 minutes 1 gram of body weight would require 0.5 cm³ of oxygen. Therefore in
1 minute 1 gram of body weight would require 0.05 cm³ of oxygen.

5 Answer **A**   *Comprehension of energy release in respiration*
The cascade model involves energy release as each successive compound loses electrons. The gain indicated in **B** and **C** represent energy retained until the next stage of energy release in the cascade occurs. The total transfer in **D** represents each end of the complete process but is also true of non-biological systems.

6 Answer **D**   *Comprehension of the cause of oxygen debt*
Glycolysis represents a fairly ready breakdown of a metabolite and a rapid release of energy. The subsequent oxidative anabolism which involves aerobic respiration represents added complexity and may be slower. Hence **D** is correct while **C** is the opposite of this. The conversion of lactic acid to glycogen in **A** involves 'paying off' the debt, not acquiring it. **B** does not have a direct bearing on the situation.

                    Knowledge of energy yield in the anaerobic respiration of
7 Answer **D**   *yeast*
The energy remaining in ethyl alcohol represents unused energy from the glucose which has been utilized by the yeast. This is considerable as the aerobic processes allow about twelve times as much energy to be obtained as that derived from the anaerobic process which produces ethyl alcohol. **A** represents an error in assuming that it is the oxygen which provides energy. **B** is irrrelevant and **C** is a teleological statement.

8 Answer **A**   *Interpretation of a respiratory quotient*
The respiratory quotient is found by

$$\frac{\text{volume of carbon dioxide produced}}{\text{volume of oxygen absorbed}}$$

In anaerobic respiration little or no oxygen is absorbed but carbon dioxide production may be high as, for example, in plants growing in oxygen-deficient, waterlogged conditions or fermentation by yeast. An RQ of 1 indicates a full aerobic respiration of carbohydrate. An RQ of 0.7 is typical of fats which require more oxygen to completely oxidize their higher proportion of carbon. An RQ below 0.5 could indicate that carbon dioxide is being retained for the formation of organic acids.

9 Answer **C**   *Knowledge of an expression of the reliability of results*
In **A**, expressing the range requires the difference between the largest and the smallest values. These are most likely exceptional because of variability of living material and experimental error. The mean deviation in **B** is the arithmetic mean of the deviations of each of the values from the mean of the sum of the values. It provides useful information of the dispersion around the mean. The standard deviation provides a more sensitive instrument for expressing the proportion between the value of the mean and the dispersal around it. Thus the smaller the standard deviation in proportion to the mean, the less dispersal and the more reliable the results. It is found by squaring the deviations of the values from the mean, adding these, dividing this sum by the number of values obtained and finding the square root. Useful approximations can also be found by simpler methods. The median value in **D** is merely the middle quantity in the range and provides no evidence on the dispersal of the results.

10 Answer **B**   *Evaluation of a procedure for estimating metabolic activity*
Assuming that aerobic respiration is taking place and that there is no oxygen debt, **B** would give the most reliable information as it is most directly related to metabolic processes. The calorific value of foods would take no account of the fraction utilized in growth and tissue repair. The respiratory quotient gives a value which represents the average for the various substrates respired but not of their rate of use. The temperature of the body surface might be influenced by the heat released by metabolic processes, but it is also influenced by the ambient temperature, loss of latent heat by evaporation and the state of circulation of body fluids to the surface. However, heat loss per unit area is a convenient method of calorimetry which can be used to give some comparison of metabolic rates.

11 Answer **C**   *Knowledge of oxygen transport in animals*
The tracheal system of insects conveys air into the tissues in such a way as to make the use of an oxygen-carrying pigment in the blood superfluous in most cases. *Amoeba* cannot be said to have tissues and, in any case, exchanges gases in solution with the water, as also does the fish. Both fishes and earthworm make use of a blood system to exchange absorbed gases between the tissues and the air.

Comprehension of the counter flow principle in the function
12 Answer **C**   *of fish gills*
The effect is that of a counterflow system in which water with the highest concentration of oxygen first encounters blood which is already fairly highly loaded with oxygen and water with less oxygen encounters blood with even less oxygen. **A** is incorrect as it would require blood and water to be flowing in the same direction. The diffusion gradients of oxygen and carbon dioxide work independently and do not interact through any form of mass flow, thus **B** is not true. **D** is the opposite of **C**.

Comprehension of diffusion in the gas exchanges of the
13 Answer **B**   *lungs of a mammal*
Gaseous exchange at the lungs depends upon physical diffusion, the rate of which depends upon maintaining concentration gradients. Thus **B** is correct. There is no mass flow of air through the alveoli as suggested in **A**, concentration differences are maintained by dilution of the residual air in the alveoli. **C** is incorrect as the gaseous exchange does not depend upon active transport. **D** is incorrect because saturation of the blood is an intrinsic figure for each gas and the extent of loading of the blood as a proportion of the saturation depends (apart from some biochemical interaction) mainly upon the partial pressure of each gas.

Comprehension of the anaerobic nature of immediate energy
14 Answer **D**   *output from muscle*
Lifting a heavy weight requires a rate of energy output which is higher than the rate of oxidative anabolism. Contraction of the muscles of the diaphragm and abdomen during weight lifting restricts breathing. Thus **D** would be advantageous and **A** would not. The effect of training is to increase the difference between heart output at rest and during exercise, hence **B** would be an undesirable starting state. **C** would have no immediate effect on muscles as they make most direct use of carbohydrate already present in their cells.

15 Answer **C** *Comprehension of lung volumes*
C represents the volume of air which cannot be emptied by the intact lungs. Its estimation requires a further gas analysis technique to obtain a calculated value. **D** is easily found by making maximum inhalation and exhalation. The differences between **D** and the upper and lower limits of tidal volume give **A** and **B**.

16 Answer **C** *Knowledge of likely residual air volume in human lungs*
This volume of air cannot be exhaled. Inspiration mixes fresh air with it so that the normal proportion of carbon dioxide in contact with the alveolar surfaces is somewhat higher than that of external air.

17 Answer **B** *Comprehension of feedback control in breathing*
As inspiration progresses, the stretch receptors send impulses which inhibit further inspiration. This is negative feedback. The lungs then empty and the inspiratory centre sends impulses to the muscles for a further inspiration. The lag between the stimulus of the receptors and the response of the medullary centres produces the oscillatory effect required for breathing movements. Alternative **D** is incorrect as homeostasis implies a steady state. **A** is incorrect as the circuit is too complex to be described as a reflex arc although there are reflex components. Positive feedback would imply some form of reinforcement which would produce an irreversible effect.

18 Answer **C** *Knowledge of the prime cause of altitude sickness*
At high altitudes the proportion of oxygen remains the same, hence **D** is incorrect. However, the amount of oxygen per volume at the decreased pressure is less. This decreases the diffusion gradient from air to blood. **B** is unchanged by altitude and **A** is the opposite of true as the diffusion gradient from blood to air is increased.

19 Answer **B** *Interpretation of a dissociation curve for oxyhaemoglobin*
The levelling of the upper part of the curve indicates that in environments of high oxygen content such as the lung capillaries, changes in the partial pressure of oxygen affect the saturation level only slightly. Thus **B** is true. **C** is false as the middle part of the curve is steep so that a small change in partial pressure of oxygen brings about a large change in the saturation level so that in an environment of decreasing oxygen pressure haemoglobin readily yields its oxygen. Alternative **A** is false because the curve does not reach the top of the graph. **D** is false as the level nature of the upper part of the curve indicates that fairly large increases in oxygen can be taken up with less rise in saturation level than in lower parts of the curve.

Comprehension of the effect of an increase of carbon dioxide
in the blood on an oxyhaemoglobin dissociation curve
20 Answer **C**
The shift of the dissociation curve is due to the intrinsic effect of carbon dioxide on the oxygen carrying capacity of haemoglobin. This has the effect of releasing more oxygen in active tissues which are producing carbon dioxide. **A** and **D** are both true but not an explanation of this phenomenon. **B** supposes a relationship between the gases in terms of simple solubility whereas there is a complex interaction between them involving the 'chloride shift' in the carriage of carbon dioxide and reversible changes in the characteristics of haemoglobin protein when involved in oxygen transport.

XII Circulation and Blood

1 Answer **C**   *Knowledge of mixing of the blood in the circulation*
The oxygen content of venous blood varies according to the activity of the organs from which it drains. Thus the posterior vena cava will have a variable content of blood according to the activity of the organs in the posterior parts of the body. The hepatic portal vein will have blood which varies according to the nature of the absorbed products of digestion. The pulmonary artery will have blood from all parts of the venous system which have been well mixed by heart action. The pulmonary vein will contain oxygenated blood.

                              Comprehension of a relationship between the pulse wave
2 Answer **C**   *and other factors in the circulation*
A is incorrect because the pulse is a shock wave which is initiated by the heart beat and which travels independently at a much faster rate than the blood itself. **B** is incorrect because all movement of blood through the closed circulation of a mammal is initiated by the heart beat. The absence of a pulse in the veins is due to the storage factor indicated in **C**. **D** is incorrect because a decrease of capillary resistance would allow the pulse wave to pass with less impedance and therefore with less amplitude in terms of arterial dilation. This would not increase the original velocity or pressure amplitude of the pulse wave.

                              Evaluation of procedures for finding the origin of the
3 Answer **A**   *excitation wave of the heart beat*
The heart beat originates in the sinu-atrial node and therefore by varying the temperature, corresponding changes in its rate of activity could be monitored. Clamping Purkinje fibres would merely interfere with transmission of the impulse and would be inconclusive. Electrical stimuli of the nerves suggested in **C** and **D** would only affect the rate of heart beat, but the initiation of heart beat stimuli would continue.

4 Answer **C**   *Knowledge of the sequence in heart action*
The pace-maker cells of the sinu-atrial node are modified muscle fibres which respond to the stretching caused by the pressure of blood entering the heart. Their contraction stimulates the slower-acting auricular muscle and, eventually, the auriculo-ventricular node. This conducts the impulse relatively slowly, thus ensuring a pause between contraction of the auricles and ventricles. The impulse is then transmitted by the Purkinje fibres through the mass of the ventricle muscle.

                              Prediction of the effect of stimulation of the vagus nerve on
5 Answer **D**   *the circulation*
Acetyl choline is released by the endings of the vagus nerve. This inhibits cardiac muscle, causing heart rate and arterial pressure to fall. Thus **A** is untrue and **B** does not follow. Acetyl choline also decreases the conductivity of the auriculo-ventricular bundle. All these changes lead to an increase in venous pressure as blood is drawn into the heart less actively.

6 Answer C

Application of data to find the region of greatest resistance in the circulation

The small volume of the arterioles indicates the greatest constriction in the system and hence the greatest resistance. The subsequent low linear velocity in the capillaries while the volume is greater than in the arterioles indicates less resistance, therefore **D** is untrue. The high linear velocity in the aorta and arteries indicates less resistance and enables their small relative volumes to transmit an adequate quantity of blood at high pressures.

7 Answer C

Application of data to find filtration pressure

A would represent the net hydrostatic pressure when the blood pressure is opposed by the pressure of the tissue fluid. **B** would represent the net osmotic pressure. Because of the attractive force exerted by osmotic pressure, the effective filtration pressure is found by the difference between **A** and **B**. **D** represents an erroneous attempt to find the value by working out a result for the capillary and tissue fluid separately and using opposite signs for the results $5 - 2 = 3$.

8 Answer A

Knowledge of the cause of lymph movement

As the lymph vessels have no direct connection with the heart nor any musculature, lymph flow depends on compression of the vessels by the surrounding tissues with the action of valves to impart directional flow. The pressure of plasma from the blood system and the facilitation of the return flow to the venous system in **C** and **D** play only a minor part. The lymph nodes, which contain fine channels, have a complex filtering action as part of their functions in protection against infection.

9 Answer A

Knowledge of a function of lymph nodes

The lymphatic vessels converge on lymph nodes before they drain into the blood system. The sinuses within the nodes provide cells which can ingest invading organisms and lymphocytes which are concerned with antibody production. Enlargement of the nodes often accompanies infection as they become active in forming barriers. Although the lymphatic vessels of the intestine transport absorbed fat, the lymph nodes are not especially concerned in this function, nor with the formation of blood. Stress conditions which stimulate adrenocortical hormones tend to diminish lymphatic tissue.

10 Answer D

Knowledge of the inheritance of the clotting capacity of the blood

The oxygen carrying capacity varies according to the rate of respiratory activity, especially in relation to the carbon dioxide present and the rate of production of red cells. The speed of circulation is adjusted by control of the heart rate through the autonomic nervous system and by certain hormones. Resistance to infection varies according to the reaction to invading pathogenic agents. On the other hand, the clotting factors are present whether they are called into operation or not.

11 Answer C

Comprehension of an osmotic effect on red blood cells

The cell membranes are semipermeable, allowing free passage of water but not of the solutes. The osmotic effect therefore causes an intake of water with the eventual rupture of the membranes and release of the cell contents. Alternative **B** is incorrect not only because exosmosis does not occur but also in assuming that osmosis involves the movement of various substances through a semipermeable membrane. Alternatives **A** and **D** suppose the membrane to be permeable, and in **D** that sodium chloride (a normal constituent of plasma) would increase permeability.

12 Answer **C**   *Knowledge of the carriage of carbon dioxide in the blood*
The formation of carbonic acid given in **A** only occurs when carbon dioxide enters
the red cells which contain carbonic anhydrase. Potassium bicarbonate is formed
within the red cells when this carbonic acid combines with potassium derived from
potassium haemoglobinate. The dissociation of the potassium bicarbonate allows
negative bicarbonate ions to diffuse from the red cells in exchange for negative
chloride ions passing inwards. These are derived from the sodium chloride in the
plasma which is decreased as the bicarbonate combines with the sodium so that
sodium bicarbonate is increased.

                            Comprehension of a relationship between carbon dioxide
13 Answer **B**   *and oxygen in the blood*
Increasing the carbon dioxide content of the blood shifts the dissociation curve to
the right which expresses the diminished oxygen-carrying power of the blood.
Arterial blood and venous blood in man contain carbon dioxide at partial
pressures of 40 and 46 mm Hg respectively. Removal of a further part of this in
either case would increase the oxygen carrying capacity of the blood. Raising the
temperature or lowering the pH value decreases the oxgen carrying capacity.
Atmospheric air at normal pressure contains oxygen at a partial pressure of 159
mm Hg. As blood is 95% saturated at a partial pressure of oxygen of 100 mm Hg
and the dissociation curve levels off above this, no extra oxygen would be carried
by increasing the atmospheric pressure.

14 Answer **D**   *Knowledge of the conditions for agglutination*
D is correct because the blood of the recipient contains sufficient antibodies to
react with the antigen of the donor red cells. **A** is incorrect because the antibodies
are in the serum. **B** and **C** are incorrect because the antigens remain on the red cells
and do not attack antibodies in the serum.

15 Answer **C**   *Knowledge of the interaction of blood groups*
The blood groups are defined by the antigen on the surface of the red cells. In
alternative **C**, antigen A on the recipient's cells can exist with antibody b in the
plasma. The donor AB has neither antibody but AB cells introduced into the
group A recipient will be affected by antibody b and agglutination will occur. The
reverse cases in alternatives **A** and **B** are unaffected because the plasma of the
donors, which contain antibodies b and a respectively, is much diluted when
mixed with the recipient's blood. Group O is a universal donor because it contains
no antigens on its cells and the plasma of this group is rapidly diluted in a
recipient's blood so that the a and b antibodies are not effective.

                            Evaluation of an hypothesis on the maintenance of placental
16 Answer **A**   *union*
B is incorrect because the genetic origins of maternal and foetal tissues are
different through sexual reproduction. **C** is untrue as the placental tissues are
derived from both embryonic and maternal sources. The antigens of different
blood groups would be likely to lead to interactions, hence **D** is wrong.

17 Answer **D**   *Knowledge of the rhesus factor*
This would have the opposite effect because the blood of the Rh negative mother
would be stimulated to produce antibodies. This effect can also occur as a result of
successive pregnancies of Rh positive infants where some leakage of foetal blood
into the maternal circulation may eventually have the same effect as a transfusion
of Rh positive blood. Thus **B** is true. **A** is also true as the antibody only develops in
response to the presence of the antigen. The inheritance of the rhesus factor as a
dominant gene implies that a rhesus negative woman must be homozygous and a
rhesus positive father may be homozygous or heterozygous.

18 Answer **D**   *Comprehension of the effect of innoculation*
The effect of the first innoculation appears to place the cells which produce
antibodies in a state of readiness to produce more on the second innoculation.
Thus **C** is unlikely and **A** does not express the typical reaction of blood which is
already sensitized. **B** is self-contradictory.

                              Application of a principle in immunology to choice of a
19 Answer **A**   *grafting procedure*
Because individual *P* produced antibodies which caused the rejection of the graft
from *Q*, it would become sensitized to any other individuals which resembled *Q*
and therefore reject grafts from them. As *R* is readily rejected, it must therefore
resemble *Q*, therefore *R* would be a good choice for skin grafting on to *Q*.
Alternative **B** is the opposite of the correct answer and alternative **C** incorrectly
interpretes rejection in the results. Alternative **D** fails to take the original rejection
of *Q* by *P* into account which relates the reactions of these two individuals.

20 Answer **D**   *Knowledge of precipitin formation*
The type of antibody formed in the blood of the rabbit is a precipitin which can
form an insoluble compound with the sensitizing substance. Similar substances
cause precipitation and are used as evidence of phylogenetic relationship. Antitoxin is an antibody which can combine with a bacterial toxin to neutralize it.
Agglutinins cause the clumping of bacteria or incompatible blood cells. Complement, according to Erlich's theory, is non-specific and is already present in nearly
all normal blood sera.

XIII Osmoregulation and Excretion in Animals

1 Answer **B**   *Application of the principle of osmoregulation*
Death would most likely be caused by a failure of osmoregulation by tissues which were originally isotonic with sea water. In fresh water, endosmosis would occur through a generally permeable body surface in the case of plants and lower animals or through gill surfaces. **A** is the opposite of the correct answer. **C** would not happen until the membranes had been denatured to some extent, **D** is unlikely to happen as the membranes of dying organisms tend to increase in permeability.

2 Answer **A**   *Comprehension of the active control of the osmotic effect*
The evidence indicates that metabolic activity dependent on aerobic respiration is probably decreased and that this activity controls the entry of sea water against an osmotic gradient. **B** is possibly true but is less directly related to the information given. **C** would produce an opposite effect by limiting the entry of water. **D** is expressed in unacceptable teleological terms, and in any case, the surface area to volume ratio would become more unfavourable.

3 Answer **B**   *Knowledge of the control of water balance in a mammal*
Although the kidneys are the main agents through which water balance operates, their action is controlled by hormones. For example, antidiuretic hormone produced in the pituitary reduces the volume of water lost from the kidneys by increasing the volume of water reabsorbed by the tubules. The amount of water absorbed by the gut depends mainly upon the volume of fluid ingested. This in turn affects the osmotic state and volume of the blood. This can affect the action of the kidneys by suppressing the production of antidiuretic hormone. Hormone from the adrenal cortex can also do this. More particularly, the salt-retaining hormone aldosterone, produced by the adrenal cortex, by regulating the sodium balance, also affects the capacity of the medulla of the kidney for resorption of water. In **C**, glomerular filtration is purely passive, depending on such physical factors as fluid pressures and osmotic relations on each side of the filtration membrane. In **D**, although sweating has some effect, it is not a controlling factor. Thus, if sweating is minimal, water balance continues to operate through the agency of the kidneys.

4 Answer **A**   *Interpretation of data on water conservation*
Uric acid is relatively insoluble and can therefore be concentrated in excretory organs without producing toxic effects. This allows conservation of water. Conversely, ammonia, which is toxic, is very soluble and can only be tolerated as an excretory product in large amounts when abundant water is present in the urine. Thus **B** and **C** are typical of aquatic organisms, especially those in fresh water where there may be a need for removing large quantities of water as part of the process of osmoregulation. **D** is an intermediate state between these extremes. Urea is soluble, but less poisonous than ammonia.

5 Answer **D** *Knowledge of urea production in mammals*
Urea is not directly produced from ammonia as suggested in **A**. The ornithine
cycle of the liver is concerned with the two-stage synthesis of the amino acid
arginine from ornithine during which ammonia is taken up. The release of urea
from arginine leaves ornithine to take up further ammonia. The oxidative
deamination of purines in **B** produces the relatively insoluble uric acid, a
convenient form of excretory storage for the bird embryo.

6 Answer **C** *Interpretation of data on kidney excretion*
Substances *c e g h* show an increase in concentration in the urine which is much
greater than that in the blood plasma. This indicates excretion. Chloride (*b*) and
water (*i*) are not included in this group because their closer proportion in plasma
and urine indicate that they are adjusted to a threshold level. Hippuric acid is not
shown in the plasma as it is formed in the kidneys, thus groups **A** and **D** are
incorrect.

7 Answer **C** *Knowledge of interaction of factors in glomerular filtration*
A is incorrect because resorption by the tubules follows filtration. The size of
protein molecules prevents their own diffusion through membranes but this does
not affect filtration which depends upon the effective hydrostatic pressure
available after it has been diminished by osmosis as in **C**. The peripheral resistance
of body capillaries increases the main blood pressure, therefore **D** is the opposite
of the correct answer.

Application of knowledge of body fluids to provide evidence
8 Answer **B** *of ultra filtration*
A comparison with the plasma would show a similar composition of solutes with a
molecular weight which is below a certain threshold but substances of high
molecular weight in the plasma are not usually found in the exudate. Comparison
with the lymph would be invalid as this is a different filtration system. Urine and
the substances resorbed as mentioned in **C** and **D** are influenced by the further
functions of the tubules.

9 Answer **A** *Knowledge of a function of the kidney tubules*
The hypertonic tissue fluid between the tubules removes water from the distal
convoluted tubules. **B**, **C** and **D** are the opposite of the actual conditions required
to produce **A**. The sodium ions necessary for the hypertonic condition of the
medulla tend to be retained by the slow rate of flow of the blood. The consequent
problem of a restricted oxygen supply is overcome by a large proportion of
anaerobic respiration.

Comprehension of filtration from a model of the artificial
10 Answer **B** *kidney*
The glomeruli of the kidneys work as filters because of the high blood pressure
within them. This is simulated by the machine. The salts added in **A** prevent excess
removal of the corresponding salts in the blood and maintain a balance of ions.
The addition of dextrose controls the osmotic pressure difference between the
plasma and the surrounding fluid which is a further factor in filtration. Circulation
of the surrounding fluid removes excretory substances as well as other substances
normally reabsorbed.

11 Answer **D**   *Knowledge of the action of antidiuretic hormone*

ADH increases the permeability of both the distal tubule walls and the collecting ducts of the kidneys. The tissue surrounding these are hyperosmotic and an increase in permeability permits an increase in the rate at which water is reabsorbed. In **B**, water is also reabsorbed by the proximal tubules but their permeability is not controlled by ADH. An increase of permeability of the glomeruli would work against the conservation of water. In **C**, water is removed from the descending limb of the loop but re-enters the nephron at the ascending limb.

Knowledge of hormone control of sodium reabsorption by
12 Answer **D**   *the kidney*

The cycle can be regarded as a self-contained negative feedback system in that it is provided with a receptor and a chain of effectors which respond to low blood pressure by causing a rise in pressure through an osmotic effect. ACTH (adrenocorticotrophic hormone) influences sodium and potassium transport through membranes not only at the kidneys but also at various glands. Removal of the anterior pituitary decreases the production of aldosterone. This action of ACTH should not be confused with ADH (anti-diuretic hormone) produced by the posterior pituitary which has a direct effect on the permeability of the distal tubules to water.

XIV Endocrine Control

1 Answer **A**   *Knowledge of the cause of cretinism*
The dwarf condition of cretinism implies an arrest of growth which must occur in infancy. In all the other conditions the body is fully grown.

2 Answer **D**   *Knowledge of the names of hormones*
Thyrotrophin is the secretion of the anterior pituitary which stimulates the activity of the thyroid gland. Calcitonin, now known to be produced by the thyroid gland, is concerned with calcium metabolism. Thyroxin and triiodothyronine are chemically similar and have similar effects but thyroxin is slower in its action.

3 Answer **B**   *Knowledge of the effect of parathormone*
The effect of parathormone is to release calcium from bone, thus raising the level of blood calcium. **D** is therefore the opposite of this. **A** and **C** would also counteract this effect and are untrue.

4 Answer **C**   *Knowledge of the hormone control of blood glucose*
Both insulin and glucagon are produced by the pancreas. Insulin promotes the uptake of glucose from the blood by the tissues while glucagon produced by the stimulus of somatotropin from the pituitary reverses this. Both thyroxin and adrenalin increase the mobilisation of glucose from liver glycogen, the first, slowly, and the second, rapidly, in conditions of stress.

                                    Comprehension of the relationship between pituitary
5 Answer **B**   *function and growth*
D represents the gene which would not be subsequently modified by endocrine activity. **B** represents the pituitary which could affect growth directly or through the thyroid **A**. **C** would represent the gonads.

6 Answer **C**   *Knowledge of pituitary control of thyroid activity*
The thyroid is influenced by thyrotrophic hormone produced by the anterior pituitary. The parathyroid gland responds directly to the level of blood calcium and the islets of Langerhans to the level of blood glucose. The hypothalamus is a brain region which controls the pituitary by secretions which pass through a direct connection of the blood system.

7 Answer **C**   *Knowledge of somatotrophic hormone function*
Somatotrophic hormone acts directly on tissues, promoting growth. All the others are trophic hormones, that is, they have another endocrine gland as their target organ. **A** and **D** are gonadotrophins and **B** acts on the adrenal cortex. In each of these cases, the response of the target organ is the secretion of another hormone.

8 Answer **B**

The experiment was carried out to determine the role of FSH and LH in ovulation. Because FSH caused ovulation in control animals but not in the experimental animal it was suggested that FSH caused the secretion of another hormone from the anterior pituitary. This is the luteinizing hormone. It is known that FSH does not stimulate this secretion directly but through the increase of oestrogen in the blood. A, C and D are the normal effects of FSH acting directly on the ovary.

9 Answer **D**   *Knowledge of the functions of oestrogen*

The corpus luteum is formed from the follicle cells which remain in the ovary after ovulation. It is under the direct control of the luteinizing hormone. Alternative **A** is the immediate effect of oestrogen after menstruation. In the course of the following two weeks the level of oestrogen increases until it inhibits FSH secretion as a form of negative feedback. Luteinizing hormone is also secreted. This stimulates the secretion of progesterone from the corpus luteum which inhibits luteinizing hormone secretion.

10 Answer **B**   *Knowledge of the function of luteinizing hormone*

Gonadotrophins FSH and LH are common to both sexes. In the male, LH acts on the interstitial cells of the testis, stimulating the production of testosterone. FSH acts on the seminiferous tubules and is responsible for the maturation of spermatozoa.

11 Answer **C**   *Comprehension of the effects of progesterone*

Progesterone influences the balance of hormone control in the female reproductive system. **B** brings about the inhibition of follicle development. This, in turn, inhibits oestrogen secretion. Thus **C** would not occur and the high progesterone levels would cause **A** and **D**. Because of the failure of oestrogen secretion, small amounts of this are added to the pill to promote repair of the uterine lining.

XV Nervous System and Sense Organs

1 Answer **A**   *Knowledge of the formation of the myelin sheath*
The Schwann cells in the embryonic stage lie adjacent to the axon. Processes then grow from them which wrap round the axon to form a spiral layer. The Schwann cells then lose most of their cytoplasm and the layers consist of plasma membrane with a high fat content, but the sheath cannot be said to consist merely of deposits of fat. Nissl's granules are present within neurons and the nodes of Ranvier interrupt the sheath.

2 Answer **C**   *Knowledge of the components of a sensory nerve system*
A, B and **D** are common components of sensory and motor nerves. In **D**, the end plate is typical of the neuromuscular junction of motor nerves only. The membrane of the muscle fibre is modified to form end plates to which dendrites are attached. The structure functions in a manner similar to a neuron-to-neuron synapse.

Interpretation of results from an experiment on nerve
3 Answer **C**   *responses*
If the synapse is subjected to a series of impulses over a period of time, the transmitter substance becomes exhausted and resynthesis cannot keep pace with its removal. This type of fatigue is also known as accommodation. This relationship between the threshold of excitation of the nerve and the rate of change in intensity of the stimulus is typical of the effect of the environment on the sensory system. Thus the stimuli are more likely to be effective if they occur suddenly and not at a constant level. **D** occurs when an impulse fails to cross a synapse but has an effect which facilitates the passage of subsequent impulses, provided that they arrive sufficiently soon after the first impulse. There is no evidence for the development of a latent period, which, in any case would be much shorter than the intervals between these stimuli. Inhibition is a process which blocks a possible nerve pathway by means of some other nerve impulse as, for instance, in the reciprocal innervation of muscles.

Comprehension of a factor affecting the velocity of a nerve
4 Answer **D**   *impulse*
Both an increase in cross-sectional area and in myelination allow a greater potential difference to be built up between the resting axon and the surrounding medium. Discharge of the resting potential produces a wave of depolarisation in which currents flow both inside and outside the axon. The effect of an increase in both of these factors is to make these currents act at a distance well ahead of the region of actual depolarisation and thus increase the velocity of transmission of the impulse. Thus the decrease given in **D** will decrease the velocity. Synapses introduce delay in nerve transmission as the substance secreted by the dendrites build up to a threshold level before the succeeding dendrites are stimulated for onward transmission. Thus **B** is the opposite of a correct answer and so is **C**.

5 Answer **C**   *Knowledge of the refractory periods of nerves and muscles*
The refractory period is the time which follows a response to a stimulus during which there is no response to a further stimulus. The refractory period of both kinds of nerves is short because nerve impulses are transmitted with sufficient frequency to maintain muscular contraction. The relatively short refractory period of striated muscle allows successive nerve impulses to maintain tetanus. The long refractory period of heart muscle allows relaxation between successive contractions, thus producing the heart beat rhythm.

6 Answer **C**   *Knowledge of the resting potential of a nerve axon*
Both **A** and **B** are aspects of the recovery process during which the axon is repolarising and is incapable of transmitting a further stimulus (refractory period). **C** represents the the resting transmembrane potential which can be discharged as a further impulse. **D** represents the condition of that part of the axon which is in the actual process of transmitting a nerve impulse which can be recorded as a negative wave which passes along its exterior.

Interpretation of a graph showing the action potential of a
7 Answer **D**   *neuron*
The action potential is the full potential difference between the resting potential of –90 millivolts and +40 millivolts giving 130 millivolts. Alternative **A** expresses only that part of the action spike which becomes positive in expression and **B** might be the difference between the positive and negative expressions around the zero level which represents the potential of the bathing solution. Alternative **C** represents the part of the spike which is negative only.

Comprehension of the effect of concentration of sodium ions
8 Answer **D**   *on the action potential of a neuron*
The action potential results from an influx of sodium ions. When more of these are present in the external medium, the more will enter as membrane permeability increases and the higher the action potential will be. In isotonic saline the action potential will be approximately that achieved in the body. In **B**, if less sodium is available it is likely that less will enter the neuron and the action potential will be lower. Thus the action potential is not a fixed value and **A** is untrue.

Interpretation of data on the control of sodium ion
9 Answer **D**   *concentration in neurons*
Assuming that the labelled sodium ions are transported in the same proportion as unlabelled sodium ions, the graph indicates that the effect of the metabolic poison is to prevent the loss of sodium ions. This supports **D** but not **A** which assumes that passage of the ions outwards is a physical process. **B** is a general statement which does not apply to the periods before and after the application of the poison. **C** is the opposite to a conclusion from the data.

Comprehension of the factor controlling the direction of a
10 Answer **D**   *nerve impulse*
The direction of flow of an electrical current in an axon is governed by the site of stimulation. Normally, the arrangement of the intact system causes the current to flow from cell body to end plates. Since the isolated neuron is merely cellular material capable of electrical conductivity, it could transmit an impulse in either direction.

11 Answer **A** *Application of the principle of reciprocal innervation*
X receives impulses from the stretch receptors in the triceps but transmission onwards to the motor neuron Y is blocked by a substance produced by the inhibitory neuron at the synapse. **B** is untrue because the inhibitory substance cannot affect impulses passing along X. **C** confuses the motor function of Y and the sensory function of X in relation to the stretch receptors. **D** is untrue because the inhibitory neuron does not transmit impulses inwards, its function being essentially one of motor control. Its inhibitory effect has already prevented impulses from passing outwards along Y as stated in **A**.

12 Answer **D** *Comprehension of the spinal reflex*
This is a spinal reflex which does not involve the brain. **A** and **B** would cut different parts of the reflex arc. **C** would destroy the cell bodies of the sensory neurones involved. **D** merely disconnects the brain and therefore does not block the spinal reflex.

13 Answer **C** *Comprehension of a function of spinal nerve roots*
If the dorsal root is cut, stimulation of the distal stump will result in stimulation of the sense organ in the skin since only a sensory pathway is operating. Thus **D** and **B** cannot be true. Stimulation of the proximal stump will transmit an impulse inwards to the spinal cord and then outwards along the ventral root to a muscle as suggested in **C**. **A** cannot be true as no impulse would reach the skin.

14 Answer **A** *Knowledge of a function of the sympathetic nervous system*
Dilation of the pupils by contraction of the radial muscles is a useful indication of the general activity of the sympathetic system. This activity also causes the opposite effects to those stated in **B, C** and **D**. Thus digestive movements are delayed and more blood is supplied to the heart wall for increasing cardiac activity. The release of glucose from the liver provides energy for 'fight or flight'.

Knowledge of neuro-secretion by parasympathetic nervous
15 Answer **C** *system*
The acetylcholine released by the parasympathetic fibres acts on particular locations where routine body maintenance must go on. Thus it stimulates peristalsis and relaxes the blood vessels to the gut. It slows down the heart rate through the parasympathetic fibres of the vagus nerve.. Adrenaline and nor-adrenaline are produced by the adrenal medulla when stimulated by the sympathetic fibres. These hormones reinforce the effects of the sympathetic system which work in opposition to the parasympathetic. Cholinesterase is the enzyme produced in tissues which rapidly destroys acetylcholine, thus limiting its effects.

16 Answer **B** *Knowledge of a function of the corpus callosum*
The corpus callosum is a tract of fibres which links the left and right cerebral hemispheres. Cutting this would result in loss of co-ordination of the motor functions of these. **D** is partly true but **B** is a more accurate statement. Sensory input reaches the cerebral hemispheres indirectly from other parts of the brain thus **A** is not acceptable. The posterior pituitary is related to the thalamencephalon and would not be directly affected.

17 Answer **B**   *Knowledge of a function of the cerebellum*
Voluntary movement is initiated in the cerebral cortex and subsequently co-
ordinated in the cerebellum. None of the sensory impulses reaching the cerebellum
attain the level of consciousness so **C** is incorrect. Reflex control of the gut,
circulatory and respiratory systems is mediated by the medulla oblongata so **D** is
incorrect.

18 Answer **C**   *Knowledge of a function of the auditory ossicles*
The auditory ossicles convey the vibrations collected from the larger area of the
tympanic membrane to the smaller area of the fenestra ovalis so that the relatively
weak force of atmospheric vibrations is concentrated. This is necessary in order to
move the dense endolymph. The auditory pinna and external auditory meatus in **A**
and **B** are more concerned with directing the sound waves than with concentrating
them. The fenestra rotunda in **D** makes compensatory movements when the
fenestra ovalis vibrates the endolymph contained in the scala vestibuli and scala
tympani.

19 Answer **A**   *Knowledge of a physical principle concerned with hearing*
The properties in **B** and **C** have no relevance for the short distances within the ear.
The property of incompressibility given in **A** allows vibrations transmitted
through the fenestra ovalis to travel through the perilymph and endolymph of the
inner ear without loss of energy. The sensory cells of the organ of Corti are thus
able to respond with the minimum loss of auditory discrimination. The collection
of sound by those animals which have a well developed pinna is not strictly a
focussing effect as might be thought from **D** but is more a form of conduction in
which waves received from a wide front are concentrated on a narrower front
when passing down the external auditory meatus with a consequent increase in
amplitude of the sound waves.

20 Answer **A**   *Knowledge of a mechanism in the organ of Corti*
Vibrations transmitted through the endolymph move the basilar membrane and
the the organ of Corti which is situated on it. Reissner's membrane is thin and is
subject to the same vibrations but its function is not clear. The dense gelatinous
tectorial membrane is relatively immobile. The hair-like processes of the cells of
the organ of Corti are attached to it and these cells are stimulated when the
particular sector of the basilar membrane vibrates.

                        Knowledge of the detection of turning movements within the
21 Answer **B**   *ear*
Acceleration of the head when turned promotes circulation of the endolymph in
the semicircular canals, but the detection of this depends upon the movement of
gelatinous material which surmounts the sensory hair cells of the crista in the
ampulla. The macula of the utricle are sensitive to the position of the otoliths of
calcium carbonate embedded in the jelly lying on the hair cells. The organ of Corti
is concerned with the reception of sound.

22 Answer **D** *Knowledge of the action of the ciliary muscles of the eye*
Contraction of the ciliary muscles does not act directly on the suspensory ligaments, but pulls the choroid and its ciliary body forwards thus decreasing the tension on the suspensory ligaments. This effect is therefore the opposite of the expressions in **B** and **C**. The tension of the choroid mentioned in **D** is exerted when the ciliary muscles are not opposing it. The internal pressures of the eye mentioned in **C** are relieved when the ciliary muscle relaxes.

23 Answer **A** *Knowledge of accommodation by the eye*
Light rays from a distance are less divergent than those from near objects and thus require less refraction through the lens system to bring them into focus on the retina. The lens curvature needs to be less for this and **A** will produce this shape. **B** is the opposite case for near vision and **C** would place two sets of muscles which normally work in a reciprocal manner both into an ineffective tension. **D** is again an effect of focussing for near vision.

24 Answer **A** *Knowledge of the function of the cones of the retina*
Cone cells are connected in small groups, or singly to ganglion cells. Thus each one or a small group of them will record very small areas of the visual image. This promotes visual acuity. On the other hand, this limited interconnection, together with a fairly high light requirement as in **B**, limits their sensitivity. Both **C** and **D** are factors for the greater sensitivity of the rods, their summative interactions in **D** expressing the effect of subthreshold stimuli, collected from a number of rods by a single ganglion cell, which are then sufficient to initiate a nerve impulse.

25 Answer **C** *Knowledge of the function of the rods of the retina*
The rods are more sensitive to low intensity illumination than the cones and tend to replace them at the periphery of the retina. **A** is untrue for most lens systems. Internal reflection given in **B** would be a disadvantage and is prevented by the light-absorbing nature of the choroid. The nerve supply is no greater at the periphery of the retina, and, in any case, it is the distribution of receptors which is the important factor.

26 Answer **D** *Knowledge of the trichromatic theory of colour vision*
Both **A** and **B** presuppose the existence of a single light-sensitive substance which is not true. **C** also makes this supposition but approaches the more usually accepted view of three different cones. It is also incorrect in assuming that each colour is represented by its own action on the light-sensitive substance. The trichromatic theory given in **D** only requires sensitivity to the three primary colours, from which the other colour sensations are derived by various mixtures of their effects.

XVI Effectors

1 Answer **B**

The ratchet-like attachment of two sets of molecules which can generate tension is also proposed for the relation between actin and myosin filaments in muscle contraction. In both cases this implies an orderly arrangement of molecules in the cell and the possibility of a biochemical explanation which is not forthcoming in the simpler physical theories of **A, C** and **D**.

2 Answer **B**   *Knowledge of relative sizes of muscle structures*

IV represents a muscle cut across to expose the ends of fibres. The connective tissue envelope of the epimysium continues as a tendon. II represents a portion of a fibre showing cross striations and its syncytial nature. III represents a small portion of a fibre at the junction with a single motor end plate. I represents the pattern of actin and myosin filaments as seen in cross section within a fibril.

3 Answer **A**   *Knowledge of changes in muscle contraction*

The myosin fibres lie within the A zone and not in the I zone which is traversed by actin fibres only. The dark areas of the A zone indicate the overlap of both sets of filaments, while the H zone is traversed by myosin filaments only. When the two sets of filaments slide together, the I zone will decrease, but the A zone, which represents the actual length of the myosin filaments, cannot become shorter. The Z zone is the septal attachment for the actin filaments and cannot change. As the actin filaments penetrate the A zone, the H zone becomes more restricted.

4 Answer **B**   *Interpretaion of traces showing muscle contraction*

In **B**, the second stimulus occurs while the the muscle is contracting in response to the first stimulus. Thus the second contraction is added to first to produce an increased shortening effect. In **A**, the recording was made with the drum stationary for each contraction, then moved on by hand. A series of separate stimuli of increasing strength have been given, producing a greater response for each separate contraction up to a maximum. This graded response appears to contradict the 'all or nothing' law, but the force of contraction of a whole muscle depends upon the number of fibres which respond. **C** represents incomplete tetanus caused by stimuli applied at short intervals. Summation occurs in the initial staircase effect, but a maximum is attained. **D** represents complete tetanus as the result of an even more rapid rate of stimulation.

5 Answer **D**   *Comprehension of muscle fatigue*

Fatigue first occurs at the neuromuscular junction as the acetylcholine secreted by the nerve endings is destroyed by cholinesterase which is abundant in the motor end plates. This effect occurs when the muscle is still capable of the response in both **A** and **B**, and the motor nerve can still transmit an impulse as in **C**.

6 Answer **D** *Knowledge of isometric muscle contraction*
Because isometric contraction involves tension without actual shortening of the muscle, no movement takes place and internal friction does not arise to any appreciable extent. This type of contraction may be shown in muscles which maintain posture. Alternative **A** is a definition of isotonic contraction in which movement does take place. **C** also applies to this. Unstriated muscle, as found in internal organs, generally does not show isometric contraction.

7 Answer **A** *Comprehension of maintenance of muscle tone*
The muscle stretch receptors (muscle spindles) are stimulated individually at different times, producing sufficient contractions to maintain muscle tone. Removal of tension removes all stimuli from these receptors. Although the sustained isometric contraction in **B** is not possible, this is an effect of **A**, not a cause. Although cutting the motor nerve, as in **C**, would also produce this effect, in this case it is the receptor mechanism which is not operating. Tetanus in **D** is the direct result of sustained contractions of the large muscle fibres, whereas muscle tone depends upon the local action of muscle spindles.

8 Answer **B** *Knowledge of the energy available in creatine phosphate*
The quantity of ATP available at any time is always small and is best regarded as material which is undergoing production and expenditure as part of the energy currency. It is the net energy released as a result of the splitting of creatine phosphate to form the stronger bonds of creatine which provides energy and phosphate for the resynthesis of ATP from ADP. This restores the ATP which has been expended in supplying energy to the protein filaments actin and myosin which bring about muscular contraction. Although glycogen and glucose may be regarded as the original providers of energy, this is neither sufficiently direct or rapid for muscular contraction.

9 Answer **B** *Knowledge of a theory of muscle contraction*
Acetyl choline increases the permeability of the sarcolemma which allows sodium and calcium ions to enter. The calcium ions activate the splitting of the ATP of an ATP-myosin complex. This allows molecular links to develop between actin and myosin which produce the tension which leads to contraction. **D** is incorrect as the subsequent binding of the calcium ions removes this effect and relaxation occurs.

Comprehension of processes which remove oxygen debt
10 Answer **C** *from muscle*
Pyruvic acid is normally rapidly removed from the muscle by conversion into lactic acid which is the prime expression of the oxygen debt. Thus **A** does not represent an answer to the problem. The lactic acid represents the accumulation of a hydrogen acceptor which is unable to pass this on at a sufficient rate. Alternative **B** operates to some extent, but if this were adequate, as in moderate exercise, there would be no oxygen debt. Removal of lactic acid by the blood allows other tissues, especially the liver, to participate in the necessary oxidation by means of the Krebs cycle while also providing some resynthesis to glucose or glycogen. Increasing the supply of phosphate would be ineffective as the essential feature of muscular action is the use of energy-providing reactions in which the energy is ultimately derived from carbohydrate by anaerobic processes which are the cause of the oxygen debt.

151

11 Answer **C** *Knowledge of processes causing heat loss from human skin*
The evaporation of water from sweat, directly through the skin and from the respiratory surfaces utilizes energy derived from body heat. This produces a cooling effect. Secretion of sweat does not, in itself, produce heat loss. The physical conditions experienced in sunbathing would be unlikely to provide much heat loss for **A** or **B**. Thus convection requires a sufficient difference between the air and skin temperatures for the necessary air currents to be established and radiation is likely to be adding heat to the skin rather than removing it.

12 Answer **B** *Comprehension of a heat-conserving mechanism*
Extremities of the body such as the pinna of the ear are likely to lose much heat. As a protection against this, shunt vessels are brought into operation which allow blood to bypass the superficial capillary plexuses of the skin. Under these conditions less heat will be lost so that **A** is incorrect. The reduced temperature of the superficial tissues and the restricted blood supply will tend to lower the metabolism of the pinna, but this is a consequence and not a cause of **B**. **D** is incorrect as the cold conditions would reduce evaporation of water.

Application of data to find heat loss by vapourization of
13 Answer **C** *water*
The daily loss of heat will be $800 \times 2\frac{1}{2}$ J $= 2000$ J. (In addition, there will be heat losses through radiation, convection, conduction, the warming of inspired air and food and heat losses in urine and faeces.)

14 Answer **D** *Knowledge of control of body temperature*
The hypothalamus is extremely sensitive to small changes of blood temperature, giving the close control required for homeostasis. There is also some response to skin receptors but this is less important than the control of deep internal temperature. The production of bradykinin by sweat glands is a local effect only and does not require the interposition of the nervous system. The mechanisms which control heat-producing hormones is not fully understood, but it is a slower response than that of the hypothalamus.

Interpretation of a graph to determine a type of heat control
15 Answer **A** *in an animal*
This endotherm is able, at first, to compensate for the falling environmental temperature, but when this has fallen further, the body temperature adjusts to a lower level and hibernation sets in. A non-hibernating endotherm as in **B**, would be expected to maintain the body temperature. In both cases of ectotherms in **C** and **D** a fall of body temperature would be closely similar to that of the environment.

XVII Animal Behaviour

1 Answer **A**
The difference would be most apparent in the pattern of the pathways. If these were strongly directional, a taxis would be indicated, while random pathways would indicate a kinesis. The counts indicated in **B** and **C** could be the results of either a kinesis or a taxis. The controls suggested in **D** would only provide evidence on the nature of the sense organs involved.

2 Answer **B**
The flatworms which move into an area which reduces the frequency of turning movements will tend to remain there. No evidence is provided for alternative **A** as the rate of turning is not necessarily related to the rate of movement. Alternatives **C** and **D** are both orientation responses which go beyond the available evidence.

3 Answer **B**
Calliphora larvae, when they are about to pupate, have two symmetrically placed light receptors on the anterior end. When this part of the body swings to the left, the left hand receptor is exposed to the light from behind and similarly for the right. These alternate swings cause the animal to move in a line which keeps the light source behind it. Thus **B** is a directed movement involving alternate testing of the stimulus on either side. Telotaxis in **A** is a movement of orientation which does not require two receptors, one being sufficient. Thus in the honey bee orientation to a light source can be achieved with one eye painted over. **D** depends on symmetrically placed receptors impulses from which are simultaneously compared by the central nervous system, producing orientation without bending from side to side. **C** refers to the type of avoiding movement which is the first part of trial and error behaviour in which an animal moves away from a stimulus and then proceeds in a random manner on a different pathway.

4 Answer **C**
A sign stimulus is inborn and is specific in producing a particular pattern of behaviour. Displacement behaviour takes place when an animal is unable to make the appropriate response to a stimulus and behaves in a way which does not appear to be related to the stimulus. A taxis is a directional response in relation to the direction of the stimulus while a kinesis is a stimulated activity which is not related to the direction of the stimulus.

5 Answer **A**   *Comprehension of displacement activity*
The displacement behaviour is not related to the rest of the behaviour pattern and
can arise from conflicting stimuli or, in this case, from lack of response by the
female. The indirect movement of the dog while conserving the stimulus is a form
of insight, indicating behaviour of a high order of complexity. By maintaining the
original compass direction when flying from a different starting point, migrating
birds are likely to fail. This indicates a fixed pattern of behaviour which is an
elaboration of a taxis. The bee dance in relation to the direction of a food source
probably indicates more than one type of stimulus for the complete orientation
process.

6 Answer **C**   *Comprehension of habituation*
B is incorrect because it would involve an association of a conditioned stimulus
with the original response. **A** is incorrect as the changes in the stimulus would not
bring about a return of the response if fatigue were present. **C** is perhaps the
simplest type of learning and is essentially the disappearance of the response upon
repeated exposure to a stimulus. Thus habituation may be said to be an elimination of a response which is not significant for the life of the animal. **D** concerns the
establishment of a social association in early life which does not apply here.

                        Comprehension of the difference between operant and
7 Answer **B**   *classical conditioning*
In operant conditioning the behaviour is spontaneous and occurs before the
'reward'. It operates to produce a certain effect and when this effect is favourable
the behaviour is reinforced. In classical conditioning the behaviour is not
spontaneous but only develops after a learning period. Alternatives **A** and **C** are
true, and alternative **D** is untrue, for both kinds of conditioning.

8 Answer **C**   *Comprehension of operant conditioning*
In the first place learning begins through random operation of the lever. The
reward of food reinforces the behaviour and this is shown by an increase in the
probability of moving the lever. Habituation is the opposite of this in that a
response progressively fails when a repeated stimulus is not significant. Conditioning in the classical sense involves the forced substitution of a new stimulus for the
original unconditioned stimulus of a simple reflex. Imprinting concerns the
establishment of a social association in early life.

                        Application of the principle of classical conditioning to draw
9 Answer **D**   *a conclusion*
This is an example of classical conditioning on the Pavlov model. **A**, **B** and **C**
would require further experiments to test them as the investigation includes two
sets of variables, namely time of application and the two different odour substances.

10 Answer **A**   *Interpretation of traces of a conditioned reflex*
The diagram indicates the process during which the conditioned reflex is being
established. Eventually it would be possible to leave out the unconditioned
stimulus **D**. The conditioned (neutral) stimulus becomes effective as it precedes the
unconditioned stimulus **D**. The conditioned stimulus is represented by the onset of
C which is immediately followed by **A**. The unconditioned stimulus **D** is still being
applied to produce the unconditioned reflex **B**. Eventually the conditioned reflex
would be demonstrated by **C** and **A** alone.

11 Answer **A**   *Comprehension of the conditions for learning a manual skill*
The exercise of motor movements in a rational person are not random even before special skill is acquired. Thus **C** is incorrect. The feedback suggested in **A** leads to correction and improvement of the early trials of the motor movements. This may lead to some facilitation of certain neural pathways, but **D** is inadequate as a simple explanation of a complex form of learning. **B** is an involuntary process which does not take place during the intentional learning of the skill although when this is highly developed the manual skill may appear so precise and rapid as to acquire some appearance of reflex behaviour.

12 Answer **D**   *Comprehension of insight learning*
Insight is the ability to organize behavioural responses from past experiences. Students are expected to carry out the two-fold task of remembering material and relating it to the particular situation of the item. Conditioning is promoted by many repetitions of a stimulus which is superimposed on an unconditioned stimulus. This is a learning situation which is lower than the intellectual level at which students are expected to operate. Trial and error learning involves an active searching for a new stimulus to release a particular behaviour. In the first instance, the search is random and it leads to operant conditioning. The freedom and repetition necessary for this is not given in these items. Perception is concerned with attaching a significance to certain sensory patterns, as, for example, recognizing biological material. In some cases it may stand close to insight.

Knowledge of the cause of dominance by the queen in a bee
13 Answer **B**   *colony*
The attention of workers to the queen is related to the secretion of substances produced by her which are distributed around the hive. Without this, the behaviour of the workers changes and certain larvae are fed with royal jelly to produce new queens. Thus **A** produces the queen, but does not maintain dominance. Although **C** is true and all workers are related to the queen in consequence, it has no effect on the dominance of the queen. It is possible, with care, to introduce a queen from another hive and once her pheromones have been accepted her dominance is established. **D** is incorrect as larval feeding which determines the development of the workers is controlled by the young nurse workers.

14 Answer **D**   *Knowledge of a term used for social organization in cattle*
The contests establish the order of dominance between the animals and this determines each individual's social rank in the hierarchy. Leadership may also be partly determined by this means but also involves attraction of the rest of the herd to follow the leader. The observations do not involve spatial considerations and therefore a territorial system was not being studied. A caste system implies the rigid organization of social insects which is determined by structural and functional differences between polymorphic types.

15 Answer **C**   *Interpretation of evidence on a pecking order in poultry*
The dominant bird is *Y* which is not pecked by any other bird. *V* pecks two other birds but is pecked by *Y*. *X* pecks two other birds but is pecked by *V*. *Z*, *T* and *U* only peck one other bird and are also pecked. *W* is lowest in the social hierarchy.

XVIII Interactions in Ecology

1 Answer **C**   *Knowledge of ecological terms*
An ecological niche represents the place occupied by a species in a community. The factors stated are required in order to establish this. The environment only takes into account the factors surrounding the organism. The ecosystem is a comprehensive term involving all of the organisms and factors. The study shown implies an autecological approach in which an individual species is studied in detail in contrast to a synecological study of the inter-relations of species in a community.

2 Answer **D**   *Comprehension of pyramids of numbers*
The main requirement for the diagram would be that the primary producers must be of small size to be most numerous. **A** appears to be a possible answer, but the dying down of the algae in late summer can give inverted pyramids. **B** is excluded as the higher plants are likely to be large and fewer and the animal species feeding on the roots smaller and more numerous. **C** is excluded because a parasitic infestation implies more organisms than the host. **D** represents organisms of increasing size which is likely to be reflected in decreasing numbers of individuals.

3 Answer **C**   *Knowledge of a condition related to the pyramid of numbers*
The fewer individuals at higher trophic levels must have a lower mortality rate, otherwise their particular trophic level would become progressively smaller. Inverted pyramids such as one based on a single tree as a primary producer or a host with many parasites also show a lower mortality rate for the larger organism. The availability of energy in **B** is not related to the number or size of the organisms, nor is obtaining food necessarily more difficult as in **D**. In **A,** predators are not necessarily larger than their prey nor are grazers necessarily larger than their food plant.

Comprehension of a condition related to an inverted
4 Answer **B**   *pyramid of numbers*
As numbers only are concerned, one or a few large primary producers would be represented by a small base to the pyramid. Small primary producers might be expected to be numerous, giving a broad base to the pyramid. Increase or dying off in these particular cases would be irrelevant.

5 Answer **D**   *Comprehension of the pyramid of energy*
With respect to the circulation of energy, an ecosystem is open, with an input of solar energy at the primary producer level and a loss at each transition to a higher level due to heat lost in respiration. Thus although there is some concentration of energy in consumers, as in **C**, this is represented at their level at its total value regardless of the number of organisms containing it. In **A** also, the size of the organisms has no direct bearing on the total energy represented at a particular trophic level. **B** is incorrect because energy stored at a given trophic level is ultimately passed to the next level or lost from the system.

6 Answer **B**   *Knowledge of the essentials of an ecosystem*
An ecosystem could consist of plants represented by **A**, which were supplied with
energy represented by **D**. Dead plant material would need to be recycled by the
decomposers **C**. Primary consumers in the form of herbivores or plant parasites
would not be essential.

7 Answer **B**   *Comprehension of relationships in an ecosystem*
C represents plants which can supply food either to the primary consumers at **D** or
to the decomposers at **B** Both primary consumers **D** and secondary consumers **A**
return food to the decomposers. The decomposers themselves break food down to
inorganic materials which are not represented on a food web.

8 Answer **A**   *Comprehension of stability in an ecosystem*
The trend towards greater diversity of species results in diverse food chains. Self
regulatory interactions between these in the form of negative feedback responses
then arise which increase the stability of the whole system. **B** is incorrect as it
would make for instability. On the contrary, the mature ecosystem tends to
produce its own environment by influencing factors such as those of soil conditions and the microclimate. The productivity of plants may be greater in immature
ecosystems, resulting in an imbalance and consequent seral changes. Thus **C** is not
a necessary characteristic of a mature ecosystem. **D** implies that decomposers are
the controlling factor of the ecosystem. This is more likely to be the producer
organisms with the activities of the decomposers adjusted to the supply of
available nutrients.

                                  Comprehension of the effect of adding fertilisers to an
9 Answer **C**   *ecosystem*
Fertilisers make the food chain more effective by providing essential nutrients
which stimulate growth of the primary producers. This does not require any
further complexity of the food web as suggested in **B**. If, in fact, the food web is
made more complex because the fertiliser is organic manure, its benefits are less
immediate as an increase in decomposers locks up a proportion of the fertiliser
material which is then not immediately available to the crop. Thus **D** indicates no
direct advantage. **A** could be partly true if organic manure is considered as a
source of energy for heterotrophic decomposers, but the main source of energy for
the crop is from solar radiation.

                                  Comprehension of the relationship between variety of
10 Answer **C**   *organisms and stability in an ecosystem*
A stable ecosystem tends to have a variety of organisms which allows alternative
pathways in food chains as the populations of the various species fluctuate. This is
best achieved in a climax community when such adjustments have developed.
Thus **D** represents a restriction on arriving at this condition. Reduction of
consumers such as predators and parasites in **A** could make for instability in the
producers and primary consumers such as grazers. This might allow population
growth which would be ultimately restricted by overcrowding or starvation which
is likely to produce instability. In **B**, the suggested equal balance of numbers takes
no account of the size of the organisms, the biomass and their productivity.

11 Answer **B**   *Interpretation of graphs illustrating interspecific competition*
Both **A** and **C** represent a predator – prey relationship. In each case, the food species *Y* declines when it is eaten. In the case of **A** this goes to extinction, followed by extinction of the dependent species *X*. In **C**, the decline of *X* allows *Y* to increase again and a series of oscillating cycles is set up. In **B**, the extinction of *Y* allows *X* to use the food source more completely as it is the successful competitor. In **D**, there is no evidence of interaction between the two species which each maintain their own stable level of population density.

12 Answer **B**   *Knowledge of an activity of denitrifying bacteria*
The reduction of nitrates to atmospheric nitrogen is carried out by denitrifying bacteria in anaerobic conditions such as waterlogged soil. Both **A** and **D** refer to the activities of putrefactive bacteria which break down complex materials. **C** is the opposite of the true answer.

13 Answer **A**   *Knowledge of a sequence in the nitrogen cycle*
Nitrosomonas and Nitrobacter act in sequence. The first part of this is represented in **A**. **B** should indicate that Nitrobacter converts nitrite to nitrate. Both Azotobacter and Clostridium can utilize atmospheric nitrogen to form organic compounds.

14 Answer **A**   *Knowledge of the effect of symbiotic nitrogen-fixing bacteria*
The protein material of the leguminous crop enters the nitrogen cycle of the soil when the crop is ploughed in. There is some evidence that other plants show benefit when grown close to leguminous plants but this would not apply in this case. **C** would suggest that root nodules could be formed by other crops, or, at least, benefit from infection. Although the root nodule bacteria can exist in the soil, they do not continue to fix nitrogen to an appreciable extent, so **D** is not acceptable.

15 Answer **A**   *Knowledge of terms used to describe nutrition*
Holophytic nutrition includes both photosynthetic and chemosynthetic organisms which both use non-organic sources of energy to fix carbon in organic compounds. Both holozoic nutrition as in animals, saprophytic nutrition and parasitic nutrition require the provision of organic compounds as energy sources and tend to degrade them to carbon dioxide.

16 Answer **D**   *Knowledge of the term "heterotrophic"*
The use of organic compounds by saprophytes places them in the heterotrophs. The other three terms relate to green plants which are autotrophs.

17 Answer **A**   *Comprehension of a sequence in nutritional relationships*
The initial association of two animals would most likely be commensalism which is a fairly loose non-physiological relationship. It may or may not be of mutual benefit to the partners. Symbiosis (or mutualism) involves a closer relationship which is of mutual benefit. Parasitism involves a parasite, which is usually the smaller organism, living on or in a larger host. Only the parasite derives benefit. Parasitic disease occurs in a host which is not well adapted to the relationsip. A further evolution of the relationship produces greater mutual adaptation with less harm to the host. Such tolerance may eventually lead to symbiosis. This is expressed in **A**, whereas **C** is the reverse of this. The series shown in **B** represents a most unlikely change in trends. In **D**, parasitism could not give rise to predation, but the reverse sequence could occcur.

18 Answer **D**   *Interpretation of data on an ecological relationship*
Each species provides the growth factor required by the other so that they are likely to grow successfully in a symbiotic relationship. **A** is incorrect as there is no competition for a growth factor. There is no evidence for incompatibility and independent growth is unlikely because of the respective deficiencies in a growth factor.

XIX Pollution

1 Answer **C**
The insecticides tend to be deposited on the plants in a dispersed form. They are concentrated in the bodies of herbivorous insects which are then destroyed. The insects may be eaten by predators or herbivores may graze on the plants and be eaten by carnivores. As the numbers of secondary consumers are smaller than the primary consumers, there is a tendency for the insecticide to concentrate in their bodies. Accumulation in detritus feeders is unlikely because they are small, numerous and have short life cycles.

2 Answer **A**   *Knowledge of a definition of polluted water*
The definition of polluted water depends upon the purpose it is to serve. Therefore no absolute standards can be applied. A high biochemical oxygen demand may be characteristic of waters with a high organic pollution, but not for other forms of pollution. Definition **C** relates pollution to human agencies only, whereas natural factors may also cause it. **D** would apply to most rivers, unpolluted or otherwise, according to rigorous modern standards.

Knowledge of the effect of suspended solids as water
3 Answer **A**   *pollutants*
The rate of settling of particles depends upon their density and size and the turbulence of the water. For similar particles, the effects of turbulence are greatest in rapid streams which tend to keep solids in suspension. The consequent opacity may interfere with photosynthesis and thereby affect the fauna. In rapid streams, also, the bottom is typically stones or gravel and if this becomes silted by deposited particles, profound changes of habitat occur for bottom-living species. Silting is a normal process in rivers and lakes and the further addition of settled particles is less important. In any case, with less turbulence, the water becomes clear more quickly.

Knowledge of the advantage of using indicator organisms
4 Answer **B**   *for estimating water pollution*
The pollution of a stream is best studied over a period of time. Physical and chemical tests made at one time may not reflect the varying range of conditions which affect the environment. The use of indicator organisms can only show the general state of pollution and it is seldom possible to relate a species to a single environmental factor. Thus **A** is not usually applicable. Identification of species is usually a problem in elementary fieldwork whereas the usual records of temperature, pH etc are more easily obtained. On the other hand detailed chemical analysis is difficult. The most useful indicator organisms are often species which occur commonly enough to give significant population counts and these may become readily identifiable. Thus **C** is only slightly less acceptable than **B**. **D** could be true for organisms which are sensitive to pollution such as trout, but certain

organisms increase in eutrophic conditions produced by some forms of pollution. Thus algae and hydrophytes may increase with a high nitrate content and organisms tolerant of low oxygen concentrations may increase in the presence of abundant detritus.

5 Answer **D**

Knowledge of a factor affecting the use of indicator organisms

Short life cycles give populations which can show rapid changes in response to the environment. Long living organisms may survive from more favourable conditions and therefore show no immediate response to prevalent conditions. Both **A** and **B** may represent some useful indicator organisms. Thus fishes which can rapidly leave or invade a stream may give fairly immediate indication of pollution. On the other hand sessile organisms and bottom feeding animals may be relatively immobile and can provide useful indicators by estimates of population density.

6 Answer **B**   *Knowledge of a sequence of organisms in a polluted stream*

The succession of animals is likely to be tubificids, chironomids, *Asellus, Gammarus*. Sewage fungus is abundant in the initial stages of pollution and therefore associated with tubificids.

7 Answer **A**

Interpretation of a curve showing biochemical oxygen demand

The first effect of the organic pollutant is to greatly increase the biochemical oxygen demand. This implies that oxygen is taken up by readily oxidizable organic substances and respiring micro-organisms. This effect steadily diminishes as a biological succession is established. The effect of the high initial biochemical oxygen demand is to produce the characteristic 'oxygen-sag' curve labelled **C**. Curve **B** represents the high initial release of ammonia from the breakdown of organic nitrogen compounds. This ammonia then provides the material for the formation of nitrate which is shown by the subsequent rise in curve **D**. The decline in nitrate which follows is dependent upon the uptake by aquatic plants.

8 Answer **C**   *Knowledge of oxidation in sewage treatment*

Apart from physical filtration, water purification refers mainly to the disposal of proteins and their derivatives by means of the nitrogen cycle. Thus **C** refers to the high oxygen environment necessary for this process. Putrefactive bacteria are largely anaerobic and are used for sludge digestion, not for treating liquid sewage. Although competitive systems between organisms are not utilized to any extent in these processes, ecosystems do develop by which a balance is achieved between the various organisms on the bacterial films.

9 Answer **B**   *Knowledge of eutrophication in lakes*

Established lakes are likely to be productive of living organisms owing to the accumulation of nutrient salts. This is the eutrophic state and the addition of further organic matter increases the rate of eutrophication. The oligotrophic state, where there is a lack of nutrients, is unproductive.

10 Answer **C**

Comprehension of a relationship between respiratory exchange and survival in polluted water

The effect of organic pollution is to decrease the oxygen content of the water. The pigments in **C** and **D** increase the oxygen-carrying capacity of the blood and in this respect haemoglobin is more efficient than haemocyanin. Because of this affinity for oxygen, the haemoglobin in the circulating blood maintains an inward invasion of oxygen when the oxygen tension of the water is low. Both **A** and **B** depend upon a high external oxygen concentration to produce a diffusion gradient inwards to the air contained in the system.

11 Answer **A**   *Knowledge of a pollutant in coal smoke*

Numerous investigations suggest that sulphur dioxide causes premature senescence in leaves and limits the development of new ones. There is little carbon monoxide in coal smoke. Experiments with deposits of carbon particles and tarry materials from typical urban smoke concentrations on leaves show negligible effect on photosynthesis or stomatal action.

12 Answer **C**   *Knowledge of a pollutant in vehicle exhaust fumes*

Sufficient carbon monoxide may be produced in heavy traffic to cause mild headaches, and, possible, slightly slower mental reactions which could be dangerous. In the presence of bright sunlight, hydrocarbons from incompletely burnt fuels may be oxidised in the atmosphere to form irritant aerosols which affect the eyes. Lead products from leaded fuels are minute in quantity and are only slowly cumulative in the body. 3:4-benzpyrene is a potent carcinogen produced by badly adjusted diesel engines, but its levels are negligible.

XX Populations

1 Answer **D**   *Knowledge of the expression of a population*
Both factors are necessary for a complete population record because each of these
can be an important variable.

2 Answer **B**   *Knowledge of a sampling procedure for a population*
Regular patterns of distribution of samples are not independent because each
sample position is determined by the position of others. Random points on the
field are truly independent and can be found by the use of random numbers. Ring
throwing is dependent on the position of the thrower and on throwing decisions.
In **D**, the sample units may have to be increased in size and the number of units
decreased, making the sampling less representative. In this case, it is better to use
the larger samples based on a regular pattern as in **A**.

Knowledge of the formula used for estimating a population
3 Answer **A**   *by the marking and recapture method*
The product of $P \times Q$ relates the two samples together so that R can be estimated
as a proportion of them. If the population size were large, the number of animals
recaptured (R) would be small. Therefore if PQ is divided by R, the smaller value
for R would give a larger answer.

Comprehension of a graphical expression of the relationship
4 Answer **A**   *between a population and an environmental factor*
The scatter diagram provides numerical information only. The distribution of the
points in a slope from left to right is a graphical expression of negative correlation
in which the increase of one variable is accompanied by a decrease in the other.
Alternative **B** would require the opposite slope. Although an inverse association
between the two sets of facts is shown, this does not demonstrate causality. Thus **C**
and **D** cannot be accepted. Both the population density and the silicate concentration may be determined independently by other causes and the association be
fortuitous.

Knowledge of a method of finding the increase of a
5 Answer **B**   *population*
A net increase is that which remains when losses have been subtracted from gains.
Thus **B** represents the sum of gains minus the sum of losses.

6 Answer **D**   *Interpretation of data to find the size of a population*

Generation	Numbers of parents		Reproductive product
1 (parents)	0	0	product
2 (F_1)	1	1	80
3 (F_2)	40	40×80	3200
	1600	1600×80	128000

7 Answer **C**
Each colony on the solid medium is formed from a single individual, although some bacteria will have failed to reproduce. Therefore there will be at least 150 bacteria in 0.1 ml of the second dilution. As the total volume of this dilution is 10 ml, there will be 150×100 bacteria in it. These were obtained from 1 ml of the first dilution in which there would be $150 \times 100 \times 10$ bacteria. These are derived from 1 ml of the original culture, therefore it contained 150 000 bacteria per ml.

8 Answer **C** *Comprehension of exponential growth by binary fission*
The exponential growth of the population of cells by binary fission follows the series 1, 2, 4, 8, 16 etc which can be expressed as $2^0, 2^1, 2^2, 2^3$ etc. Thus the index also expresses the number of generations that have occured. Therefore at n generations the number of cells is 2^n.

9 Answer **C**
The more individuals there are, the more parents there are available. There is no need to assume any change in the generation time in **A** or **B**, or the increase in reproductive capacity of the parents suggested in **D**. In favourable conditions, however, there may be some decrease in generation time as suggested in **B**.

10 Answer **B**
The representation of the stationary phase requires an expression of a zero rate of growth which is attained by a progressive decrease from the exponential phase. When numbers were small bN would be small and therefore have little effect on slowing down the rate of increase. As numbers increase, bN would increase and its effect by subtraction would become more marked to give a progressive levelling of the curve. This would apply to alternatives **B** and **C**, but the effect in **B** would be more marked because $N(a - bN) = Na - bN^2$.

11 Answer **D**
The concept of logarithmic growth usually applies to a population in a limited habitat growing under favourable conditions. These conditions are most likely to be fulfilled in **D**. Conditions of maximum dispersal and low temperature in **A** and **C** would not provide the necessary concentration or growth conditions, and the dry conditions in **A** and **B** would also be unfavourable.

12 Answer **D**
The population density of the adults is expressed on a logarithmic scale and that of larva production on an arithmetical scale. Thus **A** must be incorrect because it refers to an incorrect scale and larvae are only expressed as a rate of production, not as actual numbers. For the same reason, **B** and **C** are also incorrect. **D** expresses the information on the graph, making proper use of the two scales.

13 Answer **D**   *Interpretation of pyramids of age structure in populations*
For typical human populations the chances of survival are least in the earliest and later age groups. The mortality of the early age group is offset by the birth rate but this cannot apply for the later groups. Thus any such pyramids should taper towards the apex. This is not seen to any appreciable extent in **D**. Such a rectangular distribution would imply practically no increase in mortality in the oldest groups until a uniform maximum life-span had been attained. **A** indicates a 'young', expanding population. **B** shows an ageing population with a declining birth rate. **C** represents an expanding population in which practices to restrict births have been recently adopted.

XXI Evolution

1 Answer **A**
Knowledge of the relationship between taxonomy and studies in evolution

Alternatives **B**, **C**, and **D** are all aims of classical taxonomy which are still valid and essential. However the activities implied in **A** represent the most constructive role of the modern taxonomist in which important contributions to the study of evolutionary causation and effects can be made.

2 Answer **B**
Comprehension of the relationship between a frequency curve and the success of a variation

The most successful variants will be those which occur most frequently and this is expressed as the mode. The median represents the middle group of the range. The arithmetic mean is found by calculation and may not be actually shown in any of the data. The highest value for size of body represents one extreme of the range which is likely to have a low frequency, representing rare and therefore relatively unsuccessful individuals.

3 Answer **C**
Comprehension of a cause of variability

The variability of a species is defined as the genetic potential to produce variation. Changing environmental conditions will be unlikely to increase the genetic potential but merely select within it. Thus **A** and **D** will both limit genetic potential. Outbreeding again merely exploits the existing genetic potential by producing new combinations of alleles. Only mutation will produce the new alleles which will extend the genetic potential.

4 Answer **C**
Comprehension of adaptation

Adaptation by natural selection is implied in **C**. It assumes pre-adaptation in which 'favourable' adaptations already exist which are likely to survive in competition. **A** assumes a directional effect of the environment on the genes which is of an adaptive nature. Mutations brought about by the environment have a very small chance of being adaptive in this sense. **B** states the Lamarckian view in which the acquired characters are assumed to be inherited. In **D**, the normal conditions of development are expressed and it is a partly correct answer, but it is better expressed in the more inclusive statement of **C**.

5 Answer **B**
Comprehension of factors influencing evolution

The type of dandelion leaf is a characteristic acquired during development in response to the environment. Evidence that this type of character could be inherited is not forthcoming. It does not provide variation of the genotype upon which further selection could act. Melanism in **A** appears to have increased owing to the selective effect of predation by birds on the more visible pale varieties. This implies the existence of a pre-adaptation in a polymorphic population which is selected by a change in the environment. **C** provides an example of inherited mutation which increases the range of variation on which selection can act. **D** is an example of adaptations by the various species to particular temperature ranges by developing different surface areas in relation to heat loss. There is no evidence on the origin of these, but all the species are in the same genus which expresses a belief that they have radiated from a common stock.

6 Answer **B**   *Comprehension of a relationship between phenotype and genotype*

This depends upon the different characters being acquired in the lifetime of the individual plants. As it is generally held that such acquired characters could not be inherited, they do not form part of the genotype. In **A**, the effects of isolation might well have led to two distinct gene pools with consequent effects on the gene complement. Somatic mutations in **C** refer to changes in the genetic material even if they do not affect the next generation. In **D** the existence of a range of variation is due to the interaction of the range of genotypes with the environment. Selective breeding from such a range can produce true-breeding varieties which indicates the validity of genotypic differences.

7 Answer **D**   *Knowledge of evidence of evolutionary relationships*

The more essential features of organisms are less likely to change during evolution. They therefore provide evidence of relationship between groups which may have changed in other less essential respects. Because it carries the essential genetic information, the chromosome complement or karyotype is perpetuated with great constancy. Homologous structures, although adapted to different functions, again indicate an essential basic structure which is sufficiently conservative to indicate relationships. Vestigial structures showing an apparent loss of function provide evidence of a similar kind. Analogous structures however show no basic unity but only an acquired functional similarity.

8 Answer **D**   *Knowledge of the use of fossil evidence of evolution*

The succession of fossils in undisturbed sedimentary rocks provides evidence of the succession of living forms which produced them. Estimation of the time required for evolutionary changes is very indirect and subject to a margin of error. Evidence of relationship between species is mainly a matter for speculation, depending upon various assumptions of descent and the arrangement of fossils in series showing transitional changes. The causes of such changes are the subject of still further speculation, sometimes based upon the nature of the sediments which may indicate environmental change.

9 Answer **B**   *Comprehension of adaptive radiation*

A population undergoes adaptive radiation when it forms a number of types, each of which is suited to a particular environment. Alternative **A** expresses the converse case of convergent evolution between unrelated organisms. In **C**, evolution is counteracted by the conserving effect of the environment already present. **D** is a more general statement of a mechanism of evolution but says nothing of the direction which it is likely to take.

Comprehension of a factor restraining evolutionary change
in a flowering plant

The development of a specialized pollination mechanism is a highly integrated process and any change is likely to interfere with its operation. In **B**, high productivity produces population pressures which increase the effect of any selective processes which tend to promote new living conditions. Geographical barriers allow separation into races which do not interbreed and which are therefore likely to become distinct. In **D**, the annual habit with its short life cycle increases the chances of mutation and recombination compared with the perennial habit. The more frequent requirement to become established in a new habitat is also a strong selective factor.

11 Answer **C**

Comprehension of the use of inductive reasoning in forming
the evolutionary hypothesis

The various kinds of particular evidence which are used to support the generalization of evolution provide examples of inductive reasoning. As the evidence contains less information than the generalization, it cannot be claimed as a completely logical process. In this case, the 'theory' of evolution is in the nature of a creative hypothesis which cannot have the status of a theory in the physical sciences. There are very few 'laws' in biology. Thus **A** is incorrect, and, if evolution continues and is unrepeatable, prediction cannot be made. **B** represents the process of experimental science in which a hypothesis is tested by observations which lead to its retention or rejection. Large scale evolution is too slow for such experimentation, but in a sense, further evidence is used to test the theory of evolution. **D** is related to **B** but is false because hypotheses can never be finally proved.

12 Answer **A**

Comprehension of the relationship between discontinuous
variation and modern evolutionary theory

The original theory of natural selection assumed that progression towards a new species could occur by selection from a particular part of a range of variation in a species. It is now generally agreed that this is less likely to produce a new type than a change in the gene complement which produces a new type which stands outside of the original range of variation. Alternative **B** is related to the work of Malthus which Darwin took into account in his theory of natural selection. Alternative **C** was discussed by Darwin with, for example, sexual selection as a form of intraspecific competition. Darwin tacitly assumed that acquired characters could be inherited although this is largely refuted by modern biologists.

13 Answer **A**   *Evaluation of human characteristics related to survival*

Adaptation by behavioural changes has enabled man to occupy a wide range of habitats provided by geographical and technological variants. This plasticity of behaviour is likely to provide the means of survival in conditions of future change. **B** is an inadequate factor because of the physical limitations of world resources. The direction of human evolution in the past has been partly due to favourable selection factors operating in the environment. As the environment changes, there is no means of estimating the complex interactions of the future which may not be favourable. Thus **D** cannot be assumed. **C** takes no account of the rate of organic evolution. Although relatively rapid, one thousand years could not be expected to afford sufficient time span for appreciable change.